Witness Protection 6
Alpha Dogs

Holly Copella

Dedicated to those who proudly
served our country.

"All gave some; some gave all"

ACKNOWLEDGMENTS

Copella Books: First Paperback Edition 2018
Printed by CreateSpace, An Amazon.com Company
Cover Artist: Daniela Owergoor
Dani-owergoor.deviantart.com

PUBLISHER'S NOTE

Chapter One

The relentless sound of an alarm wailing jolted Jackie into consciousness. Her eyes barely opened. She sat in the pilot's seat and stared at the blood spatter on the windshield before her. Pain shot through her entire body as she endured the stinging sensation radiating from her left shoulder. She felt oddly paralyzed. Beyond the windshield, she could see a close-up view of the ocean rapidly passing by. Male and female screams from the fuselage could be heard above the wailing alarm. Jackie stared at the vibrating yoke in front of her. She attempted to reach for it with blood-covered hands. The pain shot through her shoulder, keeping her from getting close enough to the controls. She could do little more than watch the flashing lights on the panel.

"Stay with me, Jackie," a familiar male voice urgently shouted.

The panic in the voice wasn't something she heard often. Jackie recognized the voice, but she couldn't think straight. Her head was becoming fuzzy, and her vision was blurring. She knew she was about to pass out again. Jackie fought to stay awake as the sounds of panic from the fuselage fueled her to remain conscious. She didn't even know where she was or what she had been doing just moments before the relentless alarm started wailing.

"Dad," she gasped while struggling to stay awake. "She's going down. Pull up!"

"Jackie, stay with me!" the familiar male voice again shouted from alongside her.

The voice was coming from the co-pilot's seat. Jackie allowed her head to fall to her right shoulder and attempted to focus on the person alongside her. Her vision finally straightened. She saw Zack clutching the wheel while attempting to keep the plane from crashing into the ocean. He glanced at her. It was the first time she'd remembered seeing fear on his face. As he struggled with the controls, Jackie again attempted to reach the yoke before her. She heard the continuous screaming from the back of the plane. The passengers were terrified. She heard Zack shouting out a curse just before everything went dark.

§

Two days earlier. Salvatore Romano's Colorado Springs country mansion was nestled on a large parcel of land beyond tall, stone walls. The professionally landscaped estate didn't have a hedge out of place. Weeping willow trees and faux split rail fencing lined the long driveway. The driveway split off to circle a large fountain outside the front door, while the remaining driveway branched off to the kitchen, staff wing, and eventually to the massive, detached, eight-car garage. Toward the back of the mansion, Sal walked through the massive, blossoming garden with his daughter.

Sal Romano was a robust man, although not necessarily overweight. He held his weight well. Despite being in his mid-forties, his face had a youthful appearance and almost cherub in nature. His baby face and moderately balding head gave him an innocent appeal. His possible mafia ties had always been in question, but if he had mob ties, there was little to no evidence of it. Sal's daughter, Pinto, was an attractive woman in her mid-twenties with long, copper-colored hair. Although they had gone through a rough patch, their relationship had finally found a solid footing partially due to her future husband.

Sal hugged his daughter while smiling proudly. "I'm so glad you and Beck decided to get married here," he announced cheerfully.

"I like your new home here in Colorado. It's nicer than the one in Chicago," Pinto informed him. "I'm glad you decided to leave Chicago and move here."

"I wanted to be closer to my daughter," he admitted proudly while hugging her. "Everything will be perfect for your wedding, I promise."

"I'll admit," she remarked while hiding her devious grin, "our decision to have the wedding at your place was an underhanded plot to take some of the stress off Beck and put it on you."

Sal chuckled at his daughter's confession. "That's okay," he announced. "I don't mind." He seemed to consider the comment and appeared curious. "He's still uptight about the wedding?"

"Uptight?" she announced with a moderately nervous chuckle. "He's beyond uptight. After that last wedding we attended--"

"Don't go there," Sal warned her now turning serious. "That didn't qualify as a wedding."

She drew a deep breath and held it. It was obvious she was slightly nervous as well. "I just know he's terrified something will go terribly wrong. I know he fears our wedding will somehow be turned into a warzone," she remarked with a sigh then looked around the serene garden in the secluded countryside. "At least here, there's some control over security."

"And I'm going to hire additional security to make sure everything runs smoothly," Sal eagerly announced. He hugged her while grinning. "I can't believe my little girl is getting married in two weeks."

They heard the back, kitchen door open causing both to look across the garden to the patio. Pinto's husband-to-be, Beck Larue, stepped onto the patio. Beck was a ruggedly handsome man who stood over six feet tall with an impressive athletic build. His light brown hair was moderately rumpled and the perfect length for running fingers through. Jackie Falcone followed him onto the patio from the kitchen. Jackie was an attractive woman in her mid-twenties with her long, dark hair worn in a ponytail, although usually just when she anticipated combat.

Today, Jackie was dressed casually in a pair of worn jeans and a white tank top beneath her brown, leather bomber jacket. Beck and Jackie were laughing as they headed across the garden. Pinto grinned like a schoolgirl when she saw her husband-to-be and hurried to join him. They hugged happily after spending nearly two days apart. Sal joined them and smiled cheerfully at Jackie. Although Jackie was undeniably attractive, Sal now saw her as a second daughter. Sal saw the entire team as part of his family since his daughter started dating Beck. Even the unruly ones had a special place in his heart.

"Did Ross and Lee make their morning flight?" Sal asked Jackie.

"Despite everything, I got them to the airport in time," Jackie proudly replied.

"She broke a few sonic speeding laws," Beck teased then gingerly rubbed his sour stomach, "but it was fun living on the edge of light speed."

"I wasn't the one who forgot to wake the newlyweds," she announced while casting a glare at him.

"Guilty," Beck announced and subconsciously rubbed the back of his neck. He looked around the garden then glanced at his future wife as she clung to him. "Have you and your father mapped out the entire wedding yet?"

"We're getting there," Pinto replied then focused her attention on Jackie. "Will Holden be back in time for the wedding?"

"With a few days to spare," Jackie replied cheerfully. She didn't want to admit she was missing her husband already despite that he had only left yesterday morning. Jackie had met her husband, Holden, while she was on the run after witnessing a murder at the hands of an influential man. Their first meeting wasn't exactly love at first sight, since he was the federal agent chasing her after a botched attempt to protect her. "He's working on training some new guys, but he'll only be gone a week tops."

"I'm sure he doesn't want to miss seeing his wife in a dress," Pinto teased then giggled. "How many times will this make?"

"Me in a dress?" Jackie asked then considered the question. "My wedding; Ross' wedding; your wedding." She smiled and laughed.

"We got her in a dress a few other times," Beck announced then turned serious. "Zack's the problem."

"He's still refusing to put on a tux and be a groomsman? It doesn't seem right that he won't participate in the wedding ceremony," Pinto pouted then immediately looked at Jackie. "Can't you do something with him? Certainly, you can get him into a tuxedo."

Jackie's eyes widened as she shook her head. "No way," she announced boldly. "I'd have to call in every favor and possibly promise to let him blow up a small freighter in order to pull that off."

"Yeah, he's been a real prick since we made him work as a ship's steward that one time," Beck replied with a defeated sigh. "No one's getting him into anything that has a crease or requires ironing ever again. I even pulled rank and told him he wasn't allowed to dance with any of the pretty bridesmaids if he didn't dress up."

"That may have worked, if he didn't outrank you," Jackie muttered.

"What did he say?" Pinto asked and immediately regretted it when Beck frowned and held up his middle finger.

Sal held back his smile and attempted to keep from laughing.

Pinto glared at her father then pointed a warning finger. "And you aren't to encourage him either," she threatened. "If the two of you start conspiring, you'll have him sitting on the roof at my wedding with a sniper rifle."

Chapter Two

Three horse and riders raced along the broad path in the picturesque countryside. There wasn't a house, barn, or living soul for miles and the smooth, well-worn path seemed to extend forever. It was the perfect day for a gallop across the country. A lean, dark-haired fifteen-year-old girl on a large, black horse was in the lead. The horse, decked out in the finest western tack, dwarfed its smaller rider. A blonde fifteen-year-old girl on a bay paint gelding bolted past her and took the lead. The large white spots on the horse's otherwise dark brown coat resembled clouds, aptly spawning his name, Storm Cloud. The horse's long, black flowing tail was all the second rider saw as her blonde friend took the lead. The third rider, and sole man of the three riders, happily lagged behind on a tall, palomino mare, who didn't care about winning any race involving the bad boy horses.

The three riders slowed just past a large tree, which had been the designated finish line. Both girls waited for the handsome man to catch up and stop his horse alongside them. Bogart laughed while pushing his cowboy hat back on his head to reveal his excessively charming smile. Bogart was 'hunky actor' handsome with flowing golden-brown hair and sideburns a shade darker. The stubble on his youthful face only accentuated his dimples, adding to his charm and country boy appeal.

"I think you girls cheat," Bogart announced. "This horse is a lemon."

Monique and Colleen were the ultimate tomboys dressed in their finest blue jeans, cowboy boots, and plaid shirts. The only thing girly about either was their shoulder-length hair and even that they wore in ponytails beneath their cowboy hats. Somewhere beneath the hats and dirt were two attractive, teenage girls.

"Sorry, she's the third fastest horse at my farm," Monique, the blonde girl on the paint gelding, informed him. "We gave you a sporting chance."

"Next time I'm bringing my own horse," he announced. "Then you'll eat my dust."

"I can't believe you actually have a black Friesian stallion," Colleen, the brunette on the black horse, remarked with amazement while shaking her head. "The warhorse of the Netherlands."

Monique raised a suspicious brow while eying the handsome man. "Exactly how did you acquire a horse like that anyway?" she asked. "They cost a fortune."

"That's classified," Bogart replied without hesitation and refused to look at either girl.

"So you stole it," Colleen announced while grinning.

Bogart eyed them with surprise then frowned and shook his head. "I can't believe you girls think that way about me," he pouted playfully.

Both stared at him and raised their brows in secret comment. They knew more than he ever wanted them to know. Bogart hid his smile and rode past them, ending the interrogation. The two girls had met Bogart when former Navy SEAL team Whiskey Tango Foxtrot came to their aid a while back. Bogart had a reputation as a conman, and, despite his newly adopted family of former SEALs, he still couldn't quite shake his past. Despite what they'd heard, the two girls adored the conman. The three continued their ride at a leisurely walk, enjoying the Colorado countryside.

"I'm glad you invited me riding this weekend," Bogart announced then appeared defeated. "I needed to get away from all that wedding business."

"Fear of commitment?" Colleen teased while eyeing the handsome man.

"No, fear of boredom," Bogart replied with little enthusiasm. "I hope Pinto has some cute bridesmaids, but with my luck, they'll all be married."

"My mom's single," Colleen interjected then immediately tensed after the words left her mouth.

He eyed her suspiciously. "I hope that's not why you asked me out riding today," Bogart remarked. "We've been through this before. I'm not the sort of boy you want dating your mother. I'd do something to screw it up, and I'd be booted from your lives. I've never had a real family, and now I have several of them. I don't want to ruin a good thing."

"I understand," Colleen replied with defeat. "I realized I shouldn't have said anything the moment I said it."

Both girls appeared tense while attempting to enjoy the ride. Bogart remained happily clueless and enjoyed the scenery. Colleen nudged Monique on the horse alongside hers. Monique shifted in her saddle then looked at Bogart.

"There actually was an ulterior motive to inviting you out today," Monique announced, catching Bogart's attention.

"Oh?"

They stopped their horses and turned to face him. Their looks were serious and almost concerned.

"Someone's been spying on us," Monique informed him.

"Spying on you?" Bogart launched and immediately looked around. "Who? Where?"

"Obviously we don't know who," Monique replied, "but we've seen him several times not far from home and sometimes again later during our rides. I swear he knows the route we take."

"Have you seen him yet today?" Bogart practically demanded then squinted. "Are we talking someone your age? Or is this someone my age?"

"No, he's definitely not someone from our school," Colleen interjected. "We've encountered boys from school before. This guy definitely doesn't want to be seen."

"He's got to be at least as old as you, if not older," Monique added.

"But you're certain he's following you?" Bogart practically demanded. "It's not possible he lives nearby and is just suspicious of you two."

"No, of course not. No one lives around here," Monique replied. "He hides out near the old ghost town where we take a break before heading back home. To make matters twice as creepy; we'll sometimes see him again not far from home on the same ride."

"We think he has a four-wheeler, but we never actually hear him," Colleen added.

"Is there a specific place you've seen him hiding while spying on you within this ghost town?" Bogart asked.

"Yes, he's usually hiding near the sheriff's office at the far end of town," Monique informed him. "It's to the left as we're heading into the ghost town."

"How far is the ghost town from here?"

"It's just over that crest," Colleen replied while pointing. "Less than a mile."

"You continue toward the ghost town," Bogart informed them. "I'll catch up with you. We'll find out who's been spying on you."

§

Monique and Colleen rode at a leisurely walk into the ghost town along the main road. The dilapidated old town consisted of the main street and two side streets, though most of the buildings on the side streets were reduced to piles of rubble. The buildings along the main thoroughfare appeared almost structurally sound, having survived hundreds of years in the dry conditions. They attempted to keep their attention on each other and their ride, not wanting to think about what Bogart had planned. They stopped outside the saloon as usual and dismounted. Once on the ground, they patted their horses and stood behind them, so that they couldn't be seen by anyone hiding within the sheriff's office.

"What do you think?" Colleen asked while fidgeting.

"I'm hoping we did the right thing by confiding in Bogart," Monique muttered and leaned against her horse. "He can be sneaky, but he's not their best fighter. If there's trouble, he may need our help."

Monique removed her rifle from the saddle holster. Colleen grabbed her bullwhip, which she kept where a cattle rope should hang.

"What are the chances this guy is military grade?" Colleen asked while attempting to sound more confident. "I'm sure Bogart has enough training to take your average guy from the street down."

Monique nodded with conviction. The two girls stared at each other then frowned and groaned.

"We shouldn't have let him go alone," Monique muttered and leaned against her horse.

§

A man stood alongside the glassless window within the sheriff's office and peered outside at the girls with their horses just down the street. The sheriff's office was void of furniture and mostly rotting, as was most of the town. The floorboards were excessively dusty, although there appeared to have been a lot of foot traffic in the small room. There were old cells beyond the door to the back, although they too were hanging from the rotted wood. The man stood silently by the window while watching the girls. The girls' stalker was in his mid to late thirties. He had a full head of thick, dark hair that was in need of a trim. His facial stubble suggested he hadn't shaved in a few days, and the dark circles beneath his eyes indicated the once handsome man hadn't slept much either.

Although he was a tall, moderately muscular man, he was possibly malnourished, lacking food as well as sleep the last week. His clothes continued with the trending theme, suggesting he had been homeless for several weeks.

"I'm not sure what you're up to," Bogart announced startling the man, "but I find it a little disturbing for a man your age to be stalking two teenage girls."

The man whirled around with surprise and stared at Bogart, who casually leaned against the back entrance to the sheriff's office. Bogart stared at the man a moment, and his expression immediately dropped as he straightened.

"Ah, hell! You're Colleen's father," Bogart suddenly gasped while allowing his arms to fall to his sides, revealing the semiautomatic he'd been concealing.

The man eyed the gun in Bogart's hand but didn't seem concerned by it. "You know who I am?" he gasped with surprise. His look then turned stern. "No one can know I'm here. They can't know I'm alive."

"Maybe you shouldn't be stalking your family then," Bogart snarled, lacking sympathy to the Army deserter who'd also ran out on his family several years ago. "They've seen you lurking about, Martin. That's why they called me out here. You're scaring them."

"I didn't mean to scare them," Martin announced then fidgeted. "I just wanted to see my daughter. I miss my family."

"Why can't you tell them that yourself?" Bogart suddenly demanded.

"Because I'm wanted by the Army," he announced. "They labeled me a traitor. In some circles, they'd prefer to bring me in dead rather than alive."

"Yes, I've heard the story from your wife," Bogart snarled with annoyance. "Selling weapons to the enemy."

"I never did that," Martin insisted. "I was framed."

Bogart rolled his eyes and replaced his gun to the hidden holster in the small of his back. "Yeah, sure," he muttered with annoyance. "That's what they all say." He snorted a laugh. "I should know. It was a favorite line of mine back in the day." His look again turned serious. "If you want to see your family, you need to turn yourself in. Because this ain't cutting it."

"I can't turn myself in," he replied now seeming desperate. "You don't know the sort of men who are after me. They'd kill me before they'd ever allowed the truth to come out." His eyes pleaded with Bogart. "You don't know me, and you have no reason to believe me, but I'm telling the truth. For my family; don't tell anyone you've seen me."

"Then you need to stop stalking them," Bogart snapped sparing no sympathy. "That girl thinks her father is dead. Let her live with that delusion. Your wife went to great lengths to protect her. Don't take that from her, if you're not willing to stand trial."

Martin reluctantly nodded.

§

Bogart rode his horse down the broad road of the old ghost town toward the girls just outside the saloon. They perked up when they saw him. Bogart immediately noticed the rifle and bullwhip in their hands and stopped his horse near them.

"We're not having any of that," he announced while indicating their weapons of choice.

"We thought you might need backup," Colleen informed him while tossing the bullwhip over her shoulder.

"Did you see him?" Monique asked with concern.

"Yeah. Who was it?" Colleen asked as her eyes widened. "Did you beat the crap out of him?"

"He got away," Bogart reluctantly informed them. "I didn't get a very good look at him, but I think I scared him enough that he won't be back."

The girls were disappointed that he hadn't caught the mysterious stalker. They were quite possibly disappointed that he didn't kick any ass either.

"We should head back," Bogart announced and indicated their horses.

Monique and Colleen replaced the rifle and bullwhip then mounted their horses without use of their stirrups. All three turned and rode at a leisurely pace alongside Bogart heading back out of town.

"Should we say something to my father?" Monique asked as they reached the edge of town.

"No," Bogart replied with a defeated sigh. "There's no reason to involve your FBI father. I'm pretty sure you'll never see him again. If he shows himself again, let me know, and I'll say something to your father."

They rode several minutes away from the ghost town in silence. Bogart had a lot on his mind and seemed less enthusiastic about their return ride.

Monique cast a look at Bogart and raised her brows in question. "Can I ask you a personal question?"

Bogart shrugged. "Sure. Why not?"

"How many men have you killed?"

Colleen eagerly looked at him and awaited his answer as well. "Any with your bare hands?"

Bogart eyed both girls with some surprise then frowned and shook his head.

"You girls need to start taking an interest in boys," he muttered. "You're starting to worry me."

Chapter Three

An hour from Colorado Springs. Sebastian Cicco's mansion was sprawled across the massive, secluded estate grounds. Although only two stories, the mansion covered a lot of ground. It was early evening, and everything seemed peaceful. A woman's shrill scream broke the silence. A young woman wearing a white, satin nightgown with a matching robe ran along the mansion's second floor hallway with her robe flowing behind her. Her expensive, satin nightgown was strewn with blood near the chest and the waist. There was blood on her hands and down her legs to her bare feet. The young woman, who barely made the legal drinking age, appeared frightened to death from whoever chased her.

Lindsey Cicco was a beautiful woman with dark, nearly black flowing hair that was now pasted to her sweating neck and chest. Her expensive jewelry and the mansion hallway suggested she was as wealthy as she was beautiful. She ran along the hallway containing expensive paintings and antique tables strategically placed almost as if to hinder her escape. Lindsey heard someone following from a distance, but he was still too close. She looked behind her as she ran and held back her scream to the unseen predator. She bolted into a dimly lit nearby bedroom and slammed the door behind her.

Lindsey leaned against the door while breathing heavily then scanned the nearly dark room. She could make out the phone on the bedside table not far from her. She darted away from the door and fumbled for the nightstand, knowing it would be unwise to turn on the lights. Lindsey grabbed the phone and, with her blood-covered fingers, she pressed several buttons then placed the phone to her ear. There was a loud thump against the door, startling her. She gasped with surprise and stared at the door that seemed secure for the moment. Someone picked up on the other end.

"Daddy," she gasped into the phone. "I'm in trouble. Something's happened. He's going to kill me."

There was another thump against the door. She looked back at the door and saw it vibrate despite its thickness. Lindsey allowed a startled scream escape.

"I have to get out of here," she cried into the phone. "It's not safe here. He's going to get through. Send help!"

Lindsey tossed the phone aside and ran to the balcony door. There was a loud crack as the bedroom door broke and flew open. Lindsey gasped and spun toward the glass doors.

§

It was just after dark and Sal's back patio was brightly lit with sporadic lights extending into the garden for a romantic appeal. Several outdoor lights gave a warm glow to the extensive garden and distant gazebo. After a picnic dinner of fried chicken and coleslaw served on the expensive, fine china, Sal's guests drank wine and celebrated the upcoming nuptials of their comrade, Beck. The large patio table seated nine, including Sal and his daughter. The six men along with Jackie were seven of the eight members of Whiskey Tango Foxtrot. Their leader, Ross, was on his honeymoon.

The former Navy SEAL team Whiskey Tango Foxtrot had been under the command of Jackie's father back when they served together. He was supposed to retire, but an unfortunate incident claimed his life. When Jackie needed her father's team most, they came to her aid. She'd been a part of the team ever since. Her brother, Bogart, had finally gained acceptance with the team. Well, most of the team accepted him. Bogart had returned that afternoon from his weekend ride with their favorite teenage witnesses. Besides Ross, Beck, Jackie, and Bogart, the remainder of the team was Gil, Kirk, Monroe, and Zack.

Zack Kinsley was easily the oldest man at the table and the senior member of the team. He was shorter than average, being lucky if he made 5'8" with a moderately average physique. Non-impressive by most standards, he appeared almost innocent at first glance. He was more athletic than most people would suspect. His brown, slightly graying hair was kept short and neat, although moderately spiky on top. He seemed more cuddly than intimidating but looks were deceiving. Monroe Dallas was a tall, lanky man in his mid to late thirties with a stylish flare to his expensive wardrobe. His light brown hair was neatly trimmed, although not nearly short enough to constitute a buzz cut. He was handsome in his own rights, so his lack of female companionship was baffling.

Kirk Mandel stood an imposing 6'4" with broad shoulders and biceps the size of tree trunks. His buzz cut and thick facial stubble made him even more intimidating if it were possible. Women were drawn to Kirk's ruggedly handsome features and massive muscles. Despite his moderately loose morals, women had a tough time breaking through his frigid exterior. Gil Rafferty, although a handsome man, shared the same serious expression as his counterparts. He was on the upper end of thirty if not in his early forties. His short dark hair was peppered with gray giving him a slightly distinguished look. His serious expression was the one he wore most and had a way of keeping strangers at arm's length.

The most easily dismissed last member of the team was possibly the most temperamental. A silver sable German shepherd lay in a grassy area not far from the table and snapped at lightning bugs as they flashed past his face. Darth could be as serious as the rest of the team yet lovable when called upon or when a squeaky toy was involved. His loyalty to the team was undying, and the team felt the same way about their four-legged, furry comrade.

"Three days in Denver devoted to shopping?" Kirk remarked then eyed Beck while raising a skeptical brow. "You're not even married, and you're already--"

"Finish that sentence and die," Jackie launched across the table to the big man with more brawn than brain, which obviously included tact.

A muffled whipping sound came from one of the men at the table. Jackie's eyes narrowed as she eyed each man, but they all maintained the same mildly serious yet innocent looks on their faces. When she couldn't figure out which man it had been, there was a round of chuckles.

Pinto groaned and shook her head. "I can't believe I'm willingly marrying into this."

Beck took her hand in his and affectionately kissed it then met her gaze. "Never mind them," he announced while smiling warmly. "They're just jealous. Every single one of them would like to be whipped."

"Some more than others," Monroe muttered.

"Was that directed at me?" Bogart suddenly demanded while glaring at Monroe. "Because if anyone is whipped around here, it's you."

"Me?" Monroe practically cried out. "When have I been whipped? Figuratively or literally?"

"Literally," Zack announced and raised his hand. "A few times. Not a fan. It stings like a mother--"

"Be nice," Jackie remarked sternly.

"Well, this evening certainly took a turn in the wrong direction," Pinto scoffed.

Sal clinked his butter knife against his crystal glass, silencing everyone and directing attention on himself. He stood and raised his wineglass.

"I'd just like to say that I'm very proud to have Beck marry my daughter in two weeks," Sal announced cheerfully. "I've been blessed with a wonderful future son-in-law--" He raised his glass to Beck, who smiled and lifted his glass to Sal in response. "And to the new extended family I've always wanted." He raised his glass to the rest of the team. "To my new family!"

The entire team stood and raised their glasses to Sal and took a drink. As they returned to their seats, the butler approached the patio table. He paused near Sal and whispered something in his ear. Sal eyed his butler and appeared surprised.

"Really?" Sal announced then turned serious as he sank into thought. "Send him out."

As the butler returned to the house, the guys eyed Sal in silent question.

"What was that about?" Beck finally asked.

"An old friend I haven't heard from in years showed up unannounced at my doorstep," Sal informed them.

"What *sort* of old friend?" Monroe asked.

"Just your usual sort of old friend," Sal replied with a strange look in his eyes.

"Oh," Gil replied and shifted in his chair.

"This could get interesting," Sal announced.

They heard a gun cock. All eyes shifted to Zack. He looked innocently around the table with his semiautomatic partially hidden beneath the table and shrugged.

"What?"

"Just keep it in your pants," Beck lectured.

A neatly dressed man in his early fifties followed the butler to the patio table. Dexter Mansfield was a good-looking man with short graying hair and a clean-shaven face. He obviously had the money to take care of himself. His suit was hand tailored and cost more than the team's entire wardrobe combined. Sal stood and shook Dexter's hand then indicated the seat Pinto vacated for her father's friend. She chose to hang over Beck's shoulders instead.

"What do I owe the pleasure of your visit?" Sal asked while smiling, although it wasn't a trusting smile.

"I wish it were under better circumstances," Dexter announced then quickly eyed those at the table. He returned his attention back to Sal. "I'm here out of desperation."

"What seems to be the problem?" Sal pressed.

"My daughter recently married Vinny Cicco's boy, Sebastian," Dexter began. "I got a strange phone call from her earlier this evening. Something happened to my daughter, and Vinny is refusing to let me speak to her."

"I don't suppose the police can knock on the door," Gil muttered while resting his temple on his finger as if already knowing the story.

Dexter eyed Gil and raised his brow in response. "Vinny Cicco owns the local police," he insisted. "They tried to convince me she was fine." He shifted uncomfortably. "My daughter has, in the past, embellished a few stories. The police are trying to convince me that's all there was to it, but I'm not buying it. I need someone to rescue my daughter." He tensed and held his breath a moment. "I know something bad has happened to her. If she's fine, I want her to tell me she's fine. If she's being held against her will, or if something's happened to her, I want her out of there."

"And you came to me because you know my future son-in-law has been known for discretion in this sort of situation," Sal announced while sitting back in his chair.

"That's one way of putting it," Beck muttered humored.

"I know how desperate I sound," Dexter replied then looked around the table. "If anyone can get my daughter back, it's this team. Discretion is the last thing on my mind. I don't care if they level the entire mansion to get her out of there."

"I'm in," Zack immediately chimed in, obviously enticed by the prospect of leveling a mansion.

Beck ignored Zack's comment and leaned on the table closer to Dexter. "I'll be honest with you," he announced with little emotion. "I'm getting married in two weeks. Getting shot, maimed, or otherwise bruised before the wedding isn't an option. I'm not going on any assignments until after my honeymoon. Pinto and I have been through enough recently, and I don't want anything ruining our upcoming wedding."

"I'm willing to pay whatever you want," Dexter replied while squirming in his chair. "Maybe I'm even overreacting. Please, reconsider."

There was a tense pause. "Just because I'm not interested in any assignments," Beck announced while casually leaning back in his chair, "that doesn't mean the rest of the team wouldn't consider taking the job."

Sal and Dexter glanced at the others at the table.

"I'll do it," Zack again announced without hesitation.

"You'd dive off a cliff for the right price," Monroe remarked then looked at Dexter. "That being said; I'm in." He glanced around the table at the others.

Gil, Kirk, Bogart, and Jackie nodded.

"Then we're in agreement," Gil announced and smirked. "We're all in."

"We'll leave first thing in the morning," Monroe announced while sipping his drink.

"No, it can't wait," Dexter announced a little too eagerly. "There's no telling what's happened to my daughter. It has to be tonight."

There was a round of groans.

"He's right," Bogart announced. "His daughter could be in serious trouble."

Monroe glanced at his watch and sighed. "We can bug out in an hour."

"Thank you," Dexter gasped and seemed to relax for the first time. "If she's being held prisoner, she's at Sebastian's mansion. That's her last known location and where the phone call originated. Find her husband, and you'll find her."

Chapter Four

Sebastian Cicco's mansion seemed peaceful and serene in the midnight hour. All things considered, it seemed a little too peaceful. The estate was dimly lit on the inside as well as the outside. It didn't seem as if anyone was up, which included security. Motion sensor security cameras were mounted on the wall every twenty yards. A few cameras were aimed at the property beyond the wall, but most were directed onto the estate grounds closer to the mansion. Monroe sat on the wall while casing the massive home through night vision binoculars. He lowered the binoculars and exchanged bewildered looks with Gil, who crouched alongside him.

"Is it just me, or is this place lightly guarded for the seedy underworld type?" Monroe asked.

"Could Dexter have been wrong about Cicco's associations?" Gil remarked while looking around. "I don't even see a single guard."

"You'd think he'd have at least one," Monroe muttered and continued his scan of the estate.

Gil's lips curved into a tiny, moderately devious smile. "We could send Bogart to the front door and have him ring the bell."

Monroe chuckled then actually considered the comment. They would call that the backup plan.

"Am I missing something?" Zack's voice suddenly demanded over their ear transmitters. "Where are the bad guys? Where are the automatic weapons? I could storm this compound with harsh language."

Gil jumped and touched his ear, surprised by Zack's excessively loud response. Monroe had to remove his hidden device to keep from going deaf.

Monroe reinserted the ear transmitter and spoke in a calm voice. "Take it easy, Zack," he announced, although Zack's outrage was understandable. Something didn't feel right, and the entire team sensed it. "We came out here with limited information and not knowing what we were up against. We don't even know if she's here."

"Well, she's here," came Kirk's less than enthusiastic voice over their ear transmitters. "I have eyes on her in one of the back bedrooms on the second floor." There was an awkward silence followed by irritation. "She's watching T.V. and eating popcorn."

"Are you sure it's her?" Jackie's voice chimed in from her secured location.

"Well, it ain't her stunt double," Bogart replied from his location with Kirk.

Gil eyed Monroe alongside him and awaited his decision on their next move.

Monroe continued to stare at the mansion while deep in thought then shook his head. "Something isn't right," he remarked. "She calls her father in a state of panic, gets disconnected, and doesn't call him back to report everything is fine?"

"Do we ring the bell?" Gil teased.

Monroe gave the comment some consideration then touched his ear transmitter. "Jackie, are you up for a woman to woman talk?"

"I've never had one of those before, but I'll give it a try," she responded. "I'm going in."

§

Jackie was dressed in her finest, black stalking outfit complete with calf-high black boots. She wore her shoulder holster, which contained her semiautomatic. Her dual fighting batons were worn in a custom designed holster attached to the small of her back. As she headed across the grounds, Zack walked along the top of the wall and spray-painted the security camera lenses for her grand entrance and great escape. Although that didn't seem as if it would be nearly as harrowing as originally suspected. Jackie easily scaled the wall to the second floor balcony, landed softly in a dark corner, and peered through the glass doors into the dimly lit bedroom.

The bedroom was bigger than most homes, contained large, heavy furniture, and a large screen television mounted on the far wall. The glow from the large screen television was the only light within the bedroom. She spotted Lindsey casually reclined on the tall, canopy bed wearing frumpy sleep shorts and a tank top. She looked almost bored while flipping through the channels with the remote control. Jackie wondered if simply knocking on the front door wasn't the better plan. Dexter's daughter seemed perfectly safe and awfully comfortable.

Jackie placed an electronic device near the door lock and pressed a button. There was a small jolt of electric current, disabling the security alarm attached to the door. Jackie easily picked the lock, waited a moment, and then slipped into the dimly lit bedroom. Lindsey saw her enter the room and let out a startled scream as she sat up straight on the bed. Jackie remained close to the door and eyed the young woman only a few years younger than herself.

"Your father sent me," Jackie informed her then easily glided across the room to the bedroom door. She was able to open it, indicating it wasn't locked from the outside. Another strange find. She shut the door, turned the bolt, and eyed Lindsey with some surprise. "Your father was worried about you. You're *not* being held prisoner?"

Lindsey stared at Jackie almost unable to speak from the shock of the stranger's entrance. She suddenly came to life. "My father sent you?" she gasped and quickly moved to the side of the bed. "Did anyone see you? They're watching the grounds. It isn't safe."

"No one saw me," Jackie informed her and remained suspicious of the situation. "You called your father earlier this evening in a state of panic. You said 'he's going to kill me'. Why didn't you call him back or answer his calls? Your father thought you were in trouble."

Lindsey turned on the bedside light. Jackie was able to see the young woman up close for the first time. She had several black and blue marks on her face from being hit, choke marks on her neck, and bruises on both her wrists. Someone had clearly roughed up the girl.

"I am in trouble," she announced and moved off the bed. "They're holding me prisoner. I've tried to escape, but my father-in-law's men caught and beat me." She tilted her head and stared with concern. "Are you sure they didn't see you? There are security cameras everywhere."

"I assure you; no one saw me," Jackie informed her. "Get dressed. We're leaving."

"You don't understand," Lindsey gasped, fearful for another escape attempt. "If they catch us, they'll kill us. Even the police won't help. Unless you have an army--"

"I have an army," Jackie replied.

Lindsey stared at her a moment with distrust. The enthusiasm then showed on her face. She immediately grabbed her discarded clothes and slipped into them. Once she slipped into her shoes, she awaited further instructions. Jackie again checked the hallway.

"His men are downstairs," Lindsey informed her. "I saw two, but there could be more."

Jackie again locked the door and then indicated the balcony. "We aren't going out the front door." She tapped her ear transmitter. "The place is quiet. What's the status of the guards on ground level?"

"Blinds and curtains are closed," Monroe responded back. "We don't have eyes on them."

"No sounds on second," Jackie announced. "We're clear to move. Coming out now."

"Someone just pulled up. We've got company," Monroe suddenly announced through Jackie's ear transmitter.

Jackie paused only a moment to hear Monroe's warning. She shut off the bedroom light then rushed Lindsey onto the balcony. Gunshots were heard outside the estate. Jackie was surprised since the shots fired came from the front of the estate and her team was closer to the rear.

"Who's firing?" Lindsey suddenly gasped with a look of horror on her face.

It was a good question. "I'm not sticking around to ask," Jackie informed her and moved the young girl closer to the balcony railing.

Lindsey paused before the balcony and looked down, appearing somewhat concerned about the height. The sound of gunfire was now heard within the mansion on the first floor. Jackie indicated the emergency escape chain ladder that was now attached to the balcony for their climb. Zack had been busy while Jackie waited for Lindsey to change. Lindsey was apprehensive, but the sound of gunfire was enough to convince her to climb down the ladder. She reached the bottom where Zack waited, having held the swaying ladder steady. Jackie could now hear someone within the second floor hallway. Zack looked back up at Jackie on the balcony. Jackie was about to climb over the railing when the bedroom door vibrated only once before being kicked open.

"Jackie," Zack ordered. "Get down here!"

Jackie darted back into the dimly lit bedroom and slid behind the bed as the men entered with their semiautomatics aimed. Fortunately, they hadn't seen her. They immediately ran for the open balcony doors. Jackie silently sprang to her feet with a baton in each hand and darted onto the balcony behind them. The men were about to fire at Zack and Lindsey, who were running across the estate grounds. Jackie flicked her wrists, extending each baton to two feet. The men heard the sound and immediately spun around. Jackie kicked the first man in the chest sending him over the balcony railing and into a swan dive for the ground. The second man already had his gun aimed at her. Jackie twirled the baton and knocked the gun from his hand. He didn't seem startled enough, indicating he was a professional who was used to surprise attacks.

As Jackie swung her right baton at him, he dodged the stick and kicked her in the abdomen, sending her backward into the room.   She caught her balance and took a fighting stance with her batons while the man leaped for his discarded gun and aimed it at her.   Jackie lunged for him before he could fire, swung both batons simultaneously, and struck the man across the face with one and alongside the head with the other.   While he was disoriented, she spun into a roundhouse kick and struck him in the chest, sending him over the balcony railing and onto the estate grounds below.   Jackie darted across the balcony and for the chain ladder.   She then hesitated while listening to the silence of the mansion.

Why weren't there any other sounds?   Two men?   That was it?   The men who attacked them had obviously broken into the mansion, killing the guards who were keeping Lindsey prisoner. Why would someone shoot the mansion guards?   Obviously, they didn't work for Cicco, so who were they?   It didn't make sense.   Jackie returned her batons to her holster, climbed partway down the chain ladder, and then jumped the last few feet.   She hurried after Zack and Lindsey.   Despite their head start, Zack was having some trouble getting Lindsey up the wall. Rich girls like Lindsey weren't used to physical activity and climbing a wall was not an easy task for her.

Jackie reached the brick wall without slowing and easily scaled it as if running up a hill.   Lindsey stared with surprise at the way Jackie tackled the impressive wall.   Jackie immediately lay on top of the wall and extended her hand to assist Lindsey. Lindsey attempted to reach her hand, but it was still too high. Without warning, Zack grabbed Lindsey by the thighs just beneath her buttocks and tossed her up the wall.   She let out a startled scream in response.   Jackie caught her hands and pulled her up the rest of the way.   By the time Bogart assisted Lindsey down on the other side, Jackie and Zack were already landing near them.

They hurried her into the awaiting car just down the road where Gil, Monroe, and Kirk were already waiting.   Zack took the second car with Gil and Kirk while Jackie and Lindsey got into the car with Monroe and Bogart.

§

Once they were safely away from the mansion and there was no indication that they were being pursued, Jackie eyed the nervous woman seated in the back seat alongside her. Jackie immediately shifted her attention to Monroe, who rode shotgun while Bogart drove the getaway car.

"What happened back there?" Jackie practically demanded to Monroe. "Those men broke *into* the house and shot the guards downstairs. They weren't there to stop our rescue. They didn't even know we were there."

Monroe glanced back at Jackie as well as the young woman and remained baffled by what had just happened as well. Despite the armed men killing the guards, their escape had been a little too easy.

"Who were those men?" Monroe asked Lindsey. "They weren't Cicco's men."

Lindsey shivered slightly while rubbing her chilled arms. She finally met Monroe's gaze. "The Cicco family has many enemies," Lindsey announced somewhat timidly. "I don't know who they were. They could have been almost anyone with a grudge against Sebastian or his father."

"So Cicco's guards were killed by some unknown party." Jackie snorted a laugh. "On the bright side, they weren't there to kill us for a change," she remarked then eyed Lindsey. "Why was your husband holding you prisoner?"

Lindsey fidgeted while seeming slightly sickened at the thought of men being killed under her roof. "I don't know how much my father told you about Sebastian Cicco," Lindsey gently remarked. "So I'll start at the beginning. I married Sebastian to make my father happy. Two powerful families brought together by marriage and all that bullshit. Honestly, he seemed perfect. We spent three amazing weeks traveling Europe for our honeymoon. I thought our marriage was actually going to work. Sebastian seemed great."

Bogart eyed her through the rearview mirror from his position behind the wheel.

"After we got back from our honeymoon a few weeks ago," she continued, "Sebastian turned into a completely different person. He was cruel and insanely jealous if I talked to anyone.

He didn't even want me talking to girlfriends or my father." She drew a deep breath and shivered. "Then he started hitting me."

There was a long pause as she seemed to fade out. She fidgeted and rubbed her chilled arms. Jackie exchanged looks with Monroe in the front seat. Bogart peered at them through the rearview mirror and listened to the conversation.

"Sebastian came home late this afternoon. He'd had a little too much to drink. He became insanely jealous over my lunch with a few girlfriends. It made no sense. They were my friends since high school. He started hitting me and wouldn't stop. When I tried to defend myself, he choked me." She gently shuttered and held her breath a moment. "Next thing I knew, the butcher knife was in my hand. I stabbed him two maybe three times." She drew a labored breath. "I killed him." She shook her head as her eyes widened. "I barely remember doing it, but there he was; dead on the kitchen floor."

Monroe and Jackie again exchanged looks at the surprising twist of events they had just heard.

"One of his guards came after me," she announced. "I thought for sure he'd kill me when he caught me, but he locked me away instead. I think they were instructed to keep me there until my father-in-law got back from his trip overseas. I wouldn't doubt he intended to kill me himself. He wanted to be the one to kill me."

"So no one called the police?" Jackie asked.

She shook her head as her eyes widened. "Absolutely not! They would never call the police," she announced. "Despite owning half the police force in our little town, Vinny wouldn't want me arrested. Then I'd be in police custody with a good lawyer." She shook her head while staring at them. "No, they wanted to apply their own brand of justice."

"It's a long trip back to your father's mansion," Jackie informed her. "We'll stop at a motel about an hour from here and give you a chance to recover from your ordeal. We'll return you to your father in the morning."

"Thank you," Lindsey announced timidly and smiled for the first time. "I can't thank you enough for getting me out of there. I don't know how much longer I'd be alive if you hadn't shown up when you did."

"You're safe with us," Monroe added.

Chapter Five

The out-of-the-way motel resided close to a moderately busy highway, but the motel itself was back just far enough from the road to give it a sense of seclusion. Nothing to brag about, the motel contained ten rooms side-by-side with a plain, covered walkway. The dim lights and the missing 'T' on the sign gave the motel a creepy sort of feel, but being it was tucked away from the highway made it desirable for the team's needs. Monroe and Bogart secured two rooms for the team and Dexter's daughter. Jackie would stay with Lindsey, while the guys shared a connecting room. The rooms were nothing special and hadn't been renovated since the seventies. At least the rooms were clean. Unfortunately, Jackie had stayed at worse.

Once inside their room, Jackie unlocked the connecting door and checked on the guys. They were already engrossed in a tense game of rock, paper, scissors to see who would take first watch. Lindsey nervously paced the room and eyed the open connecting door to the guys' room.

"Are you sure we're safe here?" she asked with concern. "I can't help feeling tense."

"Your husband's guards were killed by those two intruders, whoever they were, and they've been eliminated. No one saw you leave with us, and we weren't followed," Jackie informed her. "Even if someone else shows up and discovers you're missing, there are a dozen motels between here and there. Since the guys checked us in, even the desk clerk doesn't know there are any women in these rooms. As long as we stay inside, we're safe."

"We have to leave sometime," Lindsey reminded her. "What if they do find us?"

Jackie smirked and casually shrugged. "Then I suppose heaven help them."

"You have that much confidence in those guys?" Lindsey asked with surprise while indicating the men in the connecting room.

"They range from badass to scary," Jackie replied while adding a humored chuckle. "So, yeah, I have that much confidence in them."

Lindsey attempted to relax, although her rigid body language suggested she failed miserably. "I'd feel better if I could call my dad and tell him I'm okay."

"We've already contacted your father," Jackie informed her. "The less contact we have, the safer you are. We don't know how resourceful your father-in-law is."

"Resourceful enough," Lindsey replied and stared at Jackie. "If he wants me badly enough, and I promise you he does, he'll stop at nothing until he gets me. I'm not even sure I'm safe at any of my father's safe houses."

"He knows the score, and he's already coming up with a plan to keep you out of Vinny Cicco's hands," Jackie informed her then offered a tiny, reassuring smile. "You should try to get some rest. We're leaving in a few hours just before sunup tomorrow."

Lindsey gently rubbed her chilled shoulders and shifted nervously. "That's easier said than done," she replied then looked around the room. "Maybe if I took a long, hot bath I'd be able to relax."

Jackie wondered why women always thought a hot bath was the answer to all their problems. Personally, she didn't understand the attraction. Perhaps if she had insight into how women thought, she'd understand. She had to remember to ask Pinto one day.

"The door is secure, and we'll be right outside the bathroom door," Jackie announced and offered a reassuring smile. "You'll be fine."

Lindsey finally relaxed enough to enter the bathroom and run her bathwater. Jackie made herself comfortable on the first bed closest to the secured door. Bogart appeared in the connecting room doorway and looked around.

"Where's the girl?" he asked.

"Taking a bath," Jackie replied and eyed her brother. "Are you on first watch?"

He frowned at the question and nodded. "I don't know how, but I swear they've found a way to cheat at rock, paper, scissors," Bogart remarked and entered the bedroom. He flopped down on the vacant bed, causing it to creak, and made himself comfortable.

Jackie eyed him suspiciously and wondered about his odd mood since she'd picked him up from his weekend trip. "You seem preoccupied since your visit with Monique and Colleen," she remarked. "Everything okay?"

"No, not really," Bogart remarked then groaned and sat up straight. He stared at Jackie a moment while frowning. "They asked me to go riding with them because they thought they were being stalked."

Jackie suddenly straightened as her interest was piqued. "Were they?"

"Turns out they were," Bogart replied and shifted, unable to get comfortable. The subject obviously bothered him. "It was Colleen's MIA father."

Jackie immediately jumped to the side of the bed and faced her brother. She couldn't deny she was shocked. "The one Colleen believes to be dead?"

"The Army deserter," Bogart added.

"You didn't tell Colleen, did you?"

"No, of course not," Bogart replied then groaned and again flopped down on the bed. "I told him never to come around again, or I'd turn him over to the authorities."

Jackie remained tense while deep in thought then eyed Bogart. "You made the right call."

"Did I?" he asked while eyeing her. His expression hardened. "He should be punished for his crimes."

"And then Colleen would find out her father not only didn't die a hero, but he betrayed his country and abandoned her and her mother for his own selfish reasons," Jackie remarked then vigorously shook her head. "No, you made the right call. She's at a tough age as it is. I think we should spare her the drama. Perhaps her mother will tell her one day when she's older."

Bogart groaned softly. "Yeah, that's sort of what I thought too," he replied but remained distracted. "I hate lying to the squirt, but it's not as if he's going to hurt her. I mean, he's her father."

"Just let it go, Bogart," Jackie announced and again attempted to relax. "I'm sure he'll move on now that he's been called out."

Over the next hour, Bogart spent most of his time between watching T.V. and peering out the window. He finally turned to Jackie from his position near the window.

"What do women do in the tub so long?" Bogart finally asked.

"Beats me," Jackie remarked then grinned deviously. "I only enjoy a lengthy bath when there's mixed company involved."

Bogart chuckled at the comment. "My favorite water sport."

Jackie took her cue, jumped off the bed, and approached the bathroom door. She gently knocked and waited. Lindsey didn't respond.

"Lindsey," Jackie announced through the door. "You okay in there?"

There still wasn't a response. Jackie knocked a little louder. When she didn't get an answer, she removed her lock pick and easily sprung the lock. Bogart remained a few feet back while Jackie entered the bathroom. To her surprise, the tub was filled with water, but the bathroom was empty. Jackie looked at the open window and wondered how the woman could even fit through it.

"What the hell--?" she cried out then turned to Bogart, who approached. "She flew the coup."

"What? Why?"

She shook her head. "I guess she didn't believe we could protect her," Jackie huffed then hurried past him. "She's had an hour head start, but check out back just in case. I'll wake the guys."

Bogart ran for the motel room door while Jackie headed for the connecting door.

§

Kirk and Gil each took a car and drove away from the motel in opposite directions in search of Lindsey. Zack and Bogart searched the surrounding area by foot, in case they could still locate her. Jackie waited in her motel room with Monroe, who paced the length of the room with his cell phone to his ear.

"You can tell Dexter if his daughter doesn't want to be in our protective custody, there's nothing we can do about it," Monroe insisted to the person on the other end. "That's called kidnapping. Maybe in his world that's acceptable, but that's not how we do things in the real world."

"I'm sure he doesn't want you abducting his daughter against her will," Sal commented on the phone from the other end.

"He told us to get her back even if she protested," Monroe lashed out. "That's authorizing abduction."

"I'm sure he didn't mean it that way," Sal added with a groan. "I'll talk to him. If you can't convince her to return with you, at least keep an eye on her until her father can reach you."

"Well, we would, Sal," Monroe countered with irritation, "if we knew where she went. She could have made it to the highway and hitched a ride to just about anywhere. Dexter hasn't exactly been helpful. He doesn't even know her associations in this area. Apart from checking nearby bus terminals, we don't really know where to start."

"She didn't have any identification or money," Jackie added while she stood by the motel window and stared outside.

"Jackie made a good point," Monroe announced into the phone. "She didn't have identification or money. Not even a cell phone. That means she hitched a ride. Without knowing her known acquaintances, there's no way we'll be able to find her."

There was a strange pause. "I know someone who might be able to help, but you won't like it," Sal insisted. "A former employee of Dexter's who knows the girl."

"Who's that?"

There was another long pause. "Mac."

Monroe rolled his eyes and groaned at the thought. Jackie eyed him suspiciously wondering what he was told that he'd reacted so poorly.

"That's not going to go over well," Monroe remarked while shifting uncomfortably. "We didn't exactly leave her on the best of terms."

Now Jackie was interested in the conversation. "Who?" she practically demanded.

"Mac hates us and would probably kill Zack the first opportunity she's given," Monroe informed Sal over the phone while casting a glance at Jackie.

Jackie's eyes widened in horror. "Mac?" she practically cried out and shook her head defiantly. "Oh, that's definitely not floating," she insisted. "Zack will go ballistic."

"Perhaps she's unwilling to help," Sal responded from the other end, "but it wouldn't be a bad idea to exhaust all options first before giving someone like Dexter bad news. At least let me call Mac and talk to her."

Monroe rolled his eyes and shook his head. He reluctantly sighed. "Fine," he muttered into the phone. "Call Mac and see if she's willing to help, but I'm pretty sure she won't."

Monroe disconnected the call and cast a look at Jackie. She folded her arms across her chest and glared back at him.

"Inviting Mac into our circle is a bad idea," Jackie reminded him.

"He gave me little choice," Monroe replied while flopping on the bed with disgust. "She worked for Dexter and may know Lindsey's friends."

"She's not going to help us," Jackie insisted while throwing her arms in the air. "She wants to kill Zack, and she's not overly fond of the rest of us after we abandoned her at that hotel."

"And when she tells Sal no we'll be able to say we tried," Monroe announced while straightening. "We did everything we could. If Lindsey doesn't want to be in our protection or go back to her father, we can't force her. It's that simple."

"We rescued his daughter from her captors as commissioned," Jackie informed him with confidence. "We completed our assignment. What Lindsey does with her freedom is her decision. Dexter can't make her come home to him, and we're certainly not going to abduct her for him."

"And I agree with you," Monroe insisted while staring at her. "But I also understand it from Sal's point of view. We want to be able to tell Dexter we tried everything to get her to come with us. If we don't at least talk to the girl, we won't know why she's afraid to be in our protective custody."

"At least when Mac refuses to help, it'll fall on Mac and not us," Jackie remarked with a sigh.

"Exactly."

Chapter Six

An attractive woman in her mid-thirties walked briskly through the dimly lit parking garage. It was a little after three o'clock in the morning, and the parking garage was void of life. Her soft-soled boots made little noise even though most women's boots would echo throughout all three levels. Macbeth, frequently called Mac, was a dark-haired beauty by most standards. Although her fresh face and athletic frame suggested she was a high maintenance, classy woman, the truth was less flattering. Mac approached her moderately beat up, older car and casually swung her keys. In the early morning hour, the creepy parking garage would bring about some cautiousness in most women, but Mac didn't seem the least bit concerned. She unlocked and opened her car door.

When the passenger side door opened, Mac jumped back a step with surprise. A young, shabbily dressed man stepped out of her car and immediately met her gaze across the car roof. Mac stared at the man she'd never met getting out of *her* car.

"Who the hell are you?" she demanded with a hostility that would frighten most. "And what the hell were you doing in my car?"

"I'm Kane. Just Kane," he announced almost cheerfully as he leaned on the roof of her car. "I've been looking forward to meeting you, Mac. It was late when I arrived, and I didn't want to disturb you, so I thought I'd take a little nap while I waited."

"You slept in my car? Not creepy at all," she muttered while maintaining her distance from the man who barely made the legal drinking age. "How do you know my name? I'm sure we've never met."

Kane, no last name, was oddly handsome with an almost steampunk sort of appeal. His brown hair was kept short although moderately spiky on top. He had a neatly trimmed beard that almost resembled a five o'clock shadow, although it obviously wasn't. Had he been clean-shaven, he'd probably look like a teenager. Slightly shorter than average, he didn't appear to be very muscular and not impressive in his moderately worn clothes. His piercing blue eyes were commanding and lent to his appeal. Kane casually walked around the back of Mac's car while keeping his hands in his pockets and the same strange grin on his face. Mac set her bag on the roof of the car and faced the man as he approached. Her look was stern, and her body language suggested she was fight more than flight at that moment.

"Stop right there," she announced firmly as her eyes narrowed while piercing through his. It was obvious if he got too close, she would strike. "I'm in a hurry, so I don't have time to kick your ass right now."

He smiled and chuckled in his throat. Mac tilted her head with a slightly bewildered look while studying the odd man. She started to wonder if she had met him before.

"Do I know you?" she asked. "Something about you seems familiar."

"No, we've never met," he replied and leaned against the car's back fender while folding his arms across his chest. "I'm on a quest, and I'm told you hold a piece of the puzzle."

She stared at him with mild bewilderment. "Okay," she remarked already having lost interest and shook her head. "I'm going to leave now. If you're still there when I put the car in reverse, I'm going to run you over."

"I'm looking for someone," he announced as he straightened.

"Good for you," she scoffed while opening her car door with a little added vigor.

He pushed the car door shut, stopping her from getting inside.

She glared at him through angry, hateful eyes. "You have no idea who you're fucking with," Mac snarled and flicked her wrist. The switchblade knife in her hand was already snug against his crotch although her eyes never left his. "Back the fuck off. I'm not in the mood."

His eyes fell to the knife and its location. Kane seemed oddly trusting that she wouldn't stab him and remained unusually calm under the circumstances. He casually held his hands in the air and mocked her with his charming smile. That he didn't take a step away from the blade to his crotch was almost unsettling.

"Sorry if I'm putting you on the defensive," Kane announced. "It's a bit of a character flaw, I'm afraid. Bad gene pool, or so I'm told."

Mac drew a deep breath, removed the switchblade from its undesirable location, and seemed less hostile. "What makes you think I can help you? Who are you looking for anyway?"

"Zack Kinsley."

She didn't even give the name a second thought and immediately shook her head without hesitation or flinching. "Never heard of him," she casually announced. "You may want to recheck your source."

Mac reached for the car door. He again reached for the door to stop her. Mac blocked his hand, striking it away with precision and force. He chuckled as if finding it amusing.

"Fast reflexes," he announced and gave her some space. "My source is reliable. Police saw you in a parking garage with a man who had been identified as Zack Kinsley. I believe there was a shootout in that same building the night you left with the man in question."

Mac stared at the young man and casually leaned against her car door while folding her arms across her chest. "Is that his name?" she asked while cocking her head. "I didn't ask. I wasn't in his company that long. If you did your research, you'd know we checked into a motel that evening and checked out less than two hours later. That's the extent of our relationship and the last I saw your Zack Kinsley."

"You're sure you haven't had any contact with him since?" he asked as if he didn't believe her. "It's important I find him."

"I suppose he owes you money, huh?" she remarked then smirked. "He owes me a pretty penny too. If you see him, tell him Mac wants the fifty he owes her." She raised her brows. "Now, if you don't mind, I have places to be. If you feel the need to continue this conversation, please come back another time, and I'll gladly kick your ass."

Kane chuckled at the comment. "Wow, sexy and dangerous," he announced cheerfully. "I may just take you up on that." He stepped away from her car and extended his hand to the door. "Thank you for your time, Mac. I'll see you around."

She snorted a laugh and smirked almost playfully. "Not if I see you first."

Mac opened the car door, snatched her bag from the car roof, and jumped into the driver's seat. As she backed the car out of the parking spot, she cast a look at the handsome, strange man. He smiled charmingly and waved goodbye.

§

It was a little after four o'clock in the morning when Zack and Bogart returned from their sweep of the area surrounding the motel. The weary men entered Jackie's room where the others waited and flopped on their respective beds. Jackie shifted uncomfortably and glanced at Monroe before seeing Gil and Kirk dart into the connecting room. For some reason, they didn't want to be present.

"She must have hitched a ride," Bogart announced while shutting his eyes, obviously exhausted. "We covered every inch of ground between here and the highway."

Zack appeared to be asleep already. Monroe seemed tense while running his fingers through his hair. He eyed Jackie, who only glared back at him before he turned his attention to the men sprawled out on the beds.

"Jackie and I are going for breakfast at the diner next door," Monroe informed the weary men. "We'll leave in a couple of hours, so if you two want to get some sleep--"

Zack immediately sat up on the bed. "I could use something to eat," he announced while scratching his head.

"We could bring something back for you," Jackie suggested almost too quickly. "I'm sure you're tired after being out half the night."

Zack stood without hesitation. "No, I'm good," he remarked and eyed them. "Something tells me you two need a chaperone. Whatever you two are plotting, I'd like to know about it now before it blows up in your face later."

Jackie cast a look at Monroe then headed for the motel room door.

"It's just breakfast, Zack," Monroe scoffed seeming a little defensive. "You have a nasty habit of turning everything into a conspiracy."

"Probably because everything is a conspiracy," Zack remarked casually.

Bogart suddenly sat up and eyed them. "Now I'm suspicious too," he announced. "I think I'll go with you since I'm the one you guys are always conspiring against."

Jackie groaned and left the room.

Monroe frowned and shook his head. "I don't know which of you is worse," he remarked then followed Jackie from the room.

Bogart and Zack exchanged looks. Bogart immediately nodded. "Yeah, they're up to something."

Both men left the room and followed Jackie and Monroe.

§

The small diner was unusually busy at four o'clock in the morning with mostly truck drivers needing a break. There were no more than ten tables and six booths in the diner just off the highway. The bar seating seemed to be more popular with the truck drivers and the moderately friendly waitress who flirted with them over coffee. The diner smelled of coffee and bacon despite the early hour. Jackie and the three men had cups of coffee before them while awaiting their breakfast. Although Monroe acted casual, something about the way he sat back in his chair conveyed some tension. Zack casually sipped his coffee and watched Monroe with a distrusting gaze while periodically glancing around the diner. It was as if he were waiting for something bad to happen.

Jackie watched the exchange between the two men. She often wondered how Zack was able to read minds as he did. Despite how relaxed he seemed, Monroe must have been doing something to warrant Zack's suspicious nature. What Jackie wouldn't give for just a glimpse into Zack's mind. Zack's suspicions were suddenly founded. Like a hawk, he zeroed in on his target. Although his expression didn't change, Jackie could see the explosion beyond his eyes as he stared at the woman approaching them. Mac paused before their table and smirked slyly at the four. Monroe squirmed slightly in his seat then politely stood.

"Care to join us?" Monroe asked, although he obviously knew she would since she had agreed to meet them at the diner.

Bogart stared at Mac with surprise and politely made an effort to stand, displaying his country boy manners. Once she was seated, he cast looks from Mac to Zack, as if attempting to read Zack's eyes as he stared at the woman. Zack's eyes offered nothing, but it was painfully obvious he was silently seething. Mac met his gaze and smirked almost mockingly. If looks could kill, one of them would have been dead at that moment.

"Since there's obviously not a conspiracy taking place here," Zack announced then glared at Monroe, "would you like to fill in some blanks?"

Monroe shifted uncomfortably in his chair. "Before we go back to Dexter and tell him we were unable to locate his daughter, Sal suggested we meet with someone who'd worked for Dexter and knew the family." He drew a deep breath and managed a tiny smile. "Mac was nice enough to meet us to discuss Lindsey."

"Cut the bullshit," Mac snarled while glaring at Monroe. "I can help you find Lindsey and maybe even convince her to go home to her father."

All four stared at her as if waiting for the condition that was almost certain to follow.

"And what is it you want in return?" Monroe asked suspiciously while locking eyes with her.

"I want in on the mission and my fair share of the finder's fee from Dexter," Mac announced proudly while raising an arrogant brow.

"She can't be trusted," Zack immediately interjected.

Mac glared at him through squinting eyes. "I saved your ass, you ungrateful dickhead."

"You were playing the odds," Zack snarled back. "You were going to land on whichever side won." He again glared at Monroe. "She can't be trusted."

"Neither can half the people we deal with on a daily basis," Monroe reminded him then returned his attention to Mac. "You need to understand that bringing you onboard for this mission in no way makes you part of the team."

"I'm not interested in being part of your little boys' club," Mac snapped hotly. "I don't trust you as much as you don't trust me. You've turned on me before, and I'm sure you'd do it again in a heartbeat. I just want a cut of the finder's fee and an opportunity to get back into Dexter's good graces. I need a steady job. I'd think you'd realize you can trust me, since I could just as easily find Lindsey on my own and return her to her father, keeping the finder's fee all for myself."

Monroe stared at the table and appeared to consider her proposal. Jackie frowned since she knew he'd already made up his mind to accept her offer. Zack remained casual, but he was silently distrusting of the woman who had saved his life. Monroe finally looked up and met Mac's gaze.

"Fine," Monroe announced. "We accept your assistance on this one assignment, but you don't get anything if Lindsey refuses to go back to her father of her own free will."

"Deal," Mac announced while smirking. "I already have a solid lead on your girl. We leave right after breakfast."

Jackie, Zack, and Bogart glared at Monroe. He shifted in his chair, knowing his authority had just been tested and he had to assert his dominance right away.

"Make no mistake, Mac," Monroe boldly announced while leaning across the table to meet her gaze. "I'm in charge of this mission. You tell me what information you have, and I'll say when we leave."

"Fine. Lindsey met her friend an hour ago," Mac announced with little hesitation. "She's already boarding a plane as we speak. We can't stop her at the airport here, but we can make her connecting flight in Florida if we rent a private plane."

Monroe frowned and sat back in his seat. "We leave after breakfast."

Chapter Seven

Sal walked through the garden and past the gazebo a little after eight o'clock that morning. He checked off another box on the official wedding clipboard with which his daughter had entrusted him. He looked around the garden and attempted to visualize the flowers over the gazebo archway and the seating for the wedding. His daughter's wedding was going to be perfect even if it cost a small fortune. His cell phone rang from his pocket. Sal removed the cell phone, saw Beck's name on the caller ID, and swiftly answered the call.

"Hey, Beck," he announced without his usual greeting. "You two are supposed to be enjoying your weekend in the city not checking up on the wedding venue."

"I hadn't heard from Monroe or the rest of the team," Beck announced from the other end. "Are they back? Have you heard from them?"

"No, but I'm sure they're fine," Sal reassured him then grinned. "I haven't seen them on the news yet."

"Yeah, funny," Beck remarked from the other end. "I'm not comfortable with Mac being on the mission with them. Her loyalty comes and goes with the highest bidder."

"Mac has her flaws, but she's not that bad," Sal announced with little concern by the comment. "Last time out, she saved all our asses, remember?"

"Okay, maybe I'm being a little paranoid."

"You're supposed to be enjoying yourself shopping in the city," Sal reminded him. "Just have fun. The wedding will be here before you know it. You can stress out then."

"Point taken," Beck replied from the other end. "Call if you're overwhelmed on your end."

"I'm handling your wedding details on my end perfectly fine," he announced. "Just forget about everything for two days. It's covered. Not another word. Goodbye." Sal disconnected the call then chuckled softly. "And they say the bride gets jittery before the wedding."

Sal headed across the backyard and entered the house through the kitchen entrance. Six large, muscular men armed with assault weapons and handguns immediately greeted him. They looked like a SWAT team about to conquer Sal's home. Sal jumped with surprise to see the brawny men then chuckled at his own nervousness.

"Sorry if I'm a little rattled," Sal announced to his newly hired, wedding security team. "The last time there was this many heavily armed men in my kitchen, I was standing over a dead body with three bullets in him."

A few of the men smirked at the comment, although it was uncertain if they believed his story. Sal could only wish it were fabricated for amusement.

"We've coordinated with your man in the security office and made sure the cameras catch every possible way onto the grounds," the man in charge announced. "My team will make a final sweep of the grounds this morning, and then we'll take two-man, four-hour shifts from now until after the wedding day. On the morning of the wedding, the entire team will sweep the grounds and remain on duty until the last guest leaves that night."

"Not to question your abilities, but are you sure your team of six is enough," Sal asked while raising a curious brow. "I love my son-in-law, but trouble seems to follow him and his friends. I don't want any surprises during the wedding or the reception. The last wedding we attended was a bit of a, uh, well, bloodbath."

"We've handled every type of security operation you can imagine from mob bosses to royalty," the leader replied with confidence. "My men are up to the challenge."

"I'm glad to hear," Sal replied and sighed with relief. "This is my daughter's wedding, and I don't want to see so much as a papercut."

The leader of the team chuckled. "We have it under control," he announced. "We'll make our final sweep of the grounds then report in before the first team is relieved."

Sal nodded then left the kitchen as the six men disbursed into two-man teams and headed onto the estate grounds. Sal headed down the grand hallway and entered the lounge. As with most of his mansions, the lounge was elegant yet cozy with plush sofas, a large screen television, and expensive artwork. The bar was the showpiece of the room with natural, sculpted wood and enough stools to seat eight people comfortably. Sal immediately headed behind the bar and poured himself a drink. He eyed the glass of scotch and drew a deep breath.

"It's five o'clock somewhere," he announced with a sigh. "And if this wedding goes off without a single round being fired, I'm going on a nice, long cruise by myself," he announced and raised the glass to his lips.

The sound of gunfire broke the silence. Sal nearly dropped the glass and removed a shotgun from beneath the bar. He pumped the shotgun then ran for the lounge door.

§

Two sets of security guards ran across the estate grounds in the direction of the gunfire with their automatic weapons leveled and ready to fire. They reached the front of the estate to find the first team of two men on the ground, writhing in agony from leg wounds. Two of the men crouched low to the ground and stood guard while the other two pulled their injured men safely behind the fountain. The remaining two joined their team behind the massive fountain. A man dressed entirely in black bolted across the estate grounds. Two guards fired at him, but he disappeared into the shadows. They barely saw the second man dressed in black dart across the grounds in the opposite direction.

"They're attempting to surround us," the leader announced. He indicated one of the men. "You stay here."

The leader then motioned two of the men to separate and circle around the back of the mansion while he headed inside to protect Sal. As he entered the mansion, he was greeted by Sal hidden within the lounge doorway with his shotgun aimed. Sal relaxed when he saw the team leader.

"What's going on out there?" Sal demanded. "I hit the silent alarm. The police will be here in ten minutes."

"Two of my men are down," he announced and hurried Sal into the study. "We need to keep you safe until my men can take down the trespassers."

The team leader no sooner shut and locked the door when a man in black appeared alongside him and kicked him, tossing him against the nearby wall. He attempted to aim his weapon, but the man in black was already kicking the gun from his hand. The team leader attempted to defend himself with his trained combat moves, but the man in black blocked everything he threw at him and easily took him down with a kick to the face. Sal aimed his shotgun at the man in black. Before he could pull the trigger, he heard the sound of a gun cocking only a few feet away.

"I wouldn't advise that," a male voice announced.

Sal slowly lowered the shotgun and turned toward the man seated behind his expensive, antique mahogany desk. Sal's eyes narrowed while glaring at the familiar man.

"Vinny Cicco," Sal muttered while sneering. "It's been a long time, old friend."

Vinny Cicco had the classic Italian mobster look. His black and gray hair was slicked back; his skin bronzed from conducting business on beaches and at poolside, and his mostly gray beard was perfectly trimmed. His eyes were just beady enough to make him look threatening. He was a tall, powerfully built man. Despite his wealth and social status, he had the calloused hands of a laborer. Vinny's henchman, the man dressed entirely in black, looking more like a ninja, removed Sal's shotgun from him but didn't bother aiming the weapon at him. Dawg, as he was called, didn't seem very impressive outwardly but it was painfully obvious to Sal the man was dangerous. Perhaps he was Cicco's answer to Zack. Any man who stood by a villain's right hand had to offer something, or he wouldn't be there. Dawg lacked emotion. He was a clean-cut, good-looking Korean man with dark hair kept short and neat.

Vinny casually leaned back in the expensive leather chair and set his semiautomatic on the desk in front of him. He smirked at Sal. "I don't have a quarrel with you, Sal," Vinny announced almost pleasantly. "I know Dexter solicited your son-in-law's team to break into my son's home last night. Dexter can be very persuasive, I know, but whatever he told you happened is a lie."

"His daughter called him frightened for her life," Sal remarked in a firm tone. "The guys went in to rescue her. To my knowledge, no one was hurt. Unlike your visit to my home."

"Actually there were six dead men on the property. Two of my son's guards and two unknown men were shot on the first floor. Another two men seemed to have fallen to their deaths from a second floor bedroom," Vinny remarked and offered a mildly chilling smile. "And contrary to what you may think, my men were under strict orders not to kill anyone. Trust me; if I wanted them dead; they'd be dead." His look turned mildly annoyed. "You wouldn't even be in this predicament if Dexter hadn't lied to you. That's why I'm here. I want to give you a chance to make things right and stop any unnecessary killings."

Vinny indicated the chair before the desk. Sal sat in the chair and stared at the man behind his desk.

"Your son was holding Dexter's daughter against her will," Sal informed him. "The guys rescued her. How can there be another side to that story?"

"Lindsey wasn't being held against her will," Vinny informed him. "She was hiding out until her boyfriend, Conner, could clean up the mess."

"Boyfriend? What mess?" Sal demanded.

"Conner murdered my son," Vinny informed him. "What I don't know is if Lindsey played a role in his death or if Conner did it by himself. Lindsey was cheating on my son with her old flame, and he discovered their affair. If he divorced her, she'd have to go back to her father penniless. Since her father would never approve of Conner, something had to be done."

Sal leaned back in his chair and stared at Vinny. "If what you're saying is true, why haven't I heard about your son's murder? Why aren't the police looking for her and this boyfriend?"

Vinny stared at Sal but didn't comment.

Sal nodded and gently tapped his fingertips together like some evil villain in a movie. "So you claim your son was murdered, but you have no intention of notifying the police," he announced. "You intend to handle it yourself. You want to be the judge, jury, and executioner."

"If your daughter was killed, you'd do the same," Vinny replied with little emotion.

"No, I'd notify the police, and she'd get the proper burial she deserved," Sal announced boldly and placed his hands on the arm of the chair.

"And her killer would conveniently die in prison," Vinny remarked while smirking. "I know the sort of man you are, Sal. You can't fool me."

"What do you want, Vinny?" Sal demanded. "I'm growing tired of your company."

"We both know your son-in-law's team has the girl," Vinny announced while leaning forward on the desk. "You turn her over to me, or this doesn't end well for you or Dexter." Vinny stood and walked past Sal. He paused near his chair. "Dexter's daughter killed my son. You don't want your daughter to suffer for another woman's crime."

Sal clenched his jaw and refused to look at Vinny as his fingernails dug into the wood on the chair. Vinny left the study with his armed man.

Chapter Eight

The thirty passenger, Dornier 328 turboprop-powered commuter airliner was about to leave the small airport in Florida for Costa Rico. The plane contained two seats on one side of the aisle and one seat on the other. It had two crewmembers and one stewardess. Since it was a smaller plane, there was no gangway, just the five steps embedded within the doorway entrance. Lindsey hurried onto the plane, hiding behind her dark sunglasses. She almost missed the ten A.M. flight. The stewardess closed the vault-like door behind her and secured it. Lindsey hurried along the aisle and found her seat alongside a man working on his electronic tablet. He barely acknowledged her. Two rows before her seat, Jackie lowered her magazine and eyed Bogart seated alongside her by the window. Bogart glanced from his sister then attempted to look back several rows to where Mac sat alongside Monroe.

Mac was obviously gloating that she had been right regarding Lindsey's last minute travel plans. When they didn't see her, they were initially concerned. Flying last minute to Costa Rico for no reason wasn't exactly in their plans. Thankfully, Mac had been right, and no one wanted to kill her--for now. Monroe pressed a button on his cell phone to make a quick, last minute call before their flight took off. They were already making the announcement to turn off electronic devices.

"Yeah, we have eyes on her," Monroe announced into his phone. "We'll converge when we land in Costa Rico."

"Roger that," Gil announced from the other end. "Kirk and I are preparing for take-off now. We'll probably beat you there. See you in Costa Rico."

As the stewardess approached through the aisle, Monroe disconnected his phone and altered the setting before she could comment.   The stewardess was the stereotypical blonde bombshell every man wanted on a long flight. She was almost too tall for the smaller aircraft and seemed better suited on a larger airliner. She stood an impressive 5'8" with a lean body, plenty of cleavage, and an ample backside. Her legs seemed to extend forever beneath her knee-length skirt. Monroe couldn't help but take a healthy eyeful of the attractive woman. Once the stewardess passed, Monroe shifted in his seat and eyed Mac as his seriousness returned.

"Okay, time to start sharing information," Monroe grumbled to the woman alongside him. "How did you know she'd be boarding a plane to Costa Rico?"

"That man indiscreetly sitting alongside her," Mac replied with a general nod to the barely visible heads two rows before them.

From his position, Monroe couldn't make out the man seated alongside Lindsey. Conner was boyishly good-looking with dirty blonde hair and a clean-shaven face. He was only a tick over twenty, the same as Lindsey, possibly someone she'd known since high school. Conner was average height and had the stocky build of a high school football player. By no means overweight, he had some power behind his build.

"That's her long-time friend and former boyfriend, Conner. When Sal called me, Conner was the first person I checked out. Our boy was already making travel arrangements. When he booked a last-minute flight to Costa Rico for two, I knew she was meeting him at the airport." Mac attempted to relax while watching the couple a few rows ahead of them. "So what's the plan?"

"We confront her in Costa Rico, and you convince her to return with us," Monroe casually replied. "If everything goes according to plan, Dexter has a small compound off the coast of Florida where she'll be safe from Cicco's men. Dexter is already on his way there."

"I've never been there, but I was told his sister lives at the island compound," Mac informed him. "I only met her once. She's a pleasant woman. A lot nicer than Dexter. Lindsey idolizes her. If she knows she'll be staying with her aunt, she may be more willing to cooperate."

"Ironic how familiar this feels," Monroe muttered and seemed to get lost in his own world.

"What's that?" Mac remarked becoming interested.

"Once upon a time; Jackie was on the run from a killer," he announced. "She was on her way to meet me, the former boyfriend with a plan, and we ended up at my house on an island off the coast of Florida."

"I almost forgot you and Jackie dated," Mac remarked and couldn't help but smirk. "I felt the cold chill between the two of you the first time we'd met."

"We didn't actually date," Monroe corrected then sighed. "She was young and naïve. By the time she was mature enough to handle a relationship, Holden was already pursuing her. Literally, he was *pursuing* her."

"And you were hoping she'd come back to you one day," Mac remarked while hiding her grin.

"I still hold out hope."

"I envy her," Mac muttered while casting a look to Jackie's row where she sat alongside Bogart. "She has a team of badass Navy SEALs standing in line to protect and befriend her. I had a family like that once."

Monroe cast a look at her and appeared curious. "Oh? What happened to them?"

She drew a deep breath and shifted uncomfortably in her seat. "They weren't nearly as badass as they thought," she replied. "Got themselves killed." Mac frowned while sinking into her own world. "I lost my entire family in one night."

"I'm sorry to hear," Monroe announced while studying her. "That had to be tough."

She shrugged it off, although she was still clearly bothered by it. "They were a bunch of arrogant assholes anyway," Mac snapped. "I'm better off without them."

Monroe looked away and nodded. "I'm sure you are."

Mac looked out the window and sank into her own world as they taxied down the runway.

§

The fasten seatbelt sign was only out a few seconds before the usual parade to the bathroom started. Jackie watched the first man head into the tiny closet and wondered if he'd already had too much to drink. It seemed odd that only a few minutes into a flight a healthy, young man needed to use the facilities. She never understood the attraction to drinking while flying. Then again, she was always the one behind the wheel, so drinking was never an option for her. As the man returned to his seat only a few seconds later, Jackie took a good look at him. He was just average. Average looking; average height; average weight; average suit. His hair was neatly combed, although it nearly touched his shoulder. He reminded her of a hip, modern businessman. She was also convinced he hadn't taken time to wash his hands. He wasn't in the bathroom long enough.

As he passed, another man was already making his way to the bathroom. The second man was borderline repulsive. He had a full head of thick light brown hair that seemed to go whatever direction it pleased, and his features seemed larger than his head. He didn't share the same businessman appeal as the first man.

"What's with the men with weak bladders?" Jackie muttered aloud to Bogart.

He looked up from his magazine and watched the second man enter the bathroom. "Businessmen," he informed her without care. "They probably spent too much time at the airport bar during their layover."

"I don't get the 'businessman' vibe from either," Jackie announced while watching the second man emerge from the bathroom only a few seconds after entering. "Not much for washing their hands either."

Bogart glanced up and eyed the man suspiciously. "That has to be the world's fastest piss," he remarked and strained to watch the man as he passed their row. "Might be a good idea to keep an eye on that one."

"You should probably go back and talk to Monroe," Jackie informed him. "Our girl might recognize me, but she barely saw your face in the dark car."

Both unbuckled their seatbelts since Jackie would have to let Bogart out from his window seat. Before they could even stand, they heard a man speaking behind them.

"Lindsey?" the man announced just loud enough to catch their attention.

While still seated, Jackie looked down the aisle behind them. Conner attempted to wake Lindsey in her aisle seat. She wasn't responding.

"Oh, no," Jackie gasped softly.

As Jackie stood, the stewardess hurried along the aisle to check on the unconscious woman. The second man from the bathroom was suddenly on his feet and grabbed the stewardess around the neck, pulling her against him from behind. There were several gasps as he placed a semiautomatic to her head. Several passengers screamed when they saw the gun.

"Everyone remain in your seats," the man shouted while the stewardess cried out in fear. "We're making a little detour. If you do as you're told, you may actually live."

"You're crazy," the stewardess announced. "The pilot won't open the flight deck door. They'll make an emergency landing at the first airport they reach. The plane will be surrounded."

"I sort of have other plans," the man announced then aimed the gun at one of the windows.

When the gun fired everyone screamed as the bullet went through the window, leaving behind a tiny hole. An alarm wailed as the cabin lost pressure. Jackie and Bogart exchanged stunned looks.

"He's depressurizing the cabin on purpose," Bogart announced only loud enough for Jackie to hear. "What's he thinking?"

"That the captain will take her down until the pressure stabilizes," Jackie informed him with a concerned look on her face. "He wants them to land."

"And the plane will be surrounded," Bogart insisted. "What does he hope to achieve?"

"I'm not entirely sure," Jackie replied and again watched the unfolding event.

As suspected, the plane decreased altitude until the alarm stopped wailing. Bogart watched as the first man who had used the bathroom opened the overhead compartment and removed a duffel bag. Bogart then looked out the window at their position.

"They intend to parachute from the plane," Bogart gasped just loud enough for Jackie to hear.

"Impossible," Jackie scoffed. "We're still too high and going too fast. Besides, what possible reason would they have to jump? Why board the plane in the first place? We're still over United States soil."

Both looked back to the unconscious woman then exchanged looks.

"No," Jackie boldly announced. "They couldn't possibly want her that badly. At this height and speed, they can't expect to survive that jump."

The plane suddenly shifted, tossing everyone within their seats. Jackie nearly tumbled from hers. Bogart grabbed her arm and pulled her back into her seat. They saw something outside the window. Both looked out the window and saw another plane half the size of theirs on their wing. It came dangerously close, forcing their plane to dive down to avoid hitting it.

"Oh, hell no. They're forcing us down," Bogart cried out then looked at Jackie.

Jackie bolted from her seat and charged the man with the gun, who had been thrown off balance, releasing the stewardess. As he attempted to straighten, she snap kicked him in the face, sending him backward and tumbling down the aisle. The stewardess bolted away from the action and ran for the flight deck. Jackie scanned the surrounding area for the gun, but she didn't see it. There was a round of screams as the second man to visit the bathroom pulled his gun and aimed it at Jackie. She saw a blur behind the gunman scaling the shoulders of those in the aisle seats.

Jackie threw herself to the floor as Zack's feet connected with the man's back. He was thrown forward with force, tumbled over Jackie, and crashed into several unsuspecting passengers before hitting the floor. Jackie pounced on the discarded second gun while Bogart leaped onto the fallen man in the aisle before him. Zack grabbed the first man's arm and straightened while placing his foot to the man's head. Jackie suddenly gasped at what she was certain was about to follow. Zack hesitated, saw the look on Jackie's face, and then eyed the passengers in the nearby seats. He sneered and backed off on his plan to snap the man's neck. They heard a loud boom, which was immediately followed by the plane vibrating and then jolting to the left. Jackie looked out the window and saw smoke coming from the plane's engine. The tailing plane was no longer seen.

"Did they just shoot at us?" Bogart suddenly cried out from his position on the floor over the gunman.

The sound of gunshots fired within the plane startled them. They could feel the plane jerk then rapidly descend, which could only mean one thing. Jackie leaped over Bogart's back and bolted for the flight deck. The stewardess attempted to shut the door to the cockpit to keep her out, but Jackie didn't slow her approach. She rammed the nearly closed door, sending the stewardess across the small flight deck and into the back of the pilot's seat. In the brief second Jackie stood in the flight deck doorway, she could see the pilot and co-pilot slumped in their seats. The blood spatters on the windshield before them conveyed their condition. The stewardess held the missing gun and aimed it at Jackie. Jackie fired first placing two rounds into the woman's chest and sending blood spilling out onto her neatly pressed blouse. The stewardess struck the back of the pilot's seat as her gun fired. Jackie leaped from the doorway as the shot rang out.

From his position in the aisle, Zack saw the incident within the flight deck. He swiftly snapped the man's neck beneath his foot, leaped over Bogart with his prisoner, and ran for the flight deck. Monroe and Mac stepped around the dead man and paused before Bogart. Monroe was quick to hand him a pair of plastic zip ties to secure his prisoner while Mac checked on Lindsey, who remained unconscious. Conner again attempted to wake her, although the unfolding scene within the plane had him rattled. Monroe looked out the window and saw the enemy plane once more by their right wing.

"Even if we can land the plane, they're going to be on our ass," Monroe shouted out.

"We need a diversion," Bogart responded while fumbling with the zip ties.

The man beneath him kicked out, striking Bogart in the groin. Bogart gasped while clutching himself and dropped to the aisle. The man sprang to his feet and opened an overhead bin. He removed another duffel bag, tossed it behind him, and was already prepared for Monroe's initial attack. He deflected Monroe's fist but was unprepared for the knee to his hip. Monroe punched him twice in the face, sending him backward and tumbling over Bogart, who was recovering in the aisle. Mac bolted past Monroe, leaped over Bogart, and grabbed the discarded duffel bag. She unzipped it and stared at the parachute. She looked back at Monroe with astonishment.

"The plan was to get the plane down low enough to parachute from it," Mac announced. "That's how they intended to get her from the plane. If they think she's not on the plane, maybe they'll give up chase."

Chapter Nine

Within the flight deck, Jackie and Zack removed the pilot and co-pilot's bodies from their seats. Jackie jumped into the pilot's seat while Zack took the co-pilot's spot. Jackie grabbed the controls and kept the plane from losing altitude. The plane sputtered and bucked beneath her hands.

"This is bad," Jackie informed Zack.

"Can we land?" he asked.

"If I can find a stretch of flat land," she informed him. "But the stewardess shot out the radio and we have a bogey on our right flank. They have enough firepower to shoot us out of the sky. One more shot and we're done."

Monroe appeared in the flight deck doorway. "We have a diversion for your bogey, but you're going to need to take us lower and decrease speed."

"What do you have in mind?" Zack suddenly demanded while glancing back.

"You and I are going to parachute from the plane using Mac as a decoy for Lindsey," he announced. "If it works, the tailing plane will converge on us giving Jackie and Bogart enough time to land the plane and save the passengers."

"I need to help land the plane," Zack firmly insisted. "Bogart has no experience flying planes. Jackie needs me here with her."

"Bogart has no experience skydiving either," Monroe protested then glared demandingly. "And your only experience flying planes involves crashing them."

"Which is exactly what we're doing," Zack replied while glaring back. "Anyone can jump out of a plane and pull a string."

Monroe looked at Jackie as she took the shimmying plane down to a safer altitude. "It's your call, Jackie," he informed her.

"Zack stays," she replied without looking back. "I need someone with nerves of steel."

"All right then," Monroe remarked. "I left a message on Gil's cell phone with our approximate location. Hopefully, he'll get the message before he gets too far, so he can circle back and find us once we're on the ground. You just worry about landing the plane."

Jackie nodded without looking back.

"Give us the go ahead when we're low enough," Monroe announced then hurried from the flight deck.

Zack immediately sprang from his seat, closed the flight deck door, and grabbed a first aid kit from the wall. He tore into the kit and removed some gauze pads.

"You're going to be the death of me yet," Zack snarled and pulled her jacket back to reveal her bleeding shoulder.

Jackie cringed with pain while Zack applied pressure to the gunshot wound. "Thanks for not telling him."

"You're the best chance we have of landing this plane," Zack remarked. "If Monroe knew you'd been shot, he'd make poor decisions and get us all killed."

"Can you slow the bleeding enough?" Jackie gasped while fighting the pain in her shoulder and the vibrating controls, which made the pain worse.

"As long as I keep pressure on it," he announced.

"I need you in the co-pilot's seat in order to land," she suddenly insisted.

"Just give me a two-second warning, and I'll take my seat," he replied. "Until then, I need to keep pressure on the wound."

"We're low enough," she informed Zack. "Give Monroe the signal."

Zack nodded, released pressure on her shoulder, and hurried for the cockpit door. He signaled Monroe just on the other side of the door where he, Mac, and Bogart had just finished slipping into the parachute harnesses. Conner stood alongside them by the door to assist. Once Zack disappeared into the flight deck, Monroe looked at Conner.

"We're going to attempt to lure that plane off our right flank," Monroe informed him. "Once this door is opened, there's going to be some pressure. Make sure everyone remains securely fastened in their seats."

Conner nodded and hurried into the aisle, relaying the message to the panicking passengers. More screams followed. Once Conner took one of the front seats and belted himself in, Monroe reached for the door handle.

Bogart groaned while making a face. "I really don't want to do this."

"Stop being such a big baby," Mac snapped while glaring at him. "Your chances of dying in here are just as great as they are out there."

"You're not helping," Monroe remarked.

Monroe pulled the lever and opened the door. There was a tremendous gust of air, but the plane was now low and slow enough to parachute from it safely. He grinned at Mac and extended his hand to the opening.

"Ladies first."

Mac rolled her eyes. "You're a big baby too," she announced then leaped over the threshold without hesitation.

Monroe and Bogart exchanged looks as she disappeared out of the plane. "She's got a pair on her, huh?" Monroe remarked then indicated the opening.

Bogart moved closer to the opening and looked out. He groaned and made a face. "This sucks."

"Out," Monroe snarled.

Bogart drew a deep breath and attempted to prepare himself mentally. Monroe groaned and pushed him out the opening. Bogart let out a terrified scream. Seconds after, Monroe jumped out behind him.

§

Back on the flight deck, Zack maintained pressure on Jackie's shoulder wound. Despite the blood seeping through the second set of gauze pads, neither faltered from their plan. The controls continued to vibrate in her hands. Jackie eyed the controls and remained calm despite the wailing alarm and flashing buttons.

"I'm no longer tracking the plane off our right flank," she informed Zack and briefly eyed him. "Now we need to find a place to land this heap."

Both stared out the windshield.

"What's our location?" Zack asked.

"If my calculations are correct; somewhere between screwed and fucked," Jackie informed him.

They saw the water beneath the plane and all around them. They had left the coast of Florida and were now over the ocean somewhere.

"We need to find one of those small islands off the coast of Florida," Zack remarked. "Can we make it to Monroe's island?"

"Wrong direction," she informed him. "I can't turn around either. At this point, I'm just controlling our drift and trying to keep her from losing too much altitude."

"What's the closest island to our location?"

"According to our coordinates," Jackie informed him. "We shouldn't be too far from Dexter's island. He has to have a landing field. He has a private plane."

"Dexter's island it is," Zack replied while maintaining pressure on her shoulder.

The plane continued to sputter causing both to hold their breath. Jackie was already sweating from the pain in her shoulder. She'd lost a lot of blood. Zack discarded the bloodied pads for a fresh set. They could see an island in the near distance.

"That has to be it," Jackie gasped while clinging to the controls. "I need you in the co-pilot's seat."

"A little further," Zack announced.

"Zack, take the controls," she cried out.

Zack reluctantly removed his hand from her shoulder and jumped into the co-pilot's seat. He took the controls then looked at Jackie.

"Okay, what do I--?"

Jackie released the controls and sank back in the seat already out cold. Zack stared at her with horror in his eyes.

"Jackie?"

§

Jackie opened her eyes and saw Zack leaning over her. She could feel intense pain shooting through her shoulder. For a brief instant, she saw Zack's bloody hands clutching a blood-soaked pocketknife. He caught her gaze and returned his attention to her shoulder.

"You may want to stay out for this," he announced and returned his attention to her injury.

She cried out from the intense pain. As the humming increased in her ears, everything went dark. It seemed like only seconds had passed, but it was longer than that. Jackie could feel stiffness in her shoulder as her eyes again opened. Zack sat on the flight deck floor alongside her and grinned.

"Look who's awake," he remarked in an oddly cheerful tone.

Jackie groaned and attempted to touch her throbbing shoulder. Zack caught her wrist and kept her hand away from it.

"I don't recommend that," he insisted then released her hand. "How are you feeling?"

Jackie exhaled deeply and stared at the flight deck ceiling. "My shoulder feels like it's on fire and everything hurts."

"Yeah, I've been there before," Zack muttered.

She attempted to sit up. Zack offered his hand. She clutched his now clean hand with her good, right hand, and allowed him to help her into a sitting position. Pain shot through her left shoulder. She withheld her gasp, endured the pain, and looked around the flight deck. To her surprise, the plane seemed intact. Zack handed her a travel bottle of vodka from the beverage cart.

"Is everyone okay?" she asked while accepting the bottle and drank it down in one swallow. It was all he could offer for the intense pain, and she was willing to accept it.

"Yeah, all twenty-five passengers are fine," he replied. "Just some minor scrapes and bruises." Zack smiled proudly. "I'm getting really good at this crash landing stuff."

"Were you able to fix the radio?"

"No, it's totally wasted," Zack informed her. "I saw a town as we were going down. Someone must have seen our plane buzzing overhead. I suspect someone will come to check on us soon."

"It may be beneficial if no one knows Lindsey was on the plane when help arrives," Jackie informed him.

"Way ahead of you. Her friend took her down the beach and away from the plane," Zack announced while closely watching her. "She's pretty groggy."

"She's not getting any sympathy from me," Jackie snapped while attempting to stand.

Zack stood and helped her to her feet. She clutched her left arm and endured the pain shooting through her shoulder. It seemed to radiate throughout her entire body.

"You can rest a few minutes longer," Zack informed her. "We're not really in a hurry."

"Maybe you trust Lindsey to stick around, but I don't," Jackie remarked. "I'd like to talk to her before she takes off again. I'm not in the mood to chase her around her father's island. There's a small chance I might shoot her."

"You make me so proud some days," Zack announced while sighing. "One minor detail. This isn't her father's island."

Jackie shot a look at him. "How do you know?"

"I mentioned the town to Lindsey, and she said there wasn't a town on his island," Zack replied. "She didn't recognize this beach either. His island doesn't have stretches of beach this long."

"Then where the hell are we?"

"You're the pilot," he announced teasingly. "I thought you might know."

She shook her head. "I haven't a damned clue."

Jackie headed for the open doorway. Zack followed her from the plane. The steps were on a heavy slant caused by the landing gear having been ripped off, leaving the plane's belly heavily embedded in the sand. Jackie stepped onto the ground just outside the main exit door and looked around the massive beach. There was a huge groove at least one hundred yards behind the smoldering plane with the missing wing on the tree line side. The landing gear was embedded in the sand just beyond the large groove. Several palm trees were sliced halfway down, and the beach was littered with severed wing metal and palm tree debris. Apart from the torn wing and missing landing gear, the plane was in one piece.

"Not half bad for a crash landing," Jackie informed Zack.

Zack grinned proudly. "There's nothing to flying," he remarked. "You should let me do it more often."

"Not happening," Jackie replied then joined the others on the beach.

The remaining twenty-two passengers saw her on her feet and clapped while cheering. She hid her embarrassed smile and casually waved.

Chapter Ten

Bogart lay on his back on the ground within the swampland while panting heavily. The wooded area surrounding him was thick and creepy. Despite being early summer, there were dead leaves on the bare ground, and moss-covered trees seemed to stand on their roots both in and out of the swampy land. The water was murky and frightening regarding what possibly lie beneath its dark surface. Bogart pulled himself to his hands and knees and worked on removing the parachute harness. He attempted to slip out of the harness, became caught in the nylon, and jerked and thrashed until it fell to the ground. He collected himself, slowly straightened, and placed his hands on his hips while looking around the swampland. How he missed the heavily wooded area was actually quite surprising. That he didn't land in the murky water was nothing short of an act of God.

"Well, ain't this fantastic," he snapped. "Shot out of the sky, thrown from a plane, and left to rot in the swamps of Florida. Can this day get any worse?"

Bogart heard a twig snap behind him. He turned half expecting to see Monroe. To his surprise, he saw a six-foot alligator charging him.

He cocked his head to the side and frowned at the frightening sight. "Ah, hell," Bogart moaned.

§

Monroe slipped out of his parachute harness and immediately looked around the wooded area, attempting to gain his bearings. Since he had been flying commercial, he didn't have any of his usual, useful equipment on him. A compass would have been nice. He then remembered he had an app on his cell phone. He reached into his pocket for his cell phone when he heard Bogart suddenly cry out then immediately silence. Monroe ran in the direction he'd originally heard Bogart's voice, leaping over vegetation, and dodging mud pits. He ran into a small clearing and suddenly stopped. His eyes widened in horror at what he saw before him. Bogart sat on the back of the large alligator with his belt securely around the creature's snout as he leaned on its head. Bogart saw Monroe and glared impatiently.

"Well, where the hell were you?" Bogart demanded. "A little help here!"

Monroe stared at the man on top of the alligator then removed his cell phone and took a picture.

"Damn it, help me!"

"And do what?" Monroe cried out. "We don't have alligators on my island."

"Just grab the parachute and get over here," Bogart demanded. "I'll trap it in the parachute. It'll give us enough time to get away before it frees itself."

Monroe grabbed the discarded parachute and hurried for Bogart and the alligator he sat upon. He threw the parachute over the alligator's head, allowing Bogart time to remove his belt from its snout. They tangled the creature in the parachute, giving Bogart enough time to jump off the large reptile. The creature struggled within the massive material attempting to free itself.

"What the hell are you guys doing?" Mac suddenly demanded from nearby. "While you two were over here playing games, I could have used your help back there."

They looked at the unscathed woman as she stood nearby and stared at them. Her eyes immediately strayed to the mass moving within the tangled parachute.

"Who's that?"

"Oh, I'm sorry," Bogart snarled and indicated the mass within the parachute. "Mac meet Al. Al *eat* Mac."

The alligator thrashed around and was nearly freed from the parachute. Mac jumped with surprise when she saw part of the alligator now exposed. Bogart and Monroe grabbed Mac by her arms and pulled her away.

"Time to go," Monroe announced.

§

The black SUV pulled up to Sebastian Cicco's mansion a little after nine o'clock in the morning Colorado time. It parked alongside several police cars with flashing lights. The place was alive with activity. A ruggedly handsome man in his mid-thirties got out of the SUV. Holden Falcone wasn't built excessively muscular, but he had broad shoulders and a toned chest. His neatly trimmed, nearly black hair gave him a professional appearance. Sal jumped out of the passenger seat of the official federal vehicle and hurried to catch up to Holden.

"And this Cicco guy said his daughter-in-law murdered his son?" Holden demanded as they approached the house.

"Right after he shot my security team and before he pulled a gun on me," Sal informed him. "I didn't know what else to do. He threatened my daughter if I didn't convince the guys to hand over his daughter-in-law."

"The one Jackie supposedly has in protective custody," Holden added and shook his head. He then eyed Sal. "And no one has heard from any of the guys?"

"No, I was hoping you'd heard from Jackie," Sal announced with concern. "They could still be in the air and unable to call."

"Beck's with Pinto?"

"Yes, she's safe with him," Sal remarked and shoved his hands into his pockets as they continued toward Cicco's mansion. "I told them to stay away for a while and keep a low profile."

Holden stopped Sal at the mansion steps. "You need to wait out here until we have a look around."

"Yes, of course," Sal muttered while fidgeting.

Holden approached the officers at the door and flashed his badge. "Anyone home?"

"No one answered, Agent Falcone," the officer responded. "We haven't found anyone yet, but it's a big place with plenty of ground to cover."

Sal remained outside with the officer guarding the front door and watched Holden enter the mansion. Holden seemed to be gone a long time. Sal paced the area before the front steps for nearly forty minutes before Holden finally exited the mansion. Holden shook his head as he approached Sal.

"What did you find?" Sal eagerly asked as he hurried toward him.

"Not a damned thing," Holden replied with an annoyed look on his face. "There's no one inside. We didn't see any sign of an attack or a murder. Not even a trace of blood."

"I'm sure Vinny has a crime scene clean-up crew at his disposal," Sal remarked while frowning. "The best always do."

Holden cast a look at Sal and immediately frowned. He didn't say what was on his mind. No one wanted to know about Sal's previous life and the lingering question regarding his mob ties.

"Forensics will go in with their equipment and see what they turn up, but if something had happened in there, someone took great care cleaning it up."

"What are we going to do?" Sal practically demanded. "He threatened my daughter."

"Officially, there's not much we can do without any evidence of a murder," Holden replied.

"And unofficially?"

"We continue our attempts at contacting the team and start retracing their steps," Holden informed him. "I want to find Jackie. If this guy wants his daughter-in-law as badly as you say he does, I want to make sure my wife isn't standing in his way."

"Can you bring Vinny in for questioning?" Sal eagerly asked. "He did tell me his son was murdered. Is that enough to bring him in?"

"Without a body, it's his word against yours," Holden replied and maintained his frown. "If this guy is as dangerous as you think he is, it might be best to seek out the team under the radar. We don't want to lead him right to them."

"Where do we start?" Sal asked.

"Their last known location."

"I sent Mac to the motel where they were staying," Sal informed him. "They were taking her on assignment with them. Last I heard, they were at a small airport in Florida on their way to Costa Rico."

"Then we'll start at the airport in Florida," Holden announced with a sigh. He shook his head while attempting to hide his hostility. "I can't believe Monroe was left in charge. Throw Mac into the mix, and I'm not liking this one bit."

"Why is everyone so suspicious of Mac?" Sal asked. "Yeah, sure, she's made some mistakes, but she's proven her dedication on numerous occasions."

"Well, let's see," Holden announced while mocking Sal. "She posed as a U.S. Marshal, abducted Ross' future wife, and she did try to steal fifty million dollars from you."

"Yes, and then she saved my life," he replied.

Holden didn't respond to the comment. "Let's check out the airport in Florida."

"I'll secure a private plane," Sal announced and removed his cell phone.

Chapter Eleven

Despite only being a little after twelve o'clock noon Eastern Standard Time, the plane crash survivors had a large bonfire burning nearly one hundred yards from the downed plane. Although their situation was frightening, the ocean view was spectacular. The ocean was clear with gentle waves lightly crashing to shore, and it was sunny despite what appeared to be a tropical storm system brewing in the distance. The passengers were hoping a passing ship or plane would see the fire. It had been over an hour without any sign of a rescue, which seemed odd. Jackie sat on a large duffel bag near the fire and stared at the vast ocean.

The other passengers removed the luggage from the plane's tail section and also brought the rolling beverage cart onto the beach to entertain themselves. Zack approached Jackie where she sat and extended a bottle of water, which she gladly accepted. He collapsed on the sand alongside her and shook two bottles of pills. She eyed the prescription bottles then Zack.

"What's this?"

"Compliments of your fellow castaways," he announced then eyed her. "Narcotics for the pain and antibiotics to ward off infection."

She accepted the bottles and took one of each pill then placed both bottles in her jacket pocket. She looked back at the ocean and shook her head.

"I don't get it," she remarked with a sigh. "Where's the Coast Guard? Someone from the town you saw when we crashed? Anyone."

Zack indicated the dark skies in the distance and rapidly approaching. "We're going to be in for one hell of a storm in a few hours," he informed her. "Maybe the storm system is keeping them from locating us."

"I don't like it," Jackie snapped.

"Neither do I," he remarked and cast a look at her. "But what can we do?"

She eyed him. "Hike to that town."

"I'm not leaving you," Zack informed her and seemed prepared to shut down the entire suggestion.

"You won't have to," she casually announced. "I'm going with you."

He snorted a laugh. "I don't think so." Zack looked out to the ocean and seemed unusually relaxed for a change. "For once, we're sitting this one out."

She stared at him with surprise. "Why?" Jackie demanded. "Because I've been shot?"

"Yes, because you've been shot," he replied and glared at her with an irritation she rarely saw. "There aren't any hospitals around here if something happens."

"You removed the bullet," she replied. "I'll be fine."

"I'd rather not risk it."

"We're risking it by doing nothing," Jackie insisted. "I don't see a rescue. We need to hike to that town and get someone out here."

"Not happening," Zack informed her.

She eyed him and raised her brow. "And how do you intend to stop me?"

"Normally, I'd jump at the challenge."

"Unfortunately, everything you have in mind will make my injuries worse," she replied. "So I ask. How do you intend to stop me?"

Zack groaned and frowned while looking away.

§

74

A few minutes later, the small group of six was walking along the beach and casting glances at the rapidly darkening sky. Jackie and Zack forced Lindsey to join them on their hike to town, which she wasn't thrilled. Her friend, Conner, felt compelled to tag along. Two fellow castaways, Bill and Sid, volunteered to join them on their trek to the town, which was possibly three to four miles from the plane wreckage. It would take about an hour to walk there.

"I don't understand why I had to come along," Lindsey complained while holding her head. "I'm still feeling a little out of sorts."

Jackie could feel the beach breathing as the painkillers offered maximum side effects with minimal pain relief. She really wasn't in the mood to listen to a spoiled rich girl whining about her minor discomforts.

"You're a flight risk," Jackie scoffed lacking patience for Lindsey's strife. "If I have to chase your ass through the jungle, I may end up killing you myself."

Jackie received surprised looks from all five travelers in her group. She didn't bother looking at them, and she wasn't about to apologize for her drug-induced threat. On the bright side, it silenced Lindsey for the remainder of the trek. The trek through the sand impeded their speed, so the trip to the small town took a little over an hour. By the time they reached town, the wind had picked up, the sky was black, and thunder was heard rumbling loudly in the near distance. The storm was about to hit them hard within the hour. The remainder of the crash survivors would be safe from the storm within the downed plane. Jackie and Zack's little rescue party would probably end up seeking shelter in the town until the storm passed.

All six stopped as they reached the town. To their surprise, the town appeared to have been abandoned for years. Most of the small homes were still intact, but the jungle had taken over many homes closest to the wood line. The town only contained a dozen or more homes, a small general store, a bait shop, a church, and a small bar. The few boats that had been docked at the small pier were already rotted and sinking, tugging on their ropes against the mostly rotted pier. As the rain started, they needed to make a decision and seek shelter.

"We should head to the general store for shelter," Conner announced and indicated the small, sturdy store in moderately decent condition.

"The church seems more secure," Sid announced while indicating the nearby church.

Zack ignored both and headed for the bar. Jackie eyed the five, offered a knowing smile, and followed Zack. Lindsey frowned, clung to Conner's hand, and followed them. The remaining two men had little choice but follow them.

§

The white and yellow six-passenger helicopter flew high above the palm trees within the Florida swampland. Gil and Kirk both wore their headsets, so that they could communicate above the loud hum and vibration of the helicopter. While Gil flew the helicopter, Kirk held the tracking device, which pinged on Monroe's cell phone. Even though there wasn't any cell phone coverage where they were, the tracker on Monroe's cell phone still worked. Kirk alternated looking at the tracker and scanning the area below with his binoculars. The helicopter struck the tops of the palm trees, jolting Kirk. He glared at Gil, who struggled to keep the craft just above the trees.

"Can you not get us killed?" Kirk demanded.

Darth sat up from the back seat wearing his own headset and his official, black bulletproof vest. He barked as if agreeing with Kirk.

"I'm sorry; I'm not as good behind the stick as Jackie is," Gil remarked defensively then turned concerned. "I hope she was able to land the plane. I can't believe there hasn't been any word on their plane yet."

"That's probably a good thing," Kirk remarked while continuing his scan. "If they had crashed, it'd be all over the news."

"Unless they're keeping it hush-hush," Gil responded. "If they suspect it was a terror attack, they may want to keep it out of the news."

"Let's just concentrate on what we know. Monroe and Bogart are around here somewhere. We'll find them first then worry about the plane," Kirk announced while studying the tracker. He set the tracker aside and scanned the area with his binoculars. "We need to get lower. The trees are too thick. I can't see anything."

"If they're down there, they'll hear us," Gil informed him. "We need to find a clearing and let them come to us."

"There's one to my right," Kirk announced and pointed to the clearing.

Gil veered right and headed for the clearing that was relatively dry and contained no swampy areas. They hovered over the clearing while Kirk scanned the area with his binoculars. Monroe, Bogart, and Mac ran from the swamp within the woods and into the clearing while waving their hands in the air. Both men appeared relieved when they saw the three. Gil lowered the helicopter. Another helicopter suddenly appeared on their right flank and buzzed past them. Gil attempted to control the helicopter and keep it from crashing. The rotors slashed several branches, easily cutting through them before the last one broke the heavy blade. The helicopter bucked as Kirk cried out while bracing his arms to the interior frame. Monroe, Bogart, and Mac slid to a halt and stared at the nearly disabled craft.

"Oh, shit!" Monroe cried out.

Monroe turned, dove on top of Mac, and took her to the ground, shielding her body with his. Within the helicopter, Gil attempted to lower the teetering craft while Darth bolted beneath the back seat, losing his headset. The helicopter struck the ground with a thunderous boom. Monroe, Mac, and Bogart slowly lifted their heads from the ground and looked back to where the helicopter had crashed. To their surprise, the craft was only twenty feet from them. Despite the landing rungs folding like an accordion, the craft remained intact. Gil and Kirk jumped from the helicopter and immediately threw duffel bags from the back. Darth leaped out of the craft and ran for the trees.

"Grab the gear," Gil shouted. "We need to go!"

All five grabbed a bag each and ran for the woods after the German shepherd dog. The second helicopter returned to the clearing and hovered a moment. With the crashed helicopter taking up the entire clearing, there was nowhere to land. Two ropes dropped. Two men wearing harnesses slid down the rope, released their tethers, and ran toward the disabled helicopter with their M416 assault rifles prepped for action. When they didn't find anyone inside, they motioned for the helicopter to circle and find them. Both men searched the area for traces of the men they were hunting, found a set of tracks, and ran for the woods after them.

Chapter Twelve

The hired gunmen walked cautiously in two-by-two formation through the swampy Florida land with their assault rifles prepared to fire upon the first thing that moved. The first man saw something move beneath the surface of a small water formation, which was more of a large puddle. He caught the second man's attention and indicated the bubbling beneath the water. They fired several shots into the murky water then waited. Nothing moved. Both men took several steps into the shallow water, prepared to fire. A set of eyes suddenly appeared above the surface. By the time the first man saw the set of eyes, the alligator was already lunging out of the water for him.

The alligator caught the man by the leg and pulled him into the water. The second man moved in while yelling, unable to get a clean shot as the first man attempted to break free from the alligator's grip. He was pulled beneath the surface. Water splashed in every direction, indicating the gator was taking him for a death roll. The second man was about to squeeze the trigger and fire blindly when he heard a twig snap behind him. He spun around and saw another alligator on land charging him. He screamed and attempted to aim his rifle at the creature, but he was already being thrown backward into the swampy, shallow water. His screams echoed through the woods. Bogart and Mac stood behind two trees and watched the gruesome scene from a safe distance. Mac looked at Bogart and shook her head.

"There are a lot of ways to kill a man," Mac informed him. "That has to be high on the list as one of the worst. We should have just shot them."

"Gators got to eat too," Bogart informed her. "Besides, if they want to hunt us, they have to realize there are things out here looking to hunt them as well." He indicated the woods. "We should go before the rest of the gator posse shows up."

They hurried through the woods and caught up with the rest of the team.

Kirk shook his head as the man's distant screaming subsided. "We need to get out of here," he announced. "I don't want to end up gator bait."

Gil clutched Darth's collar and looked around. "I second that," he announced while keeping the dog securely against his side. "Darth is a happy meal to an alligator."

"It's less swampy up that way," Bogart announced and indicated the area before them. "Just keep in mind, if you see a puddle, assume there's a gator in it."

They walked for nearly two miles without any sounds around them. As they approached a clearing, the team stopped and looked around.

"That helicopter is still around somewhere," Gil informed them while scanning the mostly quiet sky. "We should remain in the woods and keep out of sight."

"The woods on either side are swampy," Bogart announced with some concern. "I'm not a gator whisperer. One or two we can avoid, but if we run into a bunch of them, we're a lunch buffet."

"It's a short run to the woods on the other side," Monroe offered. "We'll hear the helicopter from a distance. We can make it to cover before they ever see us."

"When they don't hear from their men, they'll send reinforcements," Kirk reminded them. "We need to figure out where we are, find civilization, and call for extraction."

"Can we keep moving?" Mac demanded while glaring at the four men. "Or do you guys intend to stand around and jerk one another off."

Monroe smirked and indicated the clearing before them. "Ladies first."

Mac entered the clearing at a brisk jog. The guys exchanged looks and shook their heads.

"She's pleasant," Gil scoffed without emotion. "Like a snarky version of Jackie."

Bogart shrugged and grinned. "She's not without her charm."

He received several glares. The four men and Darth hurried into the clearing after Mac. They were halfway across the clearing when they heard the helicopter in the distance. All five ran through the clearing with Darth leading the way. They just made the cover of the woods as the helicopter came into view. They took positions behind trees and watched the helicopter circle the area, obviously looking for them and signs of their missing men.

"I'd love to get my hands on their bird," Gil muttered while studying the helicopter.

Kirk peered through his binoculars and raised his brows. "They have a machine gun bolted to the floor out the side door," he announced while secretly approving. "These guys are playing for keeps."

Monroe turned to face Mac while remaining hidden behind his tree. "Is there anything particular about Lindsey you'd like to share with us?" he demanded. "They're going to some pretty serious extremes to get this girl. I get that Vinny wants revenge over his dead son, but this--?"

Mac shook her head being just as baffled as the rest of the team. "There's not much to tell about Lindsey," she informed him. "When I knew her, she was eighteen or so. She was your ordinary teenager. She was love-starved over her boyfriend, Conner. They were inseparable. They visited her father's island retreat somewhere off the coast of Florida, and suddenly Conner was out of her life. I heard rumor he cheated on her. Lindsey was devastated." Mac raised her brows and considered the comment. "She turned into a complete bitch after that. I didn't want to be around her or her father any longer, so I went to work for Sal. I later heard she was engaged to Cicco's boy. Seemed a bit fast. I just assumed she was pregnant or something, although that didn't turn out to be the case."

"What's Vinny Cicco like? Have you ever met the guy?" Gil asked while casually leaning against the security of his tree and hugging his AK-47 assault rifle.

"Once or twice. He's your typical low-life thug," she casually replied. "Scumbag through and through. A real dick."

"Don't hold back," Monroe remarked. "Tell us how you really feel."

She cast a glare at him then looked back at Gil. "A lot of these mob boss types have a certain code they live by," Mac informed him. "If they kill a husband or father, they compensate the widow. Stuff like that." She wrinkled her nose while shaking her head. "Vinny is just disgusting. I know Dexter didn't care for him."

"So why did he allow his daughter to marry the guy's son?" Bogart chimed in.

"You've got me," Mac replied. "Like I said, Lindsey went off the deep end when she and Conner broke things off. If Conner had cheated on her, maybe marrying Cicco's boy was her way of punishing Conner. Maybe her father was trying to pull the two families together with the marriage of their kids. I really couldn't say. I wasn't around for the aftermath." She finally straightened and looked around. "We need to get out of gator country."

"She's right," Bogart agreed while keeping his eye on the area surrounding them. "We don't want to be anywhere near the swamps after sunset. Those boys get restless."

Kirk then indicated the darkening sky. "And there's something not so friendly brewing in those clouds," he announced. "We'll need to find civilization or shelter soon."

"At least a storm will get that helicopter off our asses for a few hours," Gil informed them.

Monroe consulted the compass Gil had conveniently packed then indicated the woods. "If we keep heading this way, we'll eventually run into a town, but I doubt we'll make it before dark."

"Then we should go," Mac snapped and headed deeper into the woods.

"By all means," Monroe scoffed with irritation after she'd walked off. "Lead the way."

Monroe looked at the guys who hid their smirks but didn't comment.

Bogart finally snorted a laugh, mocking him. "Don't look at us," he announced. "It was your idea to include her in this assignment."

"He does have a point," Kirk remarked then walked past them and followed Mac.

Chapter Thirteen

The once quaint, little bar was possibly the happening place to be on the island back when the town was in existence. Considering years of neglect, it wasn't in too bad of shape. Thick layers of dust covered everything, cobwebs hung from every corner, and some of the plaster from the ceiling and walls had chipped away. The old bar itself seemed sturdy, being made from solid wood. The bar stools looked uncomfortable but intact. Lindsey and Conner wiped off stools in front of the bar so they could sit down and rest their weary feet. For a moderately thin woman, Lindsey was surprisingly out of shape. Being Lindsey was from a rich family, it was quite possible she rarely lifted a finger for herself. Zack immediately headed behind the bar and looked around. Sid and Bill followed him and leaned on the bar looking eager.

"Any booze left behind?" Sid asked.

Sid was a handsome man of Latino descent. His jet-black hair was the perfect length combining business with youth, and his black eyebrows set off his dark eyes. He was built more athletic than muscular, but he almost certainly had some power behind him. His friend, Bill, had a younger appearance despite both being in their mid-twenties. Bill's medium brown hair was styled in that 'almost a nerd' cut. Despite his tall, lean build, his boyish smile made him seem that much younger. He had a definite boy-next-door appeal. Zack ignored the young men and continued his search. He removed a ham radio from the bottom shelf and immediately fiddled with it. Despite his creativity, the radio never came to life. He frowned with disgust. Jackie sat on one of the bar stools and eyed him.

"Did you actually think that antique would work?" she practically teased.

"Was worth a shot," Zack muttered.

"Speaking of shots," Bill announced cheerfully and grinned in suggestion.

Zack rolled his eyes and reluctantly placed a bottle of whiskey on top of the bar. He continued his search as the two men eyed the bottle. Sid groaned and made his way behind the bar for several dusty glasses. Zack headed out from behind the bar and walked through a nearby door marked 'office'. Jackie wearily slid off her bar stool and followed Zack. She entered the office and watched as he searched the small room.

"Looking for a generator?" she teased.

"That would be one small generator," he remarked then eyed her.

She smirked knowingly.

"With that storm just about on top of us, it's going to get a lot darker in here," he announced. "I'm not expecting to find any working flashlights, but with the island location, I'm hoping for kerosene lamps or candles."

"Walkie-talkies would be nice," she announced.

"The average battery shelf life isn't working in our favor," Zack reported.

She watched while he searched the office. "You know, the church probably has a ton of candles."

"Yeah, I sort of thought about that," he remarked with a sigh. "I may have to run out and grab some before the storm gets too bad."

"Want me to go with you?"

"No," he replied and eyed her. "You need to rest. You're still recovering from that gunshot wound. I can't imagine you're feeling really good right about now."

"I've felt worse," she replied.

"Take a lookout position in the bar near the door," he instructed. "I'll head out the back door for the church. I can look out back for a generator on my way through." He leaned on the desk and gave her a serious look. "Do you have the other gun from the plane?"

She nodded and raised a brow. "You?"

"Yeah, I have it," he replied. "I doubt we're in any danger, but you know the routine."

"Yeah, I know the routine," she replied. "Be careful. It's getting windy out there."

Jackie left the office and crossed the barroom. She briefly glanced at the three men and Lindsey sitting at the bar enjoying their whiskey. Jackie brushed the dust from a chair near the window and secured her stakeout position. From her position near the window, she could see a majority of the area surrounding the bar, not that she anticipated any trouble, but it was turning into a nasty habit of hers. She could hear the four talking at the bar. Since she had nothing better to do, she decided to eavesdrop and see what she could learn about her fellow castaways. Their conversation started out with the usual pleasantries but swiftly turned to their current situation.

"Why were those men after you anyway?" Sid boldly asked Lindsey, surprising his friend with his aggressive line of questioning toward the woman.

"A little personal, Sid," Bill whispered to his friend, hoping to avoid a confrontation with the woman's moderately muscular boyfriend.

Sid ignored his friend and kept his attention on Lindsey, who immediately shifted on her bar stool.

Conner came to Lindsey's defense and glared at Sid. "Listen to your friend," he remarked with some hostility. "It's personal."

Sid seemed to consider the comment. "Let me see if I have this straight," he announced. "Two armed men shoot up our flight, another plane shoots us from the sky, the pilot and co-pilot are murdered, and our plane crash lands on a deserted island." He then nodded. "Yeah, you're right. It's personal and none of our business why we were nearly killed because of your girlfriend."

Bill groaned and placed his hand over his eyes as if he knew what would happen next.

"It's not Lindsey's fault," Conner launched in anger while attempting to defend his friend.

"I didn't say *it* was," Sid snapped and raised an arrogant brow. "I'd just like to know what *it* is. Why did we nearly die today? We have a right to know why our lives are on the line."

Jackie had her head propped against her hand where she sat quietly watching the outside world. She groaned while listening to the conversation because she too knew where it was heading. As Conner continued to defend Lindsey's right to privacy, Jackie stood and approached the old pool table, which was on a severe slant. She removed one of the pool sticks and wiped the dust from it. Lindsey screamed as the sound of toppling bar stools echoed through the barroom. Bill and Lindsey were on their feet and watched as Sid and Conner had each other by the shirts while throwing punches. It was obvious neither man was a stranger to barroom brawls. Jackie always thought the grabbing of shirts was a bit dramatic. She assumed it was the guy's version of women pulling hair.

Conner threw another punch and immediately had his hand cracked by the thick end of a pool stick. He jumped back with surprise and clutched his aching hand. The hit could have been a lot harder. Sid attempted to take advantage of the incident and lunged forward only to receive a jab to the abdomen with the same pool stick. Both men clutched their sore body parts and looked at Jackie, who stood nearby holding the pool stick in a threatening manner.

"You boys want to bitch and moan about who's having the worst day?" she snarled and aggressively twirled the pool stick in one hand. She slammed it against the bar causing a loud crack and making everyone jump. Her eyes pierced through theirs. "That would be me. So if you want to play cock in the henhouse, I'd love to vent some frustration right now." She took an attack stance with the pool stick. "So bring it on or sit down and shut up."

All four stared at Jackie and the wild look in her eyes. Bill practically leaped onto his stool and clasped his hands politely on his lap. Lindsey followed suit. Sid and Conner were still slightly stunned by what had just happened but quickly gathered their stools and sat on them. Jackie relaxed her aggressive stance and lowered the pool stick.

"I want you guys to work out your differences quietly," she announced then pointed to the chair by the window. "I'll be over there enjoying the peace and quiet."

Jackie returned to her seat by the window and made herself comfortable when the lights suddenly came on within the bar. Several lightbulbs exploded, startling everyone. She guessed Zack found the generator. When he didn't return, she assumed he went to the church for some candles. Perhaps there wasn't much gasoline left, so the generator would only run for a short period of time. She stared out the dirty window a moment then rubbed the dust away to watch the storm, which was becoming steadily worse. She didn't actually mind since it matched her mood.

Despite only being about one o'clock in the afternoon, the outside world was almost as dark as night. She hoped they wouldn't be stuck in the abandoned town for long. It was possible there was already a rescue at the crash site, and it would be nice if they didn't miss it. With the massive storm beating down on them, she doubted a rescue had arrived. The winds were violent, the rain was heavy, and visibility was extremely low. Nothing was coming for them by air or sea in the foreseeable future.

Chapter Fourteen

The sky was dark and threatening over Florida's interior. The wind picked up considerably, so it was no surprise that the displaced team didn't hear the helicopter in a couple of hours. The pending bad weather had kept it grounded. Now they needed to find shelter before the storm hit. Monroe had seen plenty of tropical storms while living on a small island off the coast of Florida. This particular storm intended to be frightening, and it intended to hit them in an hour or two. Having found drier terrain, the team hadn't seen a sign of alligators either. Despite the absence of the flesh eaters, Gil refused to let Darth roam from his side.

Monroe silently seethed while watching Mac lead the way through the woods. He rarely had the opportunity to be in charge, and Mac took it upon herself to lead the team. As they got closer to a large clearing, they could feel the full force of the wind. Mac stopped by the woods edge and seemed hesitant. As the guys approached, they could see the nearly black sky and what was about to fall upon them within the hour. Their eyes immediately strayed from the threatening sky to what had caught Mac's attention. Over one hundred yards across the field was a large, abandoned stone building. The gray stone exterior of the three-story building was covered with moss and plant life.

Despite that the lower windows had been boarded, the second and third story windows were uncovered and appeared intact.

"What is this place?" Kirk asked and looked around the clearing.

The massive estate appeared to be in the middle of the woods, which was in the middle of nowhere.

"Town is a few hours' walk from here," Monroe insisted. "This place is oddly secluded."

"Looks like a private school or college," Mac remarked, unable to tear her eyes from the building. She looked at the dark sky and frowned. "Doesn't seem we have much choice. We'll need to seek shelter in that building."

Monroe glared at Mac's profile and appeared ready to lash out at the woman. He looked back at the building and studied the surrounding area. He didn't want to admit she was right, but they were about to get caught in a nasty storm.

"The area seems secure," Monroe announced as if it were his own idea. "We'll stake out the perimeter and check for breaches. Kirk and Gil will take the front. I'll take the back with Bogart and Mac."

They headed across the field and parted company nearly halfway to the facility. As they approached the front of the building, it was the first time Gil allowed Darth to run free. Both men kept an eye on their surroundings. Kirk suddenly stopped and slapped Gil's shoulder. Once he had his attention, he pointed across what was once the driveway, which was now overgrown and part of the field. Both men stared at the tall, chain-link fence barely visible through the plant life growing over it.

"I've never heard of a college surrounded by a chain-link fence before," Kirk remarked. "Who'd put a fence around a place in the middle of nowhere?"

"Plenty of private schools, colleges, and rich people have fences around their places," Gil informed him. "Even in the middle of nowhere."

"Yeah, fences or walls," Kirk insisted. "Not prison fencing."

Gil again looked at the fence beyond the plant life. "That's not prison fencing," he informed him. "There isn't any barbed wire on top. Besides, prisons usually have two sets of fence as an additional security measure."

They continued their approach to the front of the building with a renewed sense of curiosity.

"So what sort of posh place in the middle of nowhere uses industrial fencing rather than attractive fencing?" Kirk almost demanded as they approached the stone porch.

Darth jumped onto the long, broad porch and checked out the elegant double doors containing a thick chain and padlock. Gil approached the doors and looked at the moss-covered stone alongside the door. He pulled away the plant life to reveal a plaque. It read, 'Paddington Institute'. Gil looked back at Kirk and shrugged.

"I'm guessing a rehab facility," Gil announced with little emotion. "That would explain the expensive building and cheap fence."

"So would a nuthouse," Kirk muttered.

"Why do you always go to the negative?" Gil demanded while eying his teammate.

"Because this is us," Kirk informed him. "We don't get the institute for bulimic underwear models. We get psychopaths and freakish lab experiments gone astray."

Gil shook his head without comment. "Let's check out the rest of the building's exterior for breaches."

§

Monroe led Bogart and Mac around to the back of the building where they found several entrances including two large bay garage doors possibly used for deliveries. Some of the doors were boarded shut while others contained padlocks. They found no indication that anyone had attempted to gain access to the large building in years. Mac stood in the overgrown field and observed the vegetation-covered fence. She stared at what was possibly a pond or what had turned into a pond over the years.

She rubbed her chilled arms as she studied the pond and then the fence surrounding the property.

"Weird that the place is surrounded by chain-link fence," she informed them then indicated the woods from which they came. The fence had been torn down almost the entire length of the woods. "The rest of the fence must have been taken down years ago by fallen trees."

"If I were you," Bogart announced and nodded toward the murky pond, "I'd keep an eye on the water. Probably home to a dozen gators."

He walked past them and approached the kitchen entrance containing a padlock. While Bogart checked the padlock on the back door, Monroe joined Mac. He didn't seem concerned about the possibility of alligators in the pond. Instead, he glared at Mac.

"I'd like to remind you who's in charge," Monroe announced boldly.

She eyed him with surprise then raised an arrogant brow. "I know you're in charge, Monroe," she announced almost mockingly. "You don't have to keep reminding me."

"Actually, I think I do," he replied while lifting his head proudly. "You seem to keep forgetting that you're just along for the ride. Honestly, with the direction this assignment has taken, we have less need for you and your bullshit."

Her eyes immediately narrowed. "My bullshit saved your ass," she snarled defensively. "Maybe I wouldn't have to take charge quite so often if you were better at it."

Monroe's hostility rose as his patience with Mac dwindled. "Being in charge takes more than being a bull in a china shop," he snapped hotly. "There's a reason why men like Zack aren't in charge. Dangerous situations don't always require brute force and destruction. Just because you've saved the day a few times with your 'jump in with both feet' attitude that doesn't mean you won't get yourself and others killed next time."

"Hey," she launched back. "My attitude has gotten me this far. I think I know what I'm doing."

"Gotten you where?" Monroe demanded while glaring at her then shook his head. "Your attitude has cost you several jobs, financial security, and no friends to back you up. Frankly, you're not a team player."

"And Zack is?" she demanded while folding her arms across her chest then gave him a cocky look. "You just can't handle a female version of him."

"We already have a female version of Zack," he launched back, "and you're far from it." Monroe drew a deep breath while collecting his emotions. He again lowered his voice. "I don't care how you want to live, Mac. It's none of my business because you're not my problem. But while you're playing for my team, you'd better learn to listen more and check your emotions at the door."

"Can you two wrap it up?" Bogart demanded from the door that now stood open. He then indicated the dark sky. "That storm means to suck us out to Oz, and you two are in a pissing match."

Monroe looked back at Bogart and held his breath a moment. "Head around the side and see if Gil and Kirk found anything."

Bogart eyed them suspiciously then nodded and headed for the far side of the building.

Monroe looked back at Mac, who maintained her glare at him. "And you're wrong about Zack not being a team player," he informed her. "Zack would die for any one of us." His brows rose sharply. "Several times he actually had." He shook his head. "Trust me, Mac; you're no Zack."

Once Bogart returned with Gil, Kirk, and Darth, they entered the building. Each removed a flashlight from their duffel bags and checked out the excessively dark area before them. With the windows boarded, there was little light inside the building. With the approaching storm, there would have been little light anyway. They discovered they were inside the institute's massive kitchen. It contained rows and rows of counters, steel cupboards, several stoves, and two, large freezers. Despite being abandoned for many years, there was little dust or cobwebs. The place had been sealed up fairly tight, which had kept most of the elements out. Kirk locked and bolted the door behind them then secured it with several boards wedged into the corner against the hinges. Nothing short of explosives or a battering ram was getting through the door. The team continued across the kitchen and headed into the massive, grand hallway.

As they shined their flashlights around, the grand hallway gave the impression of some multi-million dollar mansion, but the kitchen screamed hospital or nursing home. The grand hallway was twenty feet across and three times as long. A coating of dust covered the tiled floor, yet there seemed to be recent activity indicated by the many footprints in the thick coating of dust. The once elegant chandeliers were hidden beneath coatings of thick cobwebs, giving the building all the appeal of a haunted house. They entered the massive lobby, which contained all its original furniture, most of which was antique.

Despite having boarded up the place, it seemed as if the owner had intended to return one day. Given the lack of a front desk, it wasn't a hotel of any kind. Apart from a small desk not far from the main entrance, there was nothing to suggest the place had been a hospital either. Perhaps it was a private hospital or some sort of private school. Gil grinned and held back his laugh as they looked around the elegant lobby.

"What did I tell you?" he announced cheerfully. "Rehab for the insanely rich."

Gil may have been right. There didn't seem to be a better explanation for the building layout. Similar to a hospital and a hotel, but it was neither. A rehab center for the wealthy did seem most plausible.

"It seems secure," Monroe informed them while studying their surroundings. "We should probably have a look around. Bottled water would be a start. Gil and Darth can take this level. Kirk and I will take the third floor." He then eyed Bogart. "You can check out the second floor with the warrior princess."

Mac sneered her disapproval.

Chapter Fifteen

Bogart and Mac entered the second floor from the stairwell and scanned the area with their flashlights. The large open area with a wall of windows looked much like a lobby or lounge of sorts, although the positioning of the desk seemed unusual. There were two elevators that also came to the lobby area. Sturdy furniture with faux leather cushions covered with dust seemed to be the theme. The remainder and majority of the floor was beyond the wall behind the desk. There were three doors leading into the area beyond the main desk. One to the right; one to the left; and one directly behind.

"Looks almost like an office floor," Bogart announced then looked at the black skies and the approaching storm beyond the wall of windows.

Mac approached the large desk while shaking her head as she scanned the area with her flashlight. "No, it's not office space," she informed him and allowed her flashlight to settle upon a binder on the desk. A large filing cabinet system looked almost like a closet. "It's a nurse's station."

Bogart did a double take, approached the desk as well, and searched with his flashlight. "So beyond those doors?"

"Patient's rooms," Mac informed him and headed for one of the doors.

She attempted to open the door, but it was locked. She studied the keycard lock. Without power, they would need a master key in order to enter the patients' area. Mac attempted to open the half door leading behind the nurse's station desk, but that too was locked. She easily scaled the half door and searched behind the desk.

"Heads up," she called out and tossed Bogart a small ring of keys.

Bogart caught the keys and approached the locked door to the patients' area while Mac jumped over the desk and joined him. He tried several keys while attempting to hold his flashlight under his arm and finally found the right key on the third try. He opened the door and peered into the vast darkness of what appeared to be a corridor. Without windows, the back area was creepy. He smiled charmingly at Mac and extended his hand.

"Ladies first."

Mac rolled her eyes then shined her flashlight into the corridor and entered. Bogart fiddled with the door hinge, preventing it from closing all the way, so they'd have a little extra light from the lobby windows. There was also a good chance the door locked from the inside as well. They roamed the hallway now resembling that of a hospital. Throughout the hallway, there were creepy wheelchairs affixed with Velcro straps for wrists and ankles. Patient's rooms were lined on either side of the corridor with the doors closed. Mac tried one, but they were also locked. Another hallway halfway across the floor led to the wing on the opposite side, which would eventually bring them back to the lobby on the far side of the nurse's station.

The connecting corridor also contained locked doors, but they had signs indicating they were supply rooms, linen closets, shower rooms, and exam rooms. Rather than taking the connecting corridor, they continued along the wing corridor until they reached the end. There was another connecting corridor, again leading to the other wing. This one was lined with patient's rooms. Mac tried another patient room door with no luck. Bogart fumbled with the keys and discovered they were marked with numbers matching the room numbers. He found the correct key, bypassing the electronic card reader, and unlocked the door.

Mac entered the patient's room and shined her light around it. Although there was a window, it contained wire within the glass. She scanned the small six-by-eight room. The walls were a bland concrete with nothing on them. There was a closet in one corner and a toilet with a sink in the corner near the door. The only privacy to the toilet was that no one could see it from the small door window. She scanned the room past the basic, metal framed cot, which was bolted to the floor. The uncomfortable looking bed contained leather straps for wrists and ankles. Mac stared a moment with some surprise.

"This isn't a posh rehab center," Mac informed Bogart. "This is a mental institution." She continued to shine her light around the room and indicated the exposed toilet. "Not a pleasant one either."

Bogart now shined his light around the room as well. "It's like a prison cell."

"Exactly," Mac remarked. "The people kept here weren't as much patients as prisoners."

He suddenly fidgeted and looked at Mac. "So this is a hospital for the criminally insane?" Bogart suddenly remarked.

"I think so."

"I think I've seen enough."

"We won't find anything in the patient rooms," Mac informed him. "There has to be a breakroom. There could be a vending machine that hadn't been cleaned out. Perhaps some bottled water left behind."

Bogart was quick to dart out the patient room door. Mac casually followed. They returned to the connecting corridor halfway across the floor and walked past the supply rooms before finally reaching the nurse's breakroom. Naturally, that was locked too. Bogart unlocked the door with the clearly marked key and both entered. The breakroom didn't offer much elegance either. Although moderately decorated, it contained the same concrete walls. There were several tables, chairs, and vending machines. A small counter contained a large coffeemaker, disposable cups, and other breakroom supplies. There was a refrigerator and several supply cabinets. Bogart checked out the vending machine while Mac routed through the supply cabinets. The vending machine was empty, leaving the team with a few power bars from their duffel bags to get them through until morning.

"Found some bottled water," Mac announced while crouched by a lower cupboard.

Bogart joined her and shined the light into the lower cabinet. There was a case of bottled water. She removed the case while Bogart checked the cupboards above the sink. He removed an unopened can of coffee and checked the expiration date.

"This place couldn't have been closed more than a couple of years," he informed her. "The coffee hasn't hit its expiration date yet."

She joined him and helped route through the cupboards. They found a few boxes of stale crackers, some cans of soup, and a box of granola bars. Mac checked the expiration date on the granola bars then removed one and opened it. She examined it first then took a bite from it. Bogart watched with anticipation to her reaction. She handed him the box of granola bars.

"They're edible," she informed him. "Let's bag up the water, soup, and bars. We'll have to eat the soup cold, but it's better than nothing."

They stuffed the items into two shopping bags they found in the cupboard then headed back into the corridor with their newly found goods. Bogart paused before the door marked exam room and stared at it a moment.

"This must be the doctor's office," Bogart informed Mac. "We should check it out."

He unlocked the door, and both entered. Upon shining their flashlights around the room, both were moderately horrified at what they saw. The room a combination of an operating room and a torture chamber. In addition to the operating table, lights, and equipment, there were other chairs around the room containing straps meant to bind patients to them. The rolling tables left behind contained instruments and probes, which couldn't be explained.

"This is charming," Mac muttered. "Looks like a science experiment gone astray."

"More like a torture chamber," Bogart muttered. "Do you think they were doing illegal experiments on their patients?"

Mac shined her light past several drains in the floor, which contained bloodstains. She immediately grimaced. "I'm going to go ahead and say 'yes' to that."

Bogart then saw the bloodstains and appeared horrified. He drew a deep breath while controlling his anxiety. "We should probably find the others."

"Yeah," Mac announced unable to look away from the bloodstains. "I'm all for that."

§

Gil and Darth checked several rooms on the main level. In addition to the lobby, there was a conference room and several offices. Each office contained a connecting room with a small bed and bathroom attached to it. Although nothing glamorous, it was functional for an office bathroom. The unusual placement of the sleeping quarters and bathrooms indicated those who worked at the facility spent frequent overnights. The only thing he didn't find on his journey was any sort of visitor's area. Perhaps visits were mostly conducted within the lobby. Darth led Gil into a small breakroom, which only consisted of two round tables that each seated four and a small counter with a sink and microwave. Gil routed through the drawers and cabinets finding little more than stored coffee, tea, and moldy dry creamer.

With everything left behind, it seemed as if they shut down in a hurry and didn't bother taking much with them. He found some stale crackers, ate a few without so much as a complaint, and gave one to Darth. Darth took the cracker from him and almost immediately spit it back out.

"Beggars can't be choosers," he informed the dog. "Better than that time I ate bugs for two days."

Darth eventually picked up the cracker and ate it. Something moved within the moderately dark breakroom. Darth suddenly snarled. Before Gil could shine his flashlight across the room, Darth took off after what he'd seen.

"Darth," he cried out. "Get back here!"

The dog was snarling from across the room in the darkness. Gil raised his weapon with his light guiding the way and hurried after the sound of the snarling dog. He shined his light past the aggressive dog to a man crouched on top of the counter to avoid Darth standing with his front paws on top near him. Darth could easily have reached the man, but he wasn't ordered to attack, so he held him there instead. Gil aimed his weapon at the man wearing a scrub uniform and lab coat. The man appeared unshaven in weeks. He held his hands up in the air defensively.

"Call off your dog," he cried out. "I work here."

"Work here?" Gil demanded. "The place has been abandoned for years."

"I know," he informed him, "but my research is very important, so I stayed on after the others had left."

"So no one knows you're here?" Gil asked with surprise.

"Not officially," he replied nervously and eyed Darth. "Can you call off your dog?"

Gil gave a slight whistle. Darth immediately returned to his side but kept an eye on the man. The man slowly moved off the counter while keeping his hands raised, since Gil kept the gun aimed in his general direction.

"Who are you?" the man asked.

"I could ask you the same question."

"I'm Dr. William Freud," he announced while slowly lowering his hands. "I conduct research in the lab in the basement."

"You have a lab in the basement?" Gil asked appearing slightly skeptical. "Most buildings in this area don't have basements because of flooding."

"The sump pump keeps the water out," Freud informed him. "I have a working generator in the basement. I could show you my lab."

"Dr. Freud, huh?" Gil muttered with some disbelief. "Yeah, okay. We'll have a look at your lab just as soon as my friends return from their sweep of the building."

"Now you know who I am," Freud remarked. "So who are you and why are you here?"

"Our transport broke down several miles from here," Gil informed him, which wasn't a lie. Broke, crashed, shot down.

It was all pretty much the same thing. "We were searching for a town, but the approaching storm forced us to take shelter here."

"Yes, I saw the black skies," Freud remarked. "I assure you; the basement is the safest place during a hurricane. I have enough supplies if you and your friends want to spend the night." He then eyed Gil and appeared curious. "Why so heavily armed?"

"We're with a special government task force," Gil informed him. "We couldn't leave our weapons behind."

"Doesn't explain why you aimed it at me though," Freud remarked then raised a curious brow. "Someone after you? I don't believe you're with the government."

"Would you believe we're a band of rogue ex-military mercenaries being hunted by the mob?"

Freud considered the comment, beamed with delight, and then nodded. "Yeah, I'd believe that," he announced enthusiastically. "You'll be safe in the basement from whoever is chasing you."

Gil eyed him suspiciously, realized he was off his rocker, and offered an almost pleasant smile. "I appreciate that. We should wait for my friends in the lobby. They'll be back soon."

Chapter Sixteen

Monroe and Kirk were the first to return from their search nearly an hour later. They entered the lobby from the fire stairs to find Gil sitting on the arm of one of the sofas while Darth kept an eye on the stranger dressed the part of a doctor. Freud seemed overly relaxed while sitting on one of the chairs and reading from a medical journal with use of a penlight. Monroe eyed the man then glanced at Gil as he approached.

"Where'd you find the creepy guy?" Monroe asked while attempting to keep his voice down.

"Lurking around in the breakroom," Gil replied then raised his brows and grinned with a humored look. "Meet Dr. *Freud*."

Monroe groaned softly and rolled his eyes. "Great," he muttered. "An escaped mental patient."

"Mental patient?" Gil asked with surprise then eyed the man engrossed in his book. "You mean--?"

"Yes, this is a mental institution for the criminally insane," Monroe informed him. "From what we've seen; a sadistic one at that. You should see what we found in the third floor exam room. Looked like a modern day torture chamber. It's no wonder the place was shut down in a hurry."

"Great," Gil groaned. "According to Sigmund Freud over there, there aren't any working phones or radios, and he doesn't have any transportation either."

"No surprise there," Monroe muttered.

"He claimed he gets supplies delivered once a month," Gil informed Monroe but now appeared defeated. "I can't believe I was actually starting to think he was telling the truth. Probably lied about the lab in the basement too. What do you want to do?"

"He seems harmless," Monroe remarked and flopped into one of the nearby chairs. "We'll just keep an eye on him. We'll be out of here by morning anyway."

The violent wind from the storm could be heard outside the building as the rain poured down. It almost sounded as if the building would be ripped off its foundation. Bogart and Mac soon appeared from the stairs with their bags of goodies. They slowed when they saw the strange man, who still sat silently reading his medical journal.

"I was going to mention that this place was creepy," Mac remarked then nodded to the man in the lab coat. "But it looks like you've figured that one out."

"Who's the creepy guy?" Bogart asked.

There was a round of snickers. "That's Dr. Freud," Gil responded with a hint of a smile. "He stayed on after the institution was shut down to conduct his 'experiments'."

Mac and Bogart simultaneously groaned.

"He's offered us shelter in his basement lab, providing there really is a basement lab," Gil informed them. "With that storm outside, it's probably not a bad idea to seek shelter underground. We should be safe there until morning."

"A basement? In this area?" Mac scoffed then chuckled while mocking Gil. "I wouldn't count on their actually being a basement lab."

"Maybe you didn't see the weird ass things we saw," Bogart announced. "If you had, you'd know a basement lab can't be a good thing."

"We'll be fine," Gil remarked. "Freud seems harmless. He claims he has a working generator, so it's worth taking a look."

§

To everyone's surprise, there was an actual basement, which contained an actual lab. The basement lab was clean and almost sterile with white walls, cement floor, and drop ceiling. There were multiple steel counters resembling workstations, which contained microscopes and other lab equipment. As promised, there was a running generator providing electric, leaving the entire basement well lit. It actually worked out to the team's benefit, since anyone searching the area would never see the lights from the basement. Even if someone checked the institution for them, they'd probably never find the basement. It seemed safe enough. Dr. Freud briefly showed them around then returned to his work. He sat at the counter and stared into a microscope. Every so often, he'd document his findings. It was hard to tell that he was faking the entire psychiatric doctor routine. He seemed somewhat believable.

There was a room just off the lab that contained sleeping quarters with enough cots for ten employees. The connecting door led to a large, four stall bathroom area and finally on to a locker room containing several private showers. Once the team had entered the sleeping quarters away from the doctor, they were able to speak freely regarding their strange host. Bogart and Kirk made themselves comfortable on the cots. Darth found his own cot, placed his head on his paws, and watched the others. Monroe, Gil, and Mac tossed their duffel bags onto empty cots, although the three remained suspicious of the entire situation.

"Even though it's only a little after three in the afternoon, we should take turns on guard duty," Monroe insisted then eyed Kirk and Bogart on their cots. "Dr. Freud is obviously some mental patient who escaped during the move. Although he seems harmless, I don't trust him."

"Darth and I will take first shift," Gil announced. "Three to nine o'clock."

"I can take second shift," Mac informed Monroe. "Six hours? So nine to three in the morning."

"Fine," Monroe replied then indicated Kirk, who appeared to be asleep already. "Kirk, you can take second watch with Mac."

Kirk gave him a thumbs up without opening his eyes.

"I'll take third watch with Bogart," Monroe remarked and eyed Bogart. He was already asleep and snoring. Monroe shook his head. "This should be fun."

"Come on, Darth," Gil announced and motioned to the door.

Darth whined then reluctantly jumped off the cot and headed into the lab with Gil.

§

The island's small town barroom contained several large candles. The candlelight compensated for the sparse lighting from the blown lightbulbs. It was about three o'clock in the afternoon, although it seemed more like three in the morning with the darkness outside. The generator remained working for the time being. As the storm continued to rage on, Jackie's four travel companions entertained themselves with games of pool on the slightly slanted pool table. They had more than enough alcohol to keep them on the verge of being drunk. Jackie took up residence on one of the booth bench seats and attempted to get a little sleep.

She had a tough time staying awake due to the pain medication, although every time she drifted off, her shoulder reminded her why she couldn't sleep. She mostly watched the violent storm outside and thought about those back at the plane. She was certain they were safe within the fuselage, despite not being able to close the main door, which had been open and severely damaged during the crash landing. Zack had a few drinks to keep his pacing to a minimum although it didn't seem to work. He was like a caged tiger within the confines of the barroom. Had it been just the two of them, he would have handled being caged better. She was almost certain he'd be asleep by now. With others around and Jackie on the injured list, he was in full-blown commando mode. There was little she could do to relax him.

The bar contained several booths, so once the weary travelers grew bored drinking and playing pool, they were able to curl up on the booth seats and take a nap. There was little else to do until the storm passed. Once the others were asleep, Zack appeared in the bar area carrying several sofa cushions he'd removed from the office. With a few throw pillows from the old sofa, he'd successfully made a comfortable bed on the floor against the wall not far from the door. He indicated the newly made bed to Jackie.

"I'm fine," she reported in a weary tone from her slightly reclined position on the booth bench while propped against the wall.

"You're not fine," he responded and again indicated the makeshift bed.

"I've been in this situation before," Jackie informed him. "I can't sleep when I'm in this much pain. I need a day or two."

"You'll collapse from exhaustion in a day or two," he snapped back and again indicated the bed.

Jackie groaned softly and attempted to move from her position against the wall within the booth. As pain shot through her entire body, she immediately regretted the action. She'd been sitting in the same position too long and had stiffened considerably. Zack easily moved the table, causing a loud squeak and woke the others. They realized it had been nothing and, after some grumbling and cursing, they went back to sleep. Zack helped Jackie from her seated position and practically guided her to the floor on his makeshift bed. She sat on the cushions a moment and endured the pain radiating outward through her body from her shoulder. Zack joined her on the floor and removed her boots. She watched him and wanted to smile, but it was difficult with how badly she felt. She attempted to lay down, but it caused too much pain. She immediately shook her head.

"This isn't going to work," she informed him.

Zack crawled behind her and gently guided her back against his chest in a moderately reclined position. He placed a small throw pillow beneath her head while he leaned against the wall to support them. She had to admit, her makeshift Zack recliner was more comfortable than the booth, and she was able to position her injured left arm in the perfect position to keep it from throbbing. She clung to his arms securely around her and felt her body swiftly give in to exhaustion.

"You're a real pain in the ass," she informed him. "I'm just glad you're my pain in the ass."

"Don't read too much into it," he muttered. "I need to sleep. If you're restless; I'm restless."

It wasn't a lie either. Zack had sleep issues stemming back from his stint as a Navy SEAL. He'd trained himself to survive on limited sleep, and his body never readjusted. After years, they'd finally found him the perfect security blanket. Unfortunately, Jackie was that security blanket. Thankfully, Holden had embraced Zack as sort of their family pet, curling up at Jackie's side when he needed much-deserved sleep. Although he never led on, Zack's demons had a strong foothold in his life.

The rest of the team had some idea what Zack had been through, but they knew it went beyond what they witnessed during their missions. Too often, Zack was off on his own securing the team's extraction and doing God knows what to achieve that goal. He'd briefly opened up to her once or twice, but she knew he was giving her the watered down version. Zack lived a nightmare, and that nightmare would haunt him for the rest of his life.

Although Jackie fell asleep almost immediately, she knew Zack was out long before her. When pressed against him, she could feel his body relax and knew exactly when he fell asleep by his heart rate and his breathing. After everything they'd been through, Jackie and Zack were inseparable. She sometimes hated to admit that he was her best friend since that honor was supposed to be reserved for her husband, but it was difficult when they relied on each other for survival. If she partnered with her husband, one of them would have been dead by now. Holden feared for her life, and that made him a bad partner. Zack was actually the only member of Whiskey Tango Foxtrot who let her take care of herself while on assignments, making him the least likely to do something to get either of them killed. He was her partner; not her protector.

§

Once the storm on the island had passed a little before five o'clock that afternoon, the sun returned. The aftermath of the hurricane was evident by the standing water, destruction, and fallen debris. The six made a quick sweep of the abandoned town but didn't find any working radios. The few homes they'd visited had been cleaned out, indicating the residents had consented to abandon the town years earlier. Jackie knew Zack had been hoping to find a rifle or shotgun, but that was wishful thinking. Their last stop was the single-story courthouse, which also contained the sheriff's headquarters. They were equally disappointed when they found no weapons or communication in the old, outdated office. Zack and Jackie routed through the desk drawers while the others poked around the remainder of the courthouse building for anything useful. Zack removed a map and placed it on the desk. Jackie hovered over him with interest.

"Well, at least we know where we crash landed," he informed her. "Hathaway Island."

She eyed the name of the island then scanned the map. Jackie frowned while pointing to the middle of the map. Zack looked where she pointed and saw an old airfield clearly marked.

"The irony escapes me," he muttered.

She studied the map and appeared curious while pointing to the far side of the island. "What's this?"

Zack glanced at the map then met her gaze. "That's a shipping port," he informed her. "I knew I heard of this island. It was a private retreat for Voyagers Cruise Lines. This was one of their stops. Passengers could spend the afternoon on their very own private island."

"So there's a port on the other side of the island?" she announced with enthusiasm. "There could be people. At the very least, some form of communication or maybe boats."

"Might be worth the lengthy hike to find out," Zack replied then gave her a curious look. "That's a three or four-hour trek. Are you up to that?"

"I'll be fine," she insisted. "We should return to the crash site first and see if the Coast Guard found the plane. We may already be rescued and don't know it yet."

"Let's collect the others and get back to the plane."

§

Bill sat behind the judge's desk in the small but cozy courtroom. The courtroom had old wooden benches possibly decades old. What resembled fencing separated the general population from the area containing the defendant and prosecutor's desks. Sid sat at the defendant's desk while Bill slammed the gavel on the judge's desk. The sound echoed off the cathedral ceiling.

"Will the accused please rise," Bill announced.

Sid stood while remaining somber.

Bill pointed the gavel at his friend. "I hereby sentence you to death by a thousand prostitutes."

Neither man could keep a straight face and started to laugh. Once their echoing laughter faded, they could hear a sharp, faint cry, catching their attention. Both men looked around with concern.

"Where are Lindsey and Conner?" Bill suddenly asked.

"I thought they were in the courtroom," Sid remarked and hurried toward the partition to the bench seating.

They heard a creak followed by a gasp. Bill and Sid looked around then met each other's gaze.

"If something happens to her, that amazingly attractive extremely frightening woman is going to hurt us," Bill informed his friend.

They heard the sound again. It was coming from the judge's chamber behind them. Sid pointed across the courtroom closer to Bill. They darted across the courtroom and attempted to open the door, but it was locked. They heard a faint, shrill scream. Sid pushed Bill aside, took a step back, and rammed his shoulder into the door. The door flew open. Sid stood in the doorway while Bill stood behind him with the gavel in his hand prepared to strike. Lindsey leaped from the desk and buttoned her shirt while Conner hurriedly pulled up his pants. Bill and Sid frowned, shook their heads, and turned away from the office. Zack stood behind them startling both men.

"Time to go," Zack announced with little emotion.

Chapter Seventeen

The six left the abandoned town around six o'clock that afternoon. They walked along the beach strewn with palm leaves, debris, and anything the strong storm winds could pick up and toss around. The surf was rough and almost deafening as it crashed to shore. Sid and Bill commented nearly the entire journey about the large waves, which would be great for surfing. At least someone still had a sense of humor. Despite making Jackie foggy, the pain pills actually seemed to help with the last dose she took, although she was pretty sure she had already taken more doses than the bottle recommended. Zack casually took in the scenery surrounding them as he led the group. Jackie was feeling less than useful since the pills were making her groggy. Despite her nap, she was still tired. Zack placed his arm around her waist and pulled her unusually close to his side, almost surprising her.

"Have you noticed our grieving widow has been awfully chummy with her former boyfriend?" Zack commented close to her ear so the others wouldn't hear.

Jackie cast a look at him then casually looked around the beach and back toward the couple bringing up the rear. They were lagging behind by several yards. Lindsey and Conner were holding hands and appeared unusually giddy. Jackie stared straight ahead and made no attempt to pull away from Zack's hold on her. Actually, she didn't mind the added support. Her legs were starting to feel a bit like jelly while trudging through the mostly wet sand and her friend made a good crutch.

"Like a couple of teenagers in love," Jackie scoffed then casually looked toward the rough surf, so their conversation seemed casual. "Are you suggesting her husband may have been somewhat jealous the night he died?"

"Just an observation," Zack replied. "Infidelity is one hell of a motivator, especially to someone like Sebastian Cicco. It could explain why he tried to kill her."

"Still," Jackie remarked. "It's no excuse for him to kill his wife."

"No, but the story makes more sense when you add a lover to the mix," Zack informed her. "Could also be a good reason why Vinny has such a hard-on for her."

Jackie suddenly eyed Zack as something occurred to her. "Do you think it's possible that her husband's death was less accidental and more premeditated?"

"I'm keeping that theory open," Zack replied. "Conner was a little too convenient in her time of need, don't you think?"

"He did show up awfully fast," she muttered then eyed him. "If Vinny thinks she murdered his son, he'd be highly motivated to want her ass."

"You mean like sending a plane to shoot a commercial airliner from the sky?" Zack remarked and raised a curious brow.

Jackie frowned. "Yeah, something like that."

§

The beach seemed quiet despite being early evening by the time Jackie and Zack returned to the crash site. All six marveled at the impressiveness of the crashed plane and the deep groove it had left when it plowed through the beach. As they passed the detached landing gear, all six eyed it as they had when they passed it on the way out. Zack focused his attention on the grounded plane and appeared almost bewildered. He seemed troubled.

"Sort of quiet, don't you think?" Zack remarked to Jackie without taking his eyes off the plane.

If her head hadn't been so fuzzy from the painkillers, she might have noticed things seemed unusually quiet surrounding the wreckage. It seemed odd that no one was outside.

Zack held his fist up at shoulder height, causing the others to stop. "Hold up," he announced. "Jackie, stay with them. I'm going to take a look."

He removed the confiscated semiautomatic from the back of his pants and was about to continue onward when Jackie caught his arm. He looked at her with surprise. She glared back at him.

"I'm not a china doll," she snapped while removing her own gun and cocked it. "Don't treat me like I'll break. I'll take point."

Zack frowned as Jackie hurried ahead of him and headed toward the cover of the woods and the main entrance to the fuselage. Jackie kept low, making certain she wasn't seen passing the windows of the plane as she approached the main entrance. She glanced back knowing Zack wouldn't be within view, but she knew he was out there somewhere. He was always out there, especially when he wasn't seen. As she approached the open fuselage door, Zack appeared on the opposite side with his gun against his chest. They exchanged looks then aimed their weapons through the opening. Zack went high while Jackie was crouched low. Both stared into the main cabin a moment unable to move. Ten of the crash survivors were slumped in their seats with blood surrounding their heads and chests. They were dead!

"Shit," Jackie softly gasped.

Jackie and Zack cautiously entered while keeping their guns leveled and eyed the cockpit as well as the galley. They didn't see anyone lurking around. It was difficult for Jackie to keep her emotions in check. The people onboard the plane weren't enemy soldiers. They were innocent men and woman who happened to be in the wrong place at the wrong time. Jackie walked down the aisle with her gun aimed while Zack kept his back to hers with his gun aimed behind them. They checked on the dead passengers while searching for whoever had shot them. The rear exit was open.

"What the hell happened?" Jackie whispered over her shoulder.

"I smell something," Zack replied then looked at the floor. He picked up a can, sniffed it, and immediately made a face. "Tear gas."

She kept her gun aimed toward the rear lavatory and the open rear exit while casting a glance over her shoulder at Zack. "Someone tossed that in here?"

"Once they were disabled, the killer simply walked through and shot everyone at point-blank range," Zack replied. "No defensive wounds. No one tried to run."

"There are only ten people here," she informed him. "There were twenty when we left. Some of them must have made it out the rear exit."

"This was a professional hit," he informed her. "We need to get back to Lindsey. We're not safe here."

They continued toward the door. "Where are we safe?" she muttered more to herself.

"On this island?" he asked. "Nowhere. I don't know if we're outmanned, but we're certainly outgunned."

§

Jackie and Zack hurried the remaining four survivors to the woods' edge and sought refuge while formulating a plan. Lindsey was in a state of panic when she heard what had happened to the other passengers. Despite being sickened by the news, Conner attempted to hold it together and keep her calm. The more she panicked, the more concerned Bill and Sid became. Both men darted looks around the woods and began backing away from the hysterical woman. They looked at her as if she were a bleeding leg in shark-infested waters.

"They're coming after me," she insisted in a shrill voice.

"This isn't good," Bill muttered to his friend. "Someone's going to hear her."

"We're not safe here," Lindsey cried out as her voice started to rise. "We have to get off this island!"

Sid grabbed his friend's arm and forced him to back up several steps with him while darting looks around the woods. Zack cast an impatient look at Jackie as if silently telling her to do something about the panicking woman or he would. Jackie didn't have to catch Zack's gaze. She was already on edge after what she'd seen in the fuselage, and she wasn't about to let the shrill screaming of a spoiled rich girl bring about their demise. Jackie took a quick step closer to Lindsey and stared her down with one look.

"And you need to calm down," Jackie snarled with a rare hostility.

"I'm the one they're after," Lindsey launched back.

"Tell that to the ten dead men and women on that airplane," Jackie snapped while glaring at her. "All of our necks are on the chopping block here. We have no idea who did this. We don't even know what happened to the others. So either you shut up and let us think, or I'm going to shoot you in the leg and really give you something to whine about."

Zack stared at Jackie with surprise by the scathing words and the threat.

She glared at him with an annoyed look. "What?" Jackie snapped.

"I'm seriously turned on right now," Zack casually replied. "You may want to tone down that dark side a notch."

Jackie rolled her eyes then ran her fingers through her hair while groaning. "We need to hike to the landing field."

"That's a two-hour trek," Sid reminded her. "What if they're waiting there for us?"

"Do you have a better idea?" Jackie demanded.

Sid held his hands in the air and took a step back. He obviously didn't want her anger directed at him after the bar incident.

"We're limited with weapons," Zack announced, "but I remember seeing some golf clubs while the others were unloading the cargo. It's not much, but it's better than nothing."

Jackie nodded then eyed the others. "You four wait here," she ordered. "Zack and I will get the golf clubs and pack a few travel bags." She pointed a warning finger at them. "Keep it quiet."

All four nodded. Jackie and Zack hurried back for the plane while keeping their guns close to their bodies and their eyes on the surrounding area. Jackie stood guard while Zack emptied two backpacks. He filled the backpacks with water and food left from the galley, which was only a few dozen little bags of pretzels. He found a working flashlight and a few airline blankets packaged in neat bundles. When he approached the golf bag, he discovered it was empty.

"What happened to the golf clubs?" he announced aloud.

Jackie stood by the nose of the plane while keeping a lookout and looked back at him. "What do you mean?"

"The bag is here, but the clubs are gone."

Lindsey suddenly screamed from the woods. Jackie and Zack ran back for the woods with their guns aimed. They found seven men and two women from their plane holding golf clubs while surrounding the other four. Everyone relaxed when they realized they were all on the same side.

"We're so glad you're back," the first man announced while lowering his club. "We thought they got you too."

"Who?" Zack asked. "Who killed the others?"

"Two men dressed in black combat gear," the man announced. "They came in through the open fuselage door during the storm. There was this smoking can. Tear gas, I guess. Those of us near the back ran out the back door, grabbing golf clubs for weapons. When we heard gunshots, we ran into the woods where we could hide. We didn't stop running until we were sure they weren't following us. Once the storm passed, we heard a helicopter, but I'm pretty sure they weren't there to rescue us, so we stayed hidden."

"We think they left," Kate, one of the two surviving women, announced. "We hadn't heard the helicopter in a while."

Kate was possibly in her mid-forties with long, strawberry blonde hair that was now mussed. Although she had been dressed business casual on the flight, she had since changed into more casual clothing, suggesting she was prepared to handle whatever was about to happen next. Jackie remembered her well after they crashed. She was the one organizing luggage.

Jackie sensed the woman was levelheaded yet possibly a little too calm for the situation. Although Jackie was moderately suspicious of the woman, she was just glad she wasn't hysterical as Lindsey had been.

"We made our way back to see if anyone else survived," the man continued. "We heard someone in the fuselage, so we stayed back. Once we saw the others hiding in the woods, we knew it was the six of you returning."

"What if they come back?" Mandy, the only other woman, asked. "What should we do?"

Mandy was possibly in her late twenties to early thirties. She looked tougher than she acted. Not considered unattractive, she just seemed like a woman who had a bit of a hard life. Her blonde hair was now untamed after their ordeal, and her casual clothes were dirty from their impromptu trek through the uncharted jungle during the storm.

"We're going on a little hike," Jackie informed them. "We'll need to take as much of the water and supplies as we can carry with us."

Zack indicated the four younger men. "You four; come with us. The rest of you wait here."

No one questioned Zack since he wasn't leaving much room for protest. Despite Zack's small stature, everyone seemed to know he wasn't someone they wanted to mess with.

Chapter Eighteen

Zack eyed Jackie several times as they walked along a slightly overgrown path in the woods. She finally caught his look and glared back at him.

"I'm fine," she snapped relaying her annoyance.

"You don't look fine," he casually replied. "Let's take a five-minute break."

"I can hike two hours, Zack," she informed him. "Stop mothering me."

"We're taking five," Zack called out to the group following them.

The group immediately stopped and sat on the ground or leaned against trees. Zack turned to face Jackie and stared into her eyes.

"I'm not your mother, and I'm not your father," he announced firmly. "I *am* your partner. That makes me the man who'll knock you on your ass if you don't get your shit together."

Jackie frowned and shifted uncomfortably. "I'm sorry," she announced almost timidly while avoiding looking him in the eyes. "It's just--" She hesitated. "I don't like being sidelined; especially when we're in this mess because of my fuck-up."

"I'm calling bullshit," Zack remarked while glaring at her. "What's really going on inside that moderately psychotic head of yours?"

She fidgeted then glared at him. "It's you," she finally blurted out.

"Me?"

"You're turning into Ross," Jackie announced with some irritation. "I don't need you worrying about me. When you stop behaving like Zack, you're going to make mistakes. I don't need you getting yourself killed because you were worrying about me. That's why we're partners. If I were partnered with Holden or Monroe, someone would be dead by now."

"Yes, and it was almost you," he demanded while glaring at her. "I nearly killed all of us with that half-assed landing. The entire way down, I kept thinking I had to stop you from bleeding to death and how Holden and the guys would blame me for not saving your ass. I've been through a lot of shit, Jackie. You have no idea how much shit. I've lost every single woman I've ever cared about. I won't lose you. You're all I've got left to live for."

Jackie stared into his eyes a long moment. Zack frowned and looked away. She placed her good arm around his neck and pulled him against her in a warm embrace. Without hesitation, Zack clung to her as if he'd never let go.

"I love you too, you mentally incompetent whack job," she whispered in his ear.

"Psycho bitch," he muttered in response.

She laughed while pulling away, met his gaze, and gently caressed his face. "Did you pack any alcohol?"

Zack grinned and removed several travel bottles from his jacket pocket. "Lady's choice."

Jackie returned the grin and snatched the bottle of vodka. She drank the entire travel bottle without taking a breath. She shut her eyes a moment and prayed the alcohol would ease the pain. She just wanted a moment of relief.

"We've all been on the injured list, Jackie," he gently informed her. "It's okay. It's not a sign of weakness to be in pain or to take it easy."

She looked away and frowned. "You're a hard act to follow," Jackie muttered. "I've seen you get shot and still take down three men."

Zack affectionately touched Jackie's face while smiling. "You're tougher than I'll ever be," he announced and allowed his hand to rest on the back of her neck.

She stared at him with surprise. "Do you honestly believe that?"

"Definitely," he replied with a serious look. "You had sex with Monroe. If that's not the definition of self-induced torture, I don't know what is."

Jackie gasped and was about to lash out when Zack grinned and kissed her quickly on the lips. He darted away from her before she could erupt verbally or physically. She shook her head and stared after him. Since finding out about her brief fling with Monroe years ago before she went off to college, the guys enjoyed torturing her with jokes about it.

"I am so kicking his ass when I'm better," she muttered under her breath.

§

After a ten-minute vodka break, the fifteen survivors continued along the narrow path in the woods in the direction of the small airfield. It would be another hour before they reached their destination. Jackie and Zack led the group, although she wasn't too surprised when she looked alongside her and saw Zack was missing. She didn't even have to look around for him since she had a pretty good idea where he went. Lindsey and Conner brought up the rear of the traveling castaways and seemed to be lagging behind as if on purpose. Lindsey giggled while clinging to Conner's arm. She seemed so much less mature than Jackie had at her age, which was only a matter of a few years.

The romantic couple stopped on the path and turned to face each other while grinning, not caring that they were being left behind. Conner leaned in to steal a kiss. A hand suddenly covered his face. Conner jumped back with surprise while Lindsey let out a startled scream. Zack stood between them and removed his hand from Conner's face.

"Kid, your timing is off," Zack snapped. "Put your enthusiasm back in your pants and fall in line."

Conner was about to protest when Zack looked toward the woods. Jackie was already staring into the woods in the same direction. When she aimed her gun into the woods, Zack shoved Conner to the ground and aimed his own weapon as someone fired upon them.

"Down!" Jackie screamed and darted behind a tree.

The others scattered and dove to the ground to avoid the gunfire. Zack took cover behind a tree while keeping his gun aimed. Neither fired their weapons since they only had a handful of bullets between the two of them. As the thirteen survivors screamed and shielded themselves within the brush, Jackie and Zack exchanged looks from nearly twenty yards away. Zack signaled to her. She nodded and looked back to the woods while Zack managed his disappearing act. Several shots were fired at Jackie, splintering her tree, giving her little advantage. The two men dressed in gray camouflage with assault rifles hid behind their own trees within the woods. When they looked back at the group taking cover on the ground, they saw Jackie standing straight and tall alongside her tree.

The first man aimed his weapon, prepared to take her down. Zack suddenly kicked the rifle from his hand then spun into a high, roundhouse kick and struck him in the face. The second man saw the attack on his partner and aimed his weapon at Zack. Jackie pulled the trigger on her weapon and shot the man in the neck. He immediately dropped. Zack kicked the first man, dropping him to the ground and aimed his weapon at the man's face. Zack smirked slyly and pulled the Bowie knife from the man's boot.

"We're going to play a little game. It's called find the digit," he informed the man and held his newly acquired Bowie knife to the man's face. "And for every answer you get wrong, I remove a finger."

"Zack," Jackie cried out from across the woods. "Don't you start cutting off fingers!"

Zack glared at her with disappointment and frowned. "You're no fun."

"You know they always pass out after the first finger," she scolded him. "We need him conscious, and we don't have smelling salts to bring him back around."

"Would you prefer if I tore off his fingernails instead?" Zack demanded. He was obviously disappointed that Jackie was spoiling his fun.

Jackie cocked her head to the side, considered the request, and sighed with defeat. "Yeah, I suppose that's okay."

"Who has the pliers?" Zack called out to the group of survivors as they cautiously moved to their feet. Their horror from the question was clearly on their faces.

Zack's prisoner stared at him with his own panic-stricken look. "I'll tell you whatever you want to know!"

§

Holden walked away from the busy airport counter in the small terminal and approached Sal, who was eager to hear what he had learned. Most of the flights had been delayed due to the hurricane that had recently passed through. Hundreds of travelers were left stranded while waiting for flights to resume. Holden and Sal were lucky they arrived in a private, chartered plane just after the hurricane had passed. As he approached Sal, Holden didn't appear happy with what he'd been told.

"What did they say?" Sal eagerly asked.

"The team was booked on the same flight to Costa Rico as Lindsey and some guy named Conner," Holden remarked with irritation. "The plane never reached its destination. Its location is unknown."

Sal stared at him with horror. "What? Were they rerouted due to the storm?"

"Communication is spotty. All she could tell me was they lost communication with Flight 316," Holden remarked while frowning. "I'll be notified when they locate the plane."

"They couldn't have crashed, right?" Sal asked obviously wanting to believe they were still alive. "The airline would know if the plane went down, wouldn't they?"

"It depends on many things," Holden replied while nervously raking his fingers through his hair. "Planes have been lost before and even crashed without a trace, particularly over oceans."

Sal groaned while staring at Holden. "There's a lot of water between Florida and Costa Rico."

Holden drew a deep breath then shook his head. "No, I refuse to believe they crashed. Jackie's story won't end like her father's."

"So what does that leave?"

Holden stared at Sal while remaining tense. "Hijacking," he replied.

"Hijacking?" Sal repeated the comment as if he thought he misunderstood Holden. "With four, highly trained, skilled fighters onboard? Impossible."

"Three," Holden corrected. "I'd hardly count Bogart as highly trained."

"I was referring to Mac."

"Yes, Mac, the wild card," he muttered. "If I actually knew what side she was playing for, I might agree with you."

"Everyone's entitled to make mistakes, Holden," Sal responded.

"Sorry I don't share your faith in that one. Any success locating Gil and Kirk?" Holden asked. "Gil's private plane was cleared for takeoff shortly before Jackie's plane took off."

"I've tried the plane's radio and their cell phones," Sal announced. "No answer from any of them."

"It's unusual that no one's answering," Holden remarked and shifted uncomfortably. "I can understand if cell phones aren't getting signals with the hurricane, but the radio in the plane should work properly."

"What about the helicopter?" Sal suggested. "Could they have used the helicopter?"

"No, they took off in the plane," Holden informed him. "Jackie's helicopter is back at the airfield in Colorado. If Gil and Kirk circled back when they lost contact, it's possible they could have rented a helicopter in Florida to search for them. I'll check into that."

"I've called every number I have for Dexter," Sal announced and frowned his disapproval. "No one seems to know where he went either."

"Someone has to know," Holden demanded with irritation. "A guy like that doesn't simply disappear without his minions knowing."

"Perhaps his minions aren't giving up his location," Sal replied. "They don't know my current relationship with Dexter. If someone's hunting his daughter, they won't trust anyone. I did get some information from his people. It would seem all his generals are unavailable at the moment. Sounds to me as if he may have put together a small army. Could he know something we don't?"

"If he's had contact with someone from that plane, it's possible," Holden remarked. "We need to see if we can figure out where Dexter and his men went on such short notice."

"Men like Dexter have safe houses everywhere," Sal informed Holden. "If he doesn't want to be found, we're going to have one hell of a time finding him."

Chapter Nineteen

The island's old abandoned airfield contained only two private planes covered with vegetation. It seemed obvious both planes had stopped working long before the landing field had been abandoned. An old hangar, which was the only standing structure, had seen better days. Part of the roof had been torn off, plant life had overtaken the entire backside, and it was evident the door would no longer close by the amount of rust. While the others remained close to the hangar, Jackie and Zack took their sole working flashlight and entered the building. Light from the open door gave visibility to the front half of the hangar, revealing a slightly larger private plane. Since the engine compartment remained open, it was a pretty good indicator the craft wasn't capable of flight. It was already eight o'clock at night, and they would rapidly lose light.

Mandy paced outside the hangar doorway while insecurely rubbing her shoulders. She periodically glanced toward her fellow survivors and the rapidly darkening woods not far from them. Kate leaned against the hangar and watched Mandy pace. Being the last two women from the group, they seemed to gravitate toward each other

"You need to relax," Kate informed her newly found friend.

"How can I relax?" Mandy demanded and again looked toward the darkening woods. "There could be more armed men out there just waiting to pick us off one-by-one. We're standing out here exposed. We should be inside the hangar, where we at least have some shelter."

"We're just waiting for Jackie and Zack to make sure the hangar is secure," Kate replied. "There are other dangerous things in the jungle too. Armed men aren't our only concern. We need to keep our heads."

Mandy frowned and looked at Kate, who seemed a little too relaxed under the circumstances. "I don't know how you can be so calm with everything that's happened in the last twelve hours. Several times today, we've cheated death."

"What doesn't kill us makes us stronger," Kate replied and straightened.

Mandy groaned and managed a tiny laugh. "I'll be honest; I really hate that saying."

"It helps me get through tougher times," Kate remarked. "I've been through a lot; I've seen a lot. Sure, this ranks pretty high up there with all-time shitty days, but I've seen some pretty bad things too."

"Really?"

Kate nodded. "I spent ten years in the Air Force," she announced proudly.

"Were you a pilot?" Mandy asked and suddenly appeared interested.

"No," Kate replied with a soft laugh, "but I did survive some pretty intense missions." She looked around. "It's going to be dark soon. The first thing we need to do is secure that hangar doorway and get a fire going."

"A fire?" Mandy asked. "Won't that alert more bad guys to our location?"

"That's why we need to cover the hanger doorway," she replied. "It'll keep the light hidden. I'd rather not spend the entire night in total darkness waiting for someone to sneak up on me."

Mandy managed a smile and nodded. "You know," she announced. "You're okay."

Jackie and Zack did their sweep of the darker half of the hangar. They found a few rolling toolboxes containing rusted tools, a rusted generator that had no hope of working, and a small office of sorts. Glass walls surrounded the office. It contained a desk with several chairs resembling a waiting room at some low-budget oil change service center. There was an old coffeepot, half a dozen dusty chairs with rusted legs, and a bathroom. Jackie boldly scanned the bathroom with the flashlight and immediately cringed. Even in its functioning days, it would have been frightening. Unfortunately, it would have to do.

Once the others were ushered inside, Zack began fiddling with the old radio he'd found within the office. It showed no signs of life, although he hadn't been holding out much hope anyway. The others made themselves somewhat comfortable on rusted chairs now moved into the naturally lit section closer to the open hangar doorway. Zack secured their prisoner in a small cage. The cage was home to welding machinery and tanks. Once the items were removed, it made for a convenient holding cell. Since the man they had captured didn't give his name, Zack happily named him 'Jail Bait'. Jail Bait looked fairly young, yet tattoos on his neck and several noticeable scars indicated he'd seen some action in a short time. While Zack made their prisoner comfortable on the concrete slab surrounded by bars, Jackie orchestrated their temporary security.

Everyone needed a break and some sleep. They decided they'd spend the night in the hangar and continued their journey to the far side of the island at sunrise. Upon Kate's suggestion, Bill and Conner cleaned out an old barrel and moved it closer to the hangar doorway beneath the hole in the roof. They collected old magazines and anything that would burn, tossing them into the burning barrel. An old pack of matches seemed useless at first, but the bottom row of matches was dry enough to ignite. Bill started a fire in the barrel, and both men slowly fed the small flame until it was burning on its own.

Bill stared at the flame now several inches above the barrel line and frowned. "We're going to die here, aren't we?" he muttered just loud enough for his friend to hear.

Sid eyed Bill then added a few more rolled up magazines to the fire. "We weren't meant to die here," he announced. "It's not our time."

Bill suddenly lifted his eyes and met his friend's gaze with a strange look. "What makes you think that?"

"We have too much to accomplish in life to die on this rock," Sid casually replied. "You have that computer program you've been working on. You're going to sell that thing for millions. Maybe even become the next computer software mogul."

Bill managed a laugh and studied his friend. "And what about you?"

"Me?" Sid announced and eyed his friend. "I'm going to exploit your wealth and help you get girls." He grinned deviously. "It's my calling in life."

Both men exchanged looks then laughed.

"I'm going to see if there are any more magazines in the office," Sid announced cheerfully. "We need to make sure we have enough material to keep this fire going throughout the night."

Bill nodded and watched his friend head toward the office across the hangar. His expression once again dropped as despair returned.

"Yeah, we're all going to die here," Bill muttered.

Kate and Mandy hung a tarp across the hangar opening, which would keep the outside world from seeing the contained fire. It would also give those inside the hangar protection while they rested. Mandy used a ladder, while Kate was forced to stand on an empty fuel barrel. Mandy hammered some nails through the tarp into what little wood she could find across the hangar doorway. Every so often, both women would cast looks at Lindsey, who appeared almost bored. Lindsey watched everyone else work on ways to keep them safe or secure and find some comfortable space for their sleepover.

"I guess her royal highness is in charge of overseeing the troops," Mandy scoffed to Kate, who helped hold the tarp in place while her counterpart tacked it up.

"The way I hear it," Kate remarked, "we're only in this mess because of Lindsey. Rumor has it; the men who shot down the plane and killed those onboard after we crashed were looking for her."

"Really?" Mandy asked with surprise. "Where did you hear that?"

"Apparently, Sid got into it with Conner when they traveled to the abandoned town," Kate replied. "With the way she's watching everyone, I swear it's like we're all working to please her or something."

"You'd think she'd help out a little, considering it's her ass they want," Mandy huffed and raised a cocky brow. "We could turn her over and possibly save ourselves. Maybe she should consider that."

"She's not thinking about anyone else but herself," Kate muttered. "I think that boyfriend of hers is in for a rude awakening one day. I'm willing to bet she'd sacrifice him just as fast."

Sid returned from the office with a pile of magazines and dumped them by Bill's feet. Bill immediately started rolling them for maximum burn ability. Sid then produced a deck of cards.

"Found these," Sid announced while grinning. "It'll give us something to do to pass the time."

"Great," Bill announced cheerfully then frowned. "I suck at card games."

Lindsey walked by, routed through the pile of magazines, found one she liked and walked away with it. Both men stared after her.

"Someone's afraid of breaking a nail," Sid scoffed and shook his head.

Zack continued to raid the hangar looking for anything useful. Jackie carried one M416 assault rifle with the second slung over her good shoulder. She approached Zack and indicated the rifle in her hand.

"This one keeps jamming," she informed him. "Maybe you can do something with it."

"That piece of crap weapon? Doubtful." Zack continued to collect objects in an old, plastic crate. "What's our ammo situation?"

"Our friends weren't exactly overly prepared," she remarked. "They had two additional magazines for each the rifles, Bowie knives in their boots, and two additional magazines for their semiautomatics." Jackie gently rubbed her sore shoulder and cringed. "They were certainly traveling lite. What did you find in their backpacks?"

Zack eyed her hand on her shoulder then met her gaze. "Canteens of water, gas masks, a couple of cans of tear gas, and functioning walkie-talkies." He shook his head. "Not even a granola bar. Either they weren't planning on staying long, or their friend with the helicopter has the rest of their gear. Why haven't we heard the helicopter? Did they land somewhere while awaiting confirmation that we're all dead?"

"Unless they have some freighter anchored off-shore, I'm guessing the pilot landed somewhere to conserve fuel," she informed him. "We're just far enough from the mainland that he'd need to ensure there's enough fuel for the return trip."

"So they're not going to sweep the island from above," Zack remarked.

"Unlikely," she replied and sighed. "They wouldn't see much through the thick jungle anyway. It'd be a waste of manpower and fuel. How far of a trek to the old port?"

"Maybe another two hours," Zack informed her. "We'll leave first thing tomorrow morning."

She then indicated the prisoner with a slight nod. "What about our friend?"

"Jail Bait?" Zack shrugged. "Leave him a bottle of water and a bag of pretzels," he casually replied. "We can't take him with us. He'll just slow us down and slit our throats the first chance he gets." He then eyed her with a curious look. "Although, if you think we should kill him; I'm not opposed to hearing you out."

Jackie rolled her eyes and walked away. Zack grinned and chuckled in his throat. He loved getting under her skin.

Chapter Twenty

An hour later, it was dark outside the hangar. Everyone had grown tired and reluctantly considered where they would sleep. The burning barrel did an excellent job of keeping the hangar's interior lit while the tarp kept anyone on the outside from seeing the burning fire. Zack found an inflatable raft in need of repairs. With some work, he was able to patch it and inflate it with a hand pump, making a comfortable bed on the concrete floor for his female travel companions. Some rope converted an old parachute into four hammocks for the guys. They would have to take turns sleeping in the hammocks, but it was better than sleeping on the concrete floor all night. Zack rolled the moderately worn desk chair across the hangar and positioned it alongside the tarp-covered entrance.

"Since you insist on taking watch," Zack announced, "you may as well be comfortable."

"If I'm too comfortable, there's a better chance I'll fall asleep," she teased. "Why don't you take the chair and get some sleep before your watch?"

They heard a commotion coming from across the hangar. Jackie and Zack left the covered entrance and hurried toward the grounded plane. Several of their fellow castaways stood around the plane's side door where Lindsey had made herself comfortable on the back seat.

"Who the hell said you get to have the only comfortable piece of furniture in this dump?" Sid proclaimed with anger while Conner remained in the doorway to keep the others from entering.

Lindsey sat proudly on the plane's back seat and held her head high. "I got here first," she insisted while eyeing them. "I'm not used to sleeping on the floor or in groups. It would be far too uncomfortable for me."

"What about everyone else?" Mandy demanded and appeared ready to lunge past Conner to reach the prissy young woman.

"There's enough room in here for Conner and me," Lindsey insisted. "I'm not concerned with what the rest of you do. It's not my problem."

Jackie rubbed her sore shoulder while shaking her head then eyed Zack. "Do we knock the princess off her pedestal?"

Zack eyed her and seemed almost enthusiastic. "Are you giving me permission?"

She frowned then sighed with disgust. "No," she muttered. "We can't have this sort of commotion. If someone is nearby, they're going to hear it."

"I'm on it," Zack groaned.

Zack moved past the others to the plane and looked at the collecting crowd. "The next person who raises their voice is getting knocked on their ass," he announced boldly and looked around to the quickly silencing masses.

"She's not special," Sid protested while pointing a demanding finger at Lindsey. "She's the reason we're all in this mess, yet she's strutting around like the goddamned island princess."

"Don't waste your breath," Lindsey scoffed and raised an arrogant brow. "He's my bodyguard."

Zack turned toward her and pointed a warning finger. "I'm no one's bodyguard," he snapped. "Tread lightly, little girl. Pissing off the angry mob is one thing. Pissing me off takes you into a whole other world of misery."

Lindsey sneered and gave Conner a nod. He pulled the side door shut and dropped the cover over the window.

"I really don't like her," Bill announced while walking away.

"Take a number," Kate scoffed.

§

It was already decided that Jackie would take watch for the first two hours, Zack would take the next four, and Bill and Sid volunteered to take the last two hours. Once the others were settled for their nap, Zack approached Jackie with the dreaded first aid kit he'd taken from the plane wreckage. She saw him with the kit and immediately groaned.

"Don't give me that look," he remarked and sat down before her near the tarp covering the hangar doorway. "Your wound needs to be checked and kept clean."

As he removed the old dressing, she tried to pretend it didn't hurt. Zack eyed the red area surrounding the stitched wound and frowned. He applied a thin layer of antibiotic ointment to the sutured wound and shook his head.

"Are you taking the antibiotics?" he practically demanded. "The wound looks inflamed."

"Yes, I've been taking them every four hours like it says on the bottle," she replied. "It's only been half a day. Antibiotics take a day to start working."

"I know I removed the entire bullet," he remarked possibly questioning himself. "Since you were out, I took my time and made sure. If it gets worse, I may have to remove a stitch and let it drain."

"That sounds pleasant," she muttered.

As he applied a fresh dressing to the wound, Jackie saw Mandy watching Zack care for her injuries. She wondered what the woman was thinking. Zack cast a look at Jackie, forcing her to meet his gaze.

"Are you sure you're up to guard duty?" he asked. "You need your rest."

"Yes, I'm fine," she replied. "I can stay awake for two hours and stare into black nothingness."

"I can do the entire six-hour shift," Zack offered. "I got some sleep this afternoon. We could volunteer some of the others as well."

"I got some sleep earlier too," she replied while glaring at him. "I'm fine. I appreciate your concern, Zack," she announced then shifted uncomfortably, "but I'd feel more comfortable doing guard duty myself than putting my life in the hands of our fellow passengers."

Zack finished taping the gauze pad to her wound. He straightened proudly and grinned. "Good as new."

She pulled her shirt over the dressing and moved her arm with some stiffness and pain. "Doesn't feel good or new." She sighed and ran her fingers through her messy ponytail. "More like old and tired."

"When I relieve you, I'll personally tip over one of the hammocks and secure you the best accommodations in the place," he announced proudly.

"I believe our overly privileged friend already secured those accommodations," Jackie muttered and nodded to the plane.

"Would you like me to throw them out?" he asked. "I'll do it."

She laughed softly while smiling at him. "That's okay," Jackie replied. "We don't want to start a war with her mob boss father over an uncomfortable bench seat in a plane."

"Be sure to let me know when you would like me to start a war with Dexter," he announced and smiled almost deviously. "I never back down from a challenge."

Jackie smiled at the comment. As he was about to stand, Jackie caught his hand. He met her gaze. She smiled and gave his hand an affectionate squeeze. Zack smiled, kissed the top of her head, and then took his position in the corner a few feet from the tarp-covered doorway. Jackie attempted to make herself comfortable in the office desk chair and briefly glanced out the hangar opening. With all the vegetation and beater planes outside the hangar, it was going to be difficult to see anyone sneaking up on them. Zack had set a few snare alarms around the perimeter, so they'd at least hear someone approaching. Mandy approached Jackie and took a seat on the floor not far from her.

"I couldn't sleep and thought you could use the company to help stay awake," Mandy announced in a hushed voice so she wouldn't wake the others.

"There's little risk that I'll fall asleep," Jackie informed her, "but I don't mind the company."

That was a lie. Jackie preferred peaceful solitude over mundane conversation. She had little in common with most women, since she didn't know many growing up. After her mother had died when she was little, it was mostly her father and the rest of Whiskey Tango Foxtrot. Over the years, the faces may have changed, but the comradery hadn't.

Mandy gave a slight nod, indicating Zack across the front of the hangar. "Your husband is fiercely devoted," she remarked while hiding her smile.

Jackie had to keep from laughing at the comment. She wasn't sure how anyone could mistake Zack for her husband. Although she supposed he was overly attentive since she'd been shot.

"Zack's not my husband," she announced while grinning. "He's my teammate and partner. We watch each other's backs."

"The others who parachuted from the plane," Mandy began. "Are they your associates as well?"

"Yes, that's my team," Jackie informed her while playing a mental game of 'can she be trusted'. She was naturally suspicious when anyone asked questions about her friends and their work.

"So you were hired to protect her royal highness?" Mandy teased while smirking as she nodded toward the plane that now creaked slightly.

Jackie hadn't noticed the sounds coming from the plane, but it was obvious what was going on inside. She managed a tiny laugh at the comment.

"Yes, we were hired to protect her snobby, little ass," Jackie countered.

Mandy laughed in response. It was easy to tell Lindsey was already the most hated person in the group. "Talk about your shit assignments, huh?" she teased.

"I know your life was put in danger the moment she boarded that plane with you," Jackie announced and honestly felt bad for those unwittingly involved, "but I really can't discuss her situation or our assignment. I can only tell you there are people who want her badly enough to sacrifice anyone who gets in their way."

"I don't want to discuss her anyway," Mandy replied surprising Jackie.

"Really?" Jackie was now becoming increasingly suspicious of the woman.

She offered a slightly embarrassed smile. "I actually wanted to ask about your friend," Mandy remarked as she blushed slightly.

Jackie stared at the woman a moment then glanced at Zack, where he rested not far from them. Although he couldn't hear their conversation, she didn't doubt he was keeping an eye on them when he should be sleeping.

"Zack?" she questioned then raised a curious brow. "You mean; ask about him as in--?"

"He seems so attentive," Mandy remarked while beaming with delight. "It's refreshing."

She stared at Mandy almost at a loss for words. "And you think he's cute?"

Mandy attempted to hide her smile, but she couldn't keep from giggling. "May as well make the best of a bad situation, don't you think?"

Jackie attempted to hold back her laugh. "Zack *is* the best in a bad situation, but certainly not the way you're thinking," she informed the woman. "While there's a fifty-fifty chance he'd hump the first woman to come along, he's not the dating type." She considered the comment. "He's more like a rogue wolf. He'll breed when he's in the mood and stray the first chance he gets."

The woman stared at Jackie with surprise to either the comment or her candor. A strange smile crossed Mandy's face. "I'm not opposed to a hit-and-run."

Jackie laughed softly, immediately catching Zack's attention, even if he couldn't hear the conversation. "By all means," she announced while attempting to control her grin, "go for it." Her expression then turned serious. "A word of advice though."

Mandy immediately perked up, leaned closer, and listened intently.

"Zack's not great on subtlety, and he's easily bored with small talk," Jackie informed her. "Flirting is lost on him. You'll need to be direct and practically grab his crotch to get his attention."

She stared with surprise then smirked. "Okay, you're just messing with me now."

Jackie sighed deeply and shook her head. "Oh, I wish I were." She offered a warm smile. "Good luck and happy hunting."

Mandy stared at her a moment then managed a tiny smile. "Thanks, I think."

Chapter Twenty-one

Mac sat in a swivel chair she had moved next to the lab door, which she left propped open to keep an eye on the basement corridor. From her position, she'd be able to hear anyone at the basement door. Since there was no light in the corridor beyond the lab, she'd hear an intruder before they noticed light coming from the basement. Kirk was positioned on the opposite side of the lab closest to the sleeping quarters. He used his guard duty time to do push-ups and sit-ups. He had his shirt off, revealing his excessively toned torso and muscular upper body. Mac spent nearly as much time gazing at Kirk's toned body as she did peering down the basement hallway.

Kirk seemed preoccupied with his exercise, but his eyes periodically strayed to Dr. Freud, who remained seated at the counter while either documenting in his notebook or staring into his microscope. It was nearly two o'clock in the morning when Freud rolled away from the counter and stood. Mac and Kirk immediately shifted their attention to him. Obviously, neither trusted the man posing as a doctor.

"Well, that's bedtime for me," Freud announced then eyed both. "You kids behave."

They each gave a general nod and watched him enter the sleeping quarters. A minute or two passed. Mac and Kirk both sprang to their feet and hurried to the counter, seemingly having the same idea. Mac reached the counter first and snatched the notebook. She began flipping through it while Kirk glanced through the microscope at what had kept the man busy the last few hours. He straightened and frowned.

"Looks like he's been staring at a piece of lint the last few hours," Kirk remarked.

Mac made a face while flipping through the pages and pages of scribbled notes. "His handwriting is worse than mine," she remarked with a huff. "I can't make out any of this. It's gibberish."

Kirk shrugged. "Score one for Monroe," he remarked. "Dr. Freud is a fraud."

She tossed the notebook down and sighed. "At least he doesn't seem dangerous." Mac ran her fingers through her hair and gazed at Kirk standing alongside her. Her eyes strayed to his bare, muscular chest. She immediately fidgeted. "I need to take a walk." She snatched her flashlight. "I'll be back in half an hour. I want to see what's happening outside with this hurricane."

Kirk grabbed his discarded shirt and took her seat by the door. "Have a nice walk."

Mac left the lab and headed down the mostly dark corridor to the stairs.

§

Monroe and Bogart entered the lab from the sleeping quarters a little before three in the morning and looked around the room. Both seemed a little surprised when they didn't see Mac. Kirk stood by the lab door while staring into the dark corridor.

"Where's Mac?" Monroe suddenly demanded.

Kirk shook his head and removed his AK-47 assault rifle from his shoulder. "She went for a walk over an hour ago and hasn't returned," he announced. "I thought I'd give her until you arrived for your shift before I went looking for her."

"An hour ago?" Monroe remarked. "I don't think she'd be gone that long, under the circumstances."

"Probably took off on us," Kirk snapped in anger then shook his head. "She can't be trusted." He raised an arrogant brow. "If she double-crosses us again, I'm putting her down myself."

"Okay, take a breath," Monroe remarked. "You just stay here. Bogart and I will look for her." His eyes then narrowed. "If anyone's going to kill her; it's going to be me."

They each grabbed their weapons and left the lab.

§

Monroe and Bogart cautiously headed through the basement door being certain to shut it behind them. Even though Monroe didn't trust Mac, he wasn't taking any chances that trouble hadn't found them. They kept their weapons aimed and prepared for the worst, even if it turned out to be unnecessary. They made their way across the massive, institutional kitchen and approached the swinging doors to a banquet hall of sorts. There was also a hallway that led to the main hallway. Monroe was about to gently push open the swinging door when Bogart snapped his fingers twice. Monroe looked at him. Bogart pointed to the hallway. Both remained still a moment and listened. They heard faint voices coming from deeper within the main level. Monroe led the way with his assault rifle while Bogart brought up the rear.

Both men continued cautiously down the broad, grand hallway and kept an eye on several doorways on either side of the hall. They could hear the voices, which were getting louder. The loudest voice was Mac's as her words became clearer.

"I told you," she announced in a commanding tone that carried. "I'm here alone. I don't even know this woman you're looking for."

Monroe and Bogart paused and crouched low near the lobby entrance. From their hidden position, they could see Mac comfortably seated on one of the sofas with her back to the boarded windows and facing the center of the lobby. Her wrists were zip-tied in front of her, although they had foolishly left her

140

ankles untied. One man dressed in black combat gear stood a few feet behind her with a gun aimed at her head while she stared at the man in front of her. Another man dressed in black lay motionless on the floor. With Mac's reputation, it seemed plausible she'd gotten the slip on one man, but she was taken prisoner when she became outnumbered.

"You jumped from the plane with two other men," the man announced in what was almost certainly a Russian accent. "Clearly you were the distraction. Don't try to deny you're not with them."

The man standing before Mac, whom she heard the others refer to as Corbin, was a tall, athletically built man in his mid to late thirties. He was what could only be described as devilishly handsome. He had dark nearly black, wavy hair that just about touched his collar, and he had amazingly dark soulful eyes. He had that typical villain smile, evil yet almost seductive. By the way he held himself and the manner in which he spoke was that of a refined gentleman even if he was anything but a gentleman. He would probably be considered Mac's type if she wasn't already in such a foul mood.

"Those creeps volunteered me to join them because, apparently, I looked like this woman you're searching for," she informed him while taking in a sweeping glance of the handsome man. She was already working on her backup plan. "Trust me; I got away from them as fast as I could. Those boys are bad news." Mac's eyes strayed to the hallway where Monroe and Bogart were barely visible. She looked back at the man standing over her. "I can tell you this much. I saw their helicopter crash right before I took off. They must have had at least a dozen heavily armed men. If they were here, your men would be dead by now." She then cocked her head and raised an arrogant brow. "Your men are wasting their time searching the second and third floor. Everything's locked up tight."

Monroe tensed a moment, realizing that comment had actually been code for him. He turned in his crouched position within the darkened hallway and faced Bogart.

"We're looking at a dozen or more heavily armed men," Monroe announced. "It sounds as if most are searching the upper floors for now. Go back to the lab and report the situation to Gil and Kirk. His men will eventually find the basement, even if they're not looking for one. We don't want to be boxed in down there."

"What about Mac?" Bogart whispered with concern. It was obvious he questioned whether Monroe intended to sacrifice her for the team.

"I'm going to monitor the situation," he replied as if reading Bogart's mind. "The moment they know we're here, it's going to turn into a war, and we're outnumbered. We need to take them out quietly."

Bogart nodded although seeming distrusting regarding Mac's fate. "She's on our side," he reminded Monroe. "Do right by her."

"Just go," Monroe huffed. "I've got this."

Chapter Twenty-two

Bogart hurried through the mostly dark kitchen while keeping low and quiet. He paused near every corner to ensure there were no bad guys lingering around. He stopped at the edge of the metal counter, remained low, and scanned the area just before the basement entrance. Although the basement door was clearly noticeable, there was nothing to indicate it led to a basement. Since basements weren't common in Florida, there would be no reason to suspect it led to one. Being the basement was a lab, the door was also designed to lock when closed automatically.

Bogart's master key would allow him access, but the men searching the building would find it difficult to enter through the basement door without making a lot of noise. He was about to continue his journey toward the basement door when he saw the light from a flashlight scan the area. Bogart ducked down and remained low to the floor while clutching his assault rifle. Even one shot fired would alert every bad guy to their presence, which made the weapon a last resort. He watched the flashlight as it scanned the area near the door then saw the man holding it come into view.

Bogart gently set down his rifle and crouched close to the floor. When the man was close enough, Bogart sprang upward while catching the weapon to keep it pointed away from him.

He immediately punched the man in the throat. When the man released the rifle and clutched his throat while wheezing, Bogart seemed surprised the throat punch had actually worked. He'd only ever seen the guys use it, and hadn't actually done it himself. He gripped the rifle barrel in both hands and swung the butt of the rifle at the man's head, striking him. The man dropped to the floor and didn't move.

"I'm getting better at this," Bogart announced then grinned proudly.

Bogart unlocked the basement door and hurried down the stairs. Kirk immediately greeted him in the doorway aiming his assault rifle at him. Bogart skidded to a stop and attempted to hide that the intimidating man startled him with the weapon aimed at him.

"Whoa," he cried out. "It's just me."

Kirk lowered his weapon and eyed Bogart. "Did you find Mac?"

"Yeah," Bogart replied. "She's entertaining some new friends. We've got a least a dozen armed men searching the building. Monroe suggested taking them out quietly, so we're not ambushed."

Kirk looked back into the lab, snapped his fingers, and pointed to the ceiling. Gil and Darth joined him in the doorway. Darth was now wearing his bulletproof vest in case they encountered danger. Dr. Freud hurried after them and appeared concerned.

"Is something wrong?"

"We have several heavily armed intruders," Kirk informed the doctor. "Stay down here and don't open the door for anyone."

Dr. Freud nodded and shut the lab door behind them. Once they heard it lock, the three men and Darth hurried for the stairs.

§

Within the lobby, Corbin paced before Mac where she remained tied. She watched Corbin pace, which was obviously meant to intimidate her, but it was actually annoying her more than anything. Mac appeared almost bored in her captive state. She finally groaned and glared at the man and his associate across the room.

"Can you at least torture me while we wait?" she finally demanded. "I'm bored out of my mind here."

The man stopped pacing and looked at Mac with some surprise. He finally chuckled. "You're a little spitfire, aren't you?"

"No," she replied with a groan. "I'm a Libra. We're just easily bored."

The man eyed her a moment, as if uncertain what to make of her, then chuckled in his throat. "Once we find your friends, I'll be more than happy to torture you," he announced while smirking. "I'd love nothing more than to make you scream."

"I told you, those guys aren't my friends," she insisted. "I have no clue why you even want this woman. Seriously? You blew a commercial plane from the sky just to get one woman?" Mac cleverly raised her brows. "What did she do? Steal your prom date?"

Corbin groaned while shutting his eyes as if in pain. "Do you ever stop talking?" he demanded.

"I'm bored," she again informed him. "I'm so bored; I'm even willing to talk to you." She cocked her head while eyeing him. "From what I heard, she pissed off this guy Cicco. What the hell could she have possibly done that your boss wants her that badly?" Mac shook her head and laughed. "She's just a kid. What could she possibly have done to warrant shooting a plane from the sky and killing all those innocent men and women?"

"Vinny Cicco? I don't know why her father-in-law wants her," Corbin announced with little interest and raised his devilish eyebrow. "But he had better not cross our path to get her because we'll crush him and his men if he gets anywhere near her. My boss wants her that badly. You're *all* expendable."

Mac stared at the man with some surprise. She attempted to cover, but it was already too late. "You don't work for Cicco?"

The man chuckled in his throat. "Hardly," Corbin scoffed then sneered with distaste. "Vinny Cicco is the slimy underbelly of the mafia world. Just a two-bit thug really."

"No argument there." She maintained her stare while attempting to process the information but was unable to connect the dots. "So who are you? Why do you want some girl barely over the legal drinking age?" Mac tilted her head and appeared curious. "Honestly, I don't get it. Did she break your heart? She stand you up at the altar? Why is everyone interested in her?"

He stared back at her a moment and maintained his grin. "You know; I almost feel sorry for you and your friends," he announced with a certain refined sophistication. "You really have no clue what you've gotten yourselves into with that wretched girl. It seems almost sad to kill you for simply being ignorant."

"I already told you," Mac insisted while groaning. "I'm an innocent bystander." She cocked her head and raised her brows. "But you've piqued my curious side. What *is* your interest in her?"

He stared at her a moment as if attempting to read her expression then turned jovial. "What the hell?" he remarked then laughed. "Perhaps if you know the truth about the girl you're protecting, you may change your mind and happily turn her over to us." The man approached Mac and casually sat in a chair across from her. He leaned forward and clasped his gun in his hands between his knees. "Your *innocent* girl stole some very important information from the Russian government. They, in turn, hired us to retrieve that information no matter what the collateral damage."

Mac stared at him and attempted not to be surprised, but she almost certainly failed. She blinked several times while attempting to process the information she'd just heard.

"She stole secrets from the Russian government?" Mac asked in as calm a tone as she could manage.

The man sitting across from her laughed while leaning back in the chair. He casually crossed his ankle to his knee while resting his gun still aimed at her on his bent knee.

"You seem surprised," he announced and casually waved the gun as if it were merely an extension of his hand. "Could it be that sweet, innocent looking girl has pulled one over on you and your friends?" His smile mocked her. "Feeling a little betrayed?"

Mac frowned while glaring back at him. "Asshole," she announced almost casually, "I live in constant betrayal. Trust me; it's nothing new to me."

He stared at her a moment as if attempting to read her then gently scratched his chin with the barrel of the gun. "A little disappointed in your friends?" Corbin teased in a tone meant to mock her.

She didn't even flinch while staring back at him. "I don't have any friends," she corrected with some bitterness. Her hostility rapidly rose. "Friends are just enemies who haven't yet stabbed you in the back. I'm interested in survival. I'm loyal to whoever signs my check."

Corbin's mind seemed to be reeling as he stared at her. He again sat forward and stared into her eyes. "I've met your kind before," he remarked almost sympathetically. "Desperately trying to fit in; willing to put your life on the line in order to find a place to call home; backing the wrong horse in hopes of being accepted."

"I don't subscribe to sentimental bullshit," she informed him. "Cold hard cash and a moderately comfortable bed are all I need." She drew a deep breath and straightened proudly. "I stopped feeling a long time ago."

"Someone with your unique talents and gritty personality would almost certainly fit in with our little family. The pay is good." He continued to stare at her then eyed the dead man on the floor before returning his gaze to her. "I believe a position recently became available." A strange smile then crossed his face as he sized her up. "And my bed is very comfortable."

Mac stared back at him a moment then allowed her eyes to fall across the moderately handsome, dangerous man. She raised a cocky brow while staring at him.

"There's a comfortable office just down the hall," she informed him. "Perhaps we could *discuss* my qualifications further in private."

He immediately shifted in his chair, almost enthusiastic by the suggestion. A humored smile crossed his face.

"You do realize, I have no intention of untying you," Corbin informed her while smirking.

"I prefer it that way," she remarked then grinned seductively.

Corbin could no longer contain his desire. He sprang up from the chair and motioned her to her feet with the gun. Mac stood, gave him a lustful once over, and then headed toward the hallway. As they entered the hall and approached the nearby office, Mac cast a look at Monroe hidden within the shadows. He stared at her with surprise. There was no telling what was about to happen next when it came to Mac, but she seemed to know what she was doing. She also left one man alone in the lobby. Monroe needed to act quickly.

§

The laundry room was half the size of a football field and contained industrial sized washers and dryers to meet the needs of a small, one-hundred-bed mental facility. In addition to the washers and dryers, there were large pressing machines used for ironing sheets and clothes, collapsible tables for folding clothes, and racks containing linens and towels. Although nothing had been used in years, everything seemed in excellent condition. A man carried an M416 assault rifle with silencer cradled in his arms as he walked through the dimly lit laundry room and scanned the area with his baton flashlight. There were dozens of dark corners big enough to hide a grown man, making his job even more difficult.

A whimpering dog was heard. The armed man spun several times while shining his light around. The glow of the flashlight caught a brief glimpse of a German shepherd dog limping behind a linen rack. In the brief moment he saw the dog, he could tell the dog's front paw was injured by the way he held it up. As the dog disappeared behind the linen rack, the man kept his weapon aimed and approached. He rounded the corner of the rack and aimed his weapon, firing several nearly silent shots. The dog wasn't there.

Someone roughly tapped him on the shoulder. The man spun around with his weapon aimed. Gil caught the barrel of the rifle and punched the man in the face twice as he twisted the weapon in his hand.

"Seriously?" Gil snarled demandingly. "You'd shoot an injured dog?"

Gil twisted the weapon around in the man's hand, forcing his finger against the trigger. The weapon fired causing the man to shoot himself with his own weapon. The large caliber bullet tore through the man's mid-section with very little sound. Gil tore the rifle from his hands as the bad guy fell to the floor while clutching his bleeding abdomen. Gil shook his head in annoyance.

"Never kill the dog," he announced while wagging his finger at the dead man. "Pisses off the wrong people."

Gil snatched the baton flashlight from the dead man's side while crouching on the floor and aimed the light into the dark corner. Darth crawled out from beneath the linen rack and panted happily while wagging his tail.

"Such a good boy," Gil announced in his best baby-talk voice.

Darth lost his limp and happily trotted to greet his human partner where he remained crouched on the floor. The dog accepted an affectionate scratch to his scruff and licked Gil's face.

"I wouldn't let the big, scary man hurt you." Gil kissed the dog on the head. He removed Darth's bulletproof vest from his shoulder and easily slipped the dog into it. Once the dog was again combat ready, Gil straightened. "Come on," he announced while maintaining his baby-talk voice. "Let's find Bogart and make sure he doesn't get himself killed. Would you like that?" Darth jumped around excitedly. "Would you? Yes, you would. Such a good boy!"

Darth barked excitedly in response.

Gil held up a warning finger. "Acht," he warned. "Use your stealth mode bark."

Darth woofed low and soft.

Gil laughed and affectionately scratched the dog's head. "That's a good boy," he announced. "If we could only train Bogart that well."

He slung his own rifle and chose to carry the dead man's weapon since it had a silencer, which would prove useful to keep his location a secret. Gil and Darth quickly and quietly crept through the laundry room and headed for the main entrance.

Chapter Twenty-three

Despite being abandoned for several years, the machinery within the maintenance department remained exactly where it had been when the facility was operational. An area not far from a large garage door appeared to be where they brought in vehicles that needed work as well as larger deliveries. The maintenance department was set up much like a garage with tool carts, an engine puller, and diagnostic machines. The rest of the large shop contained the same concrete floor. There were counters containing smaller tools, countless generators, welding equipment, and spare parts contained within dozens of plastic crates. The familiar sound of metal parts clunking against the counter seemed to radiate across the room.

A man carrying an assault rifle affixed with a silencer walked across the dimly lit maintenance room and followed the strange sound. As he entered a small clearing, he spotted Kirk sitting on a stool before the counter where he tinkered around with the old equipment. The man stopped, aimed his weapon at Kirk's back, and kept him in his sights.

"Hands in the air," the man shouted in a gruff tone.

Kirk ignored the man and continued working on his new toys. The man took a few steps closer while keeping his weapon aimed at Kirk's broad back.

"I said hands in the air or I will shoot," the armed man again announced.

His foot hit something causing him to look down. His boot was against a wire. The man's eyes followed the wire along the floor and up the side of the wall. By the time he saw that the wire was connected to a large pair of hedge clippers, it was too late. The taut wire holding it in place sprang, and the clippers shot through the air and struck him in the gut. The man gasped while dropping his rifle, which clattered when it hit the floor, and he clutched the bloodied clippers embedded in his abdomen. The man gasped, spitting up blood, and looked at Kirk, who continued with his work. As the man sank to the floor, Kirk held up a wooden four-leaf clover he'd carved by hand. Without a word, Kirk stood from the counter and approached the dead man. He tossed the four-leaf clover onto the man's chest and claimed his discarded assault rifle in exchange.

§

Monroe slipped into the dimly lit lobby while remaining within the shadows, which was technically most of the lobby. The armed man continued to patrol the area while periodically looking at his watch. Was he wondering why the rest of his team was taking so long with their sweep of the building? It couldn't be long before those on the second and third floor made their emptyhanded return. Monroe slung his assault rifle over his shoulder and removed his semiautomatic. He did not intend to fire his weapon in fear of drawing attention to their location, but he'd need it to intimidate the armed man. As he took a step closer to the armed man in the lobby, he felt the barrel of an assault rifle press against his back.

"I wouldn't advise that," a male voice announced, alerting the man within the lobby to their presence.

Monroe cursed under his breath while raising his hands in the air along with the semiautomatic. The armed man within the lobby was alerted to their presence and spun around with his weapon aimed. He saw Monroe only a few feet away with his teammate holding him prisoner at gunpoint. The man behind

Monroe snatched the pistol from his hand and placed it down the front of his pants. He then removed the assault rifle slung over Monroe's shoulder and cast it aside with a clatter.

"You idiot," the man behind Monroe exploded to his partner. "You nearly let him get the slip on you!"

The first man sneered in disgust at his teammate behind Monroe. There was the distinct possibility the two men didn't get along. Monroe watched as the man across the lobby lowered his weapon. Monroe immediately spun around while dodging the barrel of the rifle aimed at his back and caught the weapon. As the man pulled the trigger, Monroe swiftly redirected the weapon, causing the muffled shot to hit his teammate. As the large caliber bullet tore through the first man, he collapsed to the floor. Monroe kept the barrel of the assault rifle aimed away from him and elbowed the second man twice in the face. On the second hit, the man released the weapon. Before Monroe could aim the weapon at him, he was tackled to the tile floor. The assault rifle hit the floor and made a distinctive clatter that seemed to echo throughout the first floor. Monroe's gun was dislodged from the man's pants as he hit the floor.

The man punched Monroe in the face once and went for a second hit. Monroe blocked his fist, punched him in the mouth, and then tossed him off him, sending him flying across the lobby floor. Monroe sprang to his feet a second before his assailant. As the man stood, Monroe kicked him in the crotch. When he doubled over, he punched him in the face, dropping him to the floor. As Monroe reached for his discarded handgun, the supposedly disabled man on the floor kicked him in the chin. Monroe stumbled backward, tripped over the dead man, and fell to the floor. The remaining man sprang to his feet with Monroe's semiautomatic in his hand and pulled the trigger.

Monroe pulled the dead man on top of him, allowing the dead man to take both shots to the back. Monroe's assailant took two quick steps closer for a better shot. Monroe grabbed the Bowie knife from his boot and threw it at his attacker. The knife sank into the man's neck forcing him to drop the semiautomatic and clutch his bleeding neck. As the blood seeped between his fingers at an alarming rate, he stared at Monroe with a stunned look on his face then collapsed to the floor. Monroe groaned with relief then pushed his dead human shield off him while springing to his feet. Unfortunately, the others would have heard the gunfire. It would only be a matter of minutes before they came to the lobby to check on the sound. Monroe grabbed the assault rifle with silencer and reclaimed his semiautomatic before darting into the nearby hallway.

§

Mac clung to Corbin with her bound hands around his neck as he lay on top of her in a compromising position on the old leather sofa. He clung to her shoulders while holding her in a tight embrace. Both panted heavily from their brief but intense encounter. He immediately sought her mouth and kissed her with surprising warmth and passion. As he broke off the kiss, he warmly caressed her face forcing her to meet his gaze. He grinned in response.

"I'll be honest," he informed her. "I wasn't expecting you to go through with it."

She smirked slyly and chuckled in her throat while caressing his chest with her bound hands. "I figured you'd just throw me over the desk and get your jollies," she remarked. "So I guess we're both pleasantly surprised with the outcome."

"If we hadn't been pressed for time and I didn't fear you'd lay me out like my man back in the lobby," he announced, "I would have gone for some lengthy foreplay."

Mac stared at him a moment then smiled, apparently pleased to hear him say that. "Well, maybe next time," she replied then teasingly indicated her bound wrists. "When I can fully participate."

He kissed her quickly but passionately on the mouth then moved off her. As he pulled his pants up, Mac made an effort to dress with her bound wrists. She actually seemed pretty good at it. As he zipped his pants, he eyed her while she sat back down and slipped into her boots.

"Why did you really come on to me?" he finally asked with a mildly devious smile on his face.

She shrugged then finally looked at him after her boots were in place. "You're a good-looking guy with one hell of a body," she remarked then snorted a soft laugh. "And it's been a long time since I've gotten any."

He smiled at her then chuckled. The faint sounds of two gunshots from the lobby interrupted their intimate conversation. His expression immediately dropped. He grabbed his discarded semiautomatic and ran for the office door.

"I knew you were lying about your friends," he muttered with annoyance as he paused before the door.

Mac remained casually seated on the sofa with her switchblade already in her hand and easily cut through the zip ties unnoticed. Corbin threw open the office door and aimed his weapon into the corridor, prepared to shoot the first thing that moved.

"You'd think the moron would be a little more stealth," Mac remarked from alongside him.

Her sudden appearance alongside him startled Corbin. He shifted his attention to her and saw her hands were now free. Mac kicked the gun from his hand, surprising him. He attempted to lunge for her, but she was already spinning into a roundhouse kick and nailed him in the face. He was thrown several feet across the room before hitting the floor. She snatched the discarded semiautomatic and looked at the barely conscious man.

"This was fun," she informed him. "We should do it again sometime."

Mac hurried from the room and nearly collided with Monroe, who had just made his escape from the lobby.

"Are you okay?" he asked with concern.

Mac relieved him of the second assault rifle. "Never better," she remarked then glared at him. "Now that you've announced our location to nearly a dozen armed men, we'd better go before they find us."

"Hey, I was trying to save your ass," Monroe snarled.

"My ass didn't need saving," she snapped back. "I had it under control. You, on the other hand, had one job. Take out the guy in the lobby. You couldn't even do that without alerting the entire building to our presence."

"We'll argue about this later. What about their leader?" Monroe asked and indicated the room.

"Incapacitated," she replied then listened to the sound of thundering feet on the stairway. "We don't have time to worry about him right now. Let's go!"

They hurried down the dark hallway and away from the lobby before the rest of the men came to check on the sounds of gunfire.

Chapter Twenty-four

It was a little after four in the morning within the dimly lit hangar. There had been sounds coming from the other passengers throughout the night, which made sleep difficult for Jackie from her position within the raft with the other two women. The raft itself made strange noises every time one of them moved, and Jackie knew for a fact Mandy had been up to visit Zack during his watch. She witnessed the woman attempting to flirt with Zack and almost felt sorry for her. Mandy didn't bother taking Jackie's advice, which made for an awkward conversation with a man who didn't enjoy conversation.

Even if Mandy had been Zack's type, full of spitfire and danger, she'd never have lured him from his post with sexual favors. When he was in commando mode, it was best to leave him alone. After being shot down, Mandy was restless and got little sleep, which created enough noise to keep Jackie from sleeping. Mandy finally fell asleep shortly before the end of Zack's shift. Jackie remembered it well. She prayed the woman wouldn't attempt another seduction scene once Zack was relieved by Bill and Sid. That's also when Jackie was finally able to get some sleep.

Bill and Sid only had a two-hour shift leading up to sunrise. Jackie was able to sleep, but she still heard everything happening

157

around her. Strange noises kept her from a deep sleep, although with the help of the painkillers, her body was trying. Jackie wasn't sure what woke her, but it was enough to cause her to jerk in her sleep. She opened her eyes and looked around. Tear gas swiftly filled the room causing everyone to cough in their sleep. Jackie saw the can emitting smoke. She immediately held her blanket to her mouth and nose, rolled out of the raft, and across the floor. She scanned the room and saw the cage door was now open and their prisoner, Jail Bait, was gone. She didn't see Zack anywhere as smoke filled the hangar. She then saw the prisoner with a tire iron as he lunged for Bill, who had been awake and saw him.

Bill swung at him with the golf club while coughing from the tear gas. The escaped prisoner had the advantage of a facemask, indicating he'd already been through his backpack and found what he needed for his attack. Sid hadn't even noticed the escaped prisoner as he attempted to tear the tarp from the hangar opening to release the gas filling the large area. Jackie was too far from the second backpack, so she was unable to reach the second gas mask. She wrapped her lightweight blanket around her mouth and nose, removed the gun from the back of her pants, and ran across the hangar.

Bill attempted to block several swings from the tire iron, but he wasn't nearly as skilled a fighter as their prisoner was. He was swiftly losing the battle. Sid saw the attack in progress and ran to aid his friend. The blow from the tire iron, which was meant for Bill, struck Sid on the shoulder, narrowly missing his friend's head. The force of the blow was enough to send Sid to his knees.

Jackie stopped halfway across the hangar and aimed her semiautomatic at the escaped prisoner clutching the tire iron. He was about to strike Bill, his intended target. A scream distracted her. She looked across the hangar and saw one of their fellow passengers punch Lindsey in the face as he attempted to pull her from the plane doorway. Conner attempted to stop the man, but he was hit several times, knocking him to the floor.

The male passenger grabbed the now violently coughing Lindsey and tossed her over his shoulder while she was mildly incapacitated. Jackie turned just in time to see Jail Bait swing the tire iron at her, knocking the gun from her hand. He lunged at her with the tire iron.

She spun into a high, roundhouse kick and struck him in the chest, sending him back several steps. He stared at her with surprise and came at her again, not learning his lesson. He threw a punch, which she was forced to block with her arm then grabbed his wrist and kicked him several times in the side. When he was slightly disoriented, she kicked him in the face. He refused to go down and managed to come at her again, still clutching his tire iron.

Jackie blocked the blow with her forearm, jumped into the air, and caught him around the neck with her legs. She flipped him off his feet, through the air, and roughly to the concrete floor. Unfortunately, she hit the floor with less grace than usual and immediately felt the intense pain shooting through her shoulder. For a moment, she was temporarily paralyzed with pain. The tear gas was rapidly clearing from the room through the hangar opening. Sid attempted to help Jackie to her feet. She, instead, indicated the gun not far from her.

"Don't let him take her," she cried out while gasping in pain.

Sid grabbed the gun and looked across the hangar to the plane. The male passenger was already charging for the opening with Lindsey over his shoulder. Sid aimed the gun but seemed uncertain about shooting the moving target. Zack appeared out of the smoke wearing the second gas mask and kicked the man in the chest with both feet. The man and Lindsey flew across the hangar floor with tremendous force from Zack's forward momentum. Conner ran for Lindsey where she curled in a ball while gasping in pain. As the man recovered, Zack kicked him under the chin, throwing him upward and then backward. He landed harshly on his back and writhed in pain. Zack took two quick steps for the man and punched him in the face. He stopped moving, now out cold.

Zack removed the gas mask and pointed at their prisoner, Jail Bait, who writhed around not far from the entrance and attempted to get to his feet. "Don't let him escape!"

Sid turned with the gun aimed as Jail Bait made it to his feet and attempted to bolt for the opening. Sid fired two shots at the slower moving man and still managed to miss. Jackie made it to her feet and stood alongside Sid. She grabbed the gun from his hand before he could waste any more ammo, and fired at the fleeing man. Jail Bait took a bullet to his lower thigh and hit the ground.

Jackie lowered the gun while sneering with annoyance. "Drag that back in here."

Sid and Bill ran for the injured man clutching his bleeding leg and pulled him back inside the hangar. Zack turned to the unconscious man posing as one of them and flipped him onto his back. He glared at him as Jackie approached. She was in tremendous pain and was extremely pissed.

"He was posing as one of the survivors," Zack informed her then cast a glance at her. "I can't believe I didn't see him set Jail Bait free."

"You wouldn't have," Jackie informed him as she stopped near the makeshift raft bed.

She aimed the gun at Mandy's face. Mandy gasped while staring at the barrel of the gun only inches from her. The look in Jackie's eyes was unpredictable.

"This little bitch distracted you just long enough for her partner there to unlock the cage and set the prisoner free," Jackie snarled.

Mandy stared at Jackie with terror. "I didn't have a choice," she cried out. "They threatened me."

"Bullshit," Jackie lashed back. "You weren't even on the plane when it crashed, were you? During the chaos of the attack on the plane yesterday afternoon, you and your partner joined the others in the woods. When your friends with the rifles didn't succeed, you had to formulate a new plan." Jackie's eyes narrowed. "I suggest you come up with a really good reason why I shouldn't shoot you, because I'm tired, pissed, and in a lot of pain."

As Mandy stared at the unpredictable look in Jackie's eyes and the gun aimed at her, Mandy panicked slightly. "I'll tell you everything I know if you let me go."

Jackie laughed then sneered at the woman. "That's not happening," she remarked. "An hour later, you'll be trying to kill us again."

"Okay, you have to promise not to kill me," Mandy countered.

Jackie considered the deal then nodded. "Okay," she announced. "I promise *I* won't kill you."

Mandy hesitated then eyed Zack, who seemed to be sizing her up for his next meal. She immediately fidgeted.

"He can't kill me either," Mandy interjected, realizing what was happening.

Zack and Jackie exchanged looks as if being caught in something sinister.

Jackie looked back at Mandy and nodded, agreeing to her terms. "He won't kill you either." Her look turned demanding, and her eyes narrowed. "As long as you give me something worthwhile."

"Cicco's men aren't the only ones pursuing you," Mandy informed Jackie, obviously fearing for her life. "Yes, the three of us work for Vinny Cicco, and two of us were onboard before the plane crashed. We planned to intercept Lindsey in Costa Rico. The two men who hijacked the plane weren't part of our team. We'd never met them before. They were working with whoever shot us from the sky. They had to be working with the men who killed the others within the fuselage."

"And who are *they*?"

"I don't know," Mandy replied.

"Not good enough," Jackie snarled. "You haven't told me anything useful."

"Can I kill her now?" Zack asked while raising a curious brow.

"I told you everything I know," Mandy protested. "There are other men in the woods; men who don't work for Cicco. That should be good enough to keep me alive."

"What you told us doesn't change the fact that we're being hunted," Jackie insisted, "and it doesn't help us out of this situation."

Mandy fidgeted nervously and considered what other information she had to offer. She straightened proudly. "I can tell you where the helicopter is waiting for us," she quickly announced in a desperate attempt to save her life. "You're a pilot, right? There's also a working radio."

Jackie fidgeted and again looked at Zack.

Zack frowned his disappointment. "I suppose that's reason enough to keep her alive."

"You know it could be a trap," Jackie informed him, although he must have already realized that.

"I'm looking forward to it being a trap," Zack announced with a sinister grin on his face.

Chapter Twenty-five

Monroe and Mac hurried into the dark kitchen while keeping their guns aimed as they looked around. Bogart, Gil, Kirk, and Darth appeared from the connecting hallway leading from the storage and laundry areas. Mac and Monroe aimed their weapons at them then relaxed when they saw it was their own men.

"We need to get out of here," Monroe announced. "They must have trucks or jeeps we can borrow."

"Maybe one with a working radio," Kirk remarked and headed for the only door not barricaded shut.

Kirk opened the door with caution and immediately aimed his weapon out the opening. He stared a moment with little reaction then shut the door without a word. He casually turned toward his team.

"Nope," he announced. "No jeeps that way."

"They wouldn't be parked out back," Monroe insisted. "That's our only way out. We need to go out that way and head for what's left of the front driveway."

As Monroe stepped toward the door, Kirk stepped in front of it blocking his path. His look was serious.

"I don't think we want to go out that way," Kirk informed him.

Monroe eyed him suspiciously, brushed him aside, and opened the door to see for himself. Although the storm seemed to have ended, there was mass flooding. The pond out back extended into the woods toward the rear of the property and onto the institution's back patio. Several alligators had congregated on the patio not far from the door. They turned their heads just enough to spot Monroe in the doorway. As the alligators turned toward the doorway, Monroe shut the door. He stared at the shut door a moment then looked at the rest of the team.

"We need to find another way out of here," Monroe announced.

They could hear the thundering of several feet approaching the kitchen from the main hallway.

"There was a delivery entrance in the maintenance workshop," Kirk announced while pointing down the back hallway. "It's going to make a hell of a racket when we open the bay door, but we can probably get out that way. It faces the side of the building, so it's away from the overflowing pond."

"Sounds like a plan," Monroe replied and nodded the others into the hallway leading toward the maintenance and laundry areas.

All five plus Darth hurried along the broad, long hallway and entered the maintenance room in the back. They hurried to the garage door and removed the clamps. Kirk attempted to open it while the others guarded the maintenance entrance and the large doorway. Kirk pulled the large door upward only a foot or two before water spilled into the workshop. An alligator bodysurfed in with the water. Darth immediately barked at the creature. Gil was quick to pull the dog back as the alligator spun toward them with its mouth open, revealing many sharp teeth. Mac cried out while Kirk attempted to shut the large door. It creaked loudly but wouldn't budge. More water continued to spill into the maintenance workshop and quickly flooded the area.

"There's too much water," Monroe announced with concern. "We have to get to higher ground."

"The door won't close," Kirk cried out while attempting to force it closed.

They could hear voices in the corridor.

Monroe looked back at Kirk. "We don't have time," he announced. "Go, go, go!"

They hurried across the dimly lit maintenance workshop and attempted to hide out of the water's reach, but the area was quickly flooding. Two armed men entered the workshop with their weapons aimed and shined their lights around while trudging through the already calf deep water. One of the men suddenly cried out as he fell forward into the water. The second man shined his light on his partner and watched as he was pulled through the water and out the garage door. The second man stared with surprise while apparently attempting to figure out what had just happened. As he shined his light along the flooded floor, he saw two eyes along the surface of the water. He was about to pull the trigger when the alligator leaped out of the water, grabbed his leg, and pulled him under. The man screamed while randomly firing his weapon.

Gil hurried through the water while clinging to Darth's collar, guiding him toward the workshop doorway. Kirk, Bogart, Monroe, and Mac followed while attempting to keep an eye on the splashing water where the man once stood.

§

The sound of splashing water and random gunfire continued from the maintenance department for several minutes. Two more guards ran along the corridor and hurried toward the sound within the workshop. Once the men had passed, Monroe led the rest of his team back through the corridor toward the kitchen while attempting to beat the flooding water.

"We need to break open the doors in the front," Kirk announced to the others as they hurried across the kitchen.

"No," Gil replied and indicated the back stairs. "We need to go up a level."

"Up?" Kirk demanded while glaring at him. "Why would we go up? We need to get to their transports. They have to be out front."

"We'll never break through the main doors from inside. The chain is too thick," Gil insisted. "Our only hope is to get out from the second floor and make our way down to ground level."

As they hurried for the back stairs, Bogart looked back toward the vault-like basement door then eyed his teammates. "What about the doc?"

"He'll be fine as long as he doesn't come upstairs," Monroe informed him. "The basement door is watertight. In a few hours, the water will recede, and the gators will go back to their swamp."

"That's wishful thinking," Bogart muttered.

They hurried up the back stairs to the second floor.

§

The team entered the second floor lobby and approached the wall of windows. It was still mostly dark outside, although the sun could be seen on the horizon. The front of the building was fairly dry and on higher ground. They could see two SUVs parked just down the driveway near the tree line. They were obviously trying to keep the vehicles hidden for their sneak attack.

"We have to find a way to get outside from this level," Gil informed them.

"These windows weren't meant to be opened," Mac remarked and shot a look at the others. "I wouldn't doubt they're nearly 100% shatterproof."

"Nearly," Kirk replied then grinned. "There's always that small percentage that will shatter."

"We need our duffel bags in the basement," Gil informed them. "They have tools and weapons."

"We can't go back for them," Monroe insisted. "The water is already rising in the kitchen. If we open that watertight door, the water will flood the entire basement. Dr. Freud is safe where he is. We can't compromise his safety or ours. We'll need to think of something else."

"I've got some bad news for you," Bogart remarked while checking his weapon's magazine. "Our weapon situation isn't looking good. I'm nearly out of ammo."

"We'd need a lot of firepower to break those windows," Mac insisted while eyeing the guys with concern. "A few rounds each isn't going to do it."

"And a fast evacuation plan," Gil added. "The moment they hear gunfire, they'll be on top of us."

"We need a diversion," Monroe remarked.

All eyes were suddenly on Bogart. He made a face and groaned.

"Why me?" he moaned.

"Because you're gullible and expendable," Kirk announced while grinning. "Why do you think we keep you around?"

"Not funny," Bogart snarled.

Kirk playfully slapped him on the back. "Wasn't trying to be."

Chapter Twenty-six

The second floor fire door vibrated from men attempting to break through from the stairwell. The door had been barricaded in an unusual manner from the inside. One of the sofas was positioned in front of the door despite that the door opened into the stairwell. A three-foot-tall rolling medicine cart was positioned on top of the sofa braced against the door. A television cable was tied around the doorknob and around the sofa to keep the door from opening. The door continued to vibrate as the men on the other side attempted to pull it inward toward them. The cable finally came untied from the doorknob allowing the door to fly open.

As the door flew open into the stairwell, the medicine cart flew with it. The heavy medicine cart crashed through the open doorway and took out the first two men, tumbling them down the concrete steps as it crashed down the first flight. The remaining four men stood to the side, eyed their fallen men, who were obviously dead or close to it, and then continued with their mission. They shoved the sofa aside and filtered into the large, second-floor lobby. The dimly lit room was void of life and frighteningly silent. The four men scanned the area with their weapons as they approached the first locked door into the patients' area.

When they were almost certain the men they sought were beyond the locked door, they shot out the electronic lock and kicked the door open. All four filtered into the connecting patient wing corridor. Once the four men disappeared inside, Monroe slid out from beneath one of the sofas and approached the wall of windows. He looked out the window and to the ground below. It was a decent fall, but with a little assistance, they could make it. He took several steps back, aimed the assault rifle with a silencer at the window, and pulled the trigger, shooting a barrage of bullets into the safety glass. Although the firing weapon made little sound, the bullets striking the shatterproof window made more than enough noise. The glass took nearly a dozen hits before shattering. He looked back toward the patient wing doorway, but no one returned to investigate.

Monroe removed the fire hose from under the television stand and worked on securing it around the metal divider between the two windows. Once he had it secured, he tossed the rest of the fire hose out the open window. Monroe slung a pillowcase tied to the assault rifle over his shoulder. He climbed out the window and shimmied down the fire hose to the ground below, jumping the last few feet. He looked at the main door before him and removed the pillowcase from over his shoulder. He pulled a fire ax from the pillowcase, propped his assault rifle against the support beam, and hacked at the thick chain sealing the front door. It would take some doing, but he needed to open the front door for his team in case the window wouldn't be an option.

§

Two of the four armed men charged down the main corridor and checked the patient's rooms, finding all the doors were locked. They shined their lights into the rooms through the small windows but didn't find anyone. The two remaining men bringing up the rear peered over the tall nurse's station desk within the patients' area and seemed surprised when they didn't find anyone hiding behind it. They heard what sounded like shattering glass coming from the second floor lobby. When they were about to turn around to investigate, there was a strange metallic clang coming from the right side of the floor beyond the connecting corridor. Both men hurried to the right side of the floor and attempted to locate the strange sound, but it stopped just as quickly as it had started.

They continued along the hallway to the right and proceeded to check the patients' doors in an attempt to find one that hadn't been locked. Since the second floor door had been barricaded, those they sought had to be on the second floor somewhere. They heard a loud, metallic clang, being the sound they'd heard earlier only louder now. Both armed men hurried toward the sound and paused in the connecting hallway just outside the exam room. The first man pushed the door open while the second aimed his weapon inside the room.

The room clearly used for unsanctioned surgical procedures had been falsely named 'exam room'. The first man shined his flashlight around the mostly dark room beyond the surgical table. A tank of sorts, possibly an oxygen tank, lay on its side and gently rolled back and forth as if having been knocked over recently. The tank falling had been the sound they'd heard, which meant they were close to the men they sought. The armed men continued to scan the room as they entered past several pieces of tarp-covered machinery. They scanned the entire dark room.

The plastic tarp covering what appeared to be a piece of machinery slowly rose behind the second guard. The nearly silent crinkling sound of plastic alerted the armed man in the doorway. He turned with his gun aimed, but Kirk appeared from beneath the plastic and was already on top of him. He stabbed the man in the neck with a needle, dispensing the liquid into his carotid artery. The man collapsed before he even had time to gasp. As the second man hit the floor, the man in front of him was alerted to the sound and spun around.

Bogart leaped up from beneath the surgical table, jumped on the man's back, and held a mask over his nose and mouth. The armed man struggled to toss Bogart from his back. Kirk removed the plastic covering the rest of his body and struck the man in the face with the butt of his AK-47 assault rifle. Bogart rode the man to the floor while holding the gas to his nose and mouth. Kirk claimed their weapons then eyed Bogart as he jumped off the man who was uncontrollably laughing while on the floor.

Bogart tied the man's wrists behind his back with the remaining tubing then patted his shoulder. "Enjoy your trip," Bogart announced then reclaimed his weapon as well as the second man's rifle and followed Kirk from the room. They could hear the remaining two men approaching and ran for the nurse's station, diving behind the tall desk.

§

The two remaining men entered the nearby breakroom and looked around with their weapons aimed. The room appeared empty, although it was still dark enough that someone could hide in the corners. The armed men signaled each other and crossed the breakroom in opposite directions. They heard a loud clatter. The first man aimed his weapon while shining his light toward the sink area. A German shepherd dog stood on the floor among some old, scattered coffee supplies and attempted to open a bag of pretzels with its teeth and paws. The first man stared at the dog with some surprise.

"It's a dog," he announced in disbelief to his partner across the way.

"How the hell did a dog get in here?" the second man announced without looking and continued to scan the area with his weapon.

"I don't know," the man remarked, "but I think he's hungry." He removed a piece of beef jerky from his pocket and unwrapped it. "Come here, boy. I won't hurt you."

"Never mind the damned dog," the second man announced while continuing his search of the room.

Darth approached the man and sniffed the beef jerky in his hand. The man appeared pleased and offered his hand to the dog. He eyed the bulletproof vest the dog wore and appeared puzzled.

"What are you wearing?" he asked the dog.

The second man suddenly straightened and eyed his partner across the dark room.

"Wait a minute," he suddenly announced. "This area was locked, and the fire doors were closed. How did a dog get in here?"

When he looked across the room with greater concern, Gil stood directly before him and grinned. "That's because he's with me," Gil announced then punched the man in the face.

The second man immediately straightened and raised his weapon. Darth snarled at the man, surprising him. When he looked back at the dog, Mac was already standing in front of him. She spun into a high, roundhouse kick and nailed the man in the face. He fell to the floor and groaned from the hard hit. Darth licked the man's face and snatched the beef jerky from his hand.

"We need to regroup and get the hell out of here," Gil informed Mac.

§

Gil, Mac, and Darth ran into Bogart and Kirk in the doorway near the lobby nurse's station. Two men stood by the broken window with the firehose dangling through it and peered out the window. Before they were spotted, Kirk and Bogart darted behind the nurse's desk while Gil, Mac, and Darth bolted back into the patient's area.

"That's our way out," Mac whispered while hiding behind the open, broken door. "We need to go through them."

She was about to make her move when Gil stopped her from approaching the two men. She seemed surprised while glaring at Gil then looked back at the men now climbing out the window and shimmying down the fire hose. Gil and Kirk ran for the window as the last man climbed out and disappeared. Kirk untied the firehose with some effort and released it. Both men screamed as they fell to the ground.

Mac ran for the window behind them and glared at the men. "What did you do that for?" she demanded. "That was our way out."

"Monroe should have the front door opened for us by now. If those men got just one shot off, we could be looking at more men on our ass," Gil insisted.

"And then they'd be the ones cutting our lifeline and laughing while we fell to our deaths," Kirk remarked.

"We need to hurry," Gil announced and ushered them to the fire stairs.

Chapter Twenty-seven

The group of survivors left the hangar that morning just after sunrise. The injured prisoner, Jail Bait, and his accomplice were left in the cage together with some water and medical supplies. If their friends came looking for them, they would possibly get out of it alive. If Jackie and Zack killed all their friends, the two men were pretty much screwed, and they would eventually die in their six by six cage. Jackie and Zack left the remaining eleven passengers in the woods near a freshwater pond while they followed their new prisoner to the location of the helicopter. Naturally, they didn't trust Mandy, but she had more to lose than they did. Zack, who was usually fairly even-tempered, seemed a little irritated as they followed the bound woman leading them to locations unknown. Jackie eyed him several times, attempting to read his mood.

"You think I should have shot her, don't you?"

"What?" he asked with surprise while glancing at her, realized what she said, and then shook his head. "No, of course not. Finding the helicopter and a working radio is priority one."

"So what's bugging you?"

Zack groaned with disgust. "She played me," he remarked sounding oddly like sulking. "I'm usually on top of these things. I can spot a con job a mile away." He shook his head. "I must be losing my touch."

She continued to study him. "It's something more than that," Jackie remarked and appeared curious. "What's really bugging you?"

"I actually believed she was sincere with her seduction scene," Zack announced. "I've always been suspicious of any woman coming on to me, but I actually believed her." He snorted a soft laugh. "I should have known better. Normal women *don't* come on to me. I don't know why I wasn't suspicious."

"Come on, Zack," Jackie announced while grinning. "First off; when are you around normal women to know if that statement is even true?"

He didn't seem interested in her mocking analysis. Jackie playfully linked onto his arm, catching his attention and smiled sweetly.

"Women find you adorable," she announced then considered the comment. "Until they get to know you. Outwardly, you give off a loveable vibe."

"I've never heard anyone say that before," he remarked with some doubt.

"That's because you're usually in your own commando world doing your commando things," Jackie informed him. "You're good at blocking out everyday life and focusing only on the things you know."

"So what's my problem?" he asked while eyeing her. "Am I losing my touch?"

"I don't know that I would call it a problem," Jackie insisted, "but you have been a little less Zack since your last near-death experience." She studied him as they walked and raised her brows. "Did something happen when you were under Mac's care?"

"I don't want to talk about Mac," he snapped and immediately shut down the conversation.

She eyed him suspiciously. "See," Jackie remarked. "That's what I'm talking about. Something must have happened, but you won't talk about it."

He groaned with annoyance. "You know more about me than any person on this planet," Zack informed her. "You don't need to see inside my head as well."

"Honestly," she remarked. "I don't know that I'd survive the experience."

They finally reached the small, cleared field filled with lush grass yet surrounded by woods. It was an ideal location for the helicopter to remain on standby, possibly awaiting orders. Convenient yet secluded. It would stand to reason they would conserve as much fuel as possible. As it was, Cicco almost had to have a ship anchored offshore for refueling. Jackie had no doubt that Mandy would hold up her end of the bargain and take her to the helicopter. Her friends would be waiting there, so naturally, she'd want to go where someone could help her escape and complete their mission regarding Lindsey.

When they were within earshot of the craft, Zack was quick to gag Mandy and keep her from shouting a warning or alerting her friends to their presence. He roughly assisted her to the ground and bound her ankles together for good measure. She muffled a curse from under her gag. Neither paid much attention to her once she was secured. Jackie and Zack scanned the clearing for any signs of Mandy's friends. Two men dressed in gray camouflage were patrolling the area before the helicopter. Although they were armed, they weren't necessarily expecting visitors suggested by their casual body language.

Zack eyed Jackie's injured shoulder then met her gaze. "Are you okay to fight?"

"I'll be fine," she informed him while practically brushing off his concern. "There could be more armed men in the woods. We need to do this quietly."

"I can do quiet," he insisted. "As long as you're not asking that we take them alive."

"I want that helicopter," she informed him while sharply raising her brows. "I don't care how we acquire it."

Zack suddenly grinned, obviously pleased with the comment. "That's my girl."

They split up, went opposite directions, and waited for the men to continue with their patrol. A coordinated attack would take down both men, leaving less room to radio for help. Jackie felt oddly like a panther crouched in the brush stalking her prey. She sometimes felt sorry for her prey, but then she would remember they'd kill her without thinking twice. The moment the man's back was turned, Jackie sprang from the brush. She was already spinning into a roundhouse kick when he turned. She kicked him in the chest sending him roughly to the ground. Unfortunately, he didn't lose his weapon, which he fired the moment he saw her.

Jackie threw herself to the ground and rolled, immediately regretting the action. She endured the pain long enough to kick the weapon from his hand from where she lay on the ground. As the weapon flew from his hand, she followed through with a precision kick to his groin. The man clutched himself and writhed in indescribable agony. Jackie sprang to her feet with less spring than usual and kicked him in the head, stopping him from moving. She immediately clutched her injured shoulder and nearly fell to her knees from the pain. When she looked past the helicopter, she saw Zack's man lying on the ground in an unnatural position, but there was no sign of her partner. Zack had obviously gone with the silent approach and snapped the man's neck before he was even aware that Zack had been there.

Jackie wasn't much for breaking necks. It actually made her mildly nauseous. With her shoulder injury, throwing punches would be more damaging to her as well. She didn't see Zack, so she assumed he was already checking the helicopter for bad guys. As she approached the helicopter, she saw someone appear from alongside her. Jackie spun, prepared to fight, and then realized it was Zack. To her surprise, he tackled her to the ground as several gunshots struck the helicopter where her head would have been.

Her shoulder was now screaming in pain, creating a rippling effect of agonizing shockwaves throughout her body. She was forced to roll with Zack beneath the helicopter as a sniper within the woods fired at them. Zack stared at her where they remain on the ground beneath the helicopter.

"You didn't see that coming?" he practically demanded with a stunned look on his face.

She was almost at a loss for words. They'd discussed more of Cicco's men possibly nearby, but she had been so consumed with the pain in her shoulder, she failed to keep her eyes on the surrounding area.

"I'm sorry," she informed him, feeling nervous for the first time. "I wasn't thinking." She pulled the smashed hand radio from her pocket, frowned, and cast it aside. They were back to no communication.

"Not thinking?" Zack gasped, practically stunned by her words. "You don't make mistakes like that. What's wrong with you?"

She shook her head then raised demanding brows. "Can we deal with the bad guys first?" Jackie demanded. "I think this argument can wait."

"If you'd have taken the painkillers I'd given you, we wouldn't be having this conversation at all," he insisted.

"I have been taking them," she snapped back.

The sound of something dripping caught her attention. She looked at the helicopter above them. Fuel dripped to the ground.

Jackie groaned with annoyance. "Great," she scoffed. "We need to deal with this guy and plug up that hole. We need every drop of fuel she's got."

Another shot hit the ground near them, shooting up dirt close to their faces. Zack shielded Jackie with his body then pulled away just far enough to meet her gaze.

"I'll take out the prick sniper," he announced. "You plug the hole the moment it's safe."

Jackie nodded. Zack rolled beneath the helicopter and slipped out the opposite side away from the shooter. The shooting stopped, indicating there was currently only one sniper, and he was attempting to cut Zack off on the other side. Jackie rolled out from beneath the helicopter and looked around the woods while on her belly. When she didn't see anyone, she sprang to her feet and followed the bullet holes in the side of the helicopter. She found the one leaking fuel. The bullet was still lodged in the hole, preventing the fuel from pouring out. She had to hope there was a toolkit in the helicopter.

Jackie was suddenly alerted to movement. She spun around just in time to see Mandy lunging at her with a tree branch. Jackie blocked the thick branch with her forearm, preventing the woman from bashing her over the head. She kicked her twice in the side, forcing her to drop the branch. What little effort Jackie exerted was enough to cause her tremendous pain, and the constant thumping in her shoulder wasn't about to let up this time.

She saw something glisten in the woods behind Mandy. Jackie grabbed the woman by the shirt collar and waistband and positioned her in front of her as the shots were fired from a presumed second sniper. Mandy took a bullet to the back as the remaining shots struck the helicopter. Mandy stared into Jackie's eyes with surprise that she'd been shot. Jackie released Mandy, allowing her to fall to the ground, while she dived into the tall grass to avoid further gunfire. Jackie removed her semiautomatic with limited rounds remaining and stared into the nearby woods.

In the near distance, she saw the second sniper aiming his rifle at her. Jackie took the shot. The man's head snapped back as he fell to the ground. She looked back at the helicopter and frowned. Fuel was now pouring from a second hole. Jackie cursed, rolled beneath the helicopter, and looked out the opposite side. A man with an assault rifle, presumably the sniper, was now visible and heading toward the helicopter. Jackie aimed her weapon at him but waited for what she assumed would follow.

Zack suddenly appeared behind the man. He must have heard or sensed something and spun around just in time to be punched in the face. Zack blocked the rifle to keep it pointed away from him and kicked him twice in the side. He snatched the rifle from his arms and then spun into a high roundhouse kick, striking the man in the face. The sniper fell to the ground without even attempting to brace his fall. It was quite possible he was dead before he hit the ground. Jackie slid out from beneath the helicopter and looked around while keeping her gun aimed.

"We're clear," Zack informed her. "What's the helicopter situation?"

"Not good," Jackie replied while clutching her injured shoulder and led him to the other side.

They examined the new bullet hole leaking fuel that poured from the gas tank.

Jackie frowned and shook her head. "I could fix the leak," she informed Zack with disgust, "but we don't have any fuel to replace what we've lost."

The fuel leaking from the second bullet hole was slowing now.

"I'm guessing it's already empty too," Zack remarked then indicated the pilot's seat. "Try the radio." His look then turned serious. "Just remember; the channel won't be secure. Cicco's men could be listening."

"I know," Jackie replied while sighing with defeat. "We could bring them right to us, but we have to take that chance if we want to be rescued."

Zack considered the comment. "Change of plans. Go back for the others," he informed her. "Get them to the abandoned port. I'll give you a fifteen-minute head start before making the call."

"We should stick together," she insisted.

"I can move in stealth mode if I'm alone," he informed her. "A larger group is easier to spot. I'll catch up with you at the old port."

Jackie stared at him a moment then reluctantly nodded. She knew he was right. She removed the bottle of painkillers from her pocket and took one from the bottle. Zack stopped her from taking the pill and took the bottle from her. He read the label.

"Have you ever taken opiates before?" he asked while eying her.

"I've taken painkillers before," she informed him. "Mostly anti-inflammatory. Does it matter?"

He groaned softly and indicated the bottle. "This is a very strong prescription," Zack remarked. "You're probably flying high on them."

"I'm a little foggy," she replied, "but I wouldn't think I'm high." She managed a soft laugh. "Honestly, they don't do much for the pain either. Just leave me feeling cranky and miserable."

"I think you're off your game between the pain and the painkillers," he insisted. "Maybe you shouldn't take any more. Painkillers this strong aren't for everyone. If they're not helping, you may have a sensitivity to them."

"Would that make the pain worse?"

"It could," he informed her. "Your father couldn't take opiate painkillers. Made him cranky as hell."

Jackie tossed the pill over her shoulder. "They're not helping anyway," she remarked.

"You'd better get going," he instructed. "We need to get the survivors as far from here as possible. Others could show up."

She nodded and offered a tiny smile. "See you on the other side."

Zack snorted a soft laugh. Jackie took off across the field and ran for the woods. Zack watched her disappear into the woods then glanced at his watch and leaned against the helicopter. Within the tall grass near the helicopter, Mandy opened her eyes, looked beneath the helicopter, and saw Zack's legs where he relaxed. She slowly picked herself up while grabbing a discarded gun not far from her. Mandy slowly and silently maneuvered alongside the helicopter.

§

Jackie ran through the woods as fast as she could manage without tripping over rocks and exposed tree roots. Even though the run would be easy for her on most days, her shoulder was causing her enough pain to cause her to nearly fall. The pain was also draining her energy. She was starting to slow, but, thankfully, the freshwater pond wasn't far. Jackie entered the empty clearing and looked around with surprise. She panted mostly from the pain her shoulder caused as her mind reeled about the missing passengers. She heard a twig snap. Jackie spun around with her gun aimed. She was low on ammo, so she had to make each shot count. Sid stepped into the clearing and relaxed.

"It's okay," he called out to the others. "It's just Jackie. She's back."

The others came out of hiding from behind trees and the brush itself. Jackie was relieved everyone was okay.

"Where's Zack?" Bill asked with concern for the odd man they'd come to know.

"He's giving us a head start before radioing for help," she announced while attempting to catch her breath. "We need to go. The transmission won't be secure. The men responsible for all this could hear the distress call and come after us. We need to make it to that abandoned port and find someplace to hole up until help arrives." She indicated the small path. "We need to hurry."

Chapter Twenty-eight

Zack remained relaxed while leaning against the side of the helicopter although he kept an eye on the surrounding area for any additional bad guys. He glanced at his watch. He'd given Jackie plenty of time to get the others far from the area. He then straightened and approached the open pilot's side door. Unfortunately, it was only a little after six o'clock in the morning, which meant there would be few people listening to their ham radios at that hour. He had to hope the team was listening and that they were waiting for some sort of emergency call. Zack climbed onto the pilot's seat, snatched the hand mic, and fiddled with the dial.

"Reaper calling Eagle One, Whiskey Tango Foxtrot," Zack announced into the radio. "Do you copy? Over." There was no response. Zack frowned and considered changing the channel to the emergency Coast Guard channel. He hesitated and tried again. "Eagle One, Whiskey Tango Foxtrot this is the Reaper, do you copy? Over." He waited another moment then groaned with defeat. He reached for the dial to change the channel when static came over the radio.

"Reaper, this is Game Over, I copy," came an oddly familiar man's voice, although it certainly wasn't one of the guys.

Zack was bewildered by the handle, although he knew the voice sounded familiar. "Game Over? Who the hell--?"

"Is that you, Zack?" came the familiar voice from the static-filled radio. "Zack, it's Othello."

Zack suddenly grinned and laughed. "Othello, you bastard," he announced with some relief. "Am I glad you answered."

"Yeah, well, you know I don't have a life. What can I do for you, buddy?" Othello announced from the other end. "You sound a little stressed. Over."

A gun was suddenly pressed against Zack's temple. He didn't move nor respond to Othello.

Without even turning his head to look back, Zack spoke. "Well, hello, Mandy," Zack announced in a drone tone. "I didn't realize you were still alive."

"Very sloppy of you," Mandy scoffed in a tone that conveyed the amount of pain she must have been experiencing. "Release the hand receiver and don't make any sudden movements because I will shoot you, and I promise I won't miss."

Zack opened his hand and allowed the receiver to fall from it. Othello continued to speak from the radio.

"Reaper, are you there?" Othello announced over the static-filled radio. "Zack, do you copy?"

Despite her pain, Mandy managed a satisfied grin. "I'll bet you're wishing you'd taken me up on that offer now."

"Which one?" he asked with little reaction. "That clumsy attempt at seduction?" Zack chuckled in his throat and smirked. "Every time a woman has offered herself to me, it's always been followed with a gun to my head." He then considered the comment. "Well, sometimes a knife to my nuts, but you get the idea."

"Why am I not surprised?" she snarled.

"I have a confession," he announced while casting a sideways look at her and showed no emotion. "I don't like being forced to kill women. I guess I'm just old-fashioned that way."

"You don't have to worry," she replied with little concern. "You won't have the opportunity to kill me. Had I known you were such a skilled fighter, I would have killed you before that whole mess in the hangar."

"Tried," he announced boldly.

"What?"

"You would have *tried* to kill me," he casually informed her. "It wouldn't have ended well just as this won't end well for you. Of course, if you put the gun down, I won't have to kill you."

She laughed at his excessively confident statement. "Does that line ever work?"

"Sadly, no." He studied her with his sideways stare and raised a curious brow. "Do you intend to surrender or not? I'm a little pressed for time."

"As tempting as your offer to accept my surrender is, I think I'll take my chances killing you instead," she casually replied.

Zack reluctantly sighed his disappointment and shook his head. "As you wish."

Without warning, Zack snatched the gun from her hand with amazing reflexes, spun it around, and pulled the trigger before she even knew he'd taken the gun from her. Mandy gasped and looked at the blood spreading from the small bullet hole in her chest. She looked back at Zack with horror in her eyes.

"I'm sorry," Zack informed her, "but I did give you a choice."

Mandy sank to the helicopter floor in the back. Zack frowned then shook his head as he snatched the radio hand receiver.

"Othello, are you there?"

§

Gil, Kirk, Bogart, and Mac hurried down the institution stairs with Darth in the lead. Gil moved the dog aside at the closed fire door on level one and slowly pulled it open while Kirk aimed his weapon through the opening. When nothing moved within the lobby, they entered and scanned the dimly lit area. The front door opened, allowing the sunrise to spill into the lobby, brightening it for the first time. Monroe stepped into the doorway, saw his friends, and immediately motioned for them. As they hurried across the lobby, they saw an alligator meandering across the once elegant, tile floor. Darth growled at the creature, but Gil was quick to snatch his collar, keeping him from approaching the large reptile.

"Don't pick fights you can't win," Gil remarked to his four-legged partner.

"I'm so ready to leave here," Kirk muttered while keeping his weapon trained on the reptile still too far away to be of any real concern.

They reached Monroe at the front door and hurried onto the porch where they waited and assessed the situation before moving out. Despite the stormy night, the sun was coming up and would eventually give away to a beautiful day. Monroe indicated the vehicles still hidden within the tree line halfway down the driveway.

"We'll commandeer one of their vehicles and radio for extraction," Monroe informed them. "We move quickly and quietly. There's no telling how many men are still inside the facility."

"I'm guessing perhaps a ton of gator bait," Bogart announced while grinning.

They were about to leave the porch when they heard the sound of a helicopter in the near distance. They had to know the aerial assault would be coming eventually.

"Ah, hell," Kirk muttered while frowning. "That can't be good."

They dispersed and darted behind overgrown shrubs just off the main porch. As the helicopter came into view, Corbin and several armed men hurried onto the porch to greet their backup. The two men who had fallen from the second floor window limped toward the men on the porch.

"They must have gotten away," the first injured man announced while clutching his bleeding leg. "We followed them out the second floor window."

"Did you see which way they went?" Corbin demanded with little regards for his men's injuries.

Both men shook their heads. "The firehose gave way," he announced. "We were too busy falling."

"Search the grounds," Corbin shouted in anger. "They could still be close by. Guard the cars. I don't want them making their getaway in one of my vehicles."

The men nodded and were about to search the grounds while Corbin and another man hurried into the driveway and waved to the now hovering helicopter.

Corbin removed a hand radio and spoke into it. "They're still on the loose," he announced into the radio. "I need you to do a sweep of the area and find them."

Despite his order, the helicopter began its descent to Corbin's surprise. He frowned and watched the helicopter land then shut down. He approached the helicopter as the well-dressed passenger got out.

Corbin hesitated and stared at the man with some surprise. "Makar," he announced. "I didn't know you were coming out here."

Makar was a tall, sturdy man with a moderately muscular build and an intimidating appearance. His light brown hair was kept in a short, buzz cut, and his face was clean-shaven. Although his clothing suggested wealth, it was obvious he wasn't the type who needed armed guards surrounding him. He could almost certainly take care of himself.

"I've allowed you to screw things up enough for one day," Makar announced then looked around. His gaze fell upon his man. "Why haven't you found that girl?"

"It's not that easy," Corbin replied. "We thought she parachuted with our men from the plane, but they were decoys. We've been trying to catch the men helping her, but they've proven to be craftier than anticipated."

"So you've been putting all our time and effort into capturing known associates to those who actually have her?" Makar announced with annoyance then turned angry. "You should be concentrating on locating the downed plane. We'd lost radio contact with our aerial team since the hurricane passed through."

"We haven't been able to locate the plane either," Corbin replied with some concern. "It fell off radar, and no one has heard from it. Even the airline can't find it. That's why we've been concentrating our efforts on those who parachuted from the plane. They're their friends. They know something, I'm positive of that."

"You're wasting my time," Makar snarled then drew a deep breath and attempted to relax. "You'd better find that girl. Don't disappoint me again."

Nearly silent gunfire took out the armed man closest to Makar. Makar and Corbin spun around with their weapons in their hands. Corbin took a bullet to the leg and fell to the ground. Makar motioned to the pilot while jumping into the helicopter. The pilot attempted to restart the helicopter. A nearly silent shot struck the pilot in the head, causing him to slump over in the seat. Makar fired back in the direction of the building along with his remaining two men. Corbin fired back as well while all six hurried for cover behind the helicopter. Makar jumped out the opposite side and joined them. One of the men attempted to enter the back of the helicopter to reach the high-powered machine gun bolted to the floor.

"If he reaches that gun, we're dead," Monroe informed the team just loud enough for them to hear.

From their respective hiding positions, they all fired at the man attempting to reach the gun. He took several hits and fell from the back of the helicopter. The team's hiding position wouldn't offer them much cover now that their location was known. While flooding the remaining men with gunfire, the team slipped back inside the building, shutting and locking the solid door behind them.

"I counted six men still standing," Gil informed them.

"They're probably calling for reinforcements now," Monroe added. "We don't have long to take them out and get the hell out of here."

Kirk looked around and saw the alligator exploring the lobby. "We need to get to higher ground or become alligator bait."

"What we need is an alligator whisperer," Mac announced and raised a clever brow.

All eyes immediately turned to Bogart.

Bogart made a face and groaned. "Didn't I do my part already?" he whined.

"You need to lead them into alligator central," Monroe informed him. "While you're keeping them busy, the rest of us will slip out the second-floor window so Gil can prep the helicopter."

"Bad plan," Bogart insisted.

The front door vibrated. "That door won't hold much longer," Gil announced. "We need to figure something out and fast. What's the plan?"

Bogart again groaned and threw his hands down in defeat. "Fine," he scoffed. "I have a plan even if it does suck. Just don't leave without me."

Chapter Twenty-nine

Several gunshots echoed as the lobby door was torn to shreds around the lock. The door was kicked inward, revealing Makar, his four men, and Corbin. With their weapons aimed, they scanned the unusually quiet lobby.

"They're around here somewhere," Corbin announced. "The back of the building is flooded, so they must have gone to higher ground."

Several shots were fired at them. They immediately took cover then saw Bogart running through the water within the flooded hallway toward the back of the building.

"Don't let him get away," Makar cried out and indicated for the men to follow him.

"This is alligator heaven," Corbin attempted to explain to his boss. "That man is dead already. We don't need to follow him."

"If he's running into danger, he obviously has a way out," Makar insisted then glared at his man while gritting his teeth. "We need to stop him."

"We should be watching the vehicles," Corbin attempted to convince him. "If they're attempting to escape, that's where they'll go."

"Backup will be here in twenty minutes," Makar reminded him while relaying his irritation on having his authority questioned. "Have you lost your nerve, man? Certainly, we can hold them off for twenty minutes." He then looked at the others. "After that man!"

Makar followed his four armed men down the flooded hallway after Bogart. Corbin looked at his crudely wrapped leg, which bled through the gauze, then frowned.

"Bullheaded son-of-a-bitch," Corbin scoffed and reluctantly hurried after them with a pronounced limp.

§

On the second floor, Monroe, Kirk, Mac, and Gil maneuvered through the broken window and jumped the short distance to the partial roof. It was still a fantastic drop to the ground. Gil rigged television cable to Darth's bulletproof vest then lowered him to the ground and released the cable. Darth watched from the ground as the four cautiously walked along the partial overhang toward the far side of the building. The dog trotted after them while watching intently with the television cable dragging behind him. They finally encountered an overgrown tree and managed to climb down it.

Once they reached the bottom, Gil untethered Darth. The team kept low to the ground while making their run for the unguarded helicopter. Gil pulled the dead pilot from the seat while Kirk jumped behind the machine gun. Kirk aimed the large weapon at the door and waited for the first man to poke his head out so he could blow it off.

"Will she fly?" Mac asked while crouched behind Gil in the pilot's seat.

"We're not taking off yet," Gil informed her.

"What? Why not?" she demanded.

"We need to wait for Bogart," Monroe reminded her. "Besides, we have the machine gun. We have plenty of time to make our escape."

"So we're just going to sit here and wait for Bogart and hope he doesn't get eaten by an alligator?" Mac remarked with some surprise.

"Not exactly sit and wait," Gil informed her then placed the radio headset on and fiddled with several channels. "This is Whiskey Tango Foxtrot Eagle One, anyone copy? Over."

Monroe put on the extra headset as Gil fiddled with channels and continued with the message. He broadcasted for several minutes without a response. There was a distinctive crackle followed by a familiar voice.

"Eagle One," came the familiar male voice. "You son-of-a-bitch! Where have you been?"

Gil seemed surprised and eyed Monroe seated alongside him. Their matching expressions said it all.

"Othello?" Gil practically gasped into the radio. "What are you doing on this channel? Over."

"Apparently, I'm the official messenger boy these days," Othello replied over the headset. "I have word from the psycho twins."

"Jackie and Zack?" Gil asked while eyeing Monroe alongside him.

Mac and Kirk suddenly jerked and listened intently while staring at the men in front. Since the helicopter wasn't yet running, they could hear the radio broadcast clearly.

"Are they okay?" Monroe suddenly chimed in through his own headset.

"As of ten minutes ago, they were fine," Othello responded. "I have their coordinates, if you're in the air and prepping a rescue."

"We'll be airborne in fifteen minutes," Gil informed him. "What are their coordinates? Over."

"You'd better damned well give me *your* coordinates," came another familiar yet angry voice over the radio.

Darth appeared excited from where he sat alongside Mac and barked at the voice on the radio.

"You're not leaving without me," Holden demanded.

Gil and Monroe exchanged looks then frowned. "Great," both muttered.

Monroe managed a smile and spoke into his headset. "Hey, Holden," he announced almost cheerfully. "I thought you were away at some--"

"Shut the fuck up, Monroe," Holden snapped from the other end. "Tell me where you are--now!"

"I know you're upset, Holden," Monroe responded, "but we can't hold off a rescue waiting for you. Jackie may not have that kind of time."

"I'm in Florida, you son-of-a-bitch," Holden announced from the other end.

"Florida?" Monroe gasped with surprise. "How did you know we were--?"

"I traced your cell phone coordinates," Holden lashed out over the radio. "You're not the only one with expensive toys. I lost your signal last night."

"Yeah, a concrete basement will do that," Monroe muttered. "Since the bad guys are already on their way, I guess it doesn't matter that this line isn't secure. We're at an old mental institution in the middle of gator country. It's been abandoned--"

"I know exactly where you are," Holden announced impatiently. "I can be there in ten minutes."

"Oh, you're that close--"

"Over and out," Holden snapped.

Monroe and Gil exchanged looks and groaned.

"The cavalry is on its way," Monroe announced with a reluctant sigh then made a face. "Although, the cavalry may try to kill us."

"I would've warned you, man," Othello then announced over the radio. "I wanted to warn you. I got ahold of Holden a few minutes ago. I could be mistaken, but I think he's a little pissed."

"You're very perceptive, Othello," Monroe remarked while groaning. "Thanks for the assistance. Give Gil those coordinates."

Monroe removed his headset then eyed Mac and Kirk in the back of the helicopter by the machine gun. "Be ready for anything, including an irate federal agent."

§

Makar's men cautiously entered the flooded maintenance workshop where the water was two feet deep near the doorway and nearly four feet deep toward the far end by the bay doors. Makar's men kept close to the walls with their guns aimed, awaiting an attack. To their surprise, one didn't come. They finally spotted Bogart standing on a workbench across the room at the deeper end. He dropped his assault rifle into the water, grinned while waving at them, and then jumped into the four-foot deep water, disappearing beneath the surface. There appeared to be movement everywhere within the water. The four men fired into the water then saw Bogart swim for the partially open garage door. They trudged through the shallow water toward the deeper water and the garage door to get a better angle with their weapons.

The water seemed to churn all around the four men and finally caught their attention. Makar and Corbin appeared in the workshop doorway. Corbin immediately took a step back while staring with horror.

"Where did he go?" Corbin asked with concern.

"He's swimming for the open garage door," one of the men yelled back then resumed firing.

Corban watched the churning water and appeared alarmed. "It's a trap," he cried out. "Retreat!"

The men gave him a strange look and again noted the churning water near them. Corbin backed away from the workshop.

"It's not a trap," Makar snapped back while glaring at his right-hand man. "He was a decoy, you idiot. He's out here alone."

"He's not alone," Corbin insisted then hurried away from the workshop. "His backup has a lot of teeth."

Makar gave his man a strange look as he fled then looked back at the men who had stopped firing their weapons. All four were now looking at the churning water around them. One man cried out as he was pulled under the water. The other men then saw several pairs of alligator eyes as they approached. The churning water was their tails, which meant the dangerous end was already upon them. The alligators converged on the remaining three men and pulled them into the water. Two of the men were attacked by several alligators fighting for their meal. The men screamed as they were pulled under water, their weapons firing haphazardly into the air. Makar fired several shots into the water, but it was too late to save any of his men. He then saw the churning water moving toward him and appeared horrified.

"Corbin!"

Makar fired several shots and ran through the shallow water from the workshop after his man.

§

The helicopter was prepped and prepared for takeoff with Gil in the pilot's seat. Monroe kept his AK-47 assault rifle aimed at the abandoned cars near the tree line at the end of the overgrown driveway. Kirk had the machine gun aimed at the institution doorway and patiently waited. Mac alternated looking both directions from her position on the helicopter floor alongside Darth. Each time she looked toward the driveway, Darth licked her face. She frowned and pushed him away each time.

"We don't have long before Corbin's reinforcements show up," she informed them. "Screw Holden. He can meet us at the airfield."

"We need to wait for Bogart," Monroe remarked becoming irritated with her. "We have the big gun. We can hold them off."

"Someone should go after Bogart," Kirk announced while remaining steady on the gun. "He shouldn't have gone back in there alone. There were too many gators for his plan to work. We need to find him."

"We're not going back in there," Monroe insisted. "That's not the plan. Bogart had a plan. Not a great one, but give him time to execute it."

"He's going to be eaten alive," Kirk snarled while glaring at Monroe in the front seat. "He's a conman; not a soldier. He doesn't have the balls to back up his mouth."

"He'll be fine," Gil remarked while also watching with anticipation. "He's probably conning an alligator into giving up its hide for a pair of boots."

They saw an SUV appear on the overgrown driveway and speed toward them past the parked vehicles. Monroe found a pair of binoculars on the helicopter floor and looked through them at the approaching vehicle.

"Great," he muttered.

Mac turned toward the opposite side and raised her assault rifle. "Is it Corbin's men?"

"No," Monroe replied with a groan. "It's one very pissed federal agent with our favorite questionable mob boss riding shotgun." He shook his head. "I really need to re-evaluate my life choices."

"Now's not the time to find God or come out of the closet," Mac snarled at him. "We need to find Bogart and get the hell out of here before the rest of the Russian assassins show up."

All eyes were suddenly on Mac.

"Who said anything about Russian assassins?" Gil suddenly demanded.

"It's a long story," Mac informed them.

They returned their attention back to the institution. Bogart suddenly appeared in the helicopter's side doorway, startling the others. He was soaking wet and out of breath as he climbed into the helicopter.

"We need to go," Bogart cried out and collapsed onto the helicopter floor. "They're after me!"

"I thought the plan was to lose Corbin's men," Kirk snapped with annoyance.

"Not them," Bogart launched hotly then pointed toward the corner of the building. "Them!"

Six or more alligators made their way around the building and headed in their direction. Kirk aimed the machine gun at them, but Bogart stopped him before he could shoot.

"You don't need to kill them," Bogart insisted. "They're just being gators. Can we go now?"

Corbin and Makar appeared in the institution doorway and fired at the helicopter. Kirk pivoted the large machine gun bolted to the helicopter floor and fired back at them. Several shots nearly tore the door from the building. Corbin and Makar darted back inside. Kirk continued to fire a few more rounds as the SUV stopped several yards away. Holden and Sal grabbed their bags from the vehicle, kept low, and ran for the awaiting helicopter. They had barely made it inside and shut the door on their side when Gil lifted off. Two alligators snapped at the helicopter just before it left the ground.

"You took long enough," Mac snapped at them as they flew away from the institution.

"We had to divert a delivery truck heading your way," Holden informed her while Darth jumped excitedly on him, happy to see his friend. "We thought it was the reinforcements arriving. Turns out it was just a delivery truck."

"A delivery truck?" Kirk suddenly asked with surprise. "What was a delivery truck doing out here this time of morning?"

"They said they were delivering monthly supplies to a Dr. Freud at the institute," Holden replied and shook his head in disbelief. "I instructed them to call the police and avoid the place."

"Huh?" Monroe remarked with a surprised look on his face. "He really is a doctor."

"I called ahead and found us a plane at a small airfield not far from here," Holden informed Gil. "It'll be fueled and waiting for us when we get there."

Kirk patted the machine gun. "Someone needs to come up with a plan to take this baby with us," he announced. "We don't have one of these."

Holden glared at Kirk. "There's no way in hell I'm letting you walk away with a machine gun."

Kirk saw the serious look on Holden's face and chuckled, mocking him. "I was just kidding, Holden," he announced then made a face and looked away while muttering. "I forgot you were sitting there."

Chapter Thirty

Jackie and the eleven survivors paused within the woods just before the massive, sunny beach. It was nearly eight o'clock in the morning, and the brilliant sunlight was already heating up the sand. She scanned the beach but didn't see the abandoned port. She knew she was in the right area, but where was the port? It would be impossible to miss something so big. She looked back at her concerned travel companions, who also seemed to note the empty beach.

"Stay here," she instructed. "I'm going to have a look around."

"I should go with you," Sid interjected. "There's no reason for you to go it alone."

Jackie would normally protest, but she wasn't in the mood. She removed the semiautomatic from the back of her pants and handed it to Sid. He uncertainly accepted the gun, hesitated only a moment, and then put on a brave front. Her look was stern as she stared at him.

"You have three rounds," she informed him. "Use them wisely."

Sid's confidence seemed to drop at the knowledge that he had limited ammo since he didn't hit much back in the hangar. He nodded despite his lack of confidence. Jackie removed the M416 assault rifle from over her shoulder and held it as if she meant business. Her comfort with the weapon was slightly alarming to the other passengers. Sid followed her onto the beach and eyed her while managing a timid smile.

"Uh, so how many rounds do you have?" he asked in an attempt to ease his mind.

"Five," she replied.

Sid's expression dropped. "Oh."

Jackie looked along the beach to her right while Sid stared off to the left. Jackie's expression immediately dropped.

"Ah, hell," she scoffed under her breath.

The building that had once been the greeting house for cruise ships was reduced to ruins. It appeared as if a fire had burned most of it and what was left was reduced to rubble from a storm years ago. The massive dock must have burned as well, leaving supports protruding out of the water. Jackie felt defeated, and her sore shoulder seemed to throb in response. They had made the trek for nothing. Without shelter, they wouldn't last long against heavily armed men. Sid remained staring to the left with his mouth partially open and disbelief on his face.

Jackie groaned and lowered her assault rifle with disgust. "Well, that's just wonderful," she huffed while staring at the ruined welcome center. "Just fucking fantastic."

"Uh, Jackie," Sid announced without removing his eyes from where he continued to stare. "You may want to have a look at that."

She turned and looked in the direction he stared. To her surprise and possible astonishment, a massive ten-deck cruise ship was embedded in the sand by at least one deck. Given it was nearly half a mile down the beach, it had to be bigger than it looked. There was no telling how long the ship had been grounded, but it couldn't have been more than a couple of years. It appeared to be in amazing shape for an abandoned vessel. The cruise ship couldn't be more than twenty years old, which was young for a ship of that size to be rendered useless. Nearly six hundred feet in length, it had to weigh almost thirty thousand tons. Judging by its impressive size, it probably contained seven passenger levels and nearly two hundred cabins. On her last voyage, she was probably carrying over four hundred passengers and three hundred crewmembers.

"Now there's something you don't see every day," Jackie muttered then glanced at Sid and indicated the ship. "Let's check her out."

As they made the trek along the beach, both couldn't take their eyes off the massive ship embedded deep in the sand. The closer they got, the more impressive the ship became. They felt dwarfed by the massive cruise ship. Ironically, there were much larger ships sailing the ocean.

"What do you suppose happened to the ship?" Sid asked Jackie.

"A ship that size would be missed," Jackie informed him. "I'm positive the passengers and crew were abandoned long before she was grounded. I don't see any lifeboats. I guess years adrift brought it to shore."

As they got closer, what appeared to be a large rock turned out to be a huge puncture in the portside bow. The closer they got; the larger the hole became. Jackie and Sid paused before the massive hole that was twenty feet high by nearly thirty feet wide.

"Wow," Sid gasped while staring at the opening. "How did the ship stay afloat long enough to drift to shore?"

Jackie couldn't take her eyes off the opening and the darkness beyond it. "I'm guessing the ship struck something just off the coast and the captain ran her aground before she could sink to the bottom of the ocean."

"You realize there had to be at least four hundred passengers onboard," Sid informed her. "Not to mention the crew needed to man such a ship. You're sure they were rescued, right?"

Jackie cast a look at him. "I'm positive they were rescued," she remarked then sighed with relief. "Which means there must be a working radio on the bridge." She drew a deep breath and looked around the beach before returning her attention to Sid. "Go back and get the others. Find them shelter in the hull while I explore the ship."

"Not alone," Sid insisted with concern. "You don't know what sort of creatures made their home inside that thing. It could be dangerous."

"Which is exactly why you're staying with the others in the hull," she informed him. "I've got this. Go get them."

Sid seemed uncomfortable with the idea of her venturing inside the abandoned ship on her own but did as he was told. Jackie entered the opening while removing her flashlight, keeping it tight against her rifle. She aimed the light and rifle around the dark hull. Despite a lot of moss and the occasional snake, the hull appeared safe. She didn't have to roam far before finding metal steps leading up a level. Despite the moderately slippery moss coating the metal steps, there was little rust, leaving the steps intact and secure. Jackie cautiously headed up the steps to a closed, watertight door resembling that found on a sub.

The round hand wheel must have been partially rusted internally, making it nearly impossible for her to turn it. Her shoulder was killing her with minimal effort. She slipped the rifle between the spokes, prayed she wouldn't regret the idea, and put all her effort into turning the wheel. It creaked loudly and turned. She removed her rifle and easily turned it the rest of the way. Jackie opened the loudly creaking door, allowing light to shine through the opening into the hull. She entered deck four and looked around the corridor. She'd finally reached the beginning of the passenger's decks. Apart from large cobwebs covering everything, the corridor seemed almost untouched.

The ship must have been sealed tight since the accident and remained that way for however many years the ship had been abandoned. She walked along the broad corridor, which was decorated in mostly gold colors. There were paintings on the walls and couches set up sporadically throughout the hallway. Although dusty, the gold-colored carpet looked almost brand new. Until the day she was abandoned, the ship had been kept clean and tidy. Jackie tried several cabin doors, but they all remained in their locked status without power for the electronic keycard locks.

In order to gain access to the rooms, a master key would be necessary for the emergency lock override. She'd find one in the lobby or the purser's office, but that wasn't a high priority for now. She continued along the corridor before reaching the exterior door leading onto deck. She opened the door with some effort and stepped onto the deck. The broad deck contained some moss from being exposed to the elements but not enough to make it unsafe. The floor, a faux hardwood, and the heavy, metal railing seemed secure, although the once white railing was starting to rust. The metal deck stairs contained some moss, which would be slippery, so she needed to proceed carefully up them. On her return trip, she'd find the inside stairs, which would be safer.

Jackie skipped deck five and continued on to deck six. She entered the ship and roamed the sixth deck corridor while glancing at signs posted on the walls along the way. The lobby was supposedly ahead of her, which meant she was heading in the right direction. Jackie finally reached the lobby and paused to look around from her elevated position above it. Apparently, the lobby was located on deck five, but she could access it from deck six by the massive, interior staircase. The lobby was one floor below but extended another two decks above her allowing for some rooms to open to the four-story lobby. The lobby was about as glamorous as any expensive hotel and even more so with its impressive size.

Decorated mostly in white and gold, the long since abandoned lobby still had a classy appeal. There were multiple curved staircases with gold railing cascading in every direction and on multiple levels. A glass elevator allowed a bird's eye view for those who didn't want to climb all the stairs. Massive chandeliers lining the ceiling were covered in cobwebs, although the elements were kept at bay by the tightly sealed doors. There was little risk any island creatures had made their way into the ship's interior beyond the hull. A large skylight allowed for natural light to flood the entire lobby, keeping it brightly lit. She'd bring the others into the lobby for shelter until help could arrive.

Jackie had two objectives in mind as she hurried down the open staircase to the lobby below. She'd secure as many master keys as she could find as a security measure in the event of an emergency, and she needed to find a working radio. There would almost certainly be one on the bridge, but it was possible she'd find one in the purser's office near the front desk. She hurried across the abandoned yet still ritzy lobby, which contained multiple sitting areas with dusty, expensive furniture, and approached the massive front desk that encompassed nearly the entire back wall. Not interested in wasting time looking for the entrance to the area behind the desk, Jackie scaled the desk and leaped to the other side. Despite using her good arm, she immediately regretted the action, since her left arm instinctively extended for balance. She paused just behind the desk, held her left shoulder, and endured the pain shooting through her shoulder.

Once the pain subsided, she reclaimed her assault rifle and glanced at the doors behind the desk. She finally found the purser's office and entered. There was nothing glamorous or ritzy about the purser's office. It looked like any ordinary office with typical furniture. Apparently, the purser got the short end of the office stick on the fancy cruise ship. A quick search revealed there wasn't a radio, but she hadn't really expected to find one. She collapsed into the purser's leather desk chair and took a moment to enjoy the feeling of being off her feet and giving her lower back a break in a comfortable chair. She'd punished her body the last two days, and it was starting to catch up with her.

All she wanted was a hot bath, preferably with her husband. She finally sat forward and searched the desk drawers. Within the third drawer, she found a ring containing over a dozen master keys and a map of the ship, which would also come in handy. She sighed with relief at her wondrous find and immediately sprang from the chair. Her body protested, causing everything to hurt at once. She shoved the ring of keys into her jacket pocket, reclaimed her assault rifle, and headed for the door. She had one more assignment, and it was the most important one. Find a working radio.

Chapter Thirty-one

Jackie briefly glanced at the map in her hand then trotted up the interior steps. She only made it one deck when she had to stop and lean on the railing. She cringed and gently massaged her shoulder. She found it surprising how much pain she was experiencing. It wasn't as if she'd never been shot before. Perhaps she'd been pushing herself too hard. Most times in the past, Holden would force her to take it easy and not overdo it. She should have listened to Zack when he tried to tell her the same thing. She didn't know why she listened to Holden and had to be so stubborn with Zack. That was a lie. She knew the answer. She enjoyed it when Holden spoiled her. He had an amazing bedside manner.

With Zack, she always felt she needed to prove something. She too often refused to show weakness in front of him as if they were in competition to see who the bigger badass was. Obviously, that was Zack, but he set the bar pretty high. She'd already been on the ship close to an hour, but it took time getting around the massive vessel. She finally reached the bridge, which looked more like the flight deck of some spaceship than the control room for a cruise ship. She marveled at the rows of monitors, controls, and plush, tall-backed, leather seats. Windows surrounded the entire front and both sides of the bridge, allowing a panoramic view of the outside world. The bridge contained some moss since the outer door had been partially open allowing the elements inside for years. Some of the controls contained rust as a result.

Jackie looked out the many windows at the panoramic view of the island before her and took a moment to marvel at the view from deck ten. Being nine stories up, since one story was embedded in the sand, she could see over the trees with a bird's eye view. The island seemed peaceful and majestic and not the hellish nightmare she'd lived since she arrived. She'd enjoy the view later. Jackie looked around the massive control room. Operating a cruise ship was definitely not a one-man job. The plush chairs were bolted to the floor before several sections of monitors. Jackie finally found the one she was certain she had been looking for and leaped into the chair.

The leather chair was a little moist for her liking, but she tolerated the dampness on her backside long enough to scan the electronic radio equipment. As she stared at the equipment before her, she realized it was all tied into the electronics of the ship, which meant it wouldn't work without power. She needed a ham radio, and what she found wasn't going to help her. Jackie leaped from the chair with disgust. Pain shot through her shoulder and radiated throughout her body. She only had a moment to endure the pain before she heard movement. Jackie snatched the M416 assault rifle and darted behind the monitor. She scanned the room but didn't see anyone or anything.

Jackie slowly straightened and cautiously crossed the bridge while heading for the outer door. She pushed open the door and scanned the deck just outside. Nothing moved, and there was no one around. There was no telling what she may have heard. Perhaps it was some animal making a home within the walls of the bridge. Jackie drew a deep breath and turned, wanting to take the inside stairs rather than the outer ones. As she turned, she nearly collided with Zack. Jackie let out a startled scream then immediately relaxed. She hadn't been expecting him.

"You're certainly jumpy," Zack casually remarked.

Jackie stared at him with surprise. "I had a fifteen minute head start on you," she announced then shook her head. "I don't know how you got around the ship so fast."

"Actually I was nearly thirty minutes behind you," Zack corrected then grinned. "I must've made better time through the jungle."

"Well, you weren't saddled down with eleven exhausted passengers," she remarked in her defense.

She didn't know why she was making excuses. Zack was nearly twice her age yet seemed to move twice as fast. She honestly couldn't compete, and she knew it.

"When I couldn't get the radio to work in the communication office, I assumed you'd come here next in hopes of finding a working radio," he informed her.

Jackie's mind reeled a moment. Had she actually been thinking, she realized she should have gone to the communication's office first. There would probably be a radio that didn't require electric. At least Zack assumed she had gone there first, so she didn't bother correcting him.

"Yeah," she remarked under her breath. "It's a shame that one didn't work. Think you can do something with it?"

"No," Zack informed her with a bored sigh. "It doesn't matter anyway. I was able to get a message out with the helicopter radio."

"Did you get the Coast Guard?"

"Better," Zack announced and grinned slyly. "I got Othello."

"Othello?" she gasped with surprise. "That's a lucky break."

"He said he'd call the guys and try their radio as well," he replied. "I told him to alert the Coast Guard after he got a message through to the guys. I didn't know how secure the Coast Guard channel would be. It could lead Cicco's men right to us."

"We need to lock this place down," Jackie announced. "If Cicco's men find the prisoners we left in that hangar, they'll tell them where we were heading."

Zack shook his head in annoyance. "That's why you don't leave live prisoners," he informed her. "You just don't want to listen to reasoning."

"I have more of a conscience than you," Jackie corrected. "I can't kill an unarmed man."

"In some situations, it's the only way to survive," Zack informed her but didn't press the issue. "We'd better get the others and prepare for visitors." He headed for the interior door then glanced back at Jackie as she followed. A strange smile crossed his face. "You didn't know the bridge radio worked off electric when you came up here, did you?"

Jackie frowned and hid her embarrassment. "No, it hadn't occurred to me."

He chuckled and offered a mocking smile. "Your father made some pretty funny blunders when he was your age too," Zack informed her. "We've all had our moments. When I was first learning Russian, I had a lot of translation blunders. I'd accidentally sent a lot of men into the ladies restrooms."

She eyed him while frowning. "Yeah, sure," she scoffed. "My father told me about your *blunders*. He assured me you did them on purpose."

"Well, it was still funny," Zack remarked.

§

The rented Grand Caravan EX was a ten-passenger single-engine prop plane with non-retractable wheels. Its total body length was forty-one feet, and it had a wingspan of fifty-two feet. The private plane flew over the calm, blue ocean a little after nine o'clock that morning. The morning sky contained amazing colors giving away to clear blue skies. Gil piloted the plane with Holden in the co-pilot's seat. By the way Monroe glared at the back of Holden's head; it was obvious he wasn't pleased that he wasn't co-piloting. With Ross away and Beck avoiding assignments like the plague before his wedding, that left Monroe in charge. Even though his mission had been somewhat disastrous, it was still *his* mission. Gil, Kirk, and Zack never seemed to care that they weren't in charge of missions. The trio wasn't interested in the responsibilities that came with leadership.

Gil preferred receiving orders and carrying them out with his usual skill and style. Kirk didn't care what assignment he was given as long as he was able to flex his massive muscles and bang some heads together. Zack didn't exactly follow orders and had even less interest in giving them. He preferred to work behind the scenes surrounded by a shroud of mystery. Unfortunately, Jackie was usually found working in the shadows with Zack, making for a frightening and lethal duo. The team often joked that only Jackie, Zack, and the cockroaches would survive a nuclear holocaust. Holden was never amused by the reference.

The plane approached the small, long since abandoned island. As they got closer to the coast, everyone looked out the window with horror at the sight. There was a long, deep groove in the sand revealing severed palm trees and torn metal scattered everywhere. The landing gear of the small, commercial airliner appeared as if it had been neatly placed where it sat by itself. Further along the beach was the plane wreckage resting on its belly. Although most of the plane looked intact, its left wing was torn off, which was what they saw scattered along the beach. The scene was frightening yet peaceful.

"Can you land?" Holden practically demanded while unable to tear his eyes from the crashed plane. "We need to land."

"There's no safe place to land," Gil explained as they flew overhead. "I'm going to take her down for a buzz cut. Everyone keep your eyes on the ground and search for signs of survivors."

Gil flew past the horrific scene, made a sharp turn, and flew back around passing overhead a little closer with decreased speed. Everyone within the plane attempted to assess the damage and scan for signs of life. Darth joined in by placing his paws on the window and looked out as well. Sal and Mac shivered in unison at the downed plane showing no movement of life.

"I see a beverage cart on the sand next to some luggage," Kirk announced.

Mac and Sal looked at Kirk with surprise. They had been looking for actual people while the team was looking for general signs.

"A lot of luggage," Monroe added. "Neatly placed and nothing discarded."

"Meaning what exactly?" Sal asked while staring at Monroe's profile.

"More than likely the passengers removed the luggage looking for useful items," Monroe informed him. "It wasn't someone looting the plane."

The plane circled and made another pass. Everyone again looked out the windows.

"The back emergency door is open," Mac announced almost pleased with herself for noting something useful.

When she turned, Darth leaned across the seat and licked her face. She frowned and pushed the dog away. At least someone on the team appreciated her.

"No people," Holden remarked almost sedate. "They should have heard the plane. If they're alive, why haven't we seen anyone?" He again looked at Gil while turning stern. "We have to land."

"We will," Gil informed him as he flew across the island. "I just need an area big enough and flat enough to safely take her down."

"There's plenty of beach," Holden snapped. "Just pick a spot."

"If I take her down in the sand, we'll lose our landing gear just like the bigger plane," Gil informed him. "We need solid footing."

"We need to radio for help," Sal remarked while leaning forward in his seat, "but that's also going to give away our location to unwanted parties."

"I know," Gil replied with a defeated sigh. "Once we land, I'll send out a distress call. That should buy us enough time to make it to the crash site before anyone else is even off the ground. We'll have to move fast." He scanned the area. "We just need somewhere safe to land."

Mac stared out the side window by her seat and appeared surprised by what she saw. "Is that a landing field?"

Gil turned the craft to the right. To their surprise, they saw a small landing field in the near distance. The landing field was partially overgrown with plant life, but the macadam beneath appeared to be intact and mostly visible, allowing Gil to find the landing strip easily. It would be a bit of a hike to the crash site, but the overgrown landing strip was ideal.

"That's right," Gil suddenly announced and added a slight chuckle. "We're on Hathaway Island."

"Is that supposed to mean something?" Holden asked not understanding.

"It was a private island for Voyagers Cruise Line," Gil informed them. "The rich and pampered would spend the day here on their very own private beach. It shut down a few years ago." He gave the comment some consideration. "I forgot they had a landing field." He then looked around. "I thought there was a small resort or welcome center though. Maybe it's on the other side of the island."

"If there's a welcome center," Monroe announced with enthusiasm, "they could have gone there. We should check the crash site first and then head for the welcome center."

Chapter Thirty-two

Once the plane landed, Kirk and Monroe stormed down the steps with their weapons and took secured positions alongside the plane steps. They scanned the area but didn't see any movement. Monroe signaled to Kirk, indicating the hangar in the near distance. Kirk nodded and was about to move when Mac casually walked down the steps and eyed each man.

"Seriously guys," she announced boldly then groaned. "We're in the middle of fucking nowhere. Give the commando thing a rest."

Both men watched her head for the hangar without a care or even a weapon in her hand. Monroe frowned then gave Kirk a nod. Both kept low to the ground and headed for the hangar in opposite directions. If Mac wanted to play decoy, she was more than welcome. Gil, Bogart, and Holden hurried down the plane steps, armed equally heavily and scanned the area as well. Darth ran down the steps and took off after Mac. He playfully jumped at her side while licking her hand. She frowned and pulled her hand away.

Gil watched Darth with surprise then frowned. "The dog's a traitor," he muttered.

Sal appeared in the plane's doorway and looked around while clinging to his own assault rifle. "What do you want me to do?"

Gil tossed him a hand radio. "Guard the plane," he instructed. "Seal her up and keep an eye out for anything suspicious. No one gets on the plane until we return. We'll radio when we're ready to move out."

Sal nodded and pulled up the steps, sealing the entrance. Gil, Bogart, and Holden took flanking positions and hurried for the hangar behind Monroe and Kirk. Mac was already at the opening as the guys took positions on either side of the hangar. Holden took his position alongside Monroe and watched Mac fearlessly approach the opening.

"She's not going to last very long with this team," Holden remarked.

"She's not part of this team," Monroe huffed while keeping his eyes on Mac. "If she wants to dangle like bait, that's her problem."

There was an awkward silence as Holden stared at Monroe's profile. "Whatever you're thinking, Monroe," Holden suddenly announced, "just get it from your head."

Monroe shot a glare at Holden. "What are you talking about?"

"The itch in your pants for that one," he replied sternly while indicating Mac with a nod. "Scratch it somewhere else. That one will get you killed providing she's not the one actually doing the killing."

"I'm not interested in Mac," Monroe snarled then returned his attention to the woman and dog by the entrance.

Darth suddenly snarled as Mac stepped into the opening. She eyed the dog with some surprise then understood he was warning her of danger. A man suddenly leaped out of the doorway for Mac with a two foot, industrial-sized wrench. Mac blocked his arm, punched him in the face, and then spun into a roundhouse kick, knocking him to the ground. Darth leaped on top of the man's chest and snarled viciously with his teeth just inches from his face. The man stared at the dog with surprise and didn't move.

"Call him off," the man gasped almost unable to speak while staring at the dog's bared teeth.

Mac casually looked around the hangar and showed no emotion. "Yeah, about that," she announced without care. "He's not my dog, so you're sort of at his mercy."

Kirk and Monroe appeared in the entrance with their assault rifles aimed. Kirk immediately covered the man beneath the dog. Darth seemed to know he'd been relieved from holding the prisoner and jumped off the man. The man stared up the barrel of Kirk's weapon then noted the big man holding it with his finger on the trigger.

"Please don't shoot me," the man announced.

"Who the hell are you?" Kirk demanded. "What's going on here?"

"I'm Tucker Simpson," he announced nervously. "I don't know what's going on here. I had nothing to do with any of this."

Tucker Simpson was possibly in his late twenties with a few days' worth of stubble on his face. Although he acted and dressed like the average, twenty-something male traveler, he *had* attempted to brain Mac with an oversized wrench.

"Any of what?" Monroe demanded while cautiously maneuvering through the hangar, noting the makeshift beds and the recently lived in look.

Mac searched the opposite end, again looking as if she were taking a walk through the park. Holden, Bogart, and Gil entered last. Gil took a lookout position by the entrance while Holden searched the hangar for signs of his wife.

"Whatever happened to those onboard the plane," Tucker explained in a trembling voice.

Holden suddenly spun toward the man on the ground. "After *what* happened to the people on the plane?" he suddenly demanded.

Tucker nervously eyed Holden from several feet away. "The plane was attacked, and nearly everyone onboard was killed," he replied.

The entire team suddenly stopped and cast looks at the man on the ground with his hands in the air. Holden lunged at him. Kirk immediately backed off allowing Holden to snatch the man by his shirt and practically pull him to his feet.

"What happened?" Holden suddenly demanded. "Were there any survivors?"

Tucker stared at Holden with the same concern he had when Kirk had aimed his weapon at him. "It was during the hurricane," he responded. "We were seeking shelter in the fuselage when these canisters were thrown into the plane. A few of us ran for the rear exit to avoid the gas. That's when these men came charging in and started shooting everyone. A bunch of us ran into the woods." He stared at Holden with concern. "I don't know what happened to the others, but I didn't stop running until I realized I was lost and alone." Tucker held his breath a moment. "I considered going back, but I started hearing gunshots within the woods. I didn't know where they were coming from, so I just stayed away." He shook his head. "Honestly, I have no idea what's going on. I'm just trying to stay alive."

"You said others escaped," Holden growled in anger. "Who were the other survivors?"

"I don't know," he insisted and vigorously shook his head. "It happened so fast."

Holden removed his semiautomatic from his shoulder holster and aimed it at the man's forehead, surprising the others. "My wife is out there," he snarled. "You better remember something."

"Your wife?" Tucker asked with surprise and seemed to consider the comment. "She wouldn't happen to be that crazy lady piloting the plane, would she?"

Holden's expression nearly dropped. "Yes, that's my wife," he announced. "Did you see her?"

"Not since we first crashed," he replied. "She went with some of the other passengers to an old town to see about finding help. I don't know what happened to them. They weren't on the plane when we were attacked."

"She went with other passengers?" Bogart suddenly asked and appeared curious. "Was one of them a short guy with short light hair?"

"I really don't know," Tucker replied.

"Slightly unbalanced," Kirk casually added and shrugged. "Mildly menacing."

"Glued to the crazy lady's side," Mac remarked while raising a brow.

Tucker's eyes suddenly lit up. "Yeah, he was with her," he announced. "They argued a lot."

Holden lowered his gun and released the man. "Yeah, that's them."

Darth sniffed around the deflated raft containing some clothes and a few blankets from the airline. Gil looked back from his lookout position.

"Darth found something," Gil informed them.

Kirk kept his weapon aimed at the stranger while the others approached Darth by the deflated raft. Monroe picked up one of the blankets.

"These are blankets from the airline," Monroe announced. "The remaining passengers came through here."

"Darth must be picking up either Jackie or Zack's scent," Gil announced from the doorway. "He wouldn't react that way otherwise."

"Think he can track her?" Holden anxiously asked.

Mac and Bogart continued to search the hangar for any clues to their friends' welfare.

Gil remained by the open doorway and nodded. "I think so," he replied. "We need something with either of their scents on it."

Darth trotted across the hangar and paused by a discarded blanket. He sniffed the blanket and became excited. He woofed playfully.

Bogart hurried toward the dog and picked up the blanket. "I think we found something."

He tossed the blanket to Gil by the doorway. Gil caught the blanket and extended it to Darth. He said something to the dog in German. Darth became excited, ran to him, and sniffed the blanket. He again woofed and wagged his tail. They watched as the dog spun excitedly in circles and attempted to rub the blanket. Gil looked back at Holden.

"I'd say we have a winner," Gil announced.

"Guys," Mac suddenly called out from across the room. "This isn't good."

Everyone except Gil joined Mac by the open cage. She indicated a large amount of blood on the floor then eyed the others.

"Someone's been injured," she informed them.

Kirk straightened near the center of the room and sniffed the bullet casing between his fingers. "There's been some recent gunplay too," he announced and cast a look at the others. "These casings are only hours old."

"The blood too," Mac added.

"We need to find them," Holden announced with concern. "We need to go now."

Gil placed the hand radio near his mouth and spoke into it. "Sal, you copy?"

"Still here," came Sal's response over the radio.

"We're on our way," Gil announced. "Meet us outside the plane. Seal her back up."

"Copy that," Sal replied.

Gil said something to Darth in German. The dog took off out the hangar door. Monroe motioned Tucker out the door with his assault rifle.

"We're going on a little hike," Monroe informed him. "Let's go."

The team hurried after the dog with their potential prisoner in tow. They collected Sal, who waited by the plane, as well as their gear containing extra guns and ammo then entered the woods together. Darth was sniffing the ground just ahead of them. The team approached the area cautiously with their assault rifles aimed. To their surprise, they saw two men sprawled on the ground lying in bloody heaps. They'd been shot numerous times with large caliber weapons, essentially tearing their bodies to shreds. Monroe visually inspected the bodies but didn't recognize either man. Tucker appeared alarmed and took a step back.

"These injuries are fresh," Monroe announced to his teammates. "This happened earlier today." He then indicated the man dressed in gray camouflage and combat boots with his thigh wrapped, revealing an earlier injury. It was Jail Bait, the man Jackie had shot in the leg. "This man was wounded before they were gunned down. Someone shot him in the leg with a 9mm pistol." He eyed Tucker, who stared at the two men with wide, horror-filled eyes. "Do you know these men?"

"I'm pretty sure the one was a passenger on the plane," he announced then indicated the dead man with the wrapped leg. He was wearing something similar to combat gear. "I don't recognize that man."

"By the way he's dressed, I'd say he was here on a hunting trip," Kirk announced and indicated the combat gear and telltale boots.

They heard a plane flying overhead and moved to the edge of the woods attempting to spot the plane through the trees. The slightly larger plane was heading for the runway as its landing gear lowered.

"That can't be good," Sal announced while straining to see the plane.

"It's landing," Gil informed them.

"Someone searching for the missing plane?" Bogart asked while staring through the trees.

Gil motioned for everyone to move. "No, it's a private plane, which could be trouble. We need to move."

Everyone hurried through the woods to put as much distance between them and the airfield as possible. They didn't know if the passengers on the private plane were friendlies or hostiles. Gil once again sent Darth on his mission. The dog took off through the woods.

Chapter Thirty-three

The cruise ship's deck nine, panorama lounge made for the perfect safe haven for the remaining Flight 316 passengers. It contained three outer deck entrances among its wall of windows, which offered them a spectacular view of the now filthy pool at the ship's bow. The windows also allowed them to see any danger outside. A short journey down the interior hall took them past the internet cafe, the wine lounge, and the library before reaching interior stairs. There was a set of fire doors before the stairs, which was easily blocked off to keep them safe from an inside assault. The massive lounge contained seating for one hundred guests. It had a huge, circular bar in the center and another smaller bar on the port side. The smaller port side bar had its own entrance to a storage area that connected the lounge to the wine lounge on the other side of the wall.

The lounge contained three deck entrances that were easily blocked off. The lounge provided comfortable chairs and sofas, and, surprisingly, the bar remained mostly stocked with booze and bottled water. Jackie and Zack had rigged the hole in the ship's hull, so they would be alerted to anyone attempting to sneak onboard. Since their little party had gotten smaller, they had a plan in place in the event they were discovered by hostiles. Each exit came with a backup plan, so everyone would meet up in the same location if something happened.

In the event of an attack, chaos was to be expected as was being separated. Briefing everyone on what to do in the event of an emergency would ensure they'd meet at the designated rendezvous. Four of the remaining survivors were given passkeys that would manually unlock any stateroom, allowing them a safe place to hide. With the sheer number of staterooms, anyone looking for them would have to break down many doors to find them. Their safety plan was now in motion. Unfortunately, they now had little to do but wait for a rescue or an attack.

Their collection of weapons had grown since Zack's overthrow of the helicopter. Jackie and Zack had successfully armed four of the passengers, although their ammo was still limited to a few rounds each. Sid, Bill, and Conner were now armed, although Jackie had reservations regarding giving Sid another weapon. In the heat of battle, he couldn't hit shit. Conner was grateful to have a weapon to protect Lindsey, but Lindsey was feeling a little left out since she wasn't trusted with a gun. The fourth gun was given to the remaining woman in their group, Kate, who was a retired Air Force veteran, which meant she had weapons training even if she hadn't fired a gun in years.

While the remaining survivors had a drink or two to settle their nerves, Jackie and Zack left the lounge. They took lookout positions within the bridge, which was only a short journey up a set of interior stairs from the ninth floor lounge. The magnificent, panoramic view also gave them the ability to see the entire beach and woods. Anyone attempting to cross the beach for the ship would be spotted. The location of the bridge and the tinted glass also kept their position hidden from anyone sneaking around the woods with their eyes on the ship.

It was a little after ten o'clock in the morning. Zack was comfortably seated in the captain's chair. Although he appeared relaxed, he spent nearly as much time watching Jackie pace the length of the bridge as he did the beach.

"I've never seen you this fidgety before," Zack remarked. "I'll admit; it's unnerving."

"This entire situation is unnerving," Jackie informed him while only briefly glancing at him. "We usually carry the element of surprise, but this whole thing seems almost orchestrated with the odds against us."

"The attack on the plane and the one in the hangar?" Zack asked with a curious look.

"A commercial airliner is shot down and crash lands on an abandoned island," Jackie announced. "There's no rescue, yet Cicco's merry band of thugs found us, infiltrated the plane, and are hunting us?" She shook her head. "It's too orchestrated. Lindsey's problems began just two days ago. There's no way Cicco's men knew she'd be on that plane before we did. Conner only just purchased the tickets after she fled our protective custody. How could Cicco put all this together that fast?"

"Why would he do it is also a very good question," Zack remarked. "No matter how badly he wanted the girl, shooting a plane from the sky and murdering all the passengers seems a bit extreme."

"I'm glad you didn't think I was crazy," she announced then fidgeted. "It's been bothering me since we were shot down."

"Nothing personal against our mobster friends," Zack remarked, "but the men in the woods were a little too organized for the average henchman."

She spun to face him. "Any thoughts?"

Zack drew a deep breath and shifted in his chair. "This degree of organization is usually found in military operations, mercenaries for hire, or government organizations specializing in assassination."

"Why would any of those entities want Lindsey?" she suddenly demanded.

"You're being a little shortsighted, Jackie," Zack informed her and raised a brow. "Why does this have to be about Lindsey?"

"They attempted to abduct her back in the hangar," Jackie replied while giving him an arrogant look.

"Just because one person was sent after Lindsey, that doesn't mean everything that's happened has necessarily been about her," Zack corrected. "For all we know, they're after us."

She stared at him a moment with surprise which instantly turned to disbelief. "If someone intended to hunt us, they'd have plenty of opportunities to do so without shooting a commercial airliner out of the sky," she remarked, almost insulted by Zack's insistence that the downed plane could be their fault.

"Yes, they would have plenty of opportunities to go after you any other time," Zack replied and shifted in his chair. "Some of us fly a little further beneath the radar than others."

She suddenly stared at him with surprise. "You think they're after you?"

Zack shrugged. "Several countries would love to see me dead," he replied. "Especially if they knew I wasn't really dead. They're the sort of people who would have the organization, manpower, and resources to accomplish what we've seen. Government assassins are the reason I've killed off more aliases than I can remember."

"How many times have you officially been dead?" Jackie asked him with a curious look.

"Government-sanctioned or since I retired from the military?" he asked then grinned.

Jackie rolled her eyes and shook her head. "Is Zack even your real name?"

"It's my preferred name," he replied then considered the question. "I've been so many people; even I don't remember them all. The first time the government 'killed me off' was a few years after you were born. The Navy tried to retire me." He frowned and sank into thought. "That didn't work out so well. Returning to your father's SEAL team seemed to be the best way to keep everyone safe."

"Safe?" she asked with surprise.

"My past is always in my present," he informed her. "If our government hadn't killed me off so many times, everyone I ever cared about would eventually be dead. It was just safer to keep me away from the general population." He let out a throaty chuckle. "A few times, I think they even tried to retire me permanently in the name of security. I guess we'll never know since everyone who's ever tried to kill me is dead." He drifted out a moment. "I really need to consider interrogating people *before* I kill them." Zack sighed, shook his head, and relaxed in his chair. "So many character flaws." He seemed to be in his own little world.

Jackie finally sat on the control panel and stared at him. It was one of the few times he opened up to her about his past. Despite his closeness with her father and the rest of the team, she sometimes felt she knew him better than anyone did.

"Who was she?" Jackie asked delicately.

Zack shot a look at her and immediately stiffened. "There was never a 'she'," he scoffed. "You always do that. You attempt to humanize me. You want to believe there's more to me than what you see. Get over it, Jackie."

And so ended another brief moment into Zack's private life. Jackie knew she should have kept her mouth shut. When properly motivated, Zack would let things slip, and she would be able to piece together parts of his past. When she attempted to extract information from him, he'd immediately shut her down. Jackie groaned and stood.

"You're the one who needs to get over it," she muttered. "You pull me in then push me away. I feel like a yo-yo." She glared at him and raised her brows. "When I'm feeling better, we're taking it to the mats. I need to kick your ass around a little."

Zack suddenly grinned with enthusiasm. "Now that's more like it."

Jackie rolled her eyes and returned to staring outside. "We're going to die on this rock," she muttered.

§

The scenic lounge allowed the eleven remaining passengers to relax a little finally. Sid bartended while the others sat around the bar and had a drink or two to settle their frayed nerves. Ironically, it had only been twenty-four hours since their nightmare began. With everything that had happened, it seemed as if they'd been stranded on the island a week or more.

"On the bright side," Bill announced and managed a humored smile. "If we survive this, we'll probably all be famous."

He received several looks although no one was particularly enthusiastic.

"That's a mighty big 'if'," Kate muttered and sipped her drink.

"I don't know why you're complaining," one of the other men announced. "They gave you a gun."

Kate removed the gun from the back of her pants and set it on the bar. "Yeah, and I have exactly five shots," she informed him. "The people hunting us have a helicopter and automatic weapons. Five rounds in a semiautomatic is one step above using harsh language against these guys."

"Look," Sid announced while leaning on the bar. "The crazy guy said he sent out a distress message from their disabled helicopter. Worst case scenario; the Coast Guard is an hour away."

"Think the Coast Guard can handle the organization we've seen?" Conner asked while staring at Sid. "They shot a commercial airliner from the sky. Unless the Coast Guard shows up with an entire fleet, they'll be walking into a massacre."

"That's why Jackie and Zack are manning the bridge," Bill informed them. "I'm sure they have the situation under control."

"I hope you're right," Lindsey muttered and sipped her drink.

"Anything we should know about the men trying to kill us?" Kate asked while glaring at Lindsey.

"I don't know anything about the men trying to kill us," Lindsey snapped back and returned the glare. "My husband was the son of a mob boss. Two days ago, he tried to kill me in a fit of rage. Now his father wants me dead. That's the extent of what I know."

Bill shook his head with a look of disbelief on his face. "I find it hard to believe these guys are with the mob," he remarked. "They seem a little too organized."

"The mafia *is* organized," Conner interjected. "That's why they're called *organized* crime."

"I may be totally off base," Bill announced while eying the others, "but this reeks of spy stuff."

"Spy stuff?" Kate practically demanded. "What do you mean by spy stuff?"

"CIA, Mi6, KGB," Bill proclaimed. "You know; that sort of spy stuff."

"So the KGB shot a United States commercial airliner from the sky because Lindsey's abusive husband met his demise?" Sid scoffed then snorted a laugh. "You may be my friend, but you're off your rocker."

"Maybe they're not after Lindsey," Bill insisted while raising a cocky brow. "Maybe this has nothing to do with her dead mobster husband. What if they're after Jackie and Zack? What about their friends who parachuted from the plane? Who the hell parachutes from a commercial airliner? We know nothing about these people."

"I do," Lindsey announced and received several looks. She shifted uncomfortably on her stool. "My father hired them because they're former military. They're part of a team of badasses called Whiskey Tango Foxtrot."

Kate suddenly straightened in her seat and stared at Lindsey with surprise. "Whiskey Tango Foxtrot?" she practically gasped. "Are you sure?"

All eyes were suddenly on Kate.

"Does that mean something?" Bill suddenly asked.

"That depends on who you talk to," Kate remarked while shaking her head in disbelief. "Do you remember that mob wedding that turned into one major bloodbath? They were there."

"If the guys chasing us are after them," Conner announced. "Maybe we shouldn't be here. We don't need to put ourselves between them and the guys who want them dead."

Lindsey suddenly shook her head and eyed Conner. "No," she announced. "We're safer here. My father hired them. They'll protect us."

"Like they protected those on the plane?" another man remarked.

"That's not fair," Lindsey launched back. "They weren't there when that happened. If they had been, they probably would have been able to stop it. If we stay here, at least we have plenty of places to hide. Despite being outnumbered, I think Jackie and Zack are still our best chance of getting out of this alive."

"They did give us weapons," Kate informed the others. "We need to be ready to defend ourselves against the guys hunting us. Stay or go; they're still going to hunt us. Lindsey's right. We're safer here."

Chapter Thirty-four

Jackie and Zack spent nearly an hour on the bridge keeping watch for a rescue or an attack, but it was looking as if neither would happen. It was nearly eleven A.M. Jackie became bored and started playing with switches that hadn't worked in years. Zack suddenly became interested in something and slipped from the captain's chair like a cat stalking its prey. He paused near the control panel and stared outside. Jackie immediately looked up. She just saw the same woods, but something must have caught his attention.

"What is it?" Jackie asked, desperately wanting to see what he saw.

"Something glistened in the tree line," he announced while maintaining his stare. "Someone's out there."

Jackie sprang from her seat before the control panel and snatched her M416 assault rifle. She aimed it at the window and looked through the scope at the tree line. She frowned and lowered the weapon.

"The scope on this piece of shit isn't worth a damn," she informed Zack.

"Our luck. We get low-budget assassins. In order to pick them off from here, you'd have to be out on deck," Zack replied without taking his eyes from the tree line. "By the time you zeroed in on them, they'd already have you in their crosshairs."

She eyed him. "You can give me the good news any time now."

"I'm thinking a play date in the cargo hold," Zack announced then looked at her and grinned.

"You're such a predator," Jackie remarked while making a face.

"Are you coming?" he asked while snatching his assault rifle with a little too much enthusiasm.

"No, I'll keep look out from here until I see the whites of their eyes," she replied not sharing his enthusiasm. "Then I'll alert our shipmates."

A few minutes after Zack left the bridge by the interior stairs, Jackie saw the first intruder appear from the tree line. She wasn't surprised that Zack hadn't been wrong about seeing something. He had eyesight like a hawk. The man dressed in gray camouflage must have thought he was invisible with the way he scurried along the sand remaining close to the ground. Three more men dressed in similar outfits followed. Four would be enough to amuse Zack for a good fifteen minutes. When she didn't see any others, it was time to alert their fellow survivors of potential danger. With her hand radio smashed, she had no way of alerting Zack to the number of invaders approaching, but he could handle four, so she didn't need to intervene.

§

Despite Darth's excitability, Gil was able to keep the dog within view as they hurried through the woods. Kirk and Bogart kept watch behind them to ensure they didn't have any fans following them from the old airfield. Monroe kept an eye and a gun on their new friend, Tucker, who was possibly a prisoner if the circumstances were right. Sal and Mac remained in the middle of the SEAL team conga line with an awkward silence between them. There wasn't time for small talk and keeping quiet was necessary, but it was obvious the two were tense in the other's company. As they got closer to the opposite end of the island, Darth became uncontrollably excited and suddenly took off. Gil didn't dare call after him, and his soft whistle didn't bring the dog back. They had to pick up the pace to keep the dog in sight. The sound of movement behind them suddenly alerted Kirk.

"We have company," Kirk announced loud enough for Gil in the lead to hear.

Without even looking back, Gil, Mac, Bogart, and Monroe, along with his prisoner, dove behind the nearest trees. Sal was left standing on the path with a baffled look when he realized everyone had disappeared. Mac reappeared, grabbed his arm, and pulled him behind a tree with her. They aimed their weapons into the woods behind them and waited. Five or six heavily armed men dressed in black combat gear hurried along the path attempting to make as little noise as possible while searching for someone or something. More than likely, they were searching for the passengers of what they considered an enemy plane.

Mac shifted looks at the others securely hidden behind their trees. The men were nearly statuesque and didn't make a sound while waiting for those following them to get just close enough. Even Bogart seemed to have learned how to blend into any background. Monroe had mastered keeping a lookout and holding his pistol aimed at Tucker's head just in case he decided to shout out a warning. They still didn't know if he could be trusted. When the men were close enough, Monroe signaled the team. He had only taken his eye off Tucker a moment, but that was all the time he needed. Tucker caught Monroe's wrist, thrusting the gun upward to avoid being shot, and punched him in the abdomen with his free fist.

"It's a trap," Tucker shouted as he dove out from behind the tree and rolled across the ground to avoid the barrage of bullets that immediately followed as the team fired upon the armed men.

The men pursuing them fired back and attempted to take cover from the gunfire that seemed to come from out of nowhere. The newly escaped prisoner ran for the pursuing men and safety. He suddenly stopped when he got his first glimpse of the men he had just warned. His expression dropped when he realized he didn't recognize the pursuing men.

"Are you Cicco's men?" Tucker suddenly gasped.

The men didn't bother responding with words and fired several rounds into the former prisoner. Tucker took several shots to his body and fell to the ground. Despite the controlled gunfire on both side's behalf, the exchange sounded like a warzone. Kirk winged one man partially hidden behind a tree. When he fell backward from the shot, Kirk got him with the second round between the eyes. Mac kept low to the ground behind her tree and attempted to follow the gunfire exchange, but she couldn't even see the men hiding in the woods. Bullets seemed to be flying from all directions and yet coming from nowhere specific. Mac cursed at her inability to fire back. A bullet splintered the tree near her face. She gasped and took cover behind the tree. She eyed Sal alongside her.

Sal shook his head while clinging to his handgun. "I recommend you don't do that," he announced.

Mac ignored Sal and again attempted to follow the action hoping to get a round off. She saw one of the men speaking into a shortwave radio. She flattened her back against the tree and looked across the woods to Monroe.

"Hand radio," she called out to Monroe then nodded to the tree directly across the woods from her.

Monroe looked at the tree she indicated then eyed Gil and gave a nod. Monroe leaped out from behind his tree, rolled across the ground several times, and allowed the enemy to shoot at him. He landed close to the tree Mac had indicated. As the other men attempted to shoot the moving target, Gil stepped out from behind his tree and fired at the men carelessly firing at Monroe. Kirk and Bogart joined in with the barrage of bullets, taking out both men. Monroe landed in a crouched position and fired at the man with the radio. The bullet hit the radio and entered the man's face through his cheek. The last man fired at them while attempting to flee. Kirk spun around, caught the man in his sights, and fired several rounds, taking him down. When they were certain the threat had been neutralized, they checked on the dead men.

"Who do you suppose he was radioing?" Sal asked with concern. "Another plane?"

"No that was shortwave radio," Monroe informed him. "He was calling for backup from his buddies on the plane with him.   There'll be more coming this way if he got that call through.   We need to move out."

"Darth went that way," Gil announced while indicating the woods to the right.   "If we're lucky; he'll backtrack when he heard the gunfire."

Gil hurried through the woods.   The others ran after him in hopes of finding the dog that would lead them to Jackie and Zack.

Chapter Thirty-five

The first armed intruder wearing gray camouflage entered the hull through the opening. He looked around the moderately dark area but willingly kept his flashlight off until he reached a secured location behind some crates. He had only taken two steps into the hull when his foot hit a carefully hidden tripwire attached to a gun. The gun fired. The man immediately ducked when he heard the firing gun. A bullet buzzed past him but didn't even graze him. The bullet ricochet across the hull until it finally hit something wooden. The second man entered the hull while keeping low and looked around.

"Tripwire," the first man announced just loud enough for his partner to hear.

"Poorly executed," the second man remarked. "If these guys were any good, you wouldn't be standing."

"They weren't trying to kill someone with it," the first man insisted. "They knew the bullet would ricochet. It was a crude alarm to warn them of anyone entering. Clever but not very efficient."

The first man followed the thin wire to the gun mounted on a support beam. He detached the wire from the trigger and removed the gun from the wall while grinning at the second man. He noticed too late that there had been a second wire attached to the gun. When he followed the taut wire back to the support beam, an ax left loose from above and struck him in the face. He twitched and fell to the ground. The second man jumped with surprise and immediately ducked just inside the hull opening. He turned on his flashlight and shined it around the ship's hull. Despite the mess, there were no other trip wires. The two remaining men joined him at the opening with their weapons aimed.

"What happened?"

"Booby traps," the second man gasped, still shocked at what he'd witnessed.

It was a gruesome way for his teammate to die. He finally straightened and made his way into the ship. The remaining two men followed him and kept their guns aimed as they scanned the area with their flashlights. Tension was now high. The sound of whistling caught their attention. It seemed to echo from every corner of the hull. The men shined their flashlights around the dark areas to the chilling sound of Chopin's "Funeral March" being whistled. The second man immediately turned off his flashlight and moved closer to the wall. His two teammates shined their lights around then followed suit and turned them off.

"I don't think I gave this guy enough credit," the second man whispered to the others. "He's messing with us like some psycho killer."

"You're overreacting," the third man responded back, feeling less need to keep his voice down. "They're glorified bodyguards. The only one with any real military training jumped from the plane before it crashed, and he was just their communications expert. We're hunting some girl whose father was a Navy SEAL. The rest of the passengers all checked out as your average, everyday people. Only one or two even had any military background."

"You mean the daughter of a Navy SEAL did *that* to Lou?" the second man remarked while indicating the dead man with the ax still embedded in his face.

"The girl got lucky," the third man replied.

The third and fourth man headed through the cargo hold while the second man remained crouched against the wall and appeared deep in thought.

"Wait," the second man announced, although neither man listened to him. "The man who parachuted from the plane was a retired Navy SEAL as well. If the daughter of a Navy SEAL was also the one who landed the plane, she might be Jackie Remus."

"So?" the third man replied while continuing through the hull. "What difference does that make?"

"Jackie Remus married a fed," the second man informed the others as he slowly straightened and looked around, again shining his light into dark corners. "Her father's SEAL team was Whiskey Tango Foxtrot."

"So?"

"So?" the second man practically gasped. "If we're hunting Whiskey Tango Foxtrot, you'd better believe we're not the ones doing the hunting here."

The third man groaned. "I told you; the only known threat parachuted from the plane before it crashed."

The second man remained deep in thought then eyed his teammates across the hull. "Was one of the passengers named Zack?"

"I don't remember," the third man replied while scanning the area with his flashlight. "What does that matter?"

"It was rumored that Zack Kinsley never actually died," the second man responded. "I've heard talk that he still travels with his former team under different aliases."

"Zack Kinsley is an urban legend," the third man remarked without care. "He's dead and buried. His own government even wanted him dead. Trust me; he's dead."

The fourth man now appeared nervous and shined his light around the hull while turning his back to his partners. A pair of legs swung down from above, circled the third man's head, and easily snapped his neck creating a horrific crunching sound. The fourth man shined his light toward the sound. He saw his teammate standing before him with a strange look on his face as he swayed a moment before falling to the ground. The fourth man suddenly gasped and shined his light in every direction. He looked above him to the support beam. There was nothing there.

"He's dead," the fourth man called back to the second man by the hull opening.

When his teammate didn't respond, he looked back toward the opening. The second man was now sitting against the wall with a knife stuck in his throat and a fixed look of horror on his face. The fourth man shined his light around the area. When he didn't see anything move, he darted for the opening in the hull and ran back onto the beach. Once outside the ship, he spun around and aimed his weapon at the opening. Apart from the deck over three stories from the ground, there was no other way out of the grounded ship.

Several shots were fired at him from the opening in the hull. He cried out with surprise and leaped backward before exchanging gunfire. He then saw the barrel of the rifle poking through the hull. The fourth intruder aimed and fired, striking the sniper in the shoulder. There was a loud grunt as the man fell backward into the hull. The fourth man immediately hurried for the opening with his weapon aimed and stepped back into the hull. He hovered over the fallen man, prepared to put a second round into him, when he realized it was his own teammate on the floor whom he'd shot in the shoulder. He stared at his dead teammate while attempting to put it together. He realized too late that his already dead teammate had been used as a decoy.

The man spun around to see Zack standing before him. Zack kicked the rifle from his hand then spun into a roundhouse kick and struck him in the chest. The man flew from the hull opening and fell onto the sand. As Zack stepped out of the ship, the man pulled his holstered semiautomatic and aimed it at Zack. As the armed man scrambled to his feet while keeping his gun aimed at Zack, Zack's attention momentarily shifted to something behind his captor. The armed man took his eyes off Zack only a second to look behind him.

A German shepherd dog ran across the sand at full speed, surprising the man. He attempted to aim his weapon at the running dog. Darth leaped through the air, caught his forearm in his mouth, and rode the man down to the sand. Darth snarled and slung his head while holding the man's arm between his teeth. Zack approached and yelled something in German. Darth released the man as Zack stood over him with his finger on the trigger of his own semiautomatic. Zack was about to pull the trigger then hesitated. He sneered with annoyance and relaxed his trigger finger.

"Interrogation, Zack," he muttered under his breath. "Don't disappoint Jackie." He motioned to the man with his gun. "Get up."

The man slowly moved to his feet while holding his bleeding forearm. The sounds of gunfire could be heard in the near distance. Zack and Darth were alerted to the sound. Zack grabbed the man by the shirt collar and just about threw him into the hull opening. The rest of the team appeared from the woods while firing behind them. Sal was the first to see the ship and pointed.

"There!"

Zack saw his teammates and waved to them while Darth barked several times excitedly. They continued to fire into the woods then ran for the ship. Zack fired at the men dressed in black combat gear, keeping them off his friends so they could seek refuge. The sound of rapid gunfire was heard above them, driving the men back into the woods. The team ran for the opening in the hull and looked up the three stories to the deck above. Jackie fired the assault rifle into the woods, keeping the men from getting a clear shot at the team.

Once the team was safely inside the hull, Jackie ran across the deck, through a set of doors, and down the interior steps into the cargo area of the ship. She ran down the metal steps as the team was heading toward the stairs. Jackie saw Holden, tossed her assault rifle aside, ran for him, and jumped into his arms. He held her a long moment in a warm embrace before pulling away and kissing her. Darth stood before the happy couple and watched them a moment before attempting to squeeze between them and get their attention.

"I don't mean to break up this intimate moment," Bogart snarled, "but we have company on our asses."

Jackie pulled away from Holden, smiled with some embarrassment, and reclaimed her assault rifle.

"The cargo door can be locked from the other side," she informed them. "It'll buy us a little time."

The team gathered their gear, Zack's prisoner, and hurried up the steps to the next level. Holden quickly assessed Jackie and immediately noticed the large bloodstain on her left shoulder.

"You've been injured," he announced with concern.

She smiled reassuringly. "Just a scratch," Jackie replied then indicated the steps. "We should go."

He pulled her to his side and affectionately kissed her forehead while attempting to act unconcerned. "Yeah, it's always 'just a scratch' with you."

Chapter Thirty-six

Kirk had taken up residence on deck four on the other side of the sealed cargo door, in case anyone managed to slip past the snipers. Jackie, Holden, and Bogart went to the ninth deck lounge to check on their fellow passengers and keep them posted on the situation. They now had working radios, since the guys came prepared, so communication was possible without running around the entire ship playing 'whisper down the alley'. The rest of the team took up residence on the bridge to keep the intruders at bay the best they could for as long as they could. Once they found their way onboard, it would turn into a battle, and they couldn't risk the lives of the remaining crash survivors.

A gunshot rang out from the bridge deck. An armed man fell dead from a clean headshot just several feet outside the woods. There was little wiggle room for error since their new friends within the woods were wearing body armor. From their lookout positions, Gil and Zack had clean shots into the woods. With the more reliable AK-47 assault rifles the team had brought with them, they could pick the interlopers off before they even made it a few feet onto the beach. It seemed as if the invaders had given up after several deaths from sniper fire coming from the bridge. Zack and Gil remained comfortably seated behind their darkened wall of glass and kept watch on the woods' edge. Mac remained on the bridge and offered another set of eyes for the snipers. Zack remained focused on his role of sniper, but it was obvious he wasn't happy with Mac anywhere near him.

"They'll make their move once it's dark," Gil informed the others, who stood around their new prisoner.

Their prisoner from the hull was securely tied within one of the chairs on the bridge. Monroe and Sal stood over him, attempting to get some answers from him before allowing their less ethical teammates have a go at it.

"What's your name?" Monroe demanded.

The man didn't respond and refused to look at either of his captors.

Sal groaned and rolled his eyes. "He wants to do this the hard way," he announced simply while shaking his head in disgust. "I was never fond of the hard way. Sets my teeth on edge. Mostly because it involves yanking teeth from their heads."

"That's okay, Sal," Monroe announced almost cheerfully and grinned. "We have an unnamed few who enjoy interrogating prisoners."

"Darth," Gil announced, catching the dog's attention. He said something to the dog in German while pointing at the prisoner.

Darth snarled and lunged for the bound man, snapping at his crotch. The man cried out and attempted to keep his knees together, although he was tied in such a way that made it impossible. Darth's nose and teeth grazed his crotch. Gil chuckled and said something in German. Darth backed off and continued to snarl. Monroe suddenly grinned and snapped his fingers.

"I know," he announced cheerfully. "We'll call him Chew Toy." Monroe's look turned serious as he glared at the bound man. "And when he doesn't answer our questions, we'll tell Darth to get his chew toy."

The man nervously wriggled in his chair and eyed the snarling dog. "I swear," Chew Toy cried out with concern about the dog using his crotch as a squeaky toy. "I don't know those men in the woods. Cicco only had a few men in the woods, and your man killed them, including our men waiting by the helicopter. We were sent in when Cicco heard the distress call and realized his team was down."

"What about the men on the plane?" Monroe demanded while hovering over his prisoner.

"Cicco had planted two of our people onboard the plane to retrieve the girl once we reached Costa Rico," Chew Toy insisted. "She was killed near the helicopter, and we found the other with one of our men shot to death in the woods not far from the old airfield."

"What about the two men onboard the plane working with the stewardess?" Monroe again demanded. "The plane that shot us from the sky? Are you saying none of that was Vinny Cicco?"

"He didn't have anything to do with the plan to parachute from the plane or the plane being shot from the sky," Chew Toy informed him and seemed willing to blurt out everything he knew. "When our men onboard reported back with the situation, particularly the slaughter of the other passengers, he was just as surprised as anyone."

Chew Toy looked from Monroe to Sal as if expecting either one to pummel him to death. Sal put on a good intimidation act while holding a security baton he'd found. He played with the baton and casually slapped it against his free palm every so often. Those who knew Sal best would insist he was incapable of harming a fly, yet those who knew Sal best often wondered if he had them all fooled. No one really knew for sure. Monroe had roughed up their prisoner just enough to make it convincing. Had they wanted to frighten the man into confessing all his sins, they would have let Zack have him. Since it was obvious the man wasn't a mercenary, Monroe and Sal handled the situation in a less messy fashion.

"Our guys on the plane planned on intercepting the girl in Costa Rico," Chew Toy insisted. "They were just there to keep an eye on her until we landed. That's all; I swear."

"So who are these other guys?" Sal demanded. "They were willing to kill one of your guys earlier in the woods without hesitation."

"I don't know who they are," the man insisted. "They just sort of showed up. Cicco found out there was another party interested in capturing the girl. Our orders were to get the girl before they did. Whoever they are; they're highly skilled, heavily armed, and extremely organized."

Mac was now paying attention to the conversation and approached the men and their prisoner. She stared at the bound man within the chair.

"What do you know about a man named Corbin?" Mac asked while studying him.

The prisoner eyed Mac and appeared curious. "Good-looking Russian guy? Well-mannered. Polite while he's slitting your throat?"

She frowned. "Yeah, that'd be the one," she replied. "Has friends in low places."

"He works for Makar," the man informed her without hesitation. "Makar works outside the Russian government. Higher up the food chain than the Russian mafia. Makar made a name for himself while piling up the body count. Plenty of his own men as well." He suddenly looked from Mac to Monroe. "Is that who's after the girl? If she's pissed off Makar, he won't stop until he goes through every single one of you and us to get to her." His eyes widened dramatically. "That would explain the slaughter of the plane passengers. Picking off his men in the woods isn't going to help. If they called for additional backup, you'll be looking at air support and ground reinforcements within the hour. They'll kill us all; no questions asked."

Gil and Zack now looked back as well, having heard the comment.

"This tub won't hold up for long against the sort of weapons we saw on that helicopter back on the mainland," Gil informed Monroe. "There's no telling what other firepower he'll bring at us."

Sal drew a deep breath and stared at Monroe. "I've heard rumors of Makar," he announced. "That Coast Guard rescue will be short-lived if they come up against someone like that. By the time they send additional backup to fight Makar's army, we'll all be dead, and he'll be out of here."

"Maybe we're interrogating the wrong person," Zack announced boldly, catching everyone's attention.

Mac suddenly sneered. "Lindsey." She looked back at Monroe and Sal. "She's the one they want. She needs to tell us why."

"I hate to be the one offering an unpopular suggestion," Gil announced almost shamefully. "Perhaps it's best if we just turned her over to them. We need to think of the lives it'll save."

"I'd vote for that solution," Mac remarked while folding her arms across her chest.

"We're not turning her over to some hostile organization," Monroe bluntly announced, offended his team would even suggest such a thing. "They'll torture and kill her."

"If that's the case, I'm sure she's done something to warrant a death sentence," Mac informed him.

"It may not matter if you turn her over," Sal interrupted. "If Makar ordered the slaughter of a plane filled with innocent people, he's not going to let the rest of us live just because we handed over his prize. He'll take the girl and eliminate everyone onboard to cover his tracks."

"Sal's right," Zack announced from his position by the window. "He's interested in protecting his position and operation. Whether we know what's going on or not; we're a liability. At this point, he'll neutralize us whether he has the girl or not."

"Not that this hasn't been fun," Mac announced, "but I think I'm ready to go home now."

"This is what I get for helping out an old friend," Sal muttered then eyed the others. "I'll be honest with you. If I had Dexter in front of me right now, I'd probably kill him for getting us involved in this."

"I doubt he even knew what his daughter had gotten herself into," Gil muttered.

"Don't be so sure," Mac remarked with little emotion. "Dexter is notorious for spilling the blood of others to get what he wants." She eyed the others. "He just wanted his daughter back. This team was expendable."

Sal nodded then casually removed his glasses and blew dirt from the lenses. He replaced his glasses and drew a deep breath. "Yes, I'm going to kill him."

§

The sun was high over the grounded, abandoned cruise ship a little after two in the afternoon. Gil and Zack were now glued to their post while Mac and Sal paced the length of the bridge. Both were watching and waiting for what was almost sure to come. Mac and Sal would contact the others with their hand radios if the intruders made it to the hull. They had moved their prisoner, Cicco's man dubbed Chew Toy, to the library down one level. Since there was no place to lock him away safely, they left him tied to a chair in the library. He was the least of their worries.

After the revelation regarding the Russian mercenaries, the remaining passengers were sent to one of the first-class cabins with more than one escape route. It was obvious the invaders were after Lindsey. Even though they intended to wipe out anyone with any knowledge of their actions, the other passengers had a better chance of survival if their location was unknown. If locating the remaining passengers was too much of an effort, it was possible once they had Lindsey, they'd give up their quest to kill everyone and simply leave. The team didn't intend to give up Lindsey willingly, but if the men hunting her managed to find her, at least the others stood a better chance of surviving.

The sound of a helicopter approaching should have made those on the bridge feel better, but they were almost certain it wasn't the sort of backup they were anticipating. As the helicopter came into view, Zack frowned. They didn't have anything capable of bringing down the helicopter without several precision shots that they wouldn't likely get. As suspected, the helicopter flew for the abandoned cruise ship and spun sideways, revealing a man with a machine gun bolted fast to the floor in the back. He fired rapid shots at the bridge, easily shattering the glass.

All four took cover as the bridge was riddled with bullets. To no one's surprise, more than a dozen men from the woods charged across the beach for the ship's torn hull while the helicopter kept the bridge snipers occupied. Mac and Sal shouted into their hand radios, although their words weren't heard. It didn't matter what they said at that point. The sound of rapid gunfire was enough to alert those on the receiving end that the bridge was a total loss.

Zack looked at Gil where they both huddled for safety from the barrage of bullets. "You know; I never say this," Zack announced. "But I think we should retreat."

"I thought you'd never ask," Gil remarked then motioned to Sal and Mac.

Thankfully, Darth had been moved to a more secured location prior to the helicopter's arrival. Sal and Mac darted for the interior stairs and away from the machine gun fire. Gil rolled across the glass-covered floor and darted into the stairwell as well. Zack remained where he was and kept still. The firing ceased since the shooter assumed everyone had cleared the bridge. As the helicopter turned to make a pass over the abandoned cruise ship, Zack stood up, aimed his AK-47 assault rifle, and fired one round. The shot struck the tail rotor in what had to be an amazingly precise shot. The helicopter lost control and started spinning.

The pilot was able to keep the craft from going down, but he could no longer fly straight. The helicopter attempted to turn, so the man behind the machine gun could wipe out the rest of the bridge. As the craft lagged in the air, Zack appeared on deck not even attempting to shield himself. The helicopter spun just enough to reveal the machine gun. Zack raised his assault rifle and waited. With his recently acquired, precision rifle, he could make each shot count.

The man arming the machine gun rotated in Zack's direction, but it was already too late. Zack fired two carefully calculated shots. The first struck the gunner and the second hit the machine gun itself. The gun's large barrel rotated upward. As the gunner fell, his finger on the trigger jerked. Shells tore through the top of the helicopter, startling the pilot and co-pilot. Zack aimed his weapon for the fuel tank and fired several rounds. The helicopter ignited, and an explosion followed. Zack dove to the deck, shielding himself from the exploding metal and projecting flames. He lifted his head in time to watch pieces of the helicopter plummet to the sand below. The sound of another helicopter alerted him. Zack slowly moved to his knees and looked at the horizon. Another helicopter approached. He frowned and shook his head.

"That's just wrong," he muttered then ran for what was left of the bridge and headed into the stairwell.

Chapter Thirty-seven

Kirk and Bogart remained mostly hidden and watched the watertight door securing the cargo hold from the rest of the ship. The pounding against the door was almost deafening. The men on the other side had the right equipment that they'd eventually break through the nearly impenetrable door. Bogart nervously looked from the door to the frozen expression on Kirk's face as he patiently awaited the breakthrough. Bogart shifted uncomfortably while staring at Kirk's steely gaze, and the gun that remained securely cradled in his arms.

"This is Custard's last stand, isn't it?" Bogart remarked with concern. "We're going to die here, aren't we?"

"You might, if you don't shut up," Kirk informed him. "I intend to die when I'm eighty and having wild sex with a twenty-something-year-old redhead."

"You're a true romantic," Bogart muttered then returned to watching the door. "Should we be standing this close?"

Kirk groaned and glared at Bogart. "You're like the nagging wife I never wanted."

"Well, excuse me if I prefer my body parts intact," Bogart snapped.

"Just stick with the plan," Kirk huffed.

The door puckered with several hits then finally gave away. As the door flew open, it struck a wire, which sent a flame from a small welding torch into what looked like a pile of garbage. The flammable objects exploded as the men stepped through the doorway. Kirk and Bogart hit the floor to avoid a large ball of flames shooting above their heads and many pointy objects projecting across the corridor. The first few men through the doorway took the brunt of the sharp projectile objects and fell to the floor in bloody heaps. Kirk and Bogart leaped to their feet and rapidly fired into the doorway, striking several men who had taken cover from the explosion. As the first few men fell, the men behind them fired back. When a canister emitting smoke was hurled through the opening at them, Kirk and Bogart fled the scene and the pile of human remains.

"They're getting through barrier one," Kirk announced into his hand radio as he ran behind Bogart along the corridor. "Makar's men are dressed to kill in their finest SWAT uniforms. Second team, you're up."

Only moments later, nearly two dozen men dressed in black combat gear forced their way through the empty cruise ship corridors. A particularly pissed off man with a pronounced limp pushed past the others. Corbin motioned for his men to split up. Makar joined him and glared at the men.

"Remember, we want Lindsey Cicco alive," Makar shouted to his men in anger. "No witnesses left behind. Sweep and clean."

Corbin frowned but didn't comment. They broke off into four, six men teams to search the ship with a very specific mission in mind. Kill everyone they found.

§

A second helicopter flew overhead and hovered over the cruise ship's bow. More than two dozen men on cables dropped down to the deck and immediately secured their weapons while fanning out. Cicco's men were wearing gray camouflage uniforms and looked like a mini-militia. Just before the helicopter took off, the last man slid down the cable and straightened. It was Vinny Cicco. From his hidden position high on a perch above the bridge, Zack watched more than two dozen men hurry along deck and split into several groups, taking separate stairwells. Vinny Cicco had lagged just far enough behind to give Zack unhealthy thoughts. His eyes narrowed as he silently removed the Bowie knife from his boot and held the tip between his fingers. Vinny's right-hand man, Dawg, rushed to his side.

"I just got word that the other interested party is a group of Russian mercenaries," Dawg informed him. "There's no telling how many of them are on this vessel searching for the girl."

"We'd better find her first," Vinny announced. "Alert the men. Let's go."

Dawg hurried Vinny toward the stairs. Zack frowned and cursed to himself, having missed his opportunity to cut the head off the beast. Once they were out of sight, Zack replaced his Bowie knife to his boot and raised his hand radio.

"Guys, we have company," Zack announced into the hand radio. "Cicco is here with two dozen or more heavily armed Boy Scouts in gray camouflage. Might be worth stepping off to the side and letting them kill one another."

"Roger that," came Monroe's response.

Once Cicco's men had dispersed and the helicopter was flying from sight, Zack straightened and looked across the beach. Two motor rafts filled with men dressed in black and gray combat uniforms rode the waves to shore. Zack leaped from his perch and approached the railing. He raised his assault rifle and checked out the new arrivals through the riflescope.

"Oh, this just keeps getting better," Zack muttered while lowering the rifle and again raised his radio. "Uh, guys. Guess who's coming to dinner?"

"Who?" Monroe demanded through the radio.

"We have Dexter and more than a dozen armed men storming the beach," Zack informed him. "They're heading this way. Dexter's men are sporting the finest in black and gray prowling wear."

"Great," Monroe remarked. "Avoid engaging Dexter's men. They're on our side."

"Yeah, let's hope they know that," Zack remarked into his radio.

"All that's missing from this little beach war is the Coast Guard," Monroe announced through the radio.

"Copy that," Zack remarked and watched the men run for the ship. "World War III has officially started." He then turned and bolted away from the railing.

§

The ship's lobby was filled with the sound of gunfire as Cicco and Makar's men clashed in their first official meeting of the afternoon. It was approximately six-on-six since others from each group had already branched off in search of their prize. Although the lobby had withstood a few years of neglect, one afternoon of a much-anticipated war ravaged the once elegant lobby. Everything made of glass, which seemed to be just about everything, was now shattered on the floor. There wasn't a single piece of furniture that didn't contain multiple bullet holes, and several men were profusely bleeding on the once expensive carpet.

Zack remained on his perch three stories above the open lobby and watched the battle rage on below. He stayed concealed on top of the elevator, forever locked-out on deck eight, with his rifle poised for the perfect sniper shot. Since he no longer had Cicco's less accurate rifles containing their nifty silencers, he didn't want to risk involvement. Involving himself for mere sport would be foolish if it gave away his location and risked the lives of those he was protecting. He had to be amused with watching the men kill one another instead.

One of the suite doors on deck eight opened. Sid poked his head out and looked around. When he didn't see anyone, he motioned for his friend. Sid and Bill hurried along the hall with their newly acquired assault rifles courtesy of Cicco's men from the earlier hull offensive. Sid pointed toward the back stairs to avoid the war raging in the lobby. They nearly made it to the stairwell door when one of Makar's men appeared in the corridor with his weapon raised.

"Don't move," the man in black announced gruffly with his finger firm on the trigger. "Drop the weapons."

Both inexperienced men did as they were told while staring at the weapon aimed at their faces. Their weapons hit the carpeted floor with a slight clatter, and they immediately put their hands in the air. The fear on their faces indicated they weren't professionals, and Makar's man didn't need to fear them.

"Where's the girl Lindsey?" Makar's man demanded in his most intimidating voice.

"We don't know," Sid informed him. "They put her into hiding without telling us where."

"It's the truth," Bill added while trembling with his hands in the air.

"I believe you too," Makar's man replied and pressed his finger against the trigger.

The M416 assault rifle was flung in the air, shooting several rounds into the ceiling. Sid and Bill screamed while shielding themselves then seemed surprised that they hadn't been shot. Zack kicked the man in the side several times until he released the weapon. As the weapon flew to the floor, the man swung for Zack. Zack easily blocked the blow, kicked him in the groin, and caught him around the neck as he doubled over. With little exertion, Zack snapped his neck. The man dropped to the floor when he was released.

Zack glared at Bill and Sid with impatience. "If you haven't noticed, there's a war going on down there," he informed them. "You're supposed to remain inside your stateroom unless they find you."

Sid indicated the hand radio. "We tried radioing anyone, but no one responded."

"That's because we're laying low until these assholes kill one another," Zack snapped as his eyes tore through both younger men. "We don't need idle radio chatter giving away our position."

"It's the Coast Guard," Bill announced without hesitation. "We saw them through our window. They're just sitting out there. We need to contact them."

"They're sitting out there because they probably saw or heard the war happening here," Zack informed them. "They aren't going to move in without proper backup."

"How long will that be?" Bill asked.

"A few hours," Zack replied. "Go back to your stateroom and wait until we come for you." He then turned and walked away.

"But--" Sid attempted to protest.

"I'm serious, kid," Zack snarled without looking back. "I'll fucking shoot you myself."

Both men grabbed their discarded weapons and returned to their luxury suite down the hall.

Chapter Thirty-eight

Holden and Jackie patrolled the ninth deck near the ship's outdoor pool while carrying their AK-47 assault rifles. The pool was filled with murky water from several years of tropical storms. There was a foul odor wafting from the dark water, which may have had nothing to do with the dead bird floating in the center. The high-quality lounging chairs had been neatly stacked beneath the overhang of the bridge deck and were now rusted together. Not far from the stacked chairs was a small pool bar near the panoramic lounge.

Both listened to the sound of gunfire from within the ship and on lower decks. It sounded like a war. Jackie looked over the railing several times, although they had no way of knowing who was winning and how many were already dead. Holden periodically looked toward the white and red Coast Guard ship just far enough from shore to keep an eye on things within the once abandoned cruise ship. The Fast Response Cutter was more than one hundred fifty feet long and had a remote-controlled, twenty-five-millimeter chain gun as well as four, fifty caliber machine guns on the front. Despite its firepower, the ship remained docked safely offshore. The Coast Guard Cutter carried a crew of twenty-four, but that wouldn't be enough men to win the war on the old cruise ship.

"We need to get the passengers to that ship," Holden announced then nodded to the inflatable motorized rafts across the beach. "If we could get them to one of those rafts, we could load them onto the Coast Guard ship."

"It's too dangerous," Jackie reminded him. "In order to get off this ship, we need to go through the opening in the hull. By ourselves, we'd have a tough time doing that. With eleven passengers, it would be next to impossible."

The helicopter was again heard. Holden grabbed Jackie's arm and hurried her beneath the overhang and behind the deck bar. They kept low with their rifles aimed and watched the helicopter pass overhead. The machine gun exposed out the side door was intimidating.

"You're sure that's not Dexter's helicopter?" Holden asked while watching it pass.

"Unfortunately, it belongs to the other interested party," Jackie informed him.

"That guy Makar with the Russian government?" Holden questioned.

"Or so Mac claims," Jackie replied with a defeated sigh. "For such a young girl, Lindsey seems to have pissed off all the right people."

"I wonder if her father knew what you were up against when he asked you to rescue his daughter," Holden remarked and quickly turned hostile. "Did he send you in without proper intel?"

"If the answer is yes, Dexter will have us to deal with providing he survives this little coup of his," she hissed with some bitterness.

They relaxed once the helicopter made its pass. Holden turned and nearly collided with Zack, who stood behind the bar with him and turned over an empty bottle of vodka. He had a look of disappointment on his face.

"This is the worst cruise I've ever been on," Zack muttered. "That's including the one where I was shot and thrown overboard."

Holden groaned and ran his fingers through his hair. "I wish you'd stop doing that."

Zack gave Holden an innocent look. "Stop doing what?" he asked then brushed the question aside. "You saw our friends, the Coast Guard, carefully monitoring the situation from a safe distance?"

"Yeah, we saw them," Holden replied while frowning. "There's a motorized raft, but we can't get the passengers to it without passing through the warzone."

"Actually," Zack announced and offered an unsettling smile. "I was thinking we go *over* the warzone."

Holden cast a look across the beach at the helicopter making another pass. He then looked back at Zack and shook his head. "You're completely out of your mind," he remarked. "There's no way you're commandeering that bird."

"I didn't intend to commandeer it," Zack reported with an innocent look. "I thought I'd take it by brute force and maximum bloodshed."

§

Jackie and Holden followed Zack into the lounge and watched him leap over the bar toward the side of the room. He removed a decorative, metal trident from the wall. Jackie and Holden watched him with bewilderment.

"What are you doing?" Holden asked not understanding. "Are you going to throw that thing at the helicopter? In case you haven't noticed, they have a machine gun out the side door."

"I need some rope," Zack informed them.

Jackie nodded without questioning him and ran back onto deck. Holden hurried after her and watched as she opened a bench seat. She tossed old, cracked life rings aside and removed a large rope.

"How'd you know that'd be there?" Holden asked.

She smiled at him and raised her brows suggestively. "Not my first time on a ship."

As she hurried back into the lounge, Holden chased after her still not understanding. Zack held the trident over the bar and pounded on the ends with a makeshift hammer using the butt of his semiautomatic. He bent all three prongs back in separate directions until it resembled a grappling hook. He then braced the trident against one of the sturdy bar chairs and kicked the wooden handle, snapping it near the metal end. Jackie handed him the rope. He skillfully tied the rope to the makeshift grappling hook then grinned while casually swinging it in his hands.

"Let's rope us a helicopter."

"How do you intend to get close enough to use that without them shooting you?" Jackie asked and raised her brows. "They have a machine gun, remember?"

"Yeah, I know," Zack casually replied. "We're going to need live bait."

Jackie and Zack looked at Holden. He stared back at them with surprise. Jackie cringed and offered a sympathetic smile to her husband.

"You've got to be kidding?" Holden bellowed.

"Bogart's not available," Jackie explained almost timidly. "You're the next best thing."

"Hey, if you'd like," Zack announced. "I can be the bait, and you can jump into the moving helicopter."

"Fine," Holden groaned and ran his fingers through his hair. "What do you want me to do?"

Jackie and Zack exchanged looks.

"Wow," Jackie gasped with surprise. "He sounded just like Bogart."

§

The helicopter flew toward the ship for another flyby with the intent to shoot anything that moved. Holden stepped onto the deck from the lounge with an assault rifle in his hand. He fired at the helicopter as it approached. As the helicopter closed in on him just over the pool, Holden ran back into the lounge. The helicopter spun and hovered allowing the gunner to fire, striking the floor at Holden's heels. Holden ran through a back door and up a set of stairs to the bridge deck. The gunner was unaware Holden had run through a connecting doorway and continued to fire into the lounge, exploding the glass walls and doorway. As large caliber bullets tore up the interior, Zack appeared from the bench seat on deck behind the helicopter and swung his grappling hook for the skid. Neither the pilot nor the gunner noticed the sound or the helicopter's slight tilt since the machine gun was bouncing the craft around already.

Zack swiftly scaled the rope and leaped through the opposite opening, kicking the gunner in the back with both feet. The gunner flew against the wall but didn't fall out the opening. His harness tethered to the helicopter floor helped keep him in place as well. The pilot pulled his handgun while fighting to keep the craft stable as it teetered slightly from the activity in the back. Zack kicked the pistol from his hand then went after the gunner, who had already recovered. The co-pilot's door opened to the empty co-pilot's seat, startling the pilot. Jackie appeared feet first and kicked him in the chest with both feet. He slammed against the door, causing the craft to veer. Jackie jumped into the co-pilot's seat and fiddled with the controls while the pilot recovered. She activated the controls on her side as the pilot lunged at her.

Jackie removed her semiautomatic and shot the pilot in the neck. He almost immediately bled out and slumped forward against the controls. Jackie struggled to keep the craft from plummeting as the men fought in the back. The gunner swung at Zack displaying amazing fighting skills. Due to the tight quarters and the position of the machine gun, Zack was unable to use most of his kicks and had to rely on hand-to-hand combat. The gunner punched Zack, sending him backward toward the opposite opening. Zack caught the edge of the doorway and kicked the machine gun. It swiveled on its base and struck the gunner. He flew out the open doorway, but the tether on his harness prevented him from falling to the deck below.

The gunner attempted to climb his rope. Zack jumped out the doorway landing on the skid and kicked the man twice in the face. He then clung to the skid, swung his legs down, and caught the man around the neck. He tightened his legs around his head and twisted his body, snapping the man's neck. The man dangled with his head hanging limply to the side. Zack reached down and released the harness. The man plummeted into the murky pool below with a splash, sending dirty, foul-smelling water onto the deck. Holden appeared on the bridge deck in time to see the final act. Jackie turned the helicopter and approached the bridge deck. She skillfully landed the craft, shut her down, and leaped out to join Holden.

"Let's get the survivors."

Chapter Thirty-nine

"You're leaving me behind?" Lindsey suddenly squawked while staring at Jackie.

The horror clearly showed on Lindsey's face at what she was hearing. Conner stood alongside Lindsey and appeared moderately surprised as well.

Jackie showed no reaction while staring at the young woman. "We're not leaving you behind," she firmly remarked. "We need to protect you. The moment you step into the sun, they're going to shoot you in the ass. You need to stay hidden."

The remaining survivors were hole up in a two-story suite, which encompassed decks eight and nine. The living room, dining room, wet bar, and butler's pantry were located on deck eight, which had a large balcony off the port side. A brass and curved glass staircase led to the two bedrooms on the second floor, which was deck nine. One of the bedrooms had a balcony while the other had access to the ninth floor corridor. Despite a few years of abandonment, the suite was still luxurious.

Holden moved away from the main suite door and approached the two women in a face-off. His look was commanding.

"Those men intend to kill you and everyone else they come across," Holden informed Lindsey. "If they see you're not with those fleeing the ship, they're less likely to pursue and kill them." He straightened proudly and indicated the other survivors within the suite. "I'm sure you don't want to see all these innocent people die because of you."

"You mean *more* innocent people," Sid scoffed from across the room.

Sid received several looks, including those from Lindsey, Conner, and Holden. Jackie didn't flinch nor look away from the selfish woman.

"It's not my fault the other passengers died," Lindsey snarled and folded her arms across her chest in a mild temper tantrum. "I didn't ask to be pursued by those men. I didn't do anything wrong. I'm the victim here."

There was a round of sarcastic chuckles from the remaining nine passengers.

"Why do I doubt that?" Sid scoffed.

Lindsey looked at them with surprise. "I can't believe you're all taking this out on me."

"You're the reason they're here," Kate announced with some irritation. "You're the reason they shot us down. And you're the reason they're still pursuing us."

"Maybe if we turned you over, they'd leave," another man interjected.

"We're not handing her to them," Holden announced boldly then eyed Jackie, who still hadn't responded. Her silence was moderately frightening. "Right, Jackie?"

Holden touched her shoulder. Jackie flinched slightly and shook her head.

"Of course we're not turning her over," she insisted almost defensively then returned her attention to Lindsey. "Hiding you and your boyfriend on this ship will be like a needle in a haystack for the men looking for you. Your father and his men are here, and our team is still here. It's just not necessary to put the lives of the rest of the passengers in danger while we eliminate the threat."

"I don't like this plan," Lindsey scoffed while glaring at Jackie and Holden.

"You don't have to like it," Jackie snapped coldly. "As long as you cooperate and do what you're told, we'll get you out of here in one piece."

"Remain in this suite," Holden instructed while pointing a warning finger at her. "Stay hidden and keep quiet. We'll be back for you once the others are safely aboard the Coast Guard ship."

Lindsey turned toward Conner, who immediately gathered her in his arms. She pouted and sank against his chest, allowing him to hold her.

Conner cast looks between Jackie and Holden. "I hope you're right about being able to protect her," he announced while affectionately stroking Lindsey's hair. "You're asking a lot from us."

"Once the others are safely removed," Holden informed him, "we'll be able to concentrate our efforts on keeping you two safe. Trust me."

Holden returned to the door and peered out while Jackie assembled the remaining nine passengers. Once Holden gave the all clear sign, they hurried from the room and entered the empty corridor. All nine passengers were now armed with confiscated guns they'd relinquished from assorted dead men. Bill and Sid remained at the back of the group closest to Jackie and now carried their M416 assault rifles with renewed confidence. All eleven remained close to the wall. Jackie walked backward and kept an eye on their rear while Holden led the group to the bridge deck just two levels up. The faint sounds of the battle raged on, although it seemed to be further away at the moment. Most of the fighting seemed to be happening on decks five and six.

The faint sound of gunfire didn't seem to end. Their mission required radio silence, so they didn't even know who was winning at the moment. The less noise they made the better. If they could reach the bridge without gunfire, they would stand a better chance. Holden paused by the stairwell doorway and quietly opened it. He peered inside, saw everything was clear, and motioned the others to follow him. Holden slipped inside the stairwell followed by the first five passengers. The remaining four were about to follow when one of Cicco's armed men appeared in the corridor with his weapon aimed at them.

"No one move," the armed man cried out.

Jackie tensed with her weapon firmly in hand, considering her next move. In that split second, she could easily take the man out before he had a chance to squeeze the trigger. Another man dressed in gray camouflage appeared in the hall behind her. He was another of Cicco's men. Essentially, they had them boxed in now. Jackie was fairly confident she couldn't win.

"Drop the weapons," the first man announced. "We don't want to hurt anyone."

The four passengers dropped their weapons on command. Jackie was still weighing her options. She knew she couldn't possibly shoot both men with that amount of distance between them and expect to take them both out. They would almost certainly shoot her or the other passengers before she achieved her goal. She reluctantly dropped her rifle but remained focused on the gun down the back of her pants, which neither man had seen. She just needed the right moment.

"These people aren't part of this. They're just innocent bystanders," Jackie informed the men. "Just let them go, and I'll take you to the woman you want."

The first man chuckled while eying her. "You're the one they warned us about, aren't you?" the man remarked. "You can't be trusted."

"What am I going to do?" Jackie practically demanded. "You have weapons pointed at me, and I'm unarmed. Trust me; that girl's been more trouble than she's worth. I'll be happy to be rid of her."

They continued to stare at her with the same disbelieving smirks. Jackie rolled her eyes and groaned.

"So tie me, if you're afraid I might do something dramatic like bitch-slap you," she hissed in response. "What do you really think I'm going to do against two big guys armed with big guns?"

The men exchanged looks and seemed to consider the comment. The man closest to Jackie removed a pair of zip ties and approached her while the second man kept watch over the prisoners. Jackie held her hands out in front of her to prove she wasn't dangerous. As the man slung his rifle to apply the zip ties, Jackie threw herself to the floor and swept the man's feet from beneath him while drawing her hidden semiautomatic at the same time. She sat up and fired at the man in front of the other passengers, who now aimed his M416 assault rifle at her. Jackie fired two shots into the man. He took two shots to the chest, but his bulletproof vest prevented them from doing any real damage. Her idea hadn't been perfect, since she'd only ever pulled the 'drop, roll, and pull' stunt on men she intended to shoot in the chest.

The man was only momentarily set back by the shots to his vest since the gun was only a 9mm. Jackie took time to set up her shot while he again aimed his rifle at her. She fired at him, striking him in the forehead. The first two men cried out with horror and bolted through the stairwell door, nearly plowing down Holden, who had returned when he heard the gunfire. Jackie spun from her crouched position to face the man she'd initially kicked, but he had already recovered and had his weapon aimed at her.

Before she could react, she heard Sid cry out in anger. Sid charged past her and plowed into the man with a shoulder to his midsection. Sid roughly tackled the man to the corridor floor landing on top of him. Once he had the man on the floor, Sid punched him several times in the face while shouting profanities. Jackie and Bill reacted at the same time and pulled the enraged Sid off the fallen man. Holden stared with surprise then motioned them for the stairwell door. Bill handed Sid his weapon and recovered his own then rushed an energized Sid through the doorway.

Jackie headed for the stairwell as Holden shook his head and disappeared through the opening. The man on the floor groaned. Without looking back, Jackie aimed her semiautomatic behind her and squeezed the trigger. The man took the bullet to the throat and fell back to the floor. Holden returned from the stairwell and looked back at the dead man on the corridor floor as blood spilled from his neck wound. He eyed Jackie suspiciously.

Jackie glared back at him. "What?" she demanded with some irritation.

"We need to discuss all the time you spend with Zack," Holden muttered. "He's a bad influence on you."

"Yeah, well," she announced with a dramatic sigh. "Sometimes Zack makes a valid argument. One less man who'll come back and shoot us later."

Holden groaned and shook his head. He indicated the stairwell with a nod. Jackie proudly passed him and entered the stairway.

Chapter Forty

Despite being a tight fit, the nine passengers along with Holden and Zack, riding shotgun or machine gun, squeezed into the helicopter. Jackie flew the packed helicopter from the ship's bridge deck across the beach and toward the motorized raft. She couldn't fly to the Coast Guard ship since it wasn't very big and there would be no place to land. Having the passengers jump into the water didn't seem the wise move either. Jackie shut down the helicopter to allow the nine passengers safe passage from the craft to the raft. Holden loaded everyone onboard while Zack remained positioned behind the machine gun within the helicopter.

A few brave souls attempted to charge the distant helicopter, but they were quickly mowed down by Zack's rapid machine gun fire. Holden loaded seven of the nine passengers into the raft. Bill and Sid remained outside in the water to help push the raft into the surf. Holden returned to Jackie. She stared at him with some surprise.

"What are you doing?" she asked.

"Fighting alongside you."

Jackie shook her head. "No, Holden," she informed him. "Those people need your protection."

"They'll be fine," he insisted. "You're the one I need to worry about."

"Do you really think the Coast Guard ship is going to let that raft anywhere near their ship after what's been happening over there?" she remarked. "You need to pull rank and flash your badge if they're going to be allowed onboard."

"I don't like leaving you in times of danger, Jackie," Holden responded. "You've been injured already."

"I know you want to protect me, but I'm not the one who needs your protection," she insisted then indicated the passengers. "They do. Get them on that ship and order the Coast Guard to take them to safety. You know that's where you're needed."

Holden reluctantly nodded then kissed Jackie quickly but passionately on the lips. He pulled back and searched her eyes while touching her face.

"I'm coming back for you," he informed her. "If you know what's good for you, you'd better be alive and in one piece."

She smiled and nodded. "Copy that."

Holden returned to the raft and helped push it into the surf with Sid and Bill's help. All three jumped into the raft. Holden started the motor, saluted Jackie, and raced the launch for the Coast Guard ship. Jackie returned to the helicopter, started it, and remained grounded while watching the raft approach the ship. Zack remained focused on any intruders attempting to impede the rescue. As the raft neared the ship, a shot was fired into the water several yards before it. Holden cut the motor, stood up in the raft, and held his badge in the air. The men by the railing hesitated, looked through their binoculars to see what he held, and then exchanged concerned looks. The captain of the ship seemed to consider his options then motioned them to continue their approach.

Back on the beach. Jackie saw the raft dock with the ship and allowed a sigh of relief escape. She flipped several switches and gripped the control while looking back at Zack.

"Time for an aerial assault," she announced.

Zack grinned with childlike glee. "I love it when you talk dirty to me."

§

Bogart rested his head against the hall wall while panting from overexertion. He eyed Kirk who leaned against the wall alongside him. Kirk remained focused and moderately annoyed with Bogart as usual. He didn't bother looking at his bumbling partner.

"You know," Bogart announced to Kirk while innocently raising his brows. "I'm a little uncomfortable with this 'no taking prisoners' ideology. I mean; it's a little dark, don't you think?"

"Shut up," Kirk snarled without looking at Bogart and maintained his fixed stare.

"Yeah, shut up," a man dressed in black combat gear snarled and punched Bogart across the mouth.

Bogart and Kirk remained against the wall as a man with an assault rifle stood before them. The second man, who had punched Bogart, flexed his sore hand and gave his prisoner an irritated look.

"Tell us where Lindsey Cicco is, and we'll take you out quick and painless," the man announced then flashed a Bowie knife already stained with blood. "Or we can do this the fun way; one cut at a time."

Bogart stared at the bloodstained knife with concern then eyed the deranged man holding it. Bogart's brows suddenly raised in a slightly arrogant manner.

"Wow, that's a little dark," Bogart remarked. "You must be Makar's answer to Zack."

Kirk just rolled his eyes in an attempt to ignore Bogart and the trouble his mouth was about to bring upon them. "I'm *never* being paired with you again," Kirk muttered under his breath.

Bogart sighed, glanced at Kirk, and shook his head. "Why do you always have to be so negative?" he demanded then eyed the man with the knife and smiled charmingly. "You have to forgive the big guy. He's been under a lot of stress lately. It's been months since he's gotten laid."

Kirk slowly turned his head as his mouth hung open. He eyed Bogart with surprise and annoyance. "What the hell kind of stupid comment is that?" he suddenly lashed out. "Why would you even say something like that? My God! You're like a five-year-old on a sugar rush."

Bogart again looked at the man with the knife. "What did I tell you?" he announced and grinned. "Cranky."

The man punched Bogart in the abdomen causing him to gasp and double over.

Kirk casually looked away. "I swear; you enjoy this," he remarked to his teammate. "You must be a masochist or something."

Bogart remained doubled over and gasped in pain. "If there's an easier way out of these situations, I haven't found one."

As Bogart straightened, he grabbed the man's wrist and twisted it to keep the knife from slashing him then kneed him in the groin. As the man doubled over, Bogart kicked him in the face. He flew backward into the second man who was about to shoot them. Both men were knocked down to the corridor floor. Kirk casually reclaimed his weapon and shot both men in the head. Bogart cringed then shook his head while glaring at Kirk.

"We need to deal with your anger issues," Bogart remarked.

"Be happy I don't shoot you," Kirk muttered.

Several gunshots struck the wall near their heads. Bogart ducked while Kirk threw himself to the floor and sat up firing at the men down the corridor. Bogart grabbed his AK-47 assault rifle, scurried past Kirk, and ducked into the stairwell. He popped back out and fired several rounds down the corridor allowing Kirk time to retreat into the stairwell with him. They ran up the stairs to the next landing as the two men entered the stairwell behind them. Kirk and Bogart immediately took cover and fired over the railing to the landing below. Both men darted back out the door.

Kirk ran up the stairs after Bogart. Bogart threw his back against the wall alongside the door then eyed Kirk, who nodded. He pulled open the door while Kirk stepped into the doorway prepared to fire. When they didn't see anyone, they hurried onto the ninth floor deck. The sounds of a helicopter seemed to echo around the entire area surrounding the ship. The constant thumping of the rotor blades turning sounded more like white noise against the faint sounds of gunshots from inside the ship.

Bogart took a moment to look over the railing in the direction of the Coast Guard's ship. It was sailing away from the action. All that remained was the inflatable motorized raft that seemed to be heading their way, although it was hard to tell if it was manned or empty. Kirk ran along the deck and paused near the first hidden corner. Bogart hurried after him and kept watch on their backside. As Kirk rounded the corner, a man suddenly appeared as if out of nowhere, grabbed the assault rifle, and punched Kirk in the mouth.

Kirk was barely fazed by the relatively hard hit. He tore the rifle from the man's hands and struck him in the face with the butt of the rifle. The man dropped to the deck floor. The stairway door flew open, and another armed man appeared on deck behind them. Bogart fired several shots at the man, who immediately took cover and returned fire. Bogart retreated around the corner with Kirk. Two more men appeared from the opposite direction and fired at them.

Bogart made a face and groaned. "Ah, hell," he muttered as he darted for cover alongside the pool bar with Kirk. Bogart kept his back to Kirk's and had his weapon aimed at the corner. "We're about to have company up our ass."

They heard the sound of several men running down the metal steps just behind Bogart.

"Yeah, that's what was missing," Bogart announced with a defeated sigh.

The men on the steps converged on them along with the man from the stairwell, aiming their weapons at Bogart and Kirk. Kirk spun with his weapon raised, prepared to make his last stand. The helicopter suddenly appeared not far from them. The men in front and behind looked at the hovering helicopter and saw Zack's grin as he manned the machine gun. The massive weapon fired dozens of rounds, blasting the men several times each and nearly cutting them in half despite their bulletproof vests. Bogart shielded his head and screamed while Kirk watched with a cheap grin on his face.

The helicopter buzzed away with Zack screaming joyful profanities. Bogart lowered his arms and sighed with relief as he stood to join Kirk. Kirk watched the helicopter disappear around the ship and grinned. One of the wounded men appeared alongside the bar with a gun in his hand aimed at Kirk. Bogart saw him first.

"Duck," Bogart cried out.

Kirk instinctively ducked as Bogart spun into a less than graceful roundhouse kick meant to go over Kirk's head. He struck Kirk in the side of the head and threw him into the man with the gun. The man with the gun hit the bar. Kirk straightened while clutching his head, saw the man against the bar, and punched him in the face. He snatched the gun from the dazed man and shot him between the eyes. Bogart grimaced as Kirk turned toward him with a look of rage on his face while gritting his teeth.

"That didn't exactly go as planned," Bogart remarked defensively.

Kirk aimed the gun at Bogart's face. "Kick me again, and I'll shoot you!"

"I've practiced with Jackie, I swear," Bogart protested. "It's not my fault you're taller than she is."

§

As the helicopter made another sweep of the ship, Zack fired the machine gun and laughed while Cicco and Makar's men scattered like bugs from bullets raining down on them. Any man in black combat uniforms or gray camouflage was fair game as far as Zack was concerned. Jackie eyed the flashing light on the control panel.

"Playtime is over," Jackie informed Zack. "I need to set her down. We're running low on fuel."

Zack frowned and eyed the excessive amount of shells still in the feed bin. "Just another two hundred rounds," he pleaded with her.

"No, I'm putting her down," Jackie insisted. "Save those shells for a rainy day."

"Sure," he scoffed. "When's the last time you ever flew on a rainy day?"

Jackie set the helicopter down on the bridge deck and immediately shut it down. She wanted to conserve just enough fuel to get them to the abandoned airfield if necessary. Zack remained behind the machine gun until Jackie was safely out of the pilot's seat with her assault rifle in hand. He then joined her and indicated the location from which the heaviest gunfire was heard. They followed the sound of rapid gunfire coming from a level below them. Jackie and Zack slipped through the back door to the theater and darted backstage. They patiently assessed the situation. Dexter's men were in a shootout with Makar's men. It was a temptation to let them kill one another, but it was possible they needed Dexter's army in the event that Cicco's men couldn't take on Makar's assassins.

"I can't believe we're actually helping Dexter's men," Zack remarked with annoyance. "Is this the 'enemy of my enemy is my friend' bullshit?"

"No, this is picking a side," Jackie replied. "And, currently, Dexter's men are the lesser of two evils."

"Take off your Ross colored glasses, Jacklyn dear," Zack announced and raised his brows. "We don't pick sides. We sit on the sidelines and wait for the last man-standing scenario. Then we waste the last man standing."

"I appreciate the frightening insight into that devious mind of yours," she replied. "But I think we should do this old school."

He stared at her a moment then shook his head. "I knew marrying a fed would throw off your moral compass," Zack announced. "It's like I don't even know you anymore. I have right; you have left."

Both stood up and fired across the room taking out two of Makar's men. They returned to the safety of backstage and waited out the return gunfire splintering the wood near their heads.

Jackie glared at him taking offense to the comment. "I haven't changed," she insisted. "I have no idea who you think I used to be, but you're mistaken."

"I'm not mistaken," Zack snarled back. "Duck."

Jackie crouched into a tight ball while Zack fired over her head at an approaching man. She straightened without even looking at the man she assumed he'd shot behind her.

"I think all that napalm has finally gone to your head," Jackie insisted and checked the magazine in her assault rifle. "Last week, you called me Katya. Although I've never had the pleasure of meeting your Russian spy booty call, I doubt we look much alike." She tossed her assault rifle aside. It clattered when it hit the stage. "I'm out."

Jackie removed the handgun from the back of her pants and stepped out from behind backstage. She fired two shots, winged another man, and then returned backstage with Zack.

"Hey, there's a lot going on inside my head," he informed her. "You can't expect me to get your name right every time. You called me Monroe three times last month, and you didn't hear me bitching even though I had every right to bitch." He slung his rifle over his shoulder and grabbed onto a rope near them. "Seriously? Monroe? We're *nothing* alike."

Zack swiftly climbed the rope and sprang onto the catwalk above the stage. Jackie frowned and leaned her back against the wall. Zack fired nearly a dozen shots from his position on the catwalk while Jackie casually picked dirt out from under her nails. When the firing ceased, she poked her head out from backstage. Dexter's men were dumbfounded while staring at Makar's men lying dead where they had been seeking shelter. Zack leaped onto the rope, slid down it, and jumped the last few feet near Jackie. He gave her an annoyed look.

"If you're finished doing your nails," he announced in an arrogant tone, "can we end this?"

Chapter Forty-one

Sal walked across the main living area of the two-story suite and looked around while Mac swung the banister and ran up the open staircase to the second floor. She checked both bedrooms while Sal checked the downstairs bathroom and butler's pantry. Mac was heard rustling around upstairs then hurried down the stairs with her assault rifle cradled in her arms and a concerned look on her face.

"This is the right suite, isn't it?" Mac almost demanded as she approached the bottom of the stairs.

"This is where Lindsey was told to wait for us," Sal insisted then raised his brow. "We're in the right suite; Lindsey didn't wait for us."

"Where the hell would she go and why?" Mac snarled and shook her head. "Typical spoiled brat. It's no wonder everyone wants her dead."

Sal frowned and attempted the hand radio. "Jackie, do you copy?" There was no response, which wasn't too surprising. "Anyone out there copy?"

They heard gunfire through the hand radio followed by Bogart's voice. "Sort of in the middle of something, Sal," Bogart announced. "Make it quick."

"Our little chick flew the coop," Sal announced into the hand radio. "We're at her last known location, but she's not here."

They heard the main door unlock by the non-electronic, master key. Mac and Sal exchanged looks.

"That's one of us, right?" Sal asked. "We're the only one with master keys."

Mac immediately aimed her weapon at the door. "Doesn't mean someone couldn't have acquired one from somewhere else."

As the door opened, Mac motioned Sal for the stairs. They ran up the staircase to the second floor and dashed into the first bedroom as someone entered the suite below. The mostly gold toned master bedroom had a large bed with the frilly bedding still on it, a walk-in closet, and a private, master bath. The room would have been impressive if they weren't busy fighting to survive. Mac stood to the side of the partially open door holding her assault rifle while Sal held his semiautomatic. They heard voices speaking in Russian then the sound of one set of footfalls coming up the steps.

"If we make any sound, it'll alert the others downstairs," Sal whispered to Mac.

Mac nodded with understanding, handed him the rifle, and motioned him to the closet. "I've got this." She flattened herself against the wall behind the partially open door.

Sal hurried across the room and darted into the closet. The bedroom door was slowly pushed open with the barrel of an assault rifle, making a distinct scraping sound. One of Makar's men entered the room. He was about to peer behind the door when there was movement from the closet. He headed for the closet door and threw it open.

Sal held his hands up and smiled. "Hi there," he announced almost cheerfully.

Mac leaped out from behind the door. The man was alerted to the sound and spun around just in time for Mac to strike him in the throat. He gasped and wheezed. Mac snatched the assault rifle from his hand, spun into a roundhouse kick, and struck him in the face. He flew backward for the closet door. Sal gasped and leaped between the man and the fragile louver door. He caught the flying man and cushioned the hit. Sal breathed a sigh of relief and gently lay the man down on the bedroom floor. Mac eyed the M416 assault rifle affixed with a silencer and grinned.

"Time to clean house," Mac announced and hurried from the room.

She approached the railing overlooking the suite below and scanned the room through the rifle sights. She saw the first man step out of the butler's pantry. Mac caught him in her sights and fired the nearly silent shot. The man went down, striking the wall with a little more noise than she'd hoped he'd make. Another man appeared from the kitchen, saw his fallen man, and immediately aimed his weapon around the room. By the time he scanned the upper floor; Mac had him in her sights and pulled the trigger. Another nearly silent shot took down the last man. When no one else came into view, Mac motioned for Sal to follow. He slung the rifle over his shoulder and revealed a baseball bat he'd apparently found in the closet.

"This may come in handy," Sal announced while grinning almost boyishly.

Mac eyed him with the bat and raised a curious brow but didn't comment. He looked a little too at home with the baseball bat and not in the former, little league player sort of way. She led him to the corridor door located on the upper level, which would bring them out on deck nine.

§

The spa and sauna lobby consisted of mostly marble and glass with hardwood floors throughout. Plush sofas and relaxing chairs were positioned around the lobby. An elegant marble desk was located between two sets of doors, which led to the various spa facilities. Gil and Monroe ran into the spa and toward the front desk with Darth eagerly following them. They slid across the floor and rolled behind the front desk. Gil cast his assault rifle aside.

"I'm out," Gil announced with a defeated sigh and removed his semiautomatic from his shoulder holster.

Monroe ejected his empty magazine and skillfully inserted a full one. "I'm down to my last magazine," Monroe informed Gil.

When they heard noise in the corridor, Darth attempted to place his front paws on the desk to look over it. Gil pulled him back down to keep him hidden.

"Stealth mode, boy," he informed the dog.

Darth immediately crouched down, remaining unusually still and focused. They heard the sound of running feet as multiple gunmen entered the spa. Gil held up his hand revealing four fingers. Monroe nodded as if agreeing to his count of men based on the sounds of running feet. Monroe then spun his finger around and pointed to the door to their left. Gil frowned, spun his finger around and pointed to the door to the right. Monroe rolled his eyes then spun his finger around, pointed left with added vigor, and gave Gil the middle finger. Darth tilted his head while watching the men gesture their next move. Gil reluctantly nodded then listened to the sounds of footfalls as the pursuing men walked more cautiously across the spa lobby.

Four men dressed in black combat gear carrying assault rifles dispersed across the large spa lobby. Two approached the desk and the doors located on either side of it. The remaining two headed in the opposite direction, checking both sets of balcony doors in case the men had fled the room onto the large balcony. Gil and Monroe suddenly popped up from behind the desk and shot the two men closest to it. By the time the other two men had turned, they were already under fire and were forced to take cover behind strategically placed sofas. Gil, Monroe, and Darth escaped through the door to the left.

Gil slammed and locked the door behind him. Thankfully, there had been a lock. When he turned around, he stared at the long corridor containing doors to the left along the entire wall. His expression immediately dropped at their deteriorating situation.

"Oh, this is not good," Gil scoffed then glared at Monroe, who frowned while running fingers through his hair. "We should have gone through the door to the right."

"Maybe these doors lead somewhere," Monroe announced and opened the first door.

He stared at the individual massage room, which was set up with two massage tables, for couple's massages, and a private whirlpool tub.

Monroe frowned and shut the door. "Okay, they don't," he replied. "We have to move."

Darth trotted along the fancy corridor toward the back. The two men could be heard outside the door attempting to break it down. Monroe and Gil ran after Darth. Toward the back of the corridor was the beauty parlor, which contained four hair wash stations and four chairs before large mirrors. The room was decorated in various shades of pink. Not surprising, there was no exit. The corridor continued toward the right and past several dressing rooms. When they reached the other side, they discovered another corridor with only four doors, which were open. They hurried along the corridor, keeping their weapons lowered but ready.

As they looked into each room, they discovered a steam bath, sauna, whirlpool baths, and a relaxation room. Each contained hardwood floors, glass, and marble as well. None offered a way onto deck or much shelter in the event of a firefight. Gil and Monroe could hear gunfire coming from the door on the other side, which meant the men were shooting out the lock. Monroe ran into the whirlpool bath area and darted behind one of three above ground whirlpools. The water in the tubs had long since dried leaving behind a greenish black residue. Gil and Darth took position behind the open door.

Gil signaled to the dog. Darth immediately went down on his command and remained fixated on the door the same as Gil. They heard men moving within the hallway, although they were attempting to make little noise. Darth's head tilted to the sounds of approaching men. He lifted his body as if preparing to attack, alerting Gil to the closeness of the men. Gil noted the dog's body language and nodded to Monroe crouched behind the whirlpool.

As the first man entered the room with his weapon raised, Darth twitched awaiting the signal to attack. Gil held his hand out near his thigh to keep the dog from moving. Darth didn't take his eyes off the man. The first man walked toward the collection of whirlpool tubs as the second man entered the room. The second man turned toward the open door to look behind it when Monroe poked his head above the whirlpool tub and shot the first man, hitting him in the chest. The bulletproof vest prevented him from fatally injuring the man but was enough to knock him back a step.

The second man immediately fired at Monroe, who was already ducking down. Gil gave the signal. Darth leaped onto the second man and grabbed him by the arm with the gun. As the man attempted to shake the dog, Gil fired two shots striking the man in the head. The first man spun around at the same time and was about to shoot the dog. Monroe sprang up from behind the whirlpool tub and fired another shot, hitting the first man in the head as well. Darth jumped away from the fallen men. Another gunshot came close to hitting the dog and struck the floor. Darth ran across the room, leaped over the empty whirlpool tub, and joined Monroe behind it. Gil shoved his body against the door and struck the man, knocking him off balance and slightly dazing him.

As Gil stepped around the corner with his gun raised, the man recovered and struck Gil in the abdomen with his assault rifle. Gil doubled over and fell to one knee. As the man flipped the weapon in his hand prepared to shoot Gil, Darth leaped across the whirlpool tub and ran for the bad guy. The man saw the dog and aimed his weapon at Darth instead. As he fired, Darth jumped onto Gil's back, avoiding the bullet, and leaped from Gil's back for the armed man. He sailed through the air for the man, who was now unable to aim his weapon, and sank his teeth into his face as he rode him to the floor.

The man screamed and attempted to fling the snarling dog off him, but Darth had a hold of his face and refused to let go. Gil sprang to his feet and shouted at Darth in German. Darth released the man's shredded, bloody face. The man reached for his holstered semiautomatic despite his condition. Gil raised his first and shot the man in the head. Monroe slowly straightened from behind the whirlpool tub, stared at the bloodied man, and grimaced at the sight.

"I'm so glad that dog is on our side," Monroe remarked while shaking his head.

§

Mac and Sal hurried along the deck six corridor while keeping close to the wall. Mac discarded both assault rifles, since she was out of ammo, but she still had her semiautomatic. Even that only had a few rounds left. Sal had given up what few bullets he had left in his semiautomatic to allow Mac a few extra rounds. He seemed confident with his recently acquired baseball bat as his weapon of choice. They were still on their mission to find Lindsey, but it wasn't looking good. If she were hiding, she could be anywhere onboard. As they neared the lobby area from a deck above, they could hear a commotion coming from the lobby below. Mac stopped Sal and quietly approached the railing while staying out of sight. One of Makar's men punched Conner, knocking him against the front desk. She could see two armed men patrolling the area while keeping watch.

"You're going to call out your girlfriend," the man insisted. "If you don't, there won't be enough of you for her to identify."

"Fuck you," Conner cried out as blood sprayed from his mouth.

The man punched him in the abdomen, doubling him over, then laughed and looked around the lobby. "I know you're out there Lindsey," the man called out. "Come on out or your boyfriend will start losing body parts."

Mac cursed and returned to the corridor where Sal remained with his baseball bat. He stared at her with concern.

"Who do they have?" he asked.

"They have Conner," Mac informed him and looked back to the lobby opening. "That must mean she's around here somewhere. I don't think she strayed far. If she cares enough about him, she's going to turn herself in to stop them from killing him."

"I think you've misjudged her," Sal announced with a mildly defeated look on his face then raised his brows in question. "Do you honestly think she'd trade her life for his?"

Mac seemed to consider the comment and frowned. "Hard to say," she replied then drew a deep breath and stared at Sal.

"If I draw the others away, do you think you can handle the creep roughing up Conner?"

Sal eyed his baseball bat then casually swung it. A strange smile crossed his face. "Wouldn't be the first time I ruined someone's day with a baseball bat," he informed her.

"Well then," she announced and returned the grin. "Batter up. I'll wait until you're in position. When the others give chase, take care of the goon and get Conner out of here. Don't wait for me."

Sal nodded. "I'd tell you not to do anything stupid--" He then offered a tiny smile and shrugged.

"I know," she replied. "Doing something stupid is the story of my life." She slapped his arm, gave him a stern look, and pointed a warning finger at him. "You don't have three strikes. Don't miss."

Sal nodded then ran back down the hall and entered the nearby stairwell. Mac slipped along the interior hallway one level above the lobby and kept out of sight of the men patrolling. With what few shots she had left, she could possibly take out all three men but not before they'd kill Conner. She needed to divert them away, and she knew what she had to do. Mac stood near the glass elevator shaft not far from the elegant staircase to the lobby. It didn't take long for her to see Sal lurking within the lower level corridor. He was in position. The moment he had his eyes on Conner near the front desk, Mac waited for the man to punch Conner again then made her move. She poked her head around the corner from the floor above while keeping partially hidden.

"No, stop," she cried out in her best, high-pitched screech while only allowing them a glimpse of her. "Please don't hurt him!"

"It's her," the man shouted while pointing toward the glass elevator shaft on the sixth floor. "Get her!"

As if perfectly planned, both men ran for the elegant staircase and charged up them. They ran after the woman they assumed was Lindsey.

"Lindsey," Conner cried out. "Run!"

Mac took his words to heart and ran for the nearby corridor. She kept just far enough ahead of the men to keep them from shooting her or realizing she was a decoy. As the men vanished into the corridor after the imposter, Sal entered the lobby not far from the front desk. The man in black combat gear again hit Conner across the face driving him to his knees.

"I'd kill you, but I'm afraid I may still have some use for you," the man announced while shaking his sore hand. "I actually feel sorry for you. If she didn't have feelings for you, I wouldn't need to torture you to get what I want." He removed a gun from his shoulder holster and aimed it at Conner's head. "Get up. We have work to do."

"Allow me to change your mind," Sal announced from nearby.

The man spun around with his gun in his hand. The baseball bat struck the gun, launching it across the lobby. The man attempted to lunge for Sal. Sal swung hard and with precision, striking the man in the head, crushing his skull with one blow. The man hit the floor and didn't move. Blood quickly collected around his head. Sal placed the bloodied baseball bat over his shoulder and eyed Conner.

"Son, you may want to reconsider some of your choices in life," Sal casually announced. "Let's get your girlfriend and get the hell out of here before something else happens."

"Those men are chasing her," Conner practically cried out. "We have to help her."

"That wasn't Lindsey," Sal informed him. "That's a girl with a death wish and a lot of aggression issues. We need to go."

Chapter Forty-two

Mac ran into the ship's movie theater, which was a much smaller version of a regular movie theater with comfortable reclining chairs. She ran down the tacky, colorful carpet and dove into a row of seats more than halfway down the small theater. She lay on her side with her gun firmly clutched between her hands and listened for the approaching men who hadn't been far behind her. With limited ammo, she didn't need the two men coming at her from opposite ends. Despite the carpeting, their movement could be heard on the moderately crunchy carpet. The dried carpet padding also worked to her advantage. There was just enough space beneath the seats for her to see their feet as they got closer.

She drew a deep breath, shut her eyes, and exhaled softly. Her eyes suddenly popped open. Mac leaped to her knees and fired at the first man over the seats, using the seats as protection from return gunfire. She had been aiming for his head, since their body armor had used up enough of her ammunition as it was, and missed striking him in the shoulder. It was enough to stop him briefly, leaving her with the second man, who immediately shot at her. Mac ducked beneath the seats and allowed them to take the brunt of the gunfire. She crawled along the aisle and away from the shooting, but her diversion wouldn't buy her much time. She reached the end of the aisle as both men reached her aisle.

Mac gasped when she saw them and rolled along the wall aisle to avoid their gunfire. She was once again out of their line of sight. Mac again popped up and fired at them. She grazed the first man's cheek, stunning him enough that he clutched his face and fell to his knees from the hit. The second man with the injured shoulder fired several rounds at her and clicked empty. Mac heard the familiar sound and again popped up, taking a little more time to line up her shot carefully. She had him dead in her sights and squeezed the trigger. Her gun clicked empty as well almost startling her. Mac cursed, tossed her gun aside, and ran for the stage.

While the second man recovered from his grazed face shot, the first man ran for the stage from the center aisle. Mac leaped onto the stage before the movie screen, hoping to make it to the nearest exit. The first man caught up with her, leaped onto stage, and tackled her to the wooden floor. Much to his surprise, Mac rolled with the tackle and threw him off her. As he rolled across the stage, Mac rolled and then sprang to her feet. The man also leaped to his feet and immediately lunged for her.

When he got his first good look at her, he was obviously surprised she wasn't Lindsey, but he was already committed to the charge. His second surprise came when Mac didn't attempt to run from him but instead faced him. She could almost see the confusion in his eyes, but he came at her swinging anyway. Mac threw herself to the stage floor and swung her legs for his, knocking his feet out from beneath him. His forward momentum caused him to sail through the air over her and land face first. Mac sprang to her feet just in time to miss the bullet that splintered the stage where she had been positioned. She threw herself into a roll and flipped off the stage as the second shot struck the floor. She ducked behind the front row of seats then heard the familiar empty click.

Mac slowly straightened and eyed the man while raising her brow along with a devious grin. "Things are about to get very interesting," she announced and approached the man with an arrogant swagger.

As she got closer, the man removed a Bowie knife from his boot and held it in line with his wrist while clenching his fist on the handle. Mac paused a few feet before him and took a fighting stance. Her grin was slightly unsettling. The man dabbed the blood from the bullet graze on his face and eyed her.

"You're going to pay for that, bitch," he announced while sneering at her.

"Make me, you big pussy," she announced almost humored by the threat.

The man lunged at her while swinging the knife. Mac ducked the slashing knife while punching her fist upward into his abdomen. As he went for the counter swing, Mac again ducked. She then leaped onto the arm of the aisle seat and immediately kicked out, striking him in the face without losing her balance on the arm of the chair. The man flew backward into the end seat on the opposite side of the aisle. The knife flew from his hand and landed on the carpeted aisle. He straightened but didn't have time to go for the knife.

Mac leaped from the arm of the chair while spinning into a roundhouse kick and knocked him to the floor between the seats. He groaned and picked himself up more slowly, capturing his discarded knife as he straightened. The man from the stage charged Mac in the aisle. She turned just in time to see him running for her. He intended to tackle her with a lot of force. Mac leaped into a high, roundhouse kick and struck him in the face. With his forward momentum and speed, his head snapped back, and he dropped to the carpeted floor. She didn't have to check. By the position of his neck, he was obviously dead.

Mac spun back for the man she'd knocked into the row of seats. Not surprising, he was already on his feet and slashed his knife at her. She cried out and attempted to block the blow meant to impale her in the chest. She knew she'd catch it in the forearm instead, but at least she'd still be alive. A gunshot echoed through the theater. Mac gasped waiting for the sharp, hot sting of the bullet. When it didn't come, she looked at the man with the knife. He stood immobile with his knife still clutched in his hand near her. Blood seeped from the small hole between his eyes. His eyes rolled back as he collapsed against the seats then fell to the floor.

Mac turned with surprise to see who had saved her from a possibly fatal stabbing. Corbin aimed the gun at her from where he stood several yards away and limped toward her. His look was annoyed. Why he chose to shoot his own man rather than her was a mystery. Perhaps he wanted to kill her himself. Corbin stopped a couple of feet from her while keeping the gun aimed at her face.

"I should have put you down when I had the chance back at the institute," he snarled while glaring at her. "It would have been the smart thing to do."

"You wouldn't be the first man who wanted me dead," she casually replied. "What stopped you now?"

He frowned and lowered the gun. "I'm getting sentimental in my old age."

Mac released the breath she'd been holding although she didn't let him see it. "I don't know where Lindsey is," she informed him. "I was just trying to keep your men from bashing in that poor boy's brains."

"Did you ever question your loyalty?" he asked while studying her.

"Every damned day," she muttered while flexing her fists by her side. She was preparing for the worst while hoping for the best. Mac eyed him with a curious look. "Having second thoughts about Makar?"

"His orders were to kill everyone onboard," Corbin informed her and frowned at the thought. "He's not protecting his interests. He's going for maximum carnage to make his point." He drew a deep breath and sighed. "I knew if I ever defected it'd be over a woman. Of course, that'll probably be what kills me too."

Mac managed a smile and snorted a soft laugh. "Yeah, you're probably right," she announced. "I wouldn't have thought twice about killing you."

"You're welcome," Corbin remarked while chuckling then indicated the exit by the stage door. "You should probably hurry. Makar wasn't far behind me. He's going to be pissed as it is."

Mac smiled with understanding and nodded. She headed for the door then paused and looked back at Makar's handsome right-hand man.

"Hey," she announced and grinned almost seductively. "If we get out of this with all our body parts intact, I have no plans for the weekend."

He chuckled and returned the grin. "I'll look you up."

She flashed a smile then turned and hurried for the exit door. Mac left through the side door and disappeared. She was only gone a moment before Makar entered the movie theater. He saw his men laid out on the floor then looked around the small theater.

"Where'd she go?" Makar demanded while approaching his right-hand man.

Corbin frowned and returned his semiautomatic to his shoulder holster. He turned with little emotion to face his enraged boss.

"She was already gone by the time I got here," he announced and approached his boss.

"She got away?" Makar repeated with anger while glaring at his man. "I just heard the gunshot. How could she have gotten away?"

"It wasn't Lindsey," Corbin informed him. "I didn't think it was important wasting time chasing after some random woman."

"Random woman?" Makar suddenly snarled. "The same attractive woman from the institution in Florida? That random woman?"

Corbin shook his head with irritation. "Don't invent something that isn't there, Makar," he boldly announced. "I've met plenty of attractive women, and none have ever meant anything. Can we just concentrate on the woman we flew all the way out here to find?"

Corbin walked past Makar without further comment. A gunshot rang out, echoing through the theater, and forcing Corbin to stop in the aisle suddenly. He looked down and touched his bleeding abdomen. Corbin snatched his gun from shoulder holster and spun to face his boss. Makar still had his gun in his hand and fired another shot, this time hitting Corbin in the forehead. Corbin's head snapped back, and he fell to the floor. Makar replaced his gun and shook his head while frowning.

"It always ends that way, doesn't it?" Makar announced as Corbin's blood pooled on the carpeted aisle. "Men always losing their heads over some woman who means absolutely nothing to them."

Makar replaced his semiautomatic to his shoulder holster, stepped over Corbin's body as his blood spilled out onto the carpet, and headed for the main door.

Chapter Forty-three

Sal followed Conner into the children's playroom located not far from the indoor pool on deck nine. The playroom contained an area of miniature coloring tables, a large ball pit, and an indoor playground with swings and monkey bars. Conner hurried across the room and looked around while Sal secured the door and kept a tight grip on his bloodstained baseball bat.

"Lindsey," Conner called out in a hushed whisper. "Lindsey, it's me."

There was no response. Conner frantically checked several areas including the ball pit, in case she was hiding beneath the colorful balls.

"Lindsey?" Conner scanned the room from where he stood, appeared concerned, and looked back at Sal. "I don't understand where she could be. We were supposed to meet here if anything happened." Horror crossed his face. "They must have caught her!"

Conner attempted to bolt past Sal for the closed playroom door. Sal placed his hand out and stopped Conner from rushing out.

"I think you'd better slow down a moment and take time to think clearly," Sal announced in a calm tone while staring into the young man's eyes. "Don't go off half-cocked. That's how stupid people get killed."

"But she--"

Sal shut his eyes and shook his head. Conner attempted to relax and drew a deep breath. Once he was calm, he met Sal's gaze.

"We have to find her," Conner announced in a slightly calmer tone. "Everyone out there wants to kill her. She's in danger."

"Yeah, about that," Sal remarked while studying him. "Why is that?" It seemed like more of a statement than a question.

"Her husband tried to kill her," Conner reminded him. "She was forced to kill him in self-defense. Now Sebastian's father wants revenge on her. We went over all of this before." His brows rose with concern. "There's no time to explain. If he gets ahold of her--"

"And what about these Russian guys with the big toys and the long reach?" Sal questioned with a curious look. "Why are they so hell-bent on capturing her? Seems to me they want her alive, but they're willing to kill anyone--" His eyes widened with a serious look. "And I mean *anyone* whom she's even come into contact with." Sal studied Conner and tilted his head as his eyes narrowed. "Why is that? What did she do to piss off the big boys? Who are they even?"

"I don't know," he replied while vigorously shaking his head. "She said she'd explain everything after we'd gotten through this."

Sal groaned and finally looked at Conner. He placed his hand on Conner's shoulder and turned fatherly. "Son, you're being played."

Conner stared at him with surprise then turned defensive. "What? You're out of your mind," he protested. "You don't even know Lindsey."

"No, I don't," Sal replied and adjusted his small glasses, "but my former employee said she did. If you combine what Mac told me with what Cicco told me then add in what Makar told Mac, you have one hell of a Mata Hari."

The young man's eyes widened with horror and surprise. "What are you talking about?" Conner practically demanded. "What's that supposed to mean?"

"It means you have a beautiful young woman playing multiple angles for some secret agenda," Sal casually informed him. "Would you like to know why Lindsey isn't where you agreed to meet? She isn't here, because she knew you were caught. She knew the sort of people who were after her, and

she knew they would torture you into giving up her location."
He raised his brows knowingly. "And that's why she's not
here."

"Just because she feared I'd crack under pressure, that
doesn't mean she's playing me or has some secret agenda,"
Conner insisted as his eyes narrowed in anger. "You're
comparing her to a traitorous double agent. She's not. She's a
scared, innocent girl."

Sal sighed and shook his head. "You really don't see it, do
you?" he remarked with a look of defeat. "Answer me one
question, son. The night her husband allegedly tried to kill her;
did you have an alibi?"

Conner stared at Sal with some surprise. His mind was
obviously reeling. "Are you accusing me of killing her husband
for her?"

"No, I'm asking if you had an alibi," he reiterated. "Yes
or no?"

Conner folded his arms across his chest while glaring at Sal.
"No, I was waiting at the park for her to show up that
evening," he informed him. "I waited for a couple of hours.
When she didn't show up, I became worried."

"And you called her?"

"No, I was afraid to call her in case her husband had come
home," he informed him. "I never called her. She always
called me."

"And the night her husband died," Sal pressed. "Did she
call you? Did she call crying that her husband attacked her and
what she had to do to stop him?" Sal raised his brows. "Did
she beg you to come over? Did she ask you to help her dispose
of the body because she feared her father-in-law would kill her?
Did she tell you that she feared the police would suspect it
wasn't self-defense because of your affair?"

Conner couldn't take his eyes off Sal. His stunned look
indicated everything he asked was exactly what had happened the
night Sebastian Cicco died. His look then turned harsh and
angry.

"I don't know what you're suggesting," Conner remarked
while shifting uncomfortably. "It *did* happen that way. That's
the truth."

"I'm not suggesting that you're lying. I'm suggesting she set you up to take the fall," Sal informed him with brutal honesty. "I'm suggesting she plotted her husband's death weeks earlier, made amends with her cheating ex-boyfriend, and planned everything to make it look like he killed her husband in a jealous rage."

Conner stared at Sal a moment with his mouth hanging open. He then turned defensive and immediately shook his head. "No, she wouldn't do that," he protested then fidgeted. "Yes, she asked me to help her remove the body when she called around midnight. I refused to do that and convinced her we needed to go to the police. It would have worked, but her father-in-law sent men to kill her before I got there."

"No, her plan backfired when her father sent Whiskey Tango Foxtrot to her rescue," Sal insisted while raising his brows. "They foiled her perfect plan to frame you for her husband's murder, and she had to improvise just like she's improvising now. Cicco said two of Sebastian's guards were killed as well as two other men that he didn't know. I'm betting those other men were working for Lindsey. I suspect she hired them to eliminate you so she could frame you. Unfortunately, for her, Makar's men showed up first and killed her men. Face it, son; you are collateral damage. She only needed you around to save her ass and take the fall for what she'd done. Things went sideways, people were converging upon her, and she needed to flee. This time; we're all taking the fall for her."

Conner vigorously shook his head. "No, you're wrong," he protested. "Cicco's men were holding her prisoner in Sebastian's house until he could get there and torture her over his son's death. You're wrong about all of it."

"Maybe I am," Sal replied with little care. "You say she called you around midnight with the news of her dead husband, huh?"

Conner nodded.

Sal drew a deep breath then sighed and frowned. "Bad news, son. Her husband had been dead several hours by that time. Her father showed up at my mansion hours earlier expressing his concerns."

Conner stared at Sal with a look of disbelief. He seemed uncertain how to respond.

"I'm going to offer you a word of advice," Sal announced while raising his brows. "When and if you confront her, make sure you're not alone with her. Because if I'm right, she'll cut out your heart without thinking twice."

They heard someone approaching. Sal hurried Conner behind the ball pit. Cicco, Dawg, and one of his hired men entered the playroom and looked around. As the three men got closer to their hiding spot, Sal clutched his baseball bat and was about to move out from behind the ball pit to take his shot. All three men were suddenly alerted to something and bolted across the room as if evading a predator. Dexter and one of his henchmen darted into the room and fired at Cicco and his men. Conner and Sal remained hidden behind the ball pit; although it was possible they'd be discovered if the shootout continued too long.

Dexter's man took a bullet to the head, hit the jungle gym behind him, and fell against the small slide. Dexter attempted to return fire, but his gun clicked empty. He saw his dead henchman's discarded gun just a few feet from him. Unfortunately, the sound of his empty gun had been loud enough to send Cicco and his men charging across the room. Dexter lunged for the weapon. Dawg fired his own gun, shooting Dexter in the arm while preventing him from grabbing the other gun. Dexter clutched his arm while on his knees and looked up at the men standing over him. Cicco smiled deviously while staring at Dexter.

"Well, this is a stroke of luck," Vinny Cicco announced cheerfully. "If anyone can help me lure Lindsey out, it's her father."

"Leave my daughter alone," Dexter growled as blood seeped between his fingers. "Your son tried to kill her. He got what he deserved."

Cicco aimed his gun at Dexter's head and glared at him. "I'd be careful what I'd say if I were you," Cicco announced in a slightly jovial tone. "I'm in a really bad mood. It seems your little girl has pissed off some pretty resourceful people and not just me. I can't believe you're still defending her after all this. Have you seen what she caused? All this bloodshed?" He shook his head and suddenly chuckled. "She really pulled one over on all of us, didn't she? I'd ask the other interested party what she possibly did to piss them off, but those boys don't feel much like talking." Cicco eyed his right-hand man. "Dawg, round up the boys. We have all the bait we need to get Lindsey. Her daddy's going to help us find her."

Dawg nodded and hurried from the playroom leaving Cicco and his henchman alone with an unarmed and wounded Dexter.

"She didn't do anything," Dexter protested. "Somehow you created this mess. They probably want you for the things you've done."

Cicco mockingly considered the comment then grinned and shook his head. "Yeah, I don't think so." He suddenly raised his brows. "But don't you worry, I intend to ask your daughter about this entire matter when I get my hands on her." He motioned with his gun. "Now come on out. We need to find Lindsey."

Dexter slowly stood while clutching his bleeding arm. "I won't help you lure out my daughter," he proudly announced. "The men I hired to protect her probably have her far from here."

"The men you hired to protect her are probably already dead," Cicco announced then sneered. "Along with most of my men. Now let's go."

Sal suddenly appeared behind Cicco's man and swung the baseball bat. The armed man heard him, but by the time he spun around, it was already too late. Sal knocked the gun from his hand nearly breaking his arm with the bat then swung upward and struck the man in the chin. He was thrown backward. As Cicco turned, Sal knocked the gun from his hand. Cicco jumped back a step and stared at Sal with the bloodstained baseball bat.

"What the hell are you doing here?" Cicco suddenly demanded then sneered at him. "I told you what would happen if you interfered."

"What? That you'd kill my daughter?" Sal snarled and twirled the bat. "That's going to be a little difficult for you to do with your head bashed in."

Sal swung for Cicco, aiming for his head. Cicco ducked the baseball bat and saw Dexter going for the gun. Knowing he was at their mercy and would probably be killed, Vinny Cicco darted across the playroom and out the door. Dexter snatched the gun and ran after him, but it was already too late. Dexter returned to the playroom as Sal attempted to calm himself from his small rampage.

"He got away," Dexter growled then looked at his dead man with disgust. "We've got to get that bastard."

"No," Sal insisted while glaring at Dexter. "We need to keep our heads and stay out of sight. Makar will deal with Cicco. Let them kill each other. My friends will deal with whoever is left."

"We have to find my daughter," Dexter insisted. "You heard what he said. They're going to find her and kill her. She's not safe."

"Wherever she is, she's safe," Sal insisted firmly. "She's not coming out for *anyone*."

Sal cast a look at Conner. The young man wanted to comment but frowned instead. Perhaps a few of Sal's words sank in for the first time.

"I'm looking for my daughter," Dexter announced and ran from the room.

Chapter Forty-four

The faint sounds of gunfire from deep within the ship were sporadic; indicating the worst of the war was winding down just a little after seven o'clock that evening. Both sides were running out of ammunition as well as men. Lindsey remained close to the corridor wall on deck three while attempting to keep a moderately fast pace. She reached a juncture in the corridor and paused briefly to look at the ship's map. She needed to turn right, and that would take her to the employee's area, which would eventually lead to the cargo hold and freedom.

Lindsey flattened herself against the wall and peered around the corner before making any sudden movements. Horror crossed her face when she saw the once elegant corridor strewn with more than half a dozen dead men. The gold-colored carpet was now covered with so much blood it was impossible to see the original color and pattern beneath it. The blood from the dead men had soaked the entire stretch of carpet leading to the employee's stairwell. There seemed to be blood everywhere, including the walls, the plush sofa, and even a few spatters on the ceiling. Lindsey couldn't tear her eyes away from the gruesome sight. She drew a deep breath, collected her emotions, and nervously entered the horror show that was once an elegant corridor.

As she approached the first dead man, she couldn't avoid stepping in blood. The carpet squished beneath her feet, which was almost enough to make her gag. She couldn't help but stare at the first two dead men she passed. The larger caliber bullets had torn through their heads leaving gruesome wounds and exposing skull and brain. In some cases, their bulletproof vests protected them, but even their vests weren't enough for shots taken at close range. Despite seeing several assault rifles on the blood-soaked carpet, she didn't touch them. In her eyes, the weapons were massive, intimidating, and far too much weapon for her. She then saw a semiautomatic holstered and attached to one of the dead man's belts.

Lindsey hesitated, drew a deep breath, and delicately removed the handgun from his holster. She seemed almost afraid he'd leap up and grab her, although by the missing part of his skull he was almost certainly dead. She held the gun a moment and sized it up while placing her finger on the trigger. Being she never held a gun before; she was apparently clueless. She fiddled with the safety, uncertain of its function. Lindsey placed her left hand on top of the barrel and tugged on it since she knew it was supposed to make that cocking sound in order to function.

In the movies, all guns made that cocking sound. As she attempted to pull the slide back, her finger tightened on the trigger, and the gun fired narrowly missing her foot. Lindsey let out a startled cry and jumped with surprise. She released the gun, allowing it to fall to the blood-soaked, carpeted floor with a dull thud. She trembled slightly then quickly reclaimed the gun that now had blood on it from the floor. She held the gun in her hand with her finger on the trigger but made certain she didn't apply any pressure.

With how easily the gun discharged, it seemed a wonder more people didn't shoot themselves in the foot. She heard the sound of movement on the deck above her and was alarmed by the sound. Whoever was on the deck above seemed to be moving awfully fast. For a moment, she wondered why. She then eyed the gun, and it dawned on her. They heard the gunshot. Lindsey gasped and hurried through the minefield of dead bodies for her only exit. She could now hear movement coming down the stairs in front of her. She quickly turned and ran back in the opposite direction, no longer thinking about the soaked carpet beneath her feet.

Lindsey ran back for the connecting corridor and rounded it. She saw four of Makar's men running for her. They aimed their weapons but didn't fire, since she was the prize they sought, and they needed her alive. Lindsey cried out with surprise, aimed the semiautomatic in their general direction, and repeatedly pulled the trigger. As the bullets rapidly fired from the weapon, the gun seemed to bounce within her hand, and she unloaded the entire magazine at the four men. All four men had crouched down to avoid the gunfire. Not surprising, the bullets struck the walls and the ceiling but never came close to any of the men.

When the gun clicked empty, Lindsey continued to pull the trigger, uncertain why it no longer fired. When she realized she was out of bullets, she gasped with alarm and spun back for the connecting corridor. Six more of Makar's men were only a few feet from her with their weapons aimed. Lindsey could do little more than stare helplessly at them. The first man raised his hand radio.

"Makar, we have her," the man announced while grinning. "Deck three."

"I'm on my way," came the response.

§

Lindsey sat on the dusty, leather bench seat in the waiting area just inside the deck three dining room. Two men armed with assault rifles stood over her making certain she didn't move while four men kept watch over the dining room. The two-story dining room with a cathedral ceiling contained elegant chandeliers now covered in cobwebs. The main dining room had enough seating for two hundred people at small, four-person round tables. The chairs were neatly placed beneath the tables as if the dining room had been completely cleaned prior to abandoning ship.

The remaining four men stood just inside the dining room's main entrance and kept watch out the open doors. Makar and another six men in his party of mercenaries entered the dining room. Makar's eyes immediately settled on Lindsey. He grinned proudly when he saw her. He finally had his much sought after prize. Lindsey nervously coiled back on the bench seat.

"Lindsey Cicco," Makar announced almost cheerfully. "I'm so glad you remember me. Who would have thought our brief encounter would have me chasing you from Colorado to the East Coast?" He chuckled in an unsettling manner. "Certainly not me." His jovial smile faded. "I would have put a bullet in your head if I'd have known you'd be this much of a pain in my ass." He suddenly grinned then chuckled. "It must have come as a great surprise to Sebastian when he discovered you'd betrayed him." Makar then considered the comment and raised his brows. "Oh, wait. That's right. You killed him, didn't you?" He shook his head while chuckling. "You've been very busy pissing off people. Is there anyone left who doesn't want you dead?"

"The team my father hired will save me," she boldly announced with some arrogance. "They'll tear you and your men apart."

"I could be mistaken, but I think they collected your remaining crash survivors, made off with my helicopter, and left with the Coast Guard."

Lindsey stared at Makar with renewed horror at the possibility that he was telling the truth. Was it possible they had actually abandoned her? Her arrogance quickly returned as she straightened proudly on the bench seat.

"They wouldn't do that," she insisted and even managed a tiny, weak smirk. "They wouldn't double-cross my father like that."

"Why's that?" he asked with a humored look. "Do you think you're the only one allowed to double-cross influential men?"

Lindsey stared at him but didn't comment.

Makar laughed at her then removed his hand radio and spoke into it. "Helicopter two," he announced into the radio. "We need immediate extraction. Rendezvous on deck nine by the pool."

"Copy that," came the static-filled response.

"You said they stole your helicopter," Lindsey practically protested.

"My dear, I have more than a few helicopters nearby," he insisted. "My fleet is scattered from here to Costa Rico." He grinned and laughed. "See? You really did fuck with the wrong man, but I'd rather you figure that out while I'm torturing you."

He motioned to his men. They grabbed Lindsey and pulled her from the bench seat.

Chapter Forty-five

Six of Makar's men led the way along the interior corridor on deck nine with six bringing up the rear. Makar remained with Lindsey between the heavily armed men while keeping his semiautomatic aimed at her and a firm grip on her wrist. She protested his grip several times but was met with violent jerking. As they stepped onto the outer deck, several shots were fired, forcing them to retreat into the corridor. Makar pulled Lindsey into the nearby panorama lounge. The six men bringing up the rear entered with them. The lounge had a wall of shattered windows facing the pool, which was the rendezvous with Makar's extraction helicopter. Makar eyed the shattered wall of glass exposing the pool deck.

Cicco and his remaining army of nearly a dozen men appeared by the glassless doors and filtered into the lounge while firing at Makar's men. Makar pulled Lindsey to the floor with him just behind the circle bar in the middle of the lounge. Cicco's men bolted behind several larger pieces of bullet-riddled furniture. The rest of Makar's men entered the lounge while keeping their weapons aimed at the corridor doorway. They managed to shield themselves from the weapon's fire coming from the lounge before the pool deck.

"Dexter is at the outer door," one of Makar's men informed him.

"Cicco and his men are protecting the poolside doors," Makar added.

"We outnumber them," his man informed him. "We should just storm them."

"There are other ways of winning a battle," Makar informed his man. He hesitated a moment. "Vinny," he called out. "We're on the same side here. We don't need to kill each other."

"That's where you're wrong," Cicco called back. "We've never met, but you have something that belongs to me, and I'm not leaving without that girl."

"How about a momentary truce and an introduction?" Makar announced.

There was a moment of hesitation. Makar stood from behind the bar with his hands in the air. Vinny peered across the room, frowned while setting his gun aside, and stood as well. Both men kept their hands open and in front of their chests as a symbol of faith not to shoot the other.

"I'm Makar," he announced. "I work for an underground network closely related to the Russian mob."

"How do you know who I am?" Vinny demanded while studying the man with the accent. "I'm sure I'd remember meeting you."

"I know a lot of things, Vinny," Makar informed him. "I knew your son. We had a business arrangement. When things turned ugly, I did my homework on your daughter-in-law and realized she was the one we were after. I know she killed your son, and I know you want her head mounted on your wall. As I said, we're on the same side here. We don't need to kill each other."

"You're the one who shot down the airliner?" Vinny asked while raising a curious brow.

"Not me personally, but yes," Makar replied. "I have a lot of men and weapons at my disposal."

"What's your interest in Lindsey?"

"Much the same as yours, but I need a little information from her before I'm willing to remove her head," Makar informed him. "If we can come to an agreement, we can share in the spoils. I'll gladly stand aside and watch you kill her in whatever manner you wish. We just need to agree to stop trying to kill one another."

"I can't allow you to take her away without me tagging along," Vinny informed him.

"And I'm fine with that," Makar remarked while grinning. "I know a place in Costa Rico. Quiet, remote, and no one asks questions."

Cicco remained slightly suspicious but seemed to consider the bargain. "My men and I go with you and your men," he replied. "That has to be the deal."

"Absolutely," Makar announced and chuckled low in his throat. "We'll deal with her together. No more of our men need to die."

"Agreed," Cicco replied.

Makar nodded to his men. All twelve stood and lowered their weapons, although they still held them, particularly those watching the interior door for Dexter and his men. Cicco nodded to his men. Six armed men stood with their guns lowered as well while the remaining six kept their attention focused on the poolside deck. Both were now out from hiding. Makar pulled Lindsey to her feet and forced her ahead of him and closer to Cicco. She stared at Vinny with fear in her eyes. She didn't seem to know which man she feared more.

Vinny eyed her and smiled evilly. "You have every right to be worried," he casually announced then looked at Makar. "Just my curious nature. What did she steal from you? Why do you want her so badly?"

"Your son was working with our agency funneling money through our many accounts as well as other sensitive data," Makar informed him and casually leaned against the bar now behind him. "Among the data was a list of names. Names of our operatives, their aliases, and their locations all over the world. That list is worth billions to many world powers. That data alone has me pretty pissed at the girl." He eyed Lindsey who remained looking down, unable to look at either man. "But the money?" He groaned and shook his head. "Over five hundred billion dollars disappeared when your son died. She destroyed his laptop, which was the only way we could possibly have retraced his steps after she killed him. She has that information stored inside that pretty, little head of hers." Makar stroked her hair then grinned at Vinny. "And I intend to extract it by any means necessary."

Vinny shook his head while sneering at Lindsey. "So she killed my son for billions in laundered money." His attention shifted back to Makar. "Did he find out? Or was killing him part of the plan all along? I want to know exactly how and why my son died."

"Understandable. I think she needed him dead in order for her plan to work," Makar casually replied while brushing the dark hair from her shoulder. "I don't think she could have managed it with him alive. He would have killed her the moment he discovered what she'd done. She stole the classified data that morning, which would explain why she needed to get rid of him that evening before he discovered what she had done. Make no mistake; she had been planning the theft and his murder for weeks. She needed time to frame someone else if she wanted to get away with it." He sighed deeply then smiled while straightening. "Well, we have a transport arriving in fifteen minutes. We'll need to clear the deck of Dexter and what's left of his men."

"Won't be a problem," Vinny replied and snapped his fingers alerting his men. "My men and I will circle around outside. When you hear our signal, you attack through what's left of that wall here in the lounge."

"All right then," Makar announced with a little too much enthusiasm and grinned almost playfully. "We'll meet you out back in the woodshed."

Vinny's men left through the side door. Makar and his men patrolled the area near the destroyed glass windows and kept watch for Dexter's men. Sal and Conner remained hidden behind the smaller side lounge bar on the opposite end of the room, unnoticed by all sides, and watched what was about to unfold. Conner appeared deep in thought, obviously contemplating what he'd heard. Sal removed his hand radio and tried to keep his voice down.

"Guys," he announced into the radio. "We have a situation. There's a threesome in the lounge off the pool on deck nine. Makar has Lindsey, and he's just partnered with Cicco. He has air support a few minutes away. If they get here, Lindsey's as good as gone."

"We're on our way," Monroe announced through the radio.

Sal practically gasped at how loud the radio sounded and turned down the volume.

"Keep an eye on the situation, but do not intervene," Monroe continued. "Copy?"

Sal eyed his bloodstained baseball bat then spoke into the hand radio. "Considering there are two dozen men with weapons, and I'm armed with a baseball bat, I don't think you need to worry about me intervening. Over."

"What do we do?" Conner asked while shifting looks across the lounge and back at Sal.

Sal shook his head in response. "There's nothing we can do but wait for backup," he informed the young man. "Don't worry. Nothing's going to happen to her while they're busy killing one another. As long as she's on this ship, they won't kill her. She's worth too much to them alive."

Chapter Forty-six

Dexter and his remaining army of seven were scattered on the pool deck attempting to take cover behind anything that could take a hit. Cicco's men were now on both sides of the deck and opened fire on Dexter's men. Bullets were flying from every direction, splintering the wooden deck and bouncing off metal beams. Makar's men joined in on the all-out assault from the open lounge. The sound of gunfire was almost deafening as the deck was riddled with bullets from every direction. Dexter watched in horror as his seven men dropped one at a time within seconds of one another.

Some of the men fell into the murky pool, one was knocked over the railing, plummeting to the sand eight stories below, and others struck the pool deck. When the last of Dexter's men had fallen, Makar stepped into what was once the lounge doorway with a gun to Lindsey's head and smiled in a slightly psychotic manner.

"Hey, Dexter," he called out. "Looks like you're all that's left. Why don't you come on out? I may need your little girl alive, but she doesn't need all her fingers and toes to be useful to me."

Makar grabbed Lindsey's wrist and held her hand out. She closed her fingers and screamed as he held the gun to her knuckles.

"This little piggy went to market," he announced then pointed the gun to the next knuckle. "This little piggy stayed home--"

Dexter put his hands in the air and stepped out from behind the hot tub. "Don't hurt her!"

Makar eyed Dexter where he stood out in the open on deck and grinned. "That's more like it," Makar announced and chuckled. "There's nothing more special than a father-daughter bond."

Makar aimed his gun at Dexter. He was about to pull the trigger when the barrel of a gun was pressed into his back between his shoulder blades.

"Drop the gun and let the girl go," Conner snarled from behind Makar. "I won't ask twice."

Makar released Lindsey and let his gun fall to the floor. She gasped a sigh of relief and spun to face Conner. Sal immediately grabbed Lindsey by the arm and pulled her across the lounge before either group of men would have a chance to circle around. Conner quickly backed away while keeping his gun aimed at Makar, who kept his hands in the air.

Makar slowly turned to face the kid with the gun. He drew a deep breath, appeared bored, and sighed. "Kill him," he casually announced.

Makar's men opened fire on Conner, who didn't even attempt to fire back. He could have taken his shot at Makar, but it was quite possible he knew he'd miss. Conner cried out while running after Sal and Lindsey through the back door and into the interior corridor. The rear lounge door slammed shut in a foolish attempt to keep them from following. As a barrage of bullets whizzed past Makar from his own men, he wasn't even concerned that one might hit him. They ceased fire as two of his men ran through the lounge after Conner. Makar snatched his gun from the ground and turned toward Dexter. He was gone!

"What the hell?" he scoffed and glared at his remaining men on deck. "Who the hell let daddy get away?" he demanded and turned hostile while waving his gun. "Scour the deck! I want every one of them found!"

Cicco motioned to his men, who split up and took the port and aft sides of the ninth deck. Makar motioned for his men to follow him. They hurried after him heading across the destroyed lounge to the back door that led into the interior corridor. Two of his men were already at the closed lounge door attempting to open it. When they discovered it was locked, the first man easily kicked it open. Monroe stood on the other side of the doorway with his AK-47 assault rifle and sprayed them with bullets, mowing down the first two men. Monroe kicked the door shut. The remaining men fired into the door, tearing it to shreds. Makar rolled his eyes.

"Guys, conserve ammunition," Makar moaned. "Jesus, you're not even *trying* to hit anything."

The next man pushed open the door and jumped back while aiming his weapon, prepared to shoot the first thing that moved. They aimed their weapons into the corridor, but there was no one there. Gunfire suddenly came at them from the port side, lounge doorway. When they turned to return fire, Monroe was now in the port side doorway and took down another two men. He just as quickly disappeared from the doorway. Makar's men returned fire, blindly shooting at nothing. When their guns simultaneously ran out of ammo, they were left scouring for more shells.

"Damn it," Makar cried out. "I warned you! Whoever has ammo left; go get them!"

Two men left through the side door while two others went through the doorway into the interior corridor. The remaining four men tossed their M416 assault rifles aside and removed their semiautomatics. As they turned back toward the lounge interior, they saw Jackie, Zack, Mac, and Bogart standing in the broken glass opening from the pool deck. Before the men could even aim, all four opened fire and took down Makar's four men. Makar bolted into the nearby corridor to avoid being mowed down with the rest of his men.

Six of Cicco's men hurried into the lounge and were met with gunfire. They immediately returned fire. Both sides simultaneously ran out of ammo. Cicco's six men charged the four using their rifles as clubs. Mac and Zack grabbed nearby chairs to deflect the rifle clubs while Jackie took a karate stance. Her shoulder was in no condition to attempt picking up a chair let alone using it to defend herself. Bogart saw the man coming at him with the rifle club, screamed, and ran out the doorway to the pool deck with the man chasing after him. Mac, Zack, and Jackie exchanged embarrassed looks then returned to the five men coming at them.

§

Bogart ran across the pool deck with the man chasing him with his rifle club. The man caught up to Bogart and swung at him. Bogart slid on his hip to avoid the swinging rifle. The rifle missed him, but Bogart was sliding for the murky pool with bodies now floating in it. He cried out and caught the pool ladder. His forward momentum took his legs for the pool, but he was able to pull himself away from the murky water and swing around the ladder. He briefly landed on the edge of the pool and used the pool ladder to catapult his legs for the standing man. He kicked the man in the back and cast him forward into the murky water. Bogart scrambled away from the pool and stared into it.

It seemed odd that the man didn't surface. Bogart inched his way closer to the edge of the pool and peered into the dark, foul-smelling water. He seemed to be expecting the man to jump up and pull him in like some deranged serial killer in a horror movie. The man suddenly surfaced while screaming. Bogart jumped back with surprise as the man clutched and grasped for the pool edge. He didn't know what had the man screaming. There couldn't be any sharks, alligator, or piranha in the pool, but the blood surfacing above the murk was enough to force Bogart to leap back several additional steps.

When the man finally grabbed the pool ladder and pulled himself partway from the water, Bogart could see the metal pole of an old patio umbrella had impaled him. The man clutched and clawed at the pool ladder before gasping his last breath and sinking back under the water.

Bogart made a face. "Add that to my list of ways I don't want to die," he muttered.

§

Monroe ran down the long corridor and headed for the first exterior deck doors he found. He opened the doors and immediately stopped when he saw three of Cicco's men heading along deck. Thankfully, they didn't see him. Monroe turned and darted back into the corridor and took the first turn. He skidded to a halt when he saw Makar's remaining four men in the hallway checking rooms. Monroe darted into the nearby stairwell and was about to run up the stairs to the bridge deck when he heard more of Cicco's men coming down them. Monroe ran down the elegant fire steps that seemed to spiral in a never-ending cascade of steps and landings. His speed and the spiraling steps were almost enough to make him dizzy.

He bypassed the two stateroom decks and headed for deck six, where there were common areas with places to take cover. He was low on ammo and wasn't sure how much firepower the men pursuing him had. He entered the sixth deck corridor and headed for the grand lobby staircase. As he ran down the open stairs to the lobby below, the man following him was heard on the stairs. Once he reached the bottom, Monroe darted into the first room he found. It was the ship's casino. As he ran across the casino, a strange feeling of déjà vu swept over him. He darted behind a bank of slot machines, leaned against them while close to the floor, and attempted to control his breathing so he could hear the man if he entered.

When it didn't seem as if the man was still behind him, Monroe ejected the rifle magazine and checked his count. He groaned at the impressive four rounds and one in the chamber. He slapped the magazine back in place then checked his semiautomatic in his shoulder holster. The magazine contained only three rounds plus one in the chamber. Monroe replaced the handgun to his shoulder holster then concentrated on the main casino door. There wasn't any sound at all, which was almost disturbing. The sound of a gun cocking behind him close to his head caused him to immediately tense. Monroe glanced to his left and saw Chew Toy standing not far from him. He must have been hiding within the casino as well. He certainly hadn't come through either set of doors in the last few minutes. Monroe managed a smile.

"Hey, I thought you were dead," he announced almost cheerfully.

"No thanks to you leaving me tied in that chair," Chew Toy snapped while glaring at him. "Fortunately, my team found me first."

"Yes, that is fortunate," Monroe replied while maintaining his smile.

"I'm going to kill you now," Chew Toy informed him and applied pressure to the trigger.

"You do realize your team partnered with Makar's team, right?" Monroe announced showing little reaction to Chew Toy's threat to kill him.

Chew Toy's expression dropped slightly as he stared at Monroe. "What?"

"Yeah, I guess they found the girl and called for extraction." Monroe glanced at his watch. "I'm guessing the helicopter will be arriving for extraction any minute now." He tilted his head while staring at the man. "Shouldn't you be at the rendezvous?" His look turned serious. "Miss that ride, and you'll be stuck here waiting for the Coast Guard to rescue you." He then frowned. "Not much of a rescue, huh? They'll probably arrest you on sight."

"You're lying," Chew Toy launched with anger. "There's no extraction, and Cicco didn't team up with those other guys. They're a bunch of hardcore mercenary types. He'd never make a deal with them." He fidgeted while seemingly considering his options and second-guessing whether or not Monroe was telling the truth.

"Do you really want to risk missing that helicopter?" Monroe asked then sighed. "Look, there's a simple solution. You meet at the rendezvous. If the Huey is there, you climb aboard and go home. If it's not, I'll tell the Coast Guard you were helping us, and you go home. The only way this doesn't work out for you is if you kill me."

Chew Toy nervously straightened and glared at Monroe. "You better be telling the truth," he snarled.

"I'm pretty sure one of your teammates is on this deck somewhere," Monroe casually remarked. "Why don't you just find him and ask?" He shrugged and raised his brow. "What's the worst that could happen?"

"Okay, I'll do that," Chew Toy announced and removed Monroe's weapons. "You don't move until I'm gone. Follow me, and I'll shoot you myself."

Monroe casually held his hands in the air. "Hey, I'm fine right here," he announced then raised his brows. "You'd better hurry, though. I doubt they'll wait for anyone with the Coast Guard on the way."

Chew Toy collected Monroe's weapons and hurried across the casino. He ran for the main door and bolted into the corridor. Monroe shut his eyes and immediately made a face. A round of gunfire followed.

Monroe opened his eyes and cringed. "I suppose I should have mentioned they were chasing me," he muttered then sighed.

Monroe casually stood and headed for the side door rather than the main door to avoid suffering the same fate as Chew Toy. He opened the door, peered out to make sure the corridor was clear, and then slipped out of the casino. He hurried along the corridor then paused by the connecting hallway. Monroe peered down the corridor and saw the man who had been pursuing him kneeling over his dying teammate. Monroe quietly slipped down the corridor and approached the guilt-ridden man from behind. Chew Toy saw Monroe behind his teammate and attempted to gasp a warning. His teammate suddenly tensed and spun around with his weapon aimed. Monroe punched him in the face, driving him to the floor alongside Chew Toy. Chew Toy stared at him while gasping for air.

"You tricked me," Chew Toy gasped.

"Yeah," Monroe replied while grimacing. "Sorry about that." His look then turned optimistic. "Your boss did partner with Makar, and there is a transport. I told the truth about that." He shook his head and sighed softly while removing his semiautomatic from Chew Toy's pants then frowned. "I'm going to need this back though if you don't mind. You understand."

"Prick."

Chew Toy wheezed and stopped breathing.

Monroe patted him on the shoulder and sighed deeply. "Rest in peace, Chew Toy. I'll always remember the fun times we had together." Monroe then stood and hurried along the corridor.

Chapter Forty-seven

Zack held a chair leg in each hand using them like police batons while taking on two men at once. He struck each man with a baton, although it didn't seem to deter either man. Batons weren't his favorite weapons, particularly makeshift batons. He preferred weapons of the lethal variety not something he felt nuns would use on rowdy schoolboys. He finally tossed aside his 'nun' chucks and resorted to his own brute force. Mac seemed to be enjoying playtime with two men attempting to fight her at once. She kicked one man in the gut then stomped on the second man's foot just to see his reaction. Her grin revealed she was having a little too much fun.

Jackie was struggling with defeating her sole opponent, which was unusual for her. She seemed sluggish and easily winded. Her speed and reaction time was definitely suffering. When she took a punch to the chest, Zack immediately noticed. His momentary concern for Jackie left a small window for the first man he was fighting to punch him in the mouth. He took a step back and dabbed the blood from the corner of his mouth. Zack sighed and shook his head. He spun into a high roundhouse kick and struck the first man knocking him into the second man. As both men crashed against the center bar, Zack leaped through the air and kicked the second man in the chest, sending him over the bar, and crashing into the shelves behind it. The sound of breaking glass and falling objects was nearly deafening.

Zack crossed the lounge for Jackie, passing Mac with her two on one fantasy, and caught the first man's arm. He bent it

backward, snapping it, punched him in the face, and then tossed him to the ground. While holding his arm, he placed his booted foot on the man's head and snapped his neck. Mac stared at Zack with surprise and some irritation to him interrupting her fight. The distraction was enough for the second man to tackle her to the floor. She screamed as she hit the floor with the man on top of her. He attempted to punch her while he held her to the floor. Mac punched him in the throat then kneed him in the groin. As he clutched himself, she tossed him off her and sprang to her feet.

Zack's first opponent had recovered and attempted to dart after Zack. Mac spun into a roundhouse kick and used his forward momentum to break his sternum. He fell to the floor while gasping for air. Zack reached Jackie, who finally kicked her opponent and sent him back several steps. Zack stepped between them as the man attempted to lunge for Jackie. Zack held up his hand and glared at the man, stopping him in his tracks.

"Take five," Zack snapped with annoyance.

The man gave him a surprised look. "Who the fuck do you--?"

Zack punched him in the throat. The man clutched his throat while wheezing and attempting to catch his breath. "I said take five," he snarled. "I need to have a word with my friend."

While Mac continued to fight two men, Zack eyed Jackie with concern.

"Are you okay?" he asked while studying her.

She panted nearly out of breath and managed a nod. "I'm just a little dizzy," Jackie replied. "My shoulder's burning like a bastard."

"I should take a look at that," he insisted.

Jackie glared at him and raised her brows. "We're sort of in the middle of something here."

He waved off Mac, who was now struggling to handle the third man having returned to the fight. "Mac has it under control."

Jackie managed a tiny smile. "Thanks for the concern, but I'll be fine," she insisted. "Now, if you don't mind, I'd like to finish off this bastard and have a drink."

"I think there's some vodka left behind the bar," Zack announced then indicated the man who was finally able to breathe. "You kick his ass, and I'll pour you a drink."

Jackie nodded. Zack kissed her on the forehead then headed for the bar past the recovering man. He slapped the man on the shoulder.

"Don't keep a lady waiting," Zack remarked then jumped over the bar.

Mac continued to fight all three men, taking several shots from them. She saw Zack pouring vodka into a shot glass and appeared horrified.

"Hey," Mac cried out and punched the first man then kicked the second. "A little help here, you overrated psychopath!"

Zack groaned, drank down the shot then poured another. He picked up the bottle and threw it across the room, striking the first man on the head. The bottle shattered against his skull, causing glass fragments to become embedded into his scalp. The man's eyes rolled back as he sank to the floor. Mac continued to fight the remaining two men while cursing. Zack was probably just tormenting her for initially enjoying herself rather than fighting to win.

The man near the bar recovered and lunged for Jackie. She spun into a roundhouse kick, struck him in the chest, and sent him back several steps. It was a good effort, although not up to her usual standards. Jackie could feel Zack's eyes on her. If she didn't handle the situation, he would handle it for her, and she wasn't letting that happen. As the man recovered and lunged for her, Jackie threw herself into the air, caught him around the neck with her legs, and flipped him to the ground. She landed on her right side, although the sudden stop still jolted her left shoulder causing her some pain. She was able to push the pain aside, tightened her legs around his neck and gave a hard twist, snapping his neck. She cringed at the sound. It didn't get any easier, and she hated that move, but it was all she had left in her arsenal.

Zack stood behind the bar and clapped, applauding her. Jackie panted, approached the bar, and collapsed on the nearest, bullet-riddled stool. Zack pushed the shot glass in front of her, which she immediately drank down.

"Better?" he asked.

She indicated the glass with a demanding look. Zack refilled the glass. She drank the second shot then nodded. "Okay, I'm better." Jackie glanced back and saw Mac still fighting the two men. "We should probably help with that."

Zack waved her off. "She's fine."

Jackie gave him a stern look then started to stand.

Zack groaned and rolled his eyes. "Fine," he huffed then picked up a bottle of whiskey, flipped it in his hand, and threw it across the room. It struck the second man in the back of the head, sending him to the floor. Mac punched the first man, kicked him in the groin, and then snapped his neck while he was doubled over. She dropped him to the floor and approached the bar with hostility in her eyes.

"What the hell was that?" she cried out.

"I'm sorry," Zack casually replied while glaring at the irate woman. "I thought you could use some help. It's hard to tell with you."

"I could have used your help ten minutes ago," Mac launched in anger. "I regret saving your ass more and more every damned day!"

"Considering you tried to kill me once, I'd say we were even a long time ago," Zack lashed back.

Jackie stared at Zack with surprise. It wasn't often he lost his temper. He was more of the silent raging bull type. Obviously, his history with Mac was a bigger problem than anyone would have thought.

"Oh, and we're back to that again," Mac scoffed while flinging her arms in the air. "You're a pathetic excuse for a human being."

"Yes, I am," he agreed with little hesitation. "But at least people trust me."

Mac glared at him but didn't comment. Jackie groaned and covered her eyes. She didn't know if Mac and Zack needed a workout on the mats or in the bedroom. Something needed to fix their fractured relationship and fast. They heard the faint sound of a helicopter in the near distance.

"Makar's air support," Mac gasped.

Jackie and Mac ran for the shattered poolside entrance. Zack leaped over the bar and hurried after them. They paused on the pool deck just outside the lounge. Bogart saw the helicopter in the distance and joined them by what was left of the lounge doorway. The helicopter approached from the ocean, indicating it was definitely Makar's air support coming from some ship anchored offshore. Although not as fashionable as the helicopter on the bridge deck above, two men hanging out the side door with assault rifles were enough to wipe out the entire team. They needed to find a way to fight back. Monroe returned just in time to join the four and watch the helicopter nearly upon them.

"Time to take cover," Monroe announced and indicated the lounge.

As the five teammates disappeared inside the lounge and made a dash for the interior bridge stairs, Makar, Cicco, and Dawg ran along the poolside deck and paused to watch the approaching warbird.

"Let my men in the sky take care of Dexter's hired babysitters," Makar announced to Cicco. "We need to find the girl."

The helicopter got closer to the pool deck and started to turn to reveal the men hanging out the side with their weapons. Makar signaled them while Cicco and Dawg watched. As the gunmen scanned the deck for their targets, the loud rat-tat-tat of gunfire came from the bridge deck above.

On the bridge deck, Gil had raised the helicopter, hovering just a few feet above the deck, while Kirk fired the machine gun at the newly arrived aerial assault team. Both of Makar's men in the helicopter took bullets to the chest and fell from the side door, dangling by their tethered harnesses. The machine gun firing continued, striking the craft just off the ship's port side. The helicopter pilot attempted to turn the craft and flee. He didn't get very far when the helicopter emitted a ball of smoke. It quickly ignited into flames and plummeted to the beach where it exploded on impact. The explosion rocked the grounded ship, which groaned in response.

Makar and Cicco were startled by the elimination of their extraction helicopter. Cicco and Dawg made a dash for the lounge and disappeared through the interior door. Makar watched Cicco and his man flee then frowned with disgust. He was about to follow when he saw Monroe appear in the corridor on the bridge stairs just beyond the lounge. He darted out of Monroe's view.

"I've got them," Monroe shouted and ran after Cicco and his hired goon.

Makar remained hidden and watched Monroe chase after Cicco. He considered his next move now that his air support was eliminated when he saw Monroe's friends within the corridor beyond the lounge. Makar frowned and slipped away unnoticed. Jackie, Zack, Bogart, and Mac returned through the lounge and headed onto the poolside deck. Zack eagerly looked over the railing at the exploded helicopter on the beach below. He grinned deviously.

"I love a good bonfire."

Chapter Forty-eight

Cicco's remaining six men and Makar's last four men returned to the poolside deck when they heard the explosion. They saw the four standing on deck and opened fire. Jackie and Mac ran one direction while Zack and Bogart took cover in the opposite direction. Three men ran after Jackie and Mac. As the two women rounded the corner to the bow's port side, one of the men attempted to shoot Jackie at close range. She spun around and struck his arm, forcing the gun to fire away from her. She then twisted his arm and forced him to drop the weapon.

As the gun clattered to the deck floor, Jackie released his arm and kicked him in the side before spinning into a roundhouse kick and striking him in the chest. He was thrown against the wall with a loud crack. Mac fought off two men now attempting to strike her with their empty guns. She punched one while kicking the other then noticed a man appear from the nearby doorway with a gun aimed at Jackie's back. Mac gasped with horror.

"Behind you," Mac cried out while punching the first man with a little more aggression.

Jackie turned, saw the man with the gun, and leaped over the railing, disappearing over the side of the ship. The man with the gun ran for the railing and saw her hand clinging to the lower deck rail. He leaned over the railing with his gun aimed.

Jackie's legs flew up over the railing, caught the man around the neck, and continued through, tossing him over the railing. She caught the upper rail using both hands and jumped over it back onto deck. She immediately clutched her left shoulder and nearly fell to her knees in agony. The man she'd kicked into the wall recovered and leaped for her while she kneeled unaware and defenseless.

Mac saw the scene unfold. She caught the man standing behind her by the neck with both arms and used him as leverage while kicking the man coming at her for a frontal assault. She caught him with both feet to the chest. He flew backward and struck the man about to hit Jackie. The man flew into a bulkhead, cracked his skull open, and collapsed to the deck. Jackie gasped with surprise then looked back at Mac as she flipped the man over her shoulder from behind. He landed harshly on his back before Mac. She followed through with a kick to his groin and then looked at Jackie. Mac breathed heavily as she approached Jackie and extended her hand to her. Jackie managed a tiny smile, accepted her hand, and allowed her to pull her to her feet.

"You know that wound's probably infected," Mac informed her.

Jackie reluctantly nodded. "I suspected as much," she replied and gingerly touched her shoulder. "I didn't want to worry Zack."

"Trust me; he already knows," Mac replied.

They heard Bogart yelling profanities from closer to the pool where most of the activity was now happening. Mac rolled her eyes.

"Is he really your brother?" Mac demanded then groaned. "We'd better save the doofus."

Jackie and Mac hurried toward the larger portion of deck containing the pool and bar. The pool deck was officially a disaster. The glass from the wall of windows was shattered, leaving broken piles of glass around the metal frames. The deck was riddled with bullet holes, and there were dead bodies strewn all along deck, leaving puddles of fresh blood. At least four bodies now floated in the murky pool. Zack took on three men at once while Bogart barely held his own against one man. Makar remained partially hidden behind the tattered outdoor bar while frantically attempting to insert shells into the M416 assault rifle magazine. Once he had the weapon loaded, he'd be the only armed man and cut them all down.

"It's Makar," Jackie announced to Mac. "We have to stop him before he reloads."

Mac nodded. Both women ran along deck but were immediately greeted by two men charging from the lounge across the broken glass. Jackie threw herself to the deck, avoiding the first man while Mac took the aggressive approach and spun into a roundhouse kick, knocking the second man back and onto the broken glass. The shards of glass piercing his body didn't seem to faze him. He sprang to his feet and came back at Mac, attempting to throw a punch for her face. She blocked his punch but received a kick to her hip, surprising her. She jumped back and looked at the man, who now took a defensive karate stance.

She suddenly smirked in response. "Oh, you want to play?" Mac teased and took her own karate stance. "Bring it on."

The man came at Mac with a series of kicks. She dodged a couple and deflected a couple with her forearm and legs. When he took a moment to recover from his unsuccessful strikes, Mac kicked for his side. He caught her ankle and seemed overly proud that he'd stopped her first attempt. He twisted her ankle. Mac went with the twist and threw her other leg into the air, striking him in the head. He released her ankle, allowing her to drop to the deck with a little less grace than she had anticipated, but she was able to roll with it and avoid injury.

Mac sprang to her feet as the man recovered from the hard kick and came back at her. Mac delivered a series of kicks, which he successfully deflected. As his confidence rose and his grin increased, Mac changed her assault tactics and threw a punch. He blocked her punch, which was only the distraction for her knee finding his groin. The man clutched himself and dropped to his knees. Mac punched him in the face as he kneeled before her and knocked him onto the deck, driving the shards of glass deeper into his body.

Jackie managed to spring back to her feet from her roll to avoid being hit and blocked the large boot that nearly stomped on her. She couldn't deny she was slower than usual. Her arms and legs felt unusually heavy, and she couldn't seem to anticipate moves as well as she usually had. As the man came at her, her options were limited to mostly right-handed blocks and punches. One wrong move with her left shoulder and she'd be nearly disabled with pain. She couldn't count on Zack coming to her aid since he had more than enough on his own plate at the moment. Her attacker grabbed a discarded rifle by the barrel and swung at her. She jumped back and narrowly avoided a shot to the face with the non-functioning weapon. She managed to back up a few feet, positioning herself near a support beam.

When he swung again, she ducked, allowing him to strike the beam with the weapon. It was enough to jolt his entire body and knock the weapon from his hand at the same time. Jackie kicked him in the chest and sent him back a few feet, taking him off guard. She went for a return kick, which he managed to dodge. She threw a punch, which he blocked and threw his own punch in response. She managed to move just enough to avoid a chest shot and took the full force of the hit to her left shoulder. Jackie felt pain shoot through her entire body as if someone had shot her several times. Something squished beneath her gauze wrap, almost like a massive pimple bursting. Something warm and sticky seeped from her shoulder wound.

The pain was so intense; she saw a hail of darkness and heard ringing in her ears. She was almost certain she'd pass out. Jackie barely had time to clutch her injured shoulder as she sank to her knees. The man saw her clutching her bleeding shoulder and suddenly grinned. He realized she had a previous injury and found her weakness. From his position across deck, Zack saw what was about to unfold, but he was already three men deep into battle. Zack leaped into the air, caught the first man around the neck and tossed him off his feet, knocking him into the second man.

As both men fell to the deck, Zack punched the third in the abdomen. When the man doubled over, Zack caught him by the neck and swiftly broke it, allowing him to fall lifelessly to the deck. The first two men recovered, grabbed discarded rifles and came at Zack. Zack grabbed a life preserver ring and deflected blows from both men. He still couldn't find an escape to help Jackie. The man standing over Jackie pulled her bloodied hand from her left shoulder and punched her again in her injured arm. The ringing in her ears was louder, although the intense pain seemed to stop. Ironically, she didn't feel anything, but the deck floor seemed a lot closer to her face now. It took a second for her to realize she'd hit the floor, having possibly blacked out for a second. She could smell the strong odor of infection oozing from her injured shoulder. It was a horrible, unmistakable odor. She managed to look up although she was unable to move.

The man hovered over her while grinning and coiled back with his booted foot, about to kick her in the face. She managed to roll onto her back to avoid the size twelve boot to her face, although it wouldn't be far enough. She then heard a vicious, familiar snarl. Darth leaped down from the bridge deck. The man looked up as the German shepherd leaped for him, but all he saw was sharp teeth. The man suddenly gasped as the dog knocked him to the deck with his weight. Once the man's back hit the deck, Darth grabbed him by the throat, bit down, and slung his head while digging his haunches into the man's abdomen, giving the dog greater leverage.

The man could barely scream as the dog's teeth tore into his flesh. Blood sprayed across the dog and the deck surrounding the man. Once he stopped moving, Darth released him and ran for Jackie, who slowly pulled herself to her hands and knees. Darth whined and licked her nose, coating her with blood from his tongue and muzzle. Jackie managed a smile and attempted to stand.

"Good boy," she whispered now enduring the pain that seemed to return.

Another man came at Jackie, who was barely to her knees. Darth stood over her and snarled viciously while barking as blood and saliva flew from his mouth. The man backed off and bumped into someone now standing behind him. He spun around to see Gil. Gil punched the man twice in the face. As he stumbled backward, Darth darted behind the falling man's legs allowing him to topple over him and to the deck floor. Kirk leaped over the railing from the bridge deck, landing not far from Gil and hurried to Jackie's side. He linked his muscular arm beneath her good arm and pulled her to her feet. She sank against him, feeling slightly dizzy then met his gaze and smiled.

"Thanks."

"Next time you're shot, you may want to consider seeing a real doctor," Kirk informed her with little emotion. "Zack's good at digging out bullets, but his rate of after surgery infections are off the charts."

"Makar," she suddenly gasped and looked alongside the bar. Makar was gone. Jackie looked back at Gil and Kirk. "Makar was reloading an M416. He'll be the only armed person here. We need to find him."

"I have port," Gil announced to Kirk. "You take aft." He then looked at Darth and pointed at the dog. "You guard Jackie."

Both men took off across deck in separate directions, avoiding the heavy fighting still in progress by Bogart, Mac, and Zack. Jackie looked behind her to the war-torn lounge then eyed Darth.

"Come on, Darth," she announced. "I need someone to guard my aft."

Jackie swept the broken glass away with her booted foot, allowing Darth to follow her safely into the lounge.

Chapter Forty-nine

As the battle continued on the war-torn pool deck, Bogart attempted to block the fast, hard fist from Makar's man. He succeeded in not taking the full brunt of the hit, but the fist to his face was enough to drive him to his knees. He was dazed a moment and looked up at the man, who was about to deliver another hard punch. Bogart dodged the punch, dropped to his backside, whipped his legs in a circle, and swept the man's legs out from under him. The man struck the deck, landing harshly on his hip. Bogart sprang to his feet just moments before the man recovered and jumped to his feet as well. Bogart was a second faster and coiled back to punch the man. His fist was caught from behind, and he was whirled around to face a second attacker, surprising him.

Two on one was not something with which he'd had much practice or success. The man threw a punch for Bogart's face. Bogart blocked his fist and kneed him in the groin. The man behind him lunged at him. Bogart caught a glimpse of him out of the corner of his eye and spun into a backward, roundhouse kick, striking the man in the abdomen rather than the chest. The man was thrown backward. The second man recovered and threw another punch for Bogart, but Bogart couldn't maintain his balance from the kick and landed on the deck. His lack of skill allowed him to avoid the fist close to his face. While he was on the ground, he kicked the man in the knee, knocking him backward onto deck. As Bogart stood, the second man had already recovered from the kick and returned for him. Bogart punched him in the gut. As he doubled over, Bogart grabbed him around the neck. While he held the second man around the neck, the first man recovered from the knee kick and lunged for him. Bogart snap kicked the lunging man in the groin, dropping him to his knees. He then threw himself into a sitting position with a classic wrestling move and bounced the first man's head off the deck, splitting his skull.

When Bogart saw the blood spilling from the man's head, he released him and attempted to slide away. The man on his knees clutching his groin recovered and swung for Bogart while he was preoccupied with the other man's rapidly spreading blood. Bogart saw the man on his knees lunge for him. He threw both his feet in the air, catching him around the neck, and twisted his body, attempting to bring the man from his knees and to the deck. There was a loud crunching sound as the man's neck snapped from the pressure and angle. Bogart cried out while removing his legs from the man's head and saw his head wiggle freely from his broken neck. Bogart watched with horror as he hit the deck.

"Oh," Bogart cried out and attempted to spring to his feet while avoiding the blood from the first man and the sight of the second man's twisted neck. "Oh, that's disgusting!"

As Bogart turned around, he saw Zack still fighting the two remaining men. He gathered his courage and headed for Zack and his two opponents. Zack kicked the first man sending him backward several steps then threw himself to the deck floor and grabbed a discarded, three-foot piece of brass rail pipe that had broken off from the bar. As the second man came at him, Zack sprang back to his feet, twirled the brass pole above his head and lunged forward, driving the jagged metal end through the man's midsection. Bogart stopped in his tracks and stared at the gruesomeness of the kill. The man gasped several times while clutching the pole. Zack released the bar rail and turned for the second man while the first continued to struggle with the metal piece sticking out of his body.

Zack approached the second man now near the railing. The man grabbed a discarded rifle, held it like a baseball bat, and charged for Zack while coiling back to swing. He swung the rifle at Zack's head. Zack ducked the rifle then sprang back up into a high roundhouse kick. He struck the man in the chest and sent him flying backward. He hit the deck railing, jolting his body from the hard hit. Zack casually approached as the man attempted to recover, and punched him in the face, sending him backward over the railing. The man plummeted to the sand eight stories below. As Zack turned and met Bogart's gaze, Bogart fumbled for something to say.

"I had your back," Bogart announced proudly.

Zack just glared at him and continued past. He paused and looked around the deck littered with bodies, appeared curious, and looked back at Bogart.

"Where's Jackie?"

Bogart looked around as if suddenly realizing she was gone. "I, uh--?"

Zack groaned and headed for the lounge.

§

Monroe hurried through the disastrous cargo hold and cautiously approached the breach in the hull. He peered out the massive opening, but it was too late. Cicco and Dawg were already running into the woods. How they'd gotten so far ahead of him was a mystery. In the near distance, Monroe spotted two larger Coast Guard ships. They were lowering motorized rafts into the water and would soon be joining the fight. He then saw two more rafts were already on shore with men piling out of them.

"Better late than never, boys," Monroe muttered and decided to wait for them.

As nearly two dozen armed men ran across the beach toward the grounded cruise ship, Monroe spotted a familiar face in the lead. Monroe chuckled and shook his head as Holden led the way. At least it would save Monroe from having to do the usual explaining. Who he was and why he was armed. It would be nice to avoid the usual handcuffing during the Q and A portion of the meeting.

"Where's Jackie?" Holden demanded as they got closer. "Is she okay?"

"Deck nine," Monroe replied. "Like a cat stalking her prey. She's fine. Vinny Cicco and his goon managed to slip away from me though. Ran into the woods. They're probably halfway to the airfield by now."

The man in charge motioned for four of his men to head into the woods and find Cicco. The rest followed Holden and Monroe through the cargo hold.

§

Makar attempted to open the library door but found it wouldn't budge. He kicked the door several times before it finally cracked the frame and flew open. Makar entered the library with his M416 assault rifle aimed. Lindsey screamed while clinging to Conner, who immediately took her down to the floor behind a sturdy desk. Makar stepped into the room while keeping his weapon aimed and approached the desk.

"Hiding behind a desk won't save you, my dear," Makar announced with little emotion.

Sal appeared from behind the door with his bloodstained baseball bat and swung for Makar. Makar must've felt the gust of wind and spun with his weapon raised. The baseball bat connected with the rifle, keeping the weapon from firing as it fell to the hardwood floor with a clatter. Sal twirled the bat in his hand and went for a second swing. Makar spun into a roundhouse kick and struck Sal in the chest, sending him backward and into a bookcase.

The bookcase rattled beneath his weight. Sal struck the back of his head and collapsed out cold to the floor. Dexter yelled while leaping out from behind a second desk with a large, decorative lamp in his hand and swung for Makar's head. Makar went for the return kick, struck Dexter in the chest, and sent him backward, across the desk and onto the other side. Lindsey let out a terrified scream as Conner held her close to the floor behind the first desk. Makar snatched his assault rifle and approached the desk hiding the young couple.

"Come out, Lindsey, and I won't kill the boy," Makar informed her. "I don't want him. Give yourself up. He doesn't need to die because of you."

Conner clung to Lindsey, although it was evident she wasn't about to turn herself over in exchange for Conner's life. Makar paused before the desk and aimed his weapon at the cowering young man and woman.

"Sorry, kid," Makar announced to Conner. "It's nothing personal. I would have liked to take you along as leverage, but I'm a little low on men and need to travel lite."

Makar pressed his finger against the trigger when the barrel of the rifle was suddenly shoved upward causing the weapon to fire into the ceiling. Makar turned to see Jackie. She rammed her knee into his side twice then flipped him over her hip. He struck the floor with a loud thud. As she turned toward him, Makar swept her legs out from beneath her. Jackie hit the floor and felt instantaneous pain sweeping through her body from her shoulder. As Makar sprang to his feet, Darth suddenly snarled from the doorway and leaped for Makar, catching his arm and tearing into his jacket sleeve with his teeth. Makar throat punched the dog, dislodging his teeth then kicked him in the underbelly beyond his bulletproof vest.

The dog was thrown back several feet and out the open library door before catching his balance. Makar slammed the door shut before the dog could return for a second attack. Jackie endured the pain in her shoulder and saw Makar coming back for her. She managed to jump to her feet as he attempted to kick her. She deflected several kicks with her good arm and leg. He threw a punch and struck her in the ribs. She was slightly startled by the hit since she wasn't nearly as fast as she usually was. When he threw the second punch, Jackie blocked it with her left arm, immediately regretting the action as pain swept over her. She would normally have followed through with a return punch, but she couldn't complete the action. He punched her in the face, sending her stumbling backward and into the desk. She was momentarily dazed. She wasn't used to being roughed up, especially by someone with lesser skills. Makar was having a lucky day.

Darth was heard violently scratching at the door while snarling and barking as he attempted to get through. The arrogant man didn't think much of it until the doorknob started jiggling. Darth was attempting to open the door with his teeth! Makar leaped for the door as it was about to open, slammed it shut, and flipped the lock in place. Darth again snarled and scratched at the door. Makar snatched the discarded weapon and aimed it at Jackie. Fortunately, Darth had given Jackie enough time to recover from her shockwave of pain. Jackie knew she needed to end Makar's lucky day. She bolted from his path as he fired at her, striking the desk near Lindsey and Conner. Lindsey screamed from where she hid behind the desk while Conner shielded her.

Jackie bolted across the room as Makar attempted to follow her with the loaded weapon. He fired several shots, putting holes in objects behind her as she ran. She leaped onto a small end table without slowing, caught her foot on the sturdy bookshelf, and spun into a roundhouse kick through the air back for Makar. She kicked him in the face with enough force to send him sailing across the library. Jackie landed with her usual grace then immediately lost her balance and struck the floor. She writhed a moment in agony.

Makar struck the opposing bookcase not far from Sal and fell to the floor. Jackie and Makar both struggled to return to their feet. Jackie was now experiencing serious pain in her entire body. She felt weak and slightly disoriented. Her shoulder throbbed so hard; her head hurt because of it. She made it to her feet and swayed slightly while clutching her head. Was it possible she'd pass out from the pain in her shoulder? Makar seemed unsteady as well but recovered more quickly. He pulled a knife from his boot and charged for Jackie.

Jackie saw the knife in his hand and knew she couldn't duck beneath it since Makar would recover faster, and she'd be helpless on the floor. Jackie charged for him instead, tossed herself onto her hip, and slid across the floor for his legs, bowling him over. Makar fell to the floor while Jackie slid across the hardwood floor and struck the opposing bookcase with her feet not far from where Sal sat propped and unconscious. She cried out in agony while clutching her bleeding, infected shoulder.

"Get up," Conner shouted from behind the desk. "Get up, Jackie!"

She could barely hear Conner shouting his warning or Darth's snarling and scratching beyond the library door as the sound of her heart beating seemed to thump loudly in her ears. Jackie gathered all her strength while attempting to block the intense pain radiating through her body and finally made it to her feet. She spun around just in time to see Makar running for her with the knife. He was nearly on top of her, but she had nothing left. She panted heavily and just stared at the face of the man who would end her life. Sal suddenly leaped in front of her and swung the baseball bat, striking Makar in the head with his best and most powerful swing. Sal's hard swing combined with Makar's forward momentum was enough to split his head on contact, projecting blood across the room and his bat.

Makar flew across the room, struck the doorframe, and fell alongside the door. There was a tremendous crack as the door flew open alongside him revealing Zack and Darth. As the contents of Makar's head spilled out onto the floor, Zack stood in the doorway and stared at the dead man with little emotion. Jackie listened to her heart beating in her ears then the loud ringing that followed. Her eyes rolled back in her head then shut. Sal dropped his bloodied baseball bat just in time to catch Jackie as she sank to the floor.

§

Jackie heard voices over her and slowly opened her eyes.

She stared at Holden hovering over her while gently caressing her face. She managed a tiny smile and captured his hand in hers. He returned the smile.

"How are you feeling?" he asked tenderly.

"Like I've been run over by a tank," she teased then looked around the unfamiliar and moderately dingy looking medical office. "Where am I?"

"The ship's doctor's office," Holden replied. "You passed out."

Jackie allowed her eyes to roll closed as she groaned with annoyance. "You mean I'm still on the fucking ship?"

Holden chuckled softly. "Don't worry; we're leaving soon," he informed her. "I need to go over some details with the Coast Guard."

She slowly sat up against Holden's wishes and immediately clutched her shoulder, although it didn't seem to hurt nearly as bad now.

"How bad is the infection?" she asked while glancing at him.

"Could have been worse," Holden replied as he sat on the bed alongside her. "The Coast Guard medic gave you a powerful antibiotic injection and painkiller then redressed your wound."

"It's not Zack's fault," Jackie informed Holden in a defensive tone. "He did his best with what he had. The bullet had to come out."

"I know," Holden remarked and gently nodded while attempting to keep her from exerting herself. "His meatball surgery wasn't the issue. He showed me the antibiotics he'd found for you from the plane wreck. If you had a urinary infection, I'm sure it would have helped."

Jackie stared at Holden with some surprise. "You mean I wasn't taking antibiotics."

"They were antibiotics alright," Holden insisted and managed a tiny smirk. "It wasn't his fault they weren't the right kind. He's not a doctor or a field medic. He did the best he could."

She groaned lowly and rested her head on his shoulder. "I'm ready to go home now," Jackie announced while nuzzling his shoulder and clinging to his arm. "I want you to yell at me to stay in bed and nag me about the company I keep."

Holden chuckled softly then gently kissed her forehead. "Way ahead of you. Just a little while longer, I promise," he replied. "I'll take you back on deck with the others if you're ready."

"The sooner you talk to these guys, the sooner we leave, right?" she asked.

"Yes."

She immediately straightened and attempted to stand. "Then stop coddling me, and let's go," she scoffed.

Chapter Fifty

It was getting close to sunset. The team leaned against the partially destroyed pool bar and watched the Coast Guard conduct their interviews with Dexter and his daughter. It was a little after seven o'clock that night and was quite possibly the longest day any of them had ever had. The team wore matching frowns while hearing part of Dexter's recap to the Coast Guard's commanding officer. Mac sat on the deck with her back to the bar and subconsciously stroked the German shepherd's head resting on her lap. Zack sat on top of the bar with his back resting against the wall and appeared to be the only one disinterested in the entire scene.

"I'm thankful to Whiskey Tango Foxtrot for saving my daughter's life," Dexter informed the commanding officer. "The men who killed my daughter's husband are dead, and their operation is fractured. Once you turn your findings over to the CIA, I'm sure you'll discover Vinny Cicco's son was involved with a band of rogue Russian mercenaries. You'll see why they had to kill him."

"Vinny Cicco got away," the commanding officer informed Dexter. "You know your daughter isn't safe until he's captured."

"I know," Dexter replied with a defeated sigh. "That's why I'm taking my daughter someplace safe until we can go to trial against Vinny Cicco for his role in attempting to kill my little girl."

Bogart shook his head and turned away from the scene. "Unbelievable," he scoffed. "She murders her husband, and she's going to walk away."

"Even if they capture Vinny, he's the one who disposed of his son's body in his little revenge scheme," Monroe announced with disgust. "He could expose her in court, but he's the one who'll look guilty."

"She got away with it," Mac huffed with disgust as she pushed Darth aside and stood with some stiffness. "As always; money talks."

"Can we get out of here?" Kirk snarled and straightened. "I'm sick of this place."

"We're waiting for Holden," Jackie remarked while shifting uncomfortably and gingerly rubbing her shoulder. "And I wish he'd wrap it up soon." She indicated Vinny and Lindsey with a general nod. "I can't stand the sight of either of them. I've never been so angry. I may do something stupid if I don't get out of here."

Sal and Conner approached the team by the dilapidated poolside bar. They appeared to be engaged in a long, emotional conversation.

"Are you sure you want to do this?" Sal asked the young man.

Conner drew a deep, concerned breath and then nodded. "Yes," he replied and gave Sal a sympathetic look. "I know how bad it sounds, but I love Lindsey. I want to remain by her side."

Mac rolled her eyes and had to turn away. Only a few of them heard her curse. Zack slid off the bar without comment and walked away. His silent response reflected what everyone was thinking. Darth trotted after Zack.

Sal managed an uneasy laugh and shook his head. "It's your decision, kid," he announced and patted him on the shoulder. "I wish you luck."

They shook hands. Conner managed a smile at the others, who really couldn't encourage him the way Sal had. Conner shoved his hands into his pockets and headed across deck to join

Lindsey and Dexter, who were now wrapping things up with the Coast Guard.

"That kid is in for a rough life of heartache," Sal announced with a defeated sigh.

"If he survives that long," Gil muttered then looked around while running his fingers vigorously through his hair. "Where the hell is Holden anyway? I have a plane to return. Some of us still have to fly ourselves home."

"He's talking with everyone," Sal informed them. "He's going to be straightening this mess out for hours." Sal straightened proudly and offered a timid smile. "I've decided to remain behind and help him explain everything. He said the rest of you should leave. Something about less drama equals less paperwork."

"Let's hear it for drama," Mac muttered.

"Good," Kirk huffed and looked at Jackie. "Are you waiting for Holden?"

"No," she reluctantly announced while sighing then looked at Sal. "Tell Holden to call me when he's on his way, and I'll meet him at the house. He'll understand why I didn't want to wait."

Sal nodded then cleared his throat, stopping them before they could leave. "Just one more thing," he announced and handed them a check.

Monroe uncertainly accepted the check, looked at it, and rolled his eyes. He handed it back to Sal. "We don't want Dexter's money," he scoffed. "I don't care how many zeros he tacked onto it."

"Zeros?" Bogart suddenly chimed in and lunged forward to look at the check. His eyes widened in surprise then he fidgeted. "We did go to war with a mobster and Russian mercenaries. Accepting this is perfectly natural."

"It's condoning murder," Monroe snarled at Bogart and again attempted to return the check to Sal. "Tell him thanks but no thanks."

Sal shifted uncomfortably and drew a tense breath. "I think you should accept the money," he instructed Monroe. "Dexter is easily offended. It's better you keep on his good side and not start something."

"We're not starting anything," Monroe snapped. "We're washing our hands of this entire affair."

"Start what?" Jackie finally asked while eying Sal.

"Dexter knows a lot of people. *Connected* people," Sal informed them. "Right now; you're in good with every single one of them. Piss him off, and they all know your name for the wrong reason." He managed a tiny smile. "Do yourself a favor. Take the check. If you don't want the money, donate it to a charity. Listen to me, from experience, don't piss off a man like Dexter."

Monroe looked from the rest of the team, minus Zack who had again disappeared, and then back at Sal. He groaned and snatched the check from his hand.

"Fine," Monroe scoffed.

"Can we go *now*?" Kirk huffed.

"Yes, let's go," Monroe groaned and indicated the bridge deck above them to Jackie. "Can we take the helicopter to the abandoned airfield?"

"Yeah," she replied. "There's enough fuel to make it there."

"Are you okay to fly to the abandoned airfield?" Gil asked Jackie.

"Yeah, she's fine," Kirk huffed. "I'm not flying in another helicopter with you ever again."

"Yes, I'm fine," Jackie replied and hid her smile.

"We should find Zack," Bogart announced.

"Darth followed him that way," Gil announced and pointed through the destroyed lounge.

They heard the helicopter on the bridge as it started. The entire team groaned.

"I believe we're being paged," Jackie announced. "We'd better go before we have to walk."

As they headed for the outside steps to the bridge deck, Dexter, Lindsey, and Conner caught up with them. Dexter was enthusiastic and grinning.

"Are you taking the helicopter to the airfield?" he eagerly asked.

"Yes," Jackie reluctantly replied while attempting to be polite at Sal's suggestion.

"Have room for three more?" Dexter asked cheerfully while grinning.

Jackie hid her irritation, forced a smile, and nodded. "Yeah, sure."

She was the only one who was able to fake a smile, although that may have had something to do with the painkillers the Coast Guard medic gave her. Kirk sneered while watching Dexter hurry his daughter and Conner toward the outside steps for the bridge.

Mac patted his shoulder and offered a tiny smile. "Sal has a bottle of whiskey stashed on the plane," she informed him. "We'll be fine."

"Getting drunk will only increase the chances that I'll kill one or both of them," Kirk snarled.

"Why do you think I mentioned it?" Mac teased while grinning then flashed a smile and walked past him.

Chapter Fifty-one

The war-torn helicopter landed at the abandoned airfield in the center of the island. Zack was the first one off the craft and immediately headed into the hangar. He returned with a duffel bag slung over his shoulder. The others watched him with interest.

"What's in the bag?" Bogart asked.

"Provisions from the plane wreckage," Zack informed him without bothering to stop or look at him.

"Travel-sized alcohol," Jackie muttered to Bogart.

Bogart hurried after Zack and joined him on the plane. Darth ran after them while whining the entire way. The private plane that had followed them was left abandoned not far from their plane. The guys checked inside to ensure Cicco hadn't made it there and was hiding onboard. Although much larger than Sal's rental plane, Makar's plane wasn't nearly as new or luxurious. The plane looked combat ready and more for large groups of soldiers with uncomfortable seating. When all was clear, Dexter approached Monroe as Zack headed back into the hangar.

"Was that Makar's plane?" Dexter questioned while taking an interest in the private plane.

Monroe nodded. Zack returned from the hangar with a toolbox and approached the nearly disabled helicopter.

"Since he won't be needing it," Dexter announced slyly and grinned. "I suppose there's no harm if we took that one, so you wouldn't have to make any additional stops."

"Fine by me," Gil muttered while walking past.

Kirk joined Zack by the side of the helicopter, where they seemed to be having a serious discussion about something.

"Can you fly a plane?" Monroe asked the man while giving him a curious look.

"It'll be a rough landing," Dexter teased, "but I've flown in the past." He extended his hand to Monroe. "I guess this is where we part company."

Monroe eyed his hand, considered what Sal had said about keeping the peace, and sucked in his pride. He accepted Dexter's hand and shook it.

"Thank you for everything you've done," Dexter announced cheerfully.

"Yeah," Monroe remarked while forcing a smile although it couldn't have been easy. "Keep an eye on your daughter." He hesitated and didn't complete the rest of his thought. "With Cicco still out there, you'll need to keep her tucked away. Far from the world would be ideal."

"My private island is completely secluded," Dexter informed him then hesitated and gave him a knowing look. "And don't worry about Lindsey. She'll get the help she needs. I'm not completely blinded just because she's my daughter."

Monroe studied him a moment and tilted his head. "You're going to seek help for her?"

"Absolutely," Dexter replied and shook his head. "My private island isn't just about keeping people out but keeping others in."

Monroe managed a more natural smile and nodded. "Good luck," he announced with some relief.

As Monroe turned, he nearly collided with Jackie. She stared at him with a frown on her face and nervously ran her fingers through her hair. He looked past her to see what she was purposely avoiding watching. Zack and Kirk casually carried the excessively large machine gun up the steps and into the plane. They nearly got stuck once in the doorway but managed to get it inside.

Monroe rolled his eyes and groaned. "I'm through being in charge," he announced. "Let Ross or Beck deal with those two."

The team boarded their plane while Gil prepped for take-off. Dexter prepped Makar's abandoned plane, although it took him a little longer to figure things out. The team watched Lindsey and Conner in a warm embrace near their plane, nuzzling each other as if nothing had happened. The team then continued onto their nearby plane. Kirk pulled up the steps and sealed the door. He shook his head in disgust.

"I'm glad I'm no longer twenty-something and stupid," Kirk snarled and extended his hand to Mac.

She slapped the nearly full bottle of whiskey into his hand. He took the bottle and headed for the back of the plane where Zack was already camped out with his travel bottles of booze. It was unclear if Zack was willing to share or not. Jackie sank into the seat next to Darth, who was already asleep, and shook her head.

"I used to think karma took over where justice failed," Jackie remarked while petting the dog then sighed and shut her eyes. She leaned her head against the back of the seat and groaned softly. "This world officially sucks."

Monroe collapsed into a seat across from her. "Well, if it makes you feel any better, Dexter intends to lock Lindsey away on his island. It's not exactly Alcatraz, but at least she'll be removed from the general population."

"Yes, imprisoned in a mansion on an island paradise," Jackie scoffed and lazily opened her eyes. A twisted smile crossed her face. "Justice has been served."

"I don't know," Mac announced cheerfully and fell into a seat across from them. "With the way she feels about her father, she may prefer actual prison. Maybe karma wins after all."

"Nice try, Mac," Jackie muttered, "but it's still not the same."

"We're ready for take-off," Gil called back to them. "Everyone strap in."

The team took their seats, fastened their seatbelts, and prepared for take-off. Jackie stared at the second plane and frowned her disappointment. As Gil taxied the plane down the overgrown runway, Jackie released her seatbelt and headed toward the back of the plane. She collapsed between Zack and Kirk, belted herself in, and snatched the bottle from Kirk. Jackie took a large swig and returned the bottle. Zack eyed her and chuckled, grinning for the first time.

"Jackie's getting hammered," Zack teased. "This flight just got more interesting."

§

Lindsey sat within the fuselage of the less than luxurious plane alongside Conner. She had her arms folded across her chest and aggressively swung her crossed leg. They hadn't even taken off, and she was already pouting about their final destination.

"It's not going to be so bad," Conner informed her while trying to stay positive. "We've been to your father's private island before. It's a tropical paradise. It'll be a fun way to spend several months until the trial."

"He should never have made that plea deal without discussing it with me first," she snapped hotly.

"You're not going to jail," Conner insisted and placed his hand on her leg. "There's no body, remember? Cicco shot himself in the foot when he covered up the crime. It was his obsession with revenge that'll be his undoing. You'll come out looking innocent, and he'll look guilty on all counts. If you play your cards right, you'll even gain sympathy in all this." Conner then grinned and patted her hand. "And you'll get to keep all Sebastian's money. It's perfect."

"I'm glad you think so," she scoffed then turned more sympathetic while touching his arm. "I'm sorry about everything, Conner. It wasn't as bad as Cicco made it out. I wasn't planning on framing you for Sebastian's murder. I'll admit; I did exploit your feelings for me to gain your compliance, but that's all. I do love you."

Conner smiled with relief and kissed her quickly on the lips. He immediately pulled back and met her gaze. "I love you too." His smile suddenly faded. "Oh, my bag. I left it in the hangar." He sprang up from his seat and popped his head into the cockpit. "Give me a minute, Dexter. I left my bag in the hangar. There's something I don't want to leave behind."

Dexter nodded. "I'm going to need a few minutes anyway," he replied.

Conner hurried to the door and opened it, lowering the steps. He glanced back at Lindsey. "Did you want to come along and get your bag?"

"No," she replied and shifted in her chair. "There's nothing in there I need."

He nodded and left the plane. Lindsey stared out the window a moment, eyed the open door, and then released her seatbelt. She stood and approached the cockpit.

"Daddy," she announced firmly while folding her arms across her chest as she stood in the doorway. "Can we talk while Conner's gone?"

"Sure, baby," he announced and motioned for her to join him in the cockpit.

"No, I'd rather talk out here," she insisted.

Dexter released his harness and left the cockpit. He approached her in the aisle and stared at her with concern. "What is it, baby? Is something wrong? Are you having second thoughts about Conner coming with us?"

"No," she replied while drawing a deep breath. "I want to discuss this plan of yours."

"My plan?"

"The one where you lock me away on your island like some wild animal," she snapped.

"Lindsey, you're not being locked away," he insisted while smiling sympathetically. "It's for your protection. No one will find you on my island. Cicco is still out there. We can't risk him getting his hands on you. The island is the only safe place for you."

"I know it seems that way," she remarked and offered a sly smile, "but you forgot something very important."

"What's that?"

"Five hundred billion dollars," she replied matter-of-factly. "With that kind of money, I can disappear forever. No one will ever find me."

"The moment you attempt to access that money, Makar's men will be on you," Dexter informed her. "You need to let that go."

Lindsey shook her head and sighed. "You never really see the bigger picture," she remarked. "All you care about is controlling me."

"That's not true."

"Oh, please," she scoffed while sneering at him. "Just give it a rest."

Lindsey revealed a small gun in her hand and shot her father in the abdomen at close range. He clutched his bleeding midsection while staring at her in disbelief. He attempted to grab her. She leaped backward and avoided him as he collapsed to the aisle floor. Conner ran onto the plane and stared at the scene with a look of horror. Lindsey turned to Conner and smiled sweetly.

"Change of plans," she announced. "We're going to my father's island without him. We'll lay low a few weeks, get our hands on Makar's billions, and disappear forever." She smiled sweetly. "Are you in or out?"

Conner lifted his eyes from her dead father and met her gaze. He drew several deep breaths then relaxed. "Of course I'm with you," he announced. "I love you." He hesitated and again eyed her dead father. "But your father's men will be on that island. We can't take him with us. We'll need to leave his body behind as well as that gun."

Lindsey eyed the gun in her hand then her dead father. She met Conner's gaze and nodded. "Of course, you're right." She tossed the gun out the doorway and offered a smile. "Let's get him off the plane."

Conner grabbed Lindsey's father under the arms while she grabbed his ankles. "How are we going to get there? I can't fly a plane," he informed her.

"I can," she insisted cheerfully. "I've been taking lessons. I thought I might need them one day." She giggled. "Guess I was right."

They carried her dead father down the few steps from the plane and left his body not far from the landing gear. Lindsey smiled at Conner and placed her arms affectionately around his neck. He seemed tense as she kissed him. She pulled back and smiled.

"Everything is going to be fine, Conner," she insisted and gently touched his face. "We'll have everything we've ever wanted."

Conner nodded and managed a tiny smile. "Yes," he replied and rubbed her shoulders. "The money will come in handy."

He stepped away from her and the plane. Lindsey eyed him with a strange look then hesitated and looked behind her. Cicco and Dawg stood only a few feet behind her with a gun aimed at her.

She looked back at Conner and stared at him with horror. "You set me up?" Lindsey gasped.

Conner sneered and just about lunged at her. "Did you think I would forgive you for attempting to frame me in your husband's death?" he demanded in anger. "You're damned right I set you up. And by the way; it's over between us!"

"Don't worry, my dear," Cicco announced cheerfully while grinning. "Your former boyfriend is being compensated extremely well for handing you over to me. See? Everyone wins." He then reconsidered the comment. "Well, not so much you."

Chapter Fifty-two

The gazebo beyond the garden in Sal's backyard was covered with exotic flowers. Over two hundred guests sat in white, wooden folding chairs on either side of the aisle and awaited the wedding of the century. Sal's daughter was finally getting married and just about anyone with any sort of connections was in attendance. The officiator, Othello, entered the gazebo and stood in the center with an electronic tablet in his hand. Othello was a large, robust man with wild, curly black hair. Despite his size and stature, he had an innocent sort of appeal. Beck, looking dashing in his black tuxedo, was joined by his best man, Ross. Ross Madrid was a distinguished looking man in his early fifties. Despite his age, the slightly graying man still maintained an impressive build. Definitely intimidating, Ross Madrid didn't look friendly although he was considered harmless by many.

The three groomsmen, Gil, Monroe, and Kirk stood alongside Ross. The man standing at the portable keyboard played a romantic sonnet. As everyone looked back, Darth was the first to appear in the aisle with the wedding rings tied to his collar with a ribbon. He trotted excitedly and paused to greet a few of his favorite guests. Gil had to give a slight whistle to resume the dog's focus. Darth dashed up the gazebo steps and greeted Othello with a happy whimper. Othello laughed and patted his head before another whistle sent him to Gil's side. The bridesmaids were next down the aisle. They were two of Pinto's friends from college and Jackie. All three wore revealing black dresses, which Jackie secretly tugged on every so often to cover her exposed cleavage.

The bridesmaids joined the men in the gazebo on the opposite side. Jackie looked into the crowd and saw Holden, who grinned his approval of the dress. Leeann Whitley, Pinto's maid-of-honor, was the last to walk down the aisle. Lee was an attractive woman in her mid-twenties with wild, dark hair barely contained while pinned up with bobby pins and baby's breath. She wore the same black dress as the other bridesmaids, and it looked just as flattering. As Ross' wife made her way down the aisle, Jackie glanced from the groomsmen to the nearby patio roof. Zack sat casually reclined on the roof wearing his usual combat gear with his fully loaded AK-47 assault rifle set up on a sniper stand.

No one was talking Zack into wearing a suit much less getting into a tuxedo. For that reason, he was adamant about not having an active role in the wedding ceremony. The only time Jackie had ever seen Zack in formal wear was in a photo from her father's wedding. All the men were dressed in their full dress, formal, white Navy uniforms, which he seemed willing to wear at the time. When the song changed to the wedding march, all two hundred guests rose and turned to see Pinto escorted down the aisle by her father. Sal was beaming with delight while holding his daughter's hand to the crook of his arm. He looked dashing in his black tuxedo.

Pinto was breathtaking in her peach colored wedding dress with flowing train and sparkling tiara. The dress was sleeveless, which was perfect for a warm afternoon. The top was mostly lace, and the neckline plunged daringly low allowing her ample cleavage to showcase the dress. The dress was fitted through the waist then fell gently from her hips with lace and sheer mesh over top a more fitted, satin liner. Her cascading bouquet containing yellow, peach, and pink roses was large enough to conceal an Uzi comfortably. Pinto nixed the Uzi but agreed to a much smaller .22 caliber revolver. Jackie wanted to lend her the .357 Magnum she'd carried on her wedding day as her something borrowed, but Pinto was set on the much smaller weapon. To normal people attending a wedding, it would seem unheard of for the bride to be armed and a sniper on the roof, but this wasn't any ordinary wedding.

Sal kissed his daughter on the cheek and enthusiastically shook Beck's hand before turning his daughter over into his protective services. Beck walked Pinto up the gazebo steps and stopped in front of Othello. Sal took his seat in front alongside Mac, who looked stunning and particularly feminine for once. In the front row on the groom's side, Holden sat with Bogart and his two dates. Monique sat on his right while Colleen sat on his left. Both teenage girls were out of place in dresses, but they were happy to be at the wedding and even more so as Bogart's dates.

As the ceremony got underway, Beck and Pinto recited their vows and exchanged rings. It was the perfect day for an outdoor wedding. Under Zack's watchful eye and riflescope, the wedding went off without incident. Othello pronounced them husband and wife, and the eager couple kissed more passionately than normally acceptable.

§

The reception took place on the patio and inside the grand ballroom where an orchestra played. A buffet-style feast took up three tables and there was an open bar, where most of the single men seemed to hang out. There was also a portable bar on the patio, allowing the reception to float between the indoor and outdoor venues. Jackie and Holden danced several slow songs together and attempted to keep it respectable while Bogart danced with each of his young dates on a rotating basis. The two girls were in their glory and perhaps a little too smitten with Jackie's charming brother.

Gil's ex-wife gladly came as his date, and they seemed a little cozy on the dance floor. Since the entire team was staying overnight at Sal's mansion, Jackie was almost convinced Gil and his ex-wife would be having their own wedding night festivities. Kirk was becoming familiar with one of the bridesmaids, who was almost certainly warned about his commitment issues. She didn't seem to care, not seeing past his muscles. Bogart had his eye on the second bridesmaid, but he'd committed the evening to his teenager friends and intended to stick with that plan. Holden kept Jackie close as they danced and held her hand to his chest. He scanned the elegant room and everyone having a good time.

"Well," he announced with a sigh. "It would seem half the west coast mafia turned out for this little function."

"Had you seen the guest list?" Jackie muttered close to his ear. "Frightening."

"Seen it?" he teased. "I ran background checks on just about every name on the list. There are some heavy hitters here." He then cast a look at Mac and Sal slow dancing and indicated the woman. "How did Mac get an invite? I thought she was Typhoid Mary."

"She is," Jackie replied and hid her smile. "Sal invited her as his plus one against the groom's wishes. Sal thinks she deserves another chance."

"For what? To turn on you and get the entire team killed?" Holden remarked.

"Beck shut it down loud and clear," Jackie replied and nuzzled her husband's neck. "She's still ousted."

"Does she know that?"

"I couldn't say," Jackie muttered near his ear. She pulled back, met his gaze, and smiled seductively while placing both arms around his neck. "What do you say we sneak off for a quickie behind the gazebo? It's almost dark."

Holden grinned his response. "I like the way your devious mind works."

They were about to kiss when someone cleared his throat alongside them. They pulled away and looked at Monroe standing only a foot away.

"Okay, Holden," Monroe announced. "She's your wife, I get that, but I think you should let us poor dateless souls have a dance."

Holden released Jackie and placed his hand on Monroe's shoulder. "You know," he announced, "I'm feeling just sorry enough to let you have that dance."

Monroe collected Jackie in his arms and watched as Holden snickered and walked away. "I'm guessing you promised him a quickie during the reception," he muttered then eyed Jackie as they danced. "You could have done so much better."

She clung to his neck and smiled. "Oh, really?" she asked. "With you, perhaps?"

"I'm not such a bad catch," he informed her.

"No, you're a wonderful catch," she replied and straightened his tie with one hand. "You'll make some woman very happy one day."

"Does 'one day' ever come along?" he teased.

"It did for me," she replied and smiled. "When you least expect it and definitely don't want it."

"I always hoped 'one day' would be you," he remarked in a gentle, serious tone.

Jackie stared into his eyes, gently touched his face, and kissed him quickly on the lips. "Our day passed," she whispered while offering a tiny smile. "Trust me; there's some rebellious, venomous woman worse than me just waiting for you to come along."

Monroe's eyes strayed to Mac as she danced with Sal and laughed at something he'd said. Jackie's eyes suddenly widened, and she slapped Monroe gently on the face. He looked back at her with surprise.

"Don't you even consider that thought," she gasped just loud enough for him to hear. "I don't know what happened between her and Zack, but you need to stay far away from that woman."

"I wasn't thinking anything, I swear," he protested then frowned. "Well, maybe something freaky and wild, but definitely not in the way of a relationship."

"Mac is off-limits," Jackie insisted. "Don't choose her over Zack. He's liable to put you both in the ground."

§

After being passed around on the dance floor to slow dance with her father's team, minus Zack who seemed to have vanished, Jackie slipped outside for some cool air. Most of the party had ventured into the grand ballroom leaving the patio almost void of life. One couple must have had the same idea she did since she heard undeniable sounds of pleasure coming from behind the gazebo. She had to admit, she was curious, but she avoided sneaking a peek. The music could be heard almost as clearly on the patio as inside, making a romantic evening on the patio. Jackie leaned on the half wall and stared into the dimly lit garden.

"Do you have one more dance left in you?" Zack asked from nearby.

Jackie turned and saw Zack standing a few yards from her. To her surprise, he was dressed in his full dress white uniform made of certified Navy Twill. The uniform, minus the gloves and hat, consisted of a high stand-collared white tunic with shoulder boards, white trousers, and white shoes. Jackie stared at him a moment then grinned, pleased with what she saw.

"Wow," she announced while looking him over. "Do I know you?"

Zack rolled his eyes and pulled her into his arms, forcing her to dance with him on the patio. Although he held her a little too close, she didn't protest. She'd never danced with Zack before, and she wasn't going to jinx it.

"I thought you took off," Jackie remarked as he held her hand to his chest in the same affectionate manner as Holden had when they danced.

"It's Beck's wedding," he informed her. "I'm obligated to stay until after the cake is cut."

"Says who?"

"Says me," he replied then shrugged while grinning. "I like wedding cake."

Zack held Jackie tight against him almost as if he intended to smother her. It was that moment she realized something was wrong, but she couldn't push the conversation.

"You asked who 'she' was," he announced timidly. "She was an innocent, naive girl who thought she could handle my past. Mind you that was back when my past wasn't even a shadow of what it is now." He seemed to tense and fell silent a moment. "After you were born, I started thinking I could have what your father had. A life; a family; a kid named Scorpio--"

"Scorpio?" Jackie asked with surprise and nearly pulled back to see if he was serious. She knew it would end the conversation, so she decided against it.

"SEAL Team Scorpio," he replied and held his breath. "In honor of an amazing group of men we lost on a single mission." Zack sighed then snorted a soft laugh. "Me a father? And I thought she was the naïve one." He sighed gently near her ear. "I would have done anything for her. Ultimately, I did. I let the government kill me off, so she'd think I was dead. It was the only way to protect her."

Jackie considered not speaking, but she couldn't help herself. "Have you ever thought about looking her up?" she asked gently.

"Yeah," he replied softly and frowned. "I looked her up. She died the year after the government faked my death. Accidental death, they claimed." He drew a deep breath. "It wasn't an accident. Someone found her and killed her because of me; I'm almost positive of that. I sometimes visit her grave to remind myself not to invite any more innocent people into my life." He buried his face into her hair and muttered under his breath. "I'd like to go away and never come back. I was well on my way to a life of solitude on the ocean before you made your dramatic reappearance into our lives."

She pulled back and met his gaze with a stern look. "No, Zack," she insisted. "No one here is better off without you in their lives."

"Holden would be happy to get rid of me," he informed her without hesitation.

"I assure you that only applies to our bedroom," she remarked. "Not our lives."

"I feel sorry for you, Jackie," he announced and shook his head.

She stared at him with a bewildered look. "Sorry for me? Why?"

"Because you're stupid enough to care about me," he casually replied. "My past is a threat to everyone in the team and those they love. If I wasn't such a selfish bastard, I'd leave for the sake of everyone I care about. I've thought about it, but I'm afraid to leave. I'm afraid something will happen to you, and it'll be my fault for not being here to prevent it when that day comes."

Jackie stared into his eyes. "I'm selfish too," she boldly announced. "I don't want you to leave. If you try; I will find you and bring you back. It's that simple, Zack. You can't escape me. You're stuck with me."

Zack smiled and pulled her against him in a warm embrace. "I'm happy to be stuck with you." He sighed near her ear. "Besides, Gil would kill me."

She pulled back and met his gaze. "Gil? Why Gil?"

"Because if I leave; I'm taking Darth."

Jackie laughed and hugged him as if she'd never let go. "You, me, the guys. We're a team. We have each other's backs," she informed him. "Your past can't hurt us any more than it can hurt you while you're with us. We've got this. You have to trust me."

"Yep," Zack announced with a sigh. "We're one crazy ass family."

Chapter Fifty-three

Mac entered the small studio apartment still wearing her dress from the earlier wedding reception. Even without the lights on, the apartment was partially lit from streetlights filtering in through the tattered curtains. She turned on the light and immediately cast her shoes across the floor with disgust.

"Who needs them anyway," she scoffed and slammed the door behind her.

Someone banged on the wall from the apartment next door. She spun toward the banging from the wall.

"Ah, shut up!"

With the lights on, it was obvious Mac wasn't earning enough for a comfortable living. She removed a wad of cash from the cleavage of her low-cut dress and tossed it into a box on a table near the door.

"Bastards," she snarled while unzipping her dress as she crossed the slightly disheveled room for her bedroom.

She allowed the dress to fall to the floor as she paused in the bedroom doorway then violently kicked it across the bedroom.

"Two hundred dollars for some stupid dress," she lashed out. "They don't know who they're fucking with."

There was pounding from the ceiling. She looked up at the dark ceiling above her dimly lit bedroom.

"Go to hell!"

Mac turned the light on by the doorway switch brightening the moderately messy bedroom. She wore a sexy black lacy bra and thong panties. Her thigh holster contained a small caliber semiautomatic, adding to her already dangerous look. Mac stared across her room only a second, saw a man casually reclined on her bed, and immediately drew the gun from her thigh holster. Kane smiled, held his hands in the air almost mockingly, and took in a sweeping eyeful of her sexy, matching undergarments.

"I surrender," he teased. "For the record; I'm not opposed if you'd like to tie me to the bed."

Mac stared at the familiar man from their last meeting. She kept the gun aimed at him and sneered. "What the hell are you doing in my apartment?"

"Starving," he casually replied and lowered his hands. "Don't you keep any food in this place?" He then looked around. "Wouldn't hurt to pick up a little either." He raised a cocky brow. "And you could use some guest towels in the bathroom."

She stared at him with her mouth hanging open then turned angry. "How long have you been here?"

He glanced at his watch and considered the question. "Four hours and five days." He casually folded his arms across his chest and again studied her in the doorway. "If you aren't going to ravish me, could you put the gun down and maybe put on some clothes?" He wagged his finger between them. "Because *this* is sort of turning me on."

Mac lowered the gun while groaning and maintained her glare. "What the hell do you want?"

"You know what I want," he casually replied then eyed his crotch and looked back at her. "Well, you know two things I want, but let's discuss the one that won't get me shot."

"I already told you," she scoffed. "Apart from that one encounter, I haven't seen Zack Kinsley. I'm sure the bastard's probably dead by now." She raised her brows. "And if he's not, he should be."

"No love lost between you two, huh?" he teased while hiding his humor.

"Zack is incapable of loving anyone, trust me," she scoffed. "Why do you want to find him anyway?"

"We have some unfinished business, he and I." His eyes again swept over her with an approving gaze. "Are you going to put something on? I'm serious. My hormones are raging over here."

Mac rolled her eyes, snatched a discarded satin robe across her chair, and slipped into it. "You're practically a kid," she snapped. "I doubt you could impress me in that department."

He made a face. "Now that hurt," he announced while pouting. "Got to learn somewhere. Besides, I'm over the legal drinking age."

"Look, kid," she snarled. "I'm not in the mood. Not for your little quest or a three-second thrill ride in your pants. If you know what's good for you, you'll leave."

He sighed and moved off the bed. Mac didn't even flinch as he straightened. He wasn't a perceived threat to her, which he must have found amusing for some reason.

"Judging by your attitude and the past due bills piling up on your counter, I'm guessing you're low on friends and work," he informed her. "I'm starting a freelance company, and I could use someone like you. Street-smart, city savvy, and full of venom."

She stared at him with some surprise. "You're offering me a job?"

"Not a job," he insisted then grinned slyly. "A partnership. I want you to join my team."

"What team?"

He seemed pleased with himself and handed her a card. "Midnight Requisition."

Mac stared at him a moment in silence while letting the name sink in. She eyed the business card and suddenly left out a throaty laugh.

"What sort of stupid ass name is that for a business?" she practically cried out, mocking him.

He didn't seem the least bit offended by her mocking tone or callous comments. "A carefully chosen one," he replied and smiled in a somewhat devilish manner. "What do you say? Could you use a friend?"

Mac stiffened while staring at him. He seemed to have said the magic word. She finally relaxed and ran her fingers through her hair while nodding.

"Yeah, I could use a friend."

The End

Midnight Requisition
Book One

"I don't want to talk about your father," Scorpio's grandmother announced with a fearful look in her eyes that immediately turned stern. "It was your brother's obsession with that fantasy that probably got him killed."

"Probably? If there's a chance my brother is still alive, I have to find him," Scorpio remarked while staring at her grandmother. "Why would he believe our father is still alive? Why would he risk his life chasing ghosts?"

"Kane refused to believe your father was dead," her grandmother reluctantly informed her. "He never listened to anyone. Who knows what went through his head the day he picked up and left."

Scorpio continued her search of the old shoebox. She removed a black and white photo, studied it a moment, and then looked at her grandmother with surprise.

"What's this photo?"

The older woman eyed the picture of several men in uniform. The alarmed expression on her face was enough to answer the question. "That's nothing," she nervously replied. "Just an old photo your mother kept."

"According to the date on this photo, it was taken a few years after I was born," Scorpio insisted. "My mother died *before* this was taken. This wasn't hers. Where did this come from?"

"Who knows. I'm sure it's nothing," she replied while waving her off. "Must be something your brother found."

She glared demandingly at her grandmother. "It says Whiskey Tango Foxtrot. What does that mean? Who are these men?"

Her grandmother immediately fumbled on her words. "I'm not sure. I think they were some men your father knew."

"No, Grandma," she announced and indicated the picture. "My father is in this picture, isn't he? That's why my brother left. He went to find our father because he found proof he was still alive."

"Don't dig up the past, Scorpio," her grandmother begged. "Losing Kane was enough. I don't want to lose you too."

Coming Soon!

Other books by Holly Copella!
Reviews left on Amazon are appreciated!

"The Battle for Andrea Maria"

A cruise ship attack turns six survivors into overnight celebrities after they take credit for the heroic act of a stowaway who died saving them.

The cruise is just what Jess needed--a bit of harmless fun far from her daily grind. But what begins as a relaxing vacation turns into a desperate fight for her life when terrorists take over the ship and start piling up bodies. Teaming up with a mysterious stowaway, Jess attempts to send out a distress call but knows they cannot wait for help to come. If she or the few remaining passengers have any hope for survival, Jess must act now. The papers dub it "The Battle for *Andrea Maria*," but to Jess it is the moment she fought side-by-side with her enigmatic Romeo, saving the ship--and losing him. She thinks the story ends there, but really, the nightmare is just beginning...

"Insanely Deadly"

When the dead return to life, it's up to an admiral's daughter and a mildly insane, former war hero to save their small town.

Jetta Cross, a Navy Admiral's daughter, is tasked with keeping her father's comrade, a former war hero turned town crazy, grounded in the real world. Capt. John Hunter is still fighting the war in his head, where imaginary dead people are part of his world. When a viral outbreak brings about a zombie uprising, Hunter is left to his own devices. He must resume his role as a one-man commando unit in order to destroy the ravenous undead. With Hunter still fighting his own inner demons as well as the undead, the townspeople fear their zombie neighbors may not be the only threat. Stranded at the island's luxurious resort with a handful of workers, Jetta is forced to live up to her father's reputation and take charge of the deteriorating situation at the hotel. She must wage her own war against the infected before the government declares her hometown a total loss.

"Deadly Institution"

A town recluse suspected of killing his wife teams up with a young woman in order to stop a killer.

After being accused of murdering his wife, Konrad Asher turns his back on the town that once adored him. Ten years later, he still holds his grudge and the title of the most feared man in town. With the reopening of the burned mental institution, where his wife had died, former employees are now murdered one-by-one, throwing suspicion back on Asher. A young local reporter, Jacey, is forced to reveal her long-time friendship with the infamous recluse in order to clear his name not only in the recent murders but to exonerate him in the death of his wife as well. Will Jacey's relationship with Asher invite the killer closer to her? Or is the killer already in her life?

"Screenplays: The Island Collection"
"Jungle Princess", "A.L.F. Resort", "Brighton Island"

Discover how romance and fun in the sun can be downright *chilling*!

"Jungle Princess" is a romantic/thriller that leaves a teenage girl stranded on an island with two male shipmates and a creature of "unknown" origin. She soon discovers the island is home to an abandoned prison with several prisoners roaming free. What really killed over one hundred prisoners? And is it still out there--?

"A.L.F. Resort" is a romantic/thriller set on an island resort with Artificial Life Forms as the main draw. At this resort, all your fantasies come true...until a malfunction removes safety inhibitors on the A.L.F.'s. Zombies, biker gangs, and mobsters run amuck, turning fantasies into nightmares. A young reporter gets more of a story than she anticipates, but will she survive long enough to write the story?

"Brighton Island" is a romantic/thriller set on a private island. When the owner's niece brings her psychic friend to the mansion, his presence awakens the spirits' tortured souls. As the psychic attempts to solve the old murders, the niece is confronted with the possibility that she's next to join the mansion ghosts. Stranded on the island with a crazed killer, her uncle wages his own war to save them. Will his "shock and awe" tactics actually save them or get them killed?

"Death Displacement"

A grief-stricken man travels back in time to seek revenge on the woman who murdered his girlfriend but inadvertently falls in love with her.

Kane is about to marry the woman he loves. His life is perfect. A few weeks before the wedding, a vindictive woman from his girlfriend's past mysteriously arrives and kills her. He learns of a traumatic accident that happened five years earlier, which triggers Riley's hatred for his girlfriend. Distraught over his girlfriend's death, Kane uses an antique time machine to travel into the past in order to find and destroy the woman responsible. When he runs into Riley's younger self, he realizes she's not the monster she later becomes, and he can't bring himself to destroy her. With a little help from his oddball friend from the past, they formulate a plan to prevent the accident that sends Riley down her destructive path. Kane's plan backfires when he falls for the younger Riley. His new tortured existence is further complicated when future Riley, his girlfriend's killer, shows up with her own devious agenda that doesn't include him. Will he be able to stop the time ripple, which ultimately ends with his girlfriend's death? Or will future Riley take him out of the timeline forever--

"Dead Village"

After strange happenings isolate a small resort town from the rest of the world, nearly one hundred residents seek refuge at the closed hotel. Only eight survive the night. And that's just the beginning...

One day after the entire population of Fox Ridge Village disappears, a car wreck forces several unsuspecting crash victims to seek help at the closed summer hotel. Within the hotel, they discover the grisly aftermath of a brutal slaughter. Crash victims Vander and Devon, a reluctant clairvoyant, team up to solve the riddle of the "haunted hotel" and the mass hysteria plaguing the remaining survivors. By the time they discover the hotel's secret, they're already drawn into the hysteria. As the body count continues to climb, it's a race to isolate the source and bring everyone back to reality before they kill one another. Will Devon be able to communicate with the traumatized spirits before their fate becomes her own?

"Misfits, Inc."

A seemingly ordinary, young woman meets four misfits who claim she has given them supernatural powers.

While on a business trip to a remote island paradise, a bored secretary, Hailey, has her world turned upside down when her path collides with a psychic freak, Skyler. He attempts to convince her that they had met in his dreams, and she had chosen him as one of her four mystic warriors. After Skyler foresees a woman's death, they discover an unidentified creature has killed one of the guests. They are joined by a lounge pianist and a rich playboy, who also claim they had met her in their dreams. If Skyler's prophecies are genuine, the evil entity controlling the ravenous creatures needs to destroy Hailey to ensure its survival. Reluctantly accepting her fate, Hailey has to locate the last and most powerful of her chosen warriors, The Guardian. Their fate is in doubt when The Guardian turns out to be a self-absorbed, former cat burglar with a bad attitude. Can Hailey turn her company of misfits into an elite team of mystic warriors? Or will The Guardian's secret agenda destroy them all?

"Basement Dwellers"

A viral outbreak at a hospital leaves a mortician, sheriff, and coroner fighting for their lives against a horde of undead and the CDC.

After a massive car wreck leaves several survivors in critical condition at the local hospital, a surgeon uses experimental drugs on his critical patients and accidentally causes a zombie outbreak. When local mortician, Lexx, receives an infected corpse as her client, she becomes stranded in the hospital basement during CDC quarantine along with the local sheriff and the coroner. The infamous surgeon struggles to find a cure for his infectious blunder by using the other survivors as test subjects. Meanwhile, Lexx and the sheriff attempt to locate his missing sister, who's stranded somewhere in the battle zone that once was the emergency room. It's a race against time and the ravenous undead. Can they survive the undead before CDC sanitizes the hospital of all infection?

Holly Copella

"Witness Protection"
Also available in audiobook!

After witnessing an execution, a resourceful young woman attempts to disappear while being pursued by a hitman and a handsome federal agent.

A helicopter pilot, Jackie Remus, reluctantly agrees to go on a date with one of her clients, but her date is unexpectedly cut short when she witnesses a man being murdered. After narrowly escaping with her life, she is placed into protective custody. When the safe house is breached, Jackie makes a daring escape from both the hired killers and the handsome FBI agent, who wants to return her to protective custody. With a little help from her sly and crafty friend, Monroe, Jackie is convinced she can disappear until the trial. While on her journey to meet with her friend, she solicits help from a few shady but lovable characters along the way. Although she manages to stay one-step ahead of the hired killers, the federal agent remains in hot pursuit. Will Jackie reach Monroe before she's captured by the FBI and returned to protective custody? Or will the hired killers silence her first?

"Town Darling"

After surviving a brutal attack that claims the lives of those she loves, a young woman seeks revenge on a corrupt town.

Going back home is never easy, but for Casey, it means returning to her corrupt hometown where she barely survived a brutal attack. Accompanied by two family friends, she seeks justice for the night that destroyed her life. Her physical scars are nothing compared to her emotional ones, forcing the local sheriff to believe that the town darling is back for revenge. As the conspiracy for her revenge appears to be leading up to the coveted town fair, the sheriff is determined to stop her from fulfilling her vengeful scheme...but guilt over his role on that fateful night continues to haunt him. Will his desperate need for Casey's forgiveness be his undoing? Or will Casey's desire for revenge destroy them both?

360

"Unconditional"

A young woman puts her life on hold to care for an unstable, highly skilled combat soldier, who believes someone is trying to kill him.

A botched military coup leaves a team of elite fighters injured with one clinging to life in a coma. When Harlan wakes from his coma, he's left with no memory of his past life. His commander's daughter, Indy, takes it upon herself to care for the fallen war hero. She's challenged with more than just his physical care as she combats with not only his memory loss but also his newly found desire for her. His infatuation with her becomes the least of her worries when he sinks back into his role of a combat soldier. Believing his life is in danger, his fighting skills surface, turning him into an unpredictable and dangerous man. Will his memory return to him before Indy is forced to commit him? Or will he finally find his nemesis, "the coyote", and possibly claim the life of an innocent person?

"Witness Protection 2"
The Return of Whiskey Tango Foxtrot

Believing she holds the clue to millions in missing laundered money, a young woman is placed into the protective care of a former Navy SEAL team.

Feeling sorry for her recently separated co-worker, Leeann invites Wiley to join her and her friends on their night out. Little does she know that finding her co-worker murdered is just the beginning of her nightmare. Leeann unknowingly holds the key to fifty million dollars in potentially laundered mob money. With hired killers pursuing her, the FBI places her into a different kind of protective custody. Former Navy SEAL team Whiskey Tango Foxtrot reunites to keep Leeann alive at their secret hideaway. What should be an easy assignment takes an unscheduled turn when secrets, lies, and betrayal threaten to derail their mission. Is the team prepared for a war on their own doorstep? Will Leeann's misguided trust endanger the lives of those sent to protect her?

"Deadly Institution 2"

When blackmail turns into murder, a young woman finds herself caught in the killer's crosshairs.

The small town of Stony Ridge is no stranger to scandal and persecution of the innocent. When a brutal killing shakes the town's prestigious country club, Jacey McMurray seeks help from a self-proclaimed vigilante, Konrad Asher. As her professional and personal worlds collide, Jacey fears the stress of the country club killings have finally taken their toll on Asher. Can a stressed out vigilante stop the killer before he strikes again?

"Witness Protection 3"
Alpha Mike Foxtrot

A helicopter pilot risks her life to help a team of retired Navy SEALs rescue two girls from a killer.

When former Navy SEAL team Whiskey Tango Foxtrot asks for a simple favor, Jackie reluctantly offers her air-taxi services. What could go wrong? What begins as a search and rescue for two girls turns into a fight for survival against a heavily armed drug cartel. Wanted by the law with the cartel in hot pursuit and their home base breached, the team is forced to call in a favor from a questionable ally. Unfortunately, their new safe house isn't what it seems. Without knowing who the real enemy is, can Jackie and the team save their young witnesses from the hands of a killer?

"The Pen Pal"

In order to save her friend, she must enter the mind of a serial killer.

When her best friend is abducted, no one believes Jolynn saw it in a psychic vision. With nowhere to turn, Jolynn reluctantly joins Agent Harris Slade and his team on their hunt for a sadistic serial killer known only as "The Pen Pal". Finally confronted with the killer, Jolynn realizes she must enter the mind of the psychopath in order to stop the brutal killings. But when her vision reveals a particularly disturbing death, can Jolynn sacrifice her lover for her friend?

"Awaken the Dead"

A grieving innkeeper struggles to keep her haunted hotel out of foreclosure.

After losing her parents in a suspicious boating accident, Harley Brandon is determined to keep the family hotel out of foreclosure. Unfortunately, the hotel ghosts have other plans. Built with tainted money, the century old Horizon Hotel thrives on a tradition of murder, scandal, and suicide. As the paranormal activity increases to alarming levels, Harley discovers the truth about the hotel and its residents. Can Harley save her friends from the hotel's frightening hidden secrets?

"Already Dead"
Supernatural Collection

From the already dead to the undead. Three supernatural tales of "things that go bump in the night".

"Bloodletting" - A vampire themed resort allows guests to *participate* in their Bloodletting Ritual to celebrate the island's legendary vampires.

"Reaper of Souls" - A young woman must outwit an evil sorcerer in order to save her brother or become one of his minions forever.

"Already Dead" - When Flight 220 crashes, ten passengers make it to an isolated island, but only one man lives to tell the lie.

"Witness Protection 4"
O-Dark-Hundred

A simple assignment turns deadly when a retired Navy SEAL team uncovers a plot to kill a notorious mob boss.

When Whiskey Tango Foxtrot embarks on a simple stalking case, they're not prepared for a trip to a private island paradise owned by an infamous mobster. With one of their own suffering from traumatic head injuries, the team is left scrambling to decide what is real or imagined. The situation escalates even further when they uncover an assassination plot where everyone is a suspect. Now targets themselves, can the team survive their trip to paradise?

"Witness Protection 5"
Outside the Wire

After suffering several casualties on their last assignment, a retired Navy SEAL team discovers their misery is just beginning.

When Whiskey Tango Foxtrot returns home after suffering a devastating loss, they're hit with even more bad news regarding the rest of their team. Their grief is cut short when they discover their names are all on the same hit list. Hunted by relentless assassins, the scattered team must decide whether to remain safely hidden or find the man who put the price on their heads. Against the wishes of her teammates, Jackie strikes out on her own in order to save a friend who wants her dead. In a kill or be killed situation, will Jackie's emotions finally betray her?

"Once Upon a Disaster"

A young homicide detective finds herself at the mercy of a hitman in the aftermath of an earthquake

While investigating the murder of a hitman, Detective Jade Wesson pursues a lead connecting the dead man to a break-in at a computer programming company. She's drawn into the world of nightclub owner and front man for the mob, Cody Riley. Her investigation keeps pointing to Cody's right-hand man and possible hitman, Vahn Lott. Despite her efforts to keep her investigation on track, Vahn has plans of his own for the attractive detective. When an unprecedented earthquake rocks their east coast town, Jade must put her life in Vahn's hands if she wants to survive. Can she trust a man who might be the killer she's hunting?

"The Murder of Emily Fisher"

After finding their favorite teacher murdered, the lives of two teenage girls are forever changed.

Everyone loved Emily Fisher. While walking home one afternoon, two teenage girls, Sidney and Trisha, stumble upon a gruesome murder scene. The brutal murder of Emily Fisher, a young, attractive schoolteacher, shocks the small town of **Marilina**. After graduation, Sidney moves far away from the memories of the small town while Trisha retreats deeper into denial. Eight years after the murder, Sidney receives a desperate call from her childhood friend, forcing her to return home. Trisha believes Emily's killer was falsely accused and she manages to turn the entire town against her while attempting to prove it. When Trisha receives a death threat, Sidney realizes there may be some credibility to her friend's wild accusations. Is Trisha's mental breakdown a result of childhood trauma? Or is the real killer actually attempting to silence her? In order to save her friend, Sidney must answer the eight-year-old question. Who murdered Emily Fisher?

"Castle Bloodshed"
Murder Collection

From a deadly island paradise to haunted castles. Three novella length tales of murder, mystery, and malicious intent.

"Castle Bloodshed" — A tour of Wesley Castle turns into a fight for survival as six stranded tourists discover the haunting secrets within the castle walls. A mystery writer teams up with an uptight butler in order stop a killer who may already be dead. Novella length paranormal murder mystery.

"Fleshies" — Is Uncle Rutger crazy? Five years ago, four business partners died within their newly purchased, fixer-upper castle. Their bodies were never found. The surviving partner, Rutger, claims a demon keeps him as its slave. Rutger's nephew schemes to save his uncle by sacrificing the lives of a group of stranded motorists and a high-profile novelist. Novella length supernatural murder mystery.

"Demon Island" — A group of strangers are invited to a remote island for the reading of a will. The guests soon discover they were brought to the island to be executed one-by-one. It's up to a private detective and a tenacious young woman to solve the murders and find a way to escape paradise. Novella length murder mystery.

"Brighton Island"

When a psychic visits a haunted island mansion, he inadvertently awakens the ghosts' tortured souls.

Something's not right with Simon. When Jacklyn brings her eccentric friend to her uncle's island mansion, she didn't expect him to slip into psychic overload. As Simon attempts to solve a decade-old, double homicide, Jacklyn is confronted with the possibility that she could be next to join the mansion ghosts. When they find themselves stranded on the secluded island, her Uncle Hyland wages his own war to save them from a flesh and blood killer. Will her uncle's "shock and awe" military tactics save them or get them killed? Can Simon bring peace to the tortured souls or unexpectedly join them?

"A.L.F. Resort"

A fantasy vacation turns into a nightmare when the resort's artificial life forms are compromised.

Welcome to A.L.F. Resort where you can live out your fantasies with safe, state-of-the-art artificial life form robots! When a young journalist and a photographer are sent to A.L.F. Resort to do a story for their magazine, Shay and Becka believe they've hit the jackpot of all work-cations. The engineers pull out all the stops to make their fantasies memorable. Unfortunately, the newly designed A.L.F., the Gen X, is smarter than his programming and creates havoc within Shay's fantasy. A computer malfunction removes their safety inhibitors and the A.L.F.s play out their own hostile fantasies. Zombies, bikers, and mobsters run amuck, turning fantasies into nightmares. Shay gets more of a story than she anticipates, but will she survive long enough to write it?

"Jungle Princess"

While stranded on a prison island, a young woman discovers a creature of "unknown" origin.

After their cruise ship sinks, Alex and two of her shipmates are stranded on a deserted, tropical island. Unfortunately, the castaways soon realize they're not alone. They discover an abandoned prison with over two dozen inmates living on the island's south side. While avoiding the prison on the far side of the island, Alex discovers a strange but loveable creature of unknown origin. When one of her fellow castaways is in trouble, Alex reluctantly seeks help from the prisoners. After the brutal murder of several inmates, their questions surrounding the abandoned prison are about to be answered. What really killed over one hundred prisoners? And is it still out there?

"Murder in Wax"

A series of brutal murders plague a quiet farming community when beautiful women audition for the same acting job.

While all the young women in town are fighting over a once-in-a-lifetime acting opportunity, Devon Vincent is excited about her new job at the local wax museum. Although supportive of her friend's acting aspirations, Devon has a hard time understanding the rivalry among the women in town. When the aspiring actresses are brutally murdered one-by-one, Devon fears her friend may be the next victim. Devon finds herself in the middle of a murderous revenge plot that leads back to the wax museum's doorstep and possibly implicates her boss as the killer. Will Devon's newly found feelings for her boss bring a killer closer to her? Or is the killer already in her circle?

Coming Soon!
"Midnight Requisition"

ABOUT THE AUTHOR

Holly Copella has been writing since the age of twelve when her frustration at a book's poor plot drove her to author her own story. Over the last decade, she's written a number of screenplays, some of which she's now adapting into novels. Her fascination with zombies and other darker material lends an edge to her writing, which tends to lean toward horror. As a fan of Agatha Christie, she appreciates the craft of a good plot and the importance of creating significant characters.

Hailing from Pennsylvania, Copella lives in the Endless Mountains on a farm with her rescue horses and other animals. In addition to writing and reading fiction, she enjoys riding horses and traveling to Las Vegas and Disney World.

www.ingramcontent.com/pod-product-compliance
Lightning Source LLC
Chambersburg PA
CBHW071040250626
47159CB00012B/230